**HAVE FUN WITH THE FACTS.
DO YOU KNOW . . .**

1. WHAT IS THE RIM?

2. WHAT IS A LINK?

3. WHERE IS ISN (INTERSTELLAR NEWS NET-
WORK) BASED?

4. WHO ARE THE WIND SWORDS?

5. WHAT IS EARHARTS?

1. The boundary of known space

2. Communication device used by the staff of Babylon 5

3. Geneva

4. The most militant Minbari warrior caste

5. Officers' lounge aboard Babylon 5

**DON'T BE LEFT DOWN BELOW.
KNOW THE INS AND OUTS
OF THE MOST EXCITING SCI-FI SERIES TODAY.**

THE BABYLON 5 SERIES
available from Dell

The A-Z Guide to
BABYLON 5

David Bassom

Created by
J. Michael Straczynski

A DELL BOOK

Published by
Dell Publishing
a division of
Bantam Doubleday Dell Publishing Group, Inc.
1540 Broadway
New York, New York 10036

ISBN: 0-440-22385-7

Published by arrangement with Boxtree Limited

Printed in the United States of America

Published simultaneously in Canada

March 1997

10 9 8 7 6 5 4 3 2 1

OPM

Contents

A Note to the Reader

Because of the evolving nature of *Babylon 5*'s intended 5-year story arc, a number of the entries within these pages may appear incomplete. At the time of publication (three episodes into Series Three), no one, except the series creator, J. Michael Straczynski, knows exactly what will happen at the end of the 5 years. This then is the *first* edition of *The A-Z Guide to Babylon 5*.

Introduction

This book is an alphabetical guide to all the people, places and things that form the *Babylon 5* universe. As well as covering the TV series, it also incorporates the relevant background elements from the *Babylon 5* books and comic strips. In keeping with the spirit of the TV series, each entry is designed to be self-contained. Where appropriate, they refer to other entries which may provide some useful accompanying information.

As hard as I tried, I just couldn't find an Acme Handy-Dandy Micro-Helper anywhere. Consequently, I had to depend on the support, advice and guidance of many people, without whom this book would have been left for dead in Sector 45.

I would therefore like to thank the following: Tessa Kathleen O'Brien (the real TKO!); Michael and Danny O'Brien; Jake Lingwood at Boxtree (the Time Stabilizer is on the way); Jerry "Zathras" Cheung and David Richardson (a pot of Spoo to you both); Steven Grimm (whose outstanding "Lurkers' Guide to Babylon 5" must be one of the best WorldWideWeb sites in the cosmos); and Satai Bridget Cunningham (aka "The One").

Of course, I must also pay tribute to Joe Straczynski and the cast and crew of *Babylon 5*, who have worked tirelessly to create such an interesting universe for viewers to explore.

May Valen go with you all!

David Bassom
January 1996

Introduction

A Key to the Abbreviations

Throughout this book each episode/comic/novel is referred to in its shortened form below. The page numbers refer to that story's position in the Story Guide.

A-Z

A

Abbai
An alien race aboard Babylon 5 that was briefly a part of the League of Non-Aligned Worlds. Abbai are sometimes referred to as "Fishheads" due to their amphibian-like appearance. They resigned from the League in 2259. (DEATHWALKER)

Abbai 4
An Abbai world. (DEATHWALKER)

Abbot and Costello
During Colonel Ari Ben Zayne's internal investigation aboard Babylon 5 in 2258, Security Chief Garibaldi wondered if these renowned 20th-century comedians had taken command of Earthforce. (EYES)

Abbut
A Vicker occasionally employed by Ambassador Kosh. In 2258, Abbut was hired by the Vorlon to scan Talia Winters and learn how her mind functions, what scared her and how she reacted to fear, surprise, terror and reflection. Abbut claimed, falsely, to be a P23, liked Jovian Sunspots and wore a large hat to hide his cyberorganic mind. Played by Cosie Costa. (DEATHWALKER)

Abby

The senior telepath assigned to care for the young Talia Winters during her first year at the Psi Corps center. Abby would gently scan Talia to make her feel better and this partly explains her ability to form strong relationships with other women, later in life. (SPIDER)

Achilles, The

An Earthforce transport. In August 2258, the *Achilles* was attacked by Raiders to lure Babylon 5's Starfuries away from the station. When Commander Sinclair heard that the *Achilles'* cargo included nothing more valuable than hydroponic supplies, tools and atmospheric testing materials, he realized the Raiders' true intention and ordered the Starfuries to return to Babylon 5. (SIGNS)

Acme Handy-Dandy Micro-Helper

A fictitious device which supposedly makes life "easier, cleaner and all round happier." When Commander Ivanova was kidnapped by a group of green Drazi aboard the station in 2259, Security Chief Garibaldi entered their lair by posing as an Acme salesman. (GEOMETRY)

Agamemnon, The

One of the first Omega Class destroyers built after the Earth–Minbari War, the *Agamemnon's* primary task after the war was to patrol the Rim. Prior to his posting aboard Babylon 5 in January 2259, Captain Sheridan served as the *Agamemnon's* commanding officer (DEPARTURE). The ship came to Sheridan's aid a few months later, when he was kidnapped by the Streibs (ALONE).

AirDome

Earthforce fighter pilot training center. (EYES)

Akdor

The third planet in the Sh'lassan Triumvirate. In 2259, Akdor was the site of a civil war, which was later quashed by Earthforce intervention. (GROPOS)

Akshi, Gera

A dancer at the Dark Star and friend of Adira Tyree. Akshi helped Adira hide from her master, Trakis, and Ambassador Londo Mollari, when she stole the Centauri's Purple Files. Played by Laura Peterson. (PURPLE)

Al Callisto, The

A Narn starliner. Na'Toth was waiting for Narn councilor Ha'Rok to arrive on the *Al Callisto* when she spotted the infamous warleader Jha'dur. (DEATHWALKER)

Alexander, Lyta

The first commercial telepath assigned to Babylon 5. Born on Earth, 10th December 2225, Lyta Alexander was 26 years old when she joined the Psi Corps on the 18th of October 2252 (GATHERING). Lyta knew Talia Winters at the Psi Corps Academy and they spent six months working together at the Psi Corps Intern Program, during which time Lyta worked for the Psi Cops. Perhaps inevitably, she didn't like it (DIVIDED). A sixth-generation registered telepath, Lyta was rated P5 and her licensed Psi Corps telepath number was N617CC860. Prior to 2259, her record stated that she had no distinguishing marks or a criminal record (GATHERING).

Lyta arrived on Babylon 5 on 3rd January 2257 (DIVIDED). During her time on the station, she not only mediated several business deals, including a few for Ambassador Delenn (DIVIDED), but also turned down Ambassador G'Kar's pleas to help the Narn develop their own telepaths. She declined the offer to mate with the Narn diplomat and refused to provide DNA cells for cloning (GATHERING).

Most importantly, of course, Lyta Alexander reluctantly scanned the mind of the Vorlon ambassador, Kosh Naranek, to help find some way of helping the dying diplomat. Although Lyta was extremely loyal to Psi Corps and believed in keeping to the rules, she agreed to perform the illegal procedure when Dr. Kyle and Lieutenant-Commander Takashima convinced her that thousands of lives depended on finding a way to save Kosh. During the scan, the telepath saw that the ambassador had been poisoned with a skin tab applied to his hand by Commander Sinclair. Using the information gained from the scan, Dr. Kyle was able to find and analyze the poison and develop a counter-agent, while Kosh's would-be killer was later revealed to be a Minbari assassin using a Changeling Net to pose as Sinclair. (GATHERING)

According to Security Chief Garibaldi, Lyta was "never quite the same" after she entered Kosh's mind and she was recalled to Earth a mere six weeks after her assignment to Babylon 5. She was fiercely interrogated by the Psi Corps, who demanded to know what she had seen in the Vorlon's mind. All Lyta told them was that she had experienced a feeling which she couldn't put into words. She omitted several pieces of information, including the fact that ever since the scan she had felt drawn to Vorlon space and was sure that the mysterious Empire would welcome her.

In 2259, Lyta escaped from the Corps on a shuttle to Mars, where she became involved with a revolutionary movement. When she learned that the Psi Corps had placed a sleeper spy on Babylon 5, she traveled to the station to warn the command crew. Although Captain Sheridan initially found her story hard to believe, he decided to trust her when the spy tried to kill Lyta. With the captain's permission, Lyta telepathically sent the password which activates the Psi Corps–induced alternate personality into the minds of most of the station's command staff, including Ivanova, and finally unveiled Talia Winters as the unwitting mole. Before leaving the station, Lyta met with Ambassador Kosh, who left his encounter suit to reveal his true form to her. (DIVIDED)

Played by Patricia Tallman.

Alien Healing Device

Mechanism of unknown origin initially used as a form of corporal punishment. Criminals sentenced to death would have their life energy removed by the device, which would then use their life force to heal those dying from terminal diseases.

In 2256, Dr. Laura Rosen bought the alien device from a trader and, after several months, learned that by using it at a low setting, she could heal people by giving them some of her own life energy. Rosen discovered that the device could restore, renew and reinvigorate the flesh, bone and blood and could cure anything from the common cold to Stafford's Disease.

Two years later, Rosen brought the device to Babylon 5 to start an illegal clinic Down Below. When Rosen used it to save her daughter, Janice, and Dr. Franklin from a serial killer, Karl Mueller, it was turned over to station personnel. Franklin wondered if the device might one day be used to preserve someone's life like a blood donation. (MERCY)

A few months later, Franklin put the machine to the test to save Security Chief Garibaldi's life. When all traditional medical techniques failed to bring Garibaldi out of his coma, both Franklin and Captain Sheridan donated some of their life energy to revive him (REVELATIONS). Also known as The Lifegiver.

Alien Science Probe

Probe of unknown origin programmed to find and make contact with other life-forms. In 2260, it reached Babylon 5 and transmitted a recording which explained that the station's inhabitants would have to prove themselves worthy enough for contact. It then sent 600 questions on such topics as physics, genetics, molecular biology and quantum mechanics and claimed that if all questions were answered correctly within 24 hours, the probe would provide cures for every known form of disease as well as some highly advanced technology. Unfortunately, if they failed to answer all 600 questions, the probe would explode with the force of 500,000 megatonnes. Once the message was decoded, the probe began its countdown.

Although Captain Sheridan thought that the probe must have been sent by an alien race driven by natural evolution that intends to help the strong and destroy the weak, he later realized that its real function was to destroy advanced civilizations which could pose a threat to its makers. When Sheridan decided not to transmit the answers, the probe left its "inferior" inhabitants unharmed and resumed its search. It self-destructed shortly after when it was given the 600 correct answers by one of Babylon 5's security 'bots. (STRIFE)

Alien Sector

This sector contains 14 different alien atmospheres and can sustain just about every possible form of life, from methane-breathers to insectoids. Although it is widely referred to as the

"Alien Sector," those in Gray Sector actually refer to the parts of the station inhabited by humans as the "Alien Sector." (WORD)

Allan, Zack

Security officer aboard Babylon 5. Garibaldi's second in command, Zack Allan is generally good at following orders, but tends to shy away from making his own decisions. When Garibaldi was outraged by Sheridan's illegal treatment of the Shadow emissary Morden and resigned, Zack happily served Sheridan and arranged for Talia Winters to "conveniently" pass the mysterious businessman in the hope that she sensed something while in close proximity. (Z'HA'DUM)

During the Narn–Centauri War, Zack was forced to kill a Narn who refused to put down his weapon (SACRIFICE). He was later assigned to follow Ashan, the Minbari witness to the killing of Lovell by Sheridan, but was prevented from making a key breakthrough in the investigation by Lennier (HONOR).

Zack decided to join the Nightwatch simply because of the weekly payment of 50 credits (Z'HA'DUM). Clearly, he had failed to realize or even consider the real intent and function of the organization. At the end of 2259, he reluctantly corroborated stories that a shopkeeper, Xavier Darabuto, had been complaining about new import regulations. Zack was shocked when he discovered that Darabuto's shop had been closed by Nightwatch (FALL).

As a student, Zack had little interest in history and used to fall asleep in history class (Z'HA'DUM). He has something of an eye for the ladies, but subtlety is certainly not his strong point (HONOR). Zack doesn't like being poked (CONVICTIONS).

Played by Jeff Conaway.

Alpha Seven

A member of Babylon 5's Alpha Wing sent to investigate unusual tachyon emissions in Sector 14, Alpha Seven was killed when he encountered the timewarp which had trapped Babylon 4. Just before he died, he managed to scratch the letters "B4" into his belt and set his Starfury on autopilot. When his ship returned to Babylon 5, Dr. Franklin discovered that the

30-year-old pilot had died of old age and that his internal organs were like those of a 90-year-old. Played by Douglas E. McCoy. (SQUARED)

Alpha Seven
See **Mitchell, Bill**

Alpha Squad
Squadron led by Jeffrey Sinclair during the Battle of the Line. Sinclair was its only surviving member. (SKY)

Alpha Squad
One of Babylon 5's Starfury squadrons. Also known as Alpha Wing.

Alvarez
A member of the pro-Earth Homeguard movement. Contributed to a series of anti-alien attacks aboard Babylon 5 in 2258. Was later captured and sent back to Earth for trial. Played by Richard Chaves. (PRAYER)

Alyt
Title given to the acting commander of a Minbari ship when its captain is not on board. (DEPARTURE)

Amazonis Planitia
A region of Mars situated near the Mars Colony. (GRAIL)

Ambassadorial Wing
The home of Babylon 5's alien ambassadors, situated in Green-2. Each ambassador has diplomatic immunity and the quarters of each ambassador are considered to be part of their world's territory. (PARLIAMENT)

Amis
A highly-decorated GROPOS. During the Earth–Minbari War, Amis served with an intelligence-gathering unit stationed on a barren moon to monitor a Minbari command and control post. When the group built their camp on some old ruins, it was attacked by a Soldier of Darkness. The creature killed every member of the unit—all except Amis, whom he

kept alive to feed on. When a rescue party arrived, Amis weighed 85 lbs. Although Amis explained exactly how his 47 comrades were killed, his superiors didn't believe him and their deaths were officially recorded as the result of a Minbari attack. Earthforce decided that Amis was either mad or a compulsive liar.

In 2259, Amis began warning the inhabitants of Babylon 5 that judgment day was nigh and was subsequently arrested for causing a public nuisance. When he was befriended by Security Chief Garibaldi, Amis told him that the Soldier of Darkness he had encountered during the war had come aboard Babylon 5 via the *Copernicus*. He then helped Garibaldi track the creature down and destroy it. Played by Dwight Schultz. (LONG)

Amundsen, The

In 2242, the *Amundsen* became the first human ship to encounter the Minbari. Under the command of Captain Ellasai Ferdinand VI, it opened fire on them, in the process killing their leader, Dukhat. (LAW)

Antarean Flarn

An Antarean delicacy. (PARLIAMENT)

Antareans, The

An alien race aboard Babylon 5. (VOICES)

Antares Sector

The home of the Antareans. The human tech-runner Del Varner bought a Changeling Net in this sector. (GATHERING)

Anti-Agapic

A serum which retards the aging process and prevents disease. Many races and organizations are known to have tried to create an anti-agapic, including the Russian Consortium.

In 2258, the notorious war-criminal Jha'dur arrived on Babylon 5 with a universal anti-agapic, which she described as "the ultimate triumph of life." Unfortunately, one of the key ingredients of her serum couldn't be synthesized, but had to be removed from living tissues. Thus, Jha'dur hoped to plunge the galaxy into a war for immortality. However, Jha'dur's plans were cut short when the Vorlons destroyed her ship while it was en route to Earth, leaving Dr. Franklin with only a small sample of the anti-agapic. (DEATHWALKER)

Arain Station
Outpost visited by Walker Smith prior to his SportCorp boxing match with Itagi on Earth. (TKO)

AreTech
A mining corporation on Mars found to be supplying the Raiders with details of supply routes. (ACCUSATIONS)

Article 35
Earthforce regulation which states that any dispute about a new regulation must be heard by at least five senior officers. In 2258, Article 35 was invoked by Sinclair, as the commanding officer of Babylon 5, to question a new regulation which supposedly allowed Colonel Ari Ben Zayne to order telepathic scans of all of the station's command staff. Sinclair claimed that scans are only permissible when an officer faces specific charges. (EYES)

Article 52
Earthforce regulation which states that any commander found to be working against the best interests of Earth can be removed from his post. (EYES)

Ashan
A young Minbari and member of the Third Fain of Chu'Domo. In 2259, Ashan witnessed the murder of the Minbari Lovell by Captain Sheridan. Although Sheridan claimed to have killed Lovell in self-defense, Ashan stated that the Minbari was assaulted without provocation and offered to surrender before his brutal murder.

Ashan showed little respect for Ambassador Delenn, whom he called a "freak," but reluctantly cooperated with Lennier as a member of the Third Fain of Chu'Domo. When Lennier discovered that Sheridan was telling the truth and that Lovell was acting under the orders of their sect, the ambassadorial aide threatened to dishonor the sect unless Ashan told the truth. Consequently, Ashan issued a statement explaining what he really saw, while leaving Lovell's motives a mystery, in order to protect the honor of the Third Fain of Chu'Domo. Played by Sean Gregory Sullivan. (HONOR)

Ashok, Vakar

Drazi captain of a Sunhawk class ship who threatened to attack Babylon 5 unless Jha'dur was turned over to him to stand trial for war crimes. Played by Mark Hendrickson. (DEATH-WALKER)

Asimov, The

An Earth Alliance starliner named in memory of a highly regarded 20th-century writer. In 2258, the *Asimov* was en route to Babylon 5 when a fire in the ship's command and control center destroyed its navigation computer and most of its communications channels. Consequently, it was left flying blind in Raiders territory until Commander Ivanova mounted a successful rescue bid. (BELIEVERS)

B

BabCom
Babylon 5's internal communications network.

Ba-Bear-Lon 5 Teddy Bear
Teddy bear on sale at the Babylon Emporium, inspired by Captain Sheridan. When the war hero discovered that he had been immortalized as a teddy bear, he ordered the closure of the Emporium and spaced one of the bears. (HONOR)

Babylon 1
The first space station commissioned by the Earth Alliance, destroyed during construction when its infrastructure collapsed. Originally titled the Babylon Station. (GATHERING, GRAIL) (See also **Babylon Project, The**)

Babylon 2
The second Babylon station, sabotaged during construction and subsequently abandoned. (GATHERING, GRAIL) (See also **Babylon Project, The**)

Babylon 3
The third Babylon station, irreparably damaged by an explosion during construction. (GATHERING, GRAIL) (See also **Babylon Project, The**)

Babylon 4

The biggest and most expensive Babylon station, built using some of the leftover materials from the first three stations. Like its predecessors, the station was built in Sector 14. The last stages of construction were supervised by Major Lewis Krantz, who made history when the station was completed in 2254. Earthforce was in the process of choosing the station's commander when it disappeared without a trace, exactly 24 hours after it had become operational.

Four years later Babylon 4 suddenly reappeared in the very spot it had disappeared in and sent a distress signal. When Commander Sinclair arrived on the station to lead the evacuation of its skeleton crew of 12–13,000 workers, Major Krantz explained to him that Babylon 4 had been operational for 24 hours when a number of discrepancies occurred in the station's time-tracking systems. At first, everyone had assumed that it was merely the result of a computer fault, but they soon realized that they had become caught in some kind of time anomaly.

Everybody in the station experienced different visions of the past and future, which the Babylon 4 crew dubbed "The Flashes." Sinclair saw a vision of the future in which Security Chief Garibaldi was fighting an invisible and seemingly unstoppable force which was invading Babylon 5 and ordered Sinclair to leave before the station self-destructed, while Garibaldi remembered how he left his girlfriend Lise Hampton on the Mars Colony to assume the role of Babylon 5's security chief.

Sinclair and Garibaldi were also introduced to Zathras, a strange alien who claimed that his leader, known only as The One, was stealing Babylon 4 to use as a base of operations in a great war and had stopped it in 2258 for the crew to disembark. Once the station was evacuated, it disappeared (SQUARED). Earthforce confiscated all records of Babylon 5's encounter with its predecessor and officially the station was destroyed (KNIVES). It took ten hours to evacuate Babylon 4's skeleton crew and the station's Secure Code is 0010835–081677 (SQUARED). (See also **Babylon Project, The**)

Babylon 5

The fifth Babylon station, built by the Earth Alliance on the firm understanding that it would be the last.

Following the disappearance of the hugely expensive Babylon 4, the Alliance passed a slim budget for its successor and tried to build it as cheaply as possible. Even then, it could not afford to fund the station's construction on its own and required the backing of the Minbari Federation, as well as a contribution from the Centauri. To help pay for Babylon 5's maintenance, every visitor pays a fee upon boarding the station and all staff have to pay rent which is automatically deducted from their wages. Babylon 5 receives further income from those who use its local jumpgate.

In 2256, many of Earthforce's finest officers were considered as possible commanders of Babylon 5. However, the Minbari Federation rejected all of their choices, including several distinguished admirals and generals, and insisted that Commander Jeffrey Sinclair assumed the position (SIGNS). When Sinclair was reassigned to the Minbari homeworld in 2259, the Earth Alliance appointed Captain John Sheridan without the Minbari's approval (DEPARTURE).

The station's commanding officer represents the Earth Alliance on Babylon 5's Advisory Council, leaving his or her first officer to supervise the station's day-to-day operations. Most of the time, the commander acts autonomously, but is occasionally given direct instructions from the Earth Alliance. The commander has the authority to seal off the station and can grant the station's security chief full diplomatic access. (GATHERING)

As an Earth Alliance space station, English is the primary language spoken aboard Babylon 5. While most diplomats and many visiting members of the alien races learn the language, some rely on translators.

Babylon 5 became on-line in 2256 and turned fully operational in 2257 (GATHERING). The station is located in an area of neutral space, the Euphrates Sector, at Grid Epsilon 470/18/22 (MIND). It orbits a supposedly barren planet, Euphrates (also known as Epsilon 3), and its sun is Tigris (WORD). The Euphrates Sector was originally chosen as the site for Babylon 5 because it is relatively central to the five major powers (Earth Alliance, Minbari Federation, Centauri

Republic, Narn Regime and Vorlon Empire) and because nothing valuable was believed to exist in the area. However, the area erupted into a war zone in 2258 when the station learned that Epsilon 3 had once been the home of a highly advanced civilization which existed five miles beneath the planet's surface. Fortunately, the violent ownership dispute ended when Epsilon 3's guardian, Draal, announced that anyone who tried to land on the planet would be destroyed (VOICE I, II).

Given the fates of its four predecessors, few people believed that Babylon 5 would last six months. Asked to estimate the odds of the station reaching its first anniversary, Lloyds of London quoted 500-1 against, while the gambling institutions at Las Vegas and New Vegas offered customers 350-1 against and 200-1 against respectively. By 2256, the odds had improved slightly: Lloyds of London placed them at 250-1 against, while Las Vegas and New Vegas felt that they had fallen to 200-1 against and 5-1 against respectively. (WORD)

Babylon 5 functions as a free port for diplomacy, trade and commerce. The station is five miles long and its casing alone weighs 2.5 million tonnes. It can house approximately a quarter of a million inhabitants at a time and is normally visited by between 50 and 60 ships every day. 58% of Babylon 5's population is human, while the alien races account for the remaining 42%.

The station is divided into separate, color-coded sections, most of which spin to create different levels of artificial gravity. Red Sector is the center of the station's commercial and leisure activities. Among other things, it houses the Zocalo, the Zen Garden, the maze and the hydroponic gardens, as well as various hotel suites, casinos and bars. Blue Sector is the focus of station operations and contains the Observation Dome, medlabs, docking bays and customs area. Green Sector includes the Ambassadorial Wing and can be accessed by station personnel only, while the nonrotating Yellow Sector houses the zero-gravity cargo bays and the fusion engines. Gray Sector is industrial and has no living quarters. The "Alien Sector," which is adjacent, contains 14 alternate atmospheres and is capable of sustaining every possible form of life aboard B5—including methane-breathers, silicon life-forms and insectoids (GATHERING). Ironically, while the area is normally referred to as the "Alien Sector," those who visit the Gray Sector refer to the areas of the station inhabited by humans as the "Alien Sector" (WORD). Shortly after the station went on-line, the area was dubbed the "Babylon Triangle" by a number of maintenance workers who claimed to have seen strange lights and heard unusual noises in the area. There are always problems with scans and communications in Gray Sector, and several missing people were last seen there before they disappeared (KNIVES).

The station's undeveloped area is known as Down Below and plays host to the lurkers—people who come to Babylon 5 searching for new lives and new jobs, but instead find themselves homeless, unemployed and lacking the funds to return home.

In case of attack, Babylon 5 is equipped with a defense grid, blast doors and squadrons of Starfuries. When the defense grid was upgraded in 2259, the station became strong enough to battle a warcruiser. (GROPOS)

Babylon 5 falls under Earth jurisdiction. All criminals are tried and convicted by the Ombuds (GRAIL). Commercial activity is not subject to Earthforce scrutiny (SPIDER). While guests are permitted to make arms deals aboard the station, weapons cannot be brought aboard or transferred on the station (WORD, INQUISITOR).

Babylon 5 boasts thousands of entertainment and industrial channels (BELIEVERS), including the Business Channel (MEANS). While its executive and command quarters contain real water showers, the rest of the station's living quarters house vibe showers, due to the limitations of the water reclamation system (DEPARTURE). Although the station distinguishes between day and night, it does not commemorate seasons (FALL).

It would take between three and five days to evacuate Babylon 5, even if all the ships in the sector offered assistance. (VOICE II)

Despite the Earth Alliance's desire to keep Babylon 5 self-sufficient, the station's financial affairs have been dogged by controversy. When the 2258 budget failed to allocate extra money for increased dockers' pay and modern equipment, the Dockers' Guild called an illegal strike which they only ended when Commander Sinclair used the Rush Act to reallocate

1.3 million extra credits to them from the station's war budget. (MEANS)

In the first two months of 2259, station revenue dropped by 15% due to the increased presence of Earthforce military transports. In order to avoid deficit, Earthforce tried to increase Captain Sheridan and Commander Ivanova's rent for their executive suites by an extra 30 credits a week. Sheridan refused to pay or move to smaller quarters, and eventually reallocated the extra credits from the station's war-readiness budget, on the grounds that he wasn't ready to fight unless he had slept well. (RACE)

Shortly after, the Senate Oversight Committee decided that the Earth Alliance could earn over 2 million credits a year through the sale of Babylon 5 merchandise on the station. Many of the station's inhabitants, including Ambassador Mollari, felt embarrassed as Babylon 5 increasingly became a deep space franchise and Sheridan later ordered the sale of merchandise to end. (HONOR)

Although the station managed to last longer than anyone expected, opposition to Babylon 5 steadily increased on Earth. An ISN poll in March 2257 suggested that 30% of the planet's population were against the time, money and effort devoted to the station. By September 2259, that figure had risen to 41%. (WORD)

When the Narn–Centauri War broke out in 2259, it was widely recognized as the beginning of the end for Babylon 5's peace-keeping mission. However, in 2260 the station assumed a greater function as the last best hope for victory in the war against the Shadows. (TWILIGHT, FALL, MATTERS) (See also **Babylon Project, The**)

Babylon 5 Advisory Council, The
The focus of all diplomatic activity aboard Babylon 5, based on the (now defunct) United Nations Security Council. The Advisory Council comprises the representatives of the Earth Alliance, Minbari Federation, Centauri Republic, Narn Regime and Vorlon Empire, each of which has an equal vote (GATHERING). If the Council is deadlocked, then the League of Non-Aligned Worlds has the deciding vote (DEATHWALKER).

Babylon 5 Emporium, The

Shop opened on the Zocalo in 2259 to sell Babylon 5 merchandise to residents and tourists. Items on sale included Babylon 5 jackets, dolls, T-shirts, posters, alien and human masks, teddy bears and models. It offered a 20% discount to station personnel. (HONOR)

Babylon 5 Senate Oversight Committee

Advisory board responsible for keeping Babylon 5 financially self-sufficient (MEANS). In 2259, tried to compensate for the station's increasing budget deficit by charging Captain Sheridan and Commander Ivanova extra rent on their executive quarters (RACE) and subsequently suggested that the station sell merchandise (HONOR). Over time, the Committee would attempt to exert increased influence in Babylon 5's political structure (VOICES).

Babylon Park

Impressive garden aboard Babylon 5. The site of a baseball pitch regularly used by Captain Sheridan. (KNIVES)

Babylon Project, The

The Babylon Project was launched by Earth Alliance President Luis Santiago in 2249 following the conclusion of the Earth–Minbari War. The project's goal was to create an environment in which humans and aliens could resolve their differences peacefully and, above all, could avoid another war based on a misunderstanding. The project was initially proposed and pushed through the senate, by David Indiri, a senator from New Delhi, India. At the time of its inception, peace was imperative not only from an idealistic viewpoint but from a practical one: Earth's military forces had been drastically depleted in the war with the Minbari and the Alliance simply couldn't afford to fight again.

Earthforce decided to build a Babylon space station rather than a Babylon planetary base in order to allow ships incapable of entering planetary atmospheres (such as the Starfuries) to travel directly to the location. (LAW)

From the very beginning, however, the Babylon Project faced serious resistance from members of the Alliance who believed that it was a naive and pointless waste of time, money and resources, and opposed the idea that humans should develop closer ties to alien species. As a result, the first three Babylon stations were sabotaged and destroyed during construction.

Support for the Babylon Project steadily continued to dwindle over the years. As Earthforce rebuilt its military strength, the public increasingly began to believe that the project was no longer necessary or valid. The mysterious disappearance of Babylon 4 in 2254 only served to undermine the project's credibility. Consequently, the Earth Alliance agreed to finance Babylon 5 on the condition that it would be the last of the Babylon stations.

When President Santiago was killed on January 1st 2259, the Babylon Project lost its leading patron. When the Narn–Centauri War broke out a few months later, many considered it to be the final nail in the Babylon Project's coffin. (WORD) (See also **Babylon 1, Babylon 2, Babylon 3, Babylon 4** and **Babylon 5**)

Babylon Station, The
See **Babylon 1**

Bagna Cauda
An Italian fondue, the main ingredients of which include a pint of olive oil, butter, salt, bread, garlic and anchovies. Alfredo Garibaldi cooked *bagna cauda* for his son, Michael, every year on his birthday. Ever since Alfredo died, Garibaldi has cooked it every year as a tribute to his father. The ingredients are hard to come by aboard Babylon 5, especially when the station's chief medical officer is determined to stop you from eating *bagna cauda*. (DISTANT)

Balus
An alien world and a member of the League of Non-Aligned Worlds. Balus was invaded by the Dilgar and later liberated by Earth Alliance. (DEATHWALKER)

Battle of Na'Shok, The
A war in the mid-22nd century, during which the Eye was lost. (SIGNS) (See also **Eye, The**)

Battle of Salos, The
The Earth Alliance's decisive victory during the war against
the Dilgar. Afterward, the remaining Dilgar fled and the notorious warmaster Jha'dur disappeared. (DEATHWALKER)

Battle of the Line, The
The final conflict during the Earth–Minbari War. The
Minbari had brought the Earth Alliance to its knees and went
past many of its colonies and outposts to attack Earth (TWI-
LIGHT). Earth mounted a defense of 20,000 fighters, but
they were outgunned and outmanned, and found that they
could not "hold the line" around their homeworld against the
Minbari. However, shortly after the Battle of the Line, the
Minbari surrendered to Earth (SKY).

The 200 survivors of the Battle of the Line became heroes.
They included Jeffrey Sinclair. (DARKNESS) (See also
Earth–Minbari War, The)

Bay 11
Docking port in Babylon 5 in which Ambassador Kosh's ship
first arrived. Kosh was poisoned by a Minbari assassin just
outside the bay. (GATHERING)

Bay 13
Docking port in Babylon 5 which normally plays host to Ambassador Kosh's ship. By 2259, Bay 13 was quarantined because the last maintenance crew assigned there refused to
ever enter the bay again. Each member claimed to have had
dreams about Kosh's ship and that it talked to them in their
sleep. (HUNTER)

Beldon, Alisa
Born on Earth. Following the death of her mother in 2250
and father in 2257, Alisa lived Down Below and used to steal
to pay for food.

She was stealing jewelry from a boutique on the Zocalo in
2258 when she suffered a mindburst. When Alisa was found
to be a strong telepath (possibly a high P10) Talia Winters and
Commander Ivanova argued over her fate; while Talia was
keen for her to join the Psi Corps, Ivanova was determined to
find another option.

Alisa turned down a lucrative offer from the Narn Regime to work as a telepath and help contribute to the genetic creation of telepathic Narns. When she discussed her situation with Ambassador Delenn, she accidentally scanned her mind and realized that the Minbari had stolen the missing body of the war leader Branmer. She also saw one word in Delenn's mind—"chrysalis."

After a great deal of thought, Alisa decided to take Delenn's offer and traveled to Minbar to work as an instrument of communication between humans and Minbari. Played by Grace Una. (LEGACIES)

Beldon, Eliot

Husband of Esperanza, father of Alisa. Brought her to Babylon 5 in 2256 when he was offered a job as a construction worker. He was killed in an accident the following year, thus leaving his daughter to fend for herself. (LEGACIES)

Beldon, Esperanza

Wife of Eliot, mother of Alisa Beldon. Died in 2250 of Stafford's Disease. (LEGACIES)

Benson

A security officer aboard Babylon 5 in 2258. When he ran up a large debt in the casino, Benson was ordered to justify his actions to Commander Sinclair and Security Chief Garibaldi. Although Benson claimed that he always stayed close to the official 50 credits a week gambling limit but had never broken it, Sinclair and Garibaldi realized that he must have been participating in unregistered gambling to get into such debt. Consequently, they decided that he was a security risk and took him off active duty.

Benson later supplied the Bureau 13 operatives Knights One and Two with an energy pod in return for 15,000 credits, which he used to pay off his debts. As a result, Garibaldi's aide Jack decided to put him back in action during the search for Sinclair. When Benson discovered that the energy pod was being used to power the Virtual Reality Cybernet in which Sinclair had been placed, he was killed by Knight One. Played by Jim Youngs. (SKY)

Ben Zayne, Ari (Colonel)

An Earthforce war veteran who served in Israel, New Jerusalem and Syrius 3, Colonel Ari Ben Zayne was one of the leading candidates to command Babylon 5. When the post was offered to Jeffrey Sinclair, Zayne became enraged with jealousy. Zayne's close personal friends included the sinister Psi Cop Bester, who personally assigned Harriman Gray as his aide. He doesn't drink because he believes that it makes a soldier weak.

In 2258, Zayne seized the opportunity to discredit Sinclair when he was assigned by the Earthforce Bureau of Internal Affairs to investigate the station's senior command staff. Arriving on the station, he posed as a businessman, Aaron Franks, to gain as much information as he possibly could before revealing his true intentions. Zayne ordered Security Chief Garibaldi to help him with his inquiries, saying that he liked Garibaldi's style.

During the course of the investigation, Zayne revealed that he thought Sinclair was a "hotshot hero" who had been promoted through the ranks without any real leadership ability. He then assumed command of Babylon 5 using Article 52. Ultimately, Zayne was betrayed by Gray, who exposed his unstable mental state. Played by Gregory Martin. (EYES)

"Be Seeing You"

Catchphrase of the new order on Earth. First used by the sinister Psi Cop Bester (MIND) and then by Garibaldi's traitorous aide, Jack (REVELATIONS).

Bester

A ruthless Psi Cop who only cares about himself and the good of Psi Corps, Bester is referred to as one of the Corps' "most valued members" in its propaganda (RACE, PSI). He is more than willing to kill and illegally scans most of those around him (RACE).

Bester first traveled to Babylon 5 in 2258 to hunt for the rogue telepath Jason Ironheart. Bester was initially reluctant to divulge any information to the station's command staff, but was subsequently forced to cooperate when Sinclair threatened to accuse him of endangering the station and blame him for the death of Kelsey. Consequently, Bester corroborated

Sinclair's story that Ironheart was killed leaving the station. (MIND)

Bester made his second visit to the station the following year to search for an underground railroad of unregistered telepaths. He seemed intrigued by Talia Winters and was keen to enlist her support. Ultimately, Talia joined forces with the unregistered telepaths to make Bester believe that he had killed all of the unregistered telepaths with Talia's help. (RACE)

Bester prefers telepathic communication and finds talking a very slow process (MIND). He is married with a five-year-old daughter. When he is home on Mars, Bester and his family spend their Sundays together at Syria Planum, watching the stars come out (RACE).

Played by Walter Koenig.

Beta System
Region of space conquered by the Centauri Republic in nine days at the height of its power. (GATHERING)

Beta 7
Site of an ice-mining operation from which Robert J. Carlsen stole explosives. (CONVICTIONS)

Biggs, Malcolm
A former lover of Commander Ivanova, Malcolm Biggs tried to rekindle their passion aboard Babylon 5 in 2258. Although Biggs told Ivanova that he was setting up a business on the station, he neglected to mention the fact that he was actually a member of the vicious pro-Earth group, the Homeguard.

When Ivanova and Commander Sinclair expressed anti-alien sentiments, Biggs invited them to join the Homeguard and revealed that he intended to coordinate the assassination of the station's four alien ambassadors. This, in turn, would act as a signal to other members of the Homeguard to terminate the other alien emissaries on Earth. Ivanova and Sinclair then turned on the group and ordered their arrest. Later, Biggs was sent back to Earth for trial. Played by Tristan Rogers. (PRAYER)

Black Light Cammo Suit
A black costume which allows an individual to appear invisible in dark and shadowy places. Earthforce Research and Development prototypes of black light cammo suits were used by Homeguard in 2258 to commit a series of vicious and unprovoked attacks on aliens. (PRAYER)

Black Omega Squad
Earth Alliance interceptor squadron of Black Omega Starfuries with Psi Corps connections. Several of its fighters were destroyed while pursuing rogue telepath Jason Ironheart in 2258. (MIND)

Black Omega Starfury
An extremely expensive class of Starfury used for surveillance and infiltration missions.

Black Star, The
The Minbari flagship destroyed during the Earth–Minbari War by Captain John Sheridan, who mined an asteroid field between Jupiter and Mars and sent a distress signal which lured the ship and three heavy cruisers to their destruction. Although the Earth Alliance captain achieved the impossible by destroying the ship, the Minbari perceived it as a dishonorable victory and dubbed Sheridan "Starkiller" (DEPARTURE, HONOR). When the *Black Star* was destroyed, many members of the Third Fain of Chu'Domo were aboard, as well as several of Lennier's relatives (HONOR). At Christmas 2259, Commander Ivanova gave Sinclair a fragment of the *Black Star* to remind him that sometimes the impossible is possible (FALL).

Blast Doors
Exterior panels used to shield Babylon 5 from attack.

Blue Sector
The focus of all station operations, Blue Sector incorporates the Observation Dome and medlabs, as well as Babylon 5's docking bays and customs area.

Bonehard Maneuver, The

Desperate strategem devised by Earthforce during the Earth–Minbari War, the Bonehard Maneuver refers to the extremely risky procedure of opening a jumppoint within a jumpgate. The plan was abandoned by Earthforce, who concluded it was suicidal because not even its fastest ships could escape the explosion.

In 2260, Captain Sheridan used the Bonehard Maneuver to destroy a Shadow ship, obliterating Sector 45's local jumpgate in the process. Fortunately, the *White Star* was fast enough to escape from the tremendous force of the blast. (MATTERS)

Book of G'Quan, The

The basis of G'Quan's teachings. Each book is copied precisely by hand from the original, complete with every note and line (MATTERS). In his book, G'Quan outlines a Great War against the Shadows. He also reveals that they dwelled at the rim of known space on a planet called Z'ha'dum (REVELATIONS) and set up a base in one of the Narn homeworld's southern continents (MATTERS). (See also **G'Quan**)

Book Universe

Bookstore situated in the Zocalo.

Brainwipe

A painless but controversial procedure also known as the "death of personality" used as a punishment for criminals. The offender has all his personality and memories erased, and is then reprogrammed with a new set of memories in order to serve the community harmlessly. A telepath is required to scan the subject before and after brainwipe to check that the procedure has worked correctly. (MERCY)

In 2258, the crew of Babylon 5 discovered that a Na'ka'leen feeder is also capable of removing all normal brainwave activity associated with personality or memory. (GRAIL)

Brakiri, The

Alien race aboard Babylon 5. (SURVIVORS, TWILIGHT, STRIFE)

Branmer

Branmer is widely regarded as one of the greatest Minbari warleaders who ever lived. Branmer's father was a member of the warrior caste, while his mother was a member of the religious caste. As the religious caste generally takes precedence over the warrior caste, Branmer was raised as a member of the religious caste and subsequently became a high priest.

Following the death of Dukhat, Branmer believed that the war against Earth was righteous. He fought with honor, bravery and vision. Toward the end of the war, he planned and led the Minbari during the historic Battle of the Line and commanded one of the warcruisers which destroyed Commander Sinclair's squadron.

Branmer obeyed the Grey Council's order to surrender, but did not agree with it. Although he became a hero to his people, Ambassador Delenn felt that he was always a priest in his heart. He once told her that he wanted a quiet funeral and didn't want his body displayed as a monument to war.

When Branmer died suddenly during a diplomatic tour, Shai Alyt Neroon deliberately disobeyed his wishes and intended to display his former commander's body to all Minbari from the Euphrates Sector to homeworld. As a result, Delenn stole Branmer's body when it was about to be displayed on Babylon 5 and, as per his request, cremated his body and had his ashes scattered in space near the Minbari homeworld. The disappearance almost sparked another war between the humans and Minbari until Delenn ordered Neroon to support her story that Branmer's body was transformed to allow him to take his place with the gods. (LEGACIES)

Breathers

Oxygen masks used in alien environments, including Babylon 5's alien sector.

Brivare

A Centauri beverage. Ambassador Mollari's lifelong friend Urza Jaddo was almost legendary for his ability to drink Brivare. (KNIVES)

Buffer
A GROPOS who served with his best friend, Large, for more than 25 years, until he was killed during the 2258 Mars Rebellion. Buffer used to say that "a GROPOS who ain't scared is either dead or stupid." (GROPOS)

Bureau 13
A covert organization which operates within the Earth Alliance government, Bureau 13 is a dirty tricks squad which deals in starchamber justice and black projects. Captain Sheridan first heard of its existence in 2253 and learned its name three years later. Shortly after, his informant died. Bureau 13 is controlled by a mysterious woman known only as 13. She was once a Psi Cop and had been declared dead by Earth Alliance records. (SPIDER)

Two of its operatives, Knight One and Knight Two, believed that the Minbari had chosen to build a "fifth column" on Earth to corrupt and destroy the Earth Alliance from within and believed that Commander Sinclair was a leading member of the organization. In 2258, they kidnapped Sinclair and tried to find evidence of their theory, but were cut short by the commander's escape. (SKY)

The following year, Captain Sheridan discovered that Bureau 13 had developed Earthforce's Project : Lazarus to create cyberorganic agents out of dying human beings. One such operative was Abel Horn, who had been instructed to kill Taro Isogi (thus preventing a peaceful solution to the Mars crisis) and destroy the Free Mars movement from within. However, the Bureau's plans suffered a setback when Talia Winters touched Horn's mind and made him consider what he had become. Naturally, Horn self-destructed when he was killed, thus destroying any evidence or further clues. (SPIDER)

Following the breach in its operations, Bureau 13 destroyed many of its records, and changed its name, eventually re-emerging with other covert operations on Earth.

C

C-15
An explosive compound used by Homeguard supporters Nolan and Cutter. (SURVIVORS)

Caliban
An old Mutari who helped Walker Smith enter the Mutai and, together with Security Chief Garibaldi, served as his Ka'Ti during his championship fight against the Sho'Rin, Gyor. Following Smith's victory, Caliban said that he would stand Ka'Ti again if the human ever returned to the Mutai. Played by Don Stroud. (TKO)

Cardial Stimulator
Device used to stimulate heart activity. Naturally, it can be fatal if used on a healthy individual. Nelson Drake killed a customs guard with a cardial stimulator in order to smuggle Ikaaran artifacts onto Babylon 5. (INFECTION)

Carlsen, Robert J.
When Robert J. Carlsen lost his wife, his job and apartment he was told by everyone around him that it was nothing personal, just a sign of the "chaotic" times. The trauma pushed Carlsen over the edge and he decided to become "an instrument of chaos" and strike fear into the hearts of others, courtesy of random bombings.

Using a batch of explosives stolen from the ice-mining operation on Beta 7, Carlsen carried out a series of bombings on Proxima 3 before he was hired by Babylon 5's Engineering and Station Maintenance Division on 11th January 2260. According to his record, Carlsen was a quiet and solitary individual who had a bad temper. While working on Babylon 5, he received several disciplinary notes for not paying attention to his work. Captain Sheridan and Security Chief Garibaldi later discovered why he couldn't pay attention when they realized that he was planting bombs at random points on the station.

Carlsen took Sheridan hostage and tried to bargain his way to freedom using a bomb near the station's fusion reactor. However, the device was found and moved away from the station before it exploded. Played by Robert Kilpatrick. (CONVICTIONS)

Carnellian Bed Sheets
Brought to Babylon 5 by Carolyn Sykes in 2257. She had heard that they were "completely frictionless." (GATHERING)

Cartagia
The nephew of Centauri Emperor Turhan, who succeeded his uncle when he died in 2259. Cartagia was maneuvered into the position by Lord Refa and his associates, who set policy while he acted as a figurehead. (SHADOWS, TWILIGHT)

Cartee, The
A Markab transport used in 2259 to take 200 Markabs away from their homeworld in the hope that they would escape the spread of Drafa. Unfortunately for the *Cartee*'s passengers, somebody aboard the ship was already carrying the plague. As a result, the *Cartee* was found drifting in Sector 23, Grid 230,9,40, with everyone aboard dead. (CONFESSIONS)

Carter, Amanda
The granddaughter of John Carter, Amanda Carter was always a strong supporter of Mars independence. In 2244, she fell in love with Abel Horn, who introduced her to the Free Mars movement. However, when Free Mars became violent, Carter left the organization and split up with Horn.

As a member of Mars Colony Business Affairs Committee, Carter was sent to Babylon 5 in 2259 to discuss Taro Isogi's proposed peaceful settlement to the Mars crisis. When Isogi was murdered, Carter discovered that the killer was none other than Abel Horn, who had been transformed into a cyberorganic agent of Bureau 13. Following the destruction of Horn, she decided to pursue Isogi's plan as a tribute to his memory. Played by Adrienne Barbeau. (SPIDER)

Carter, John

John Carter won a place in human history when he piloted the first colony ship to Mars. The grandfather of Amanda Carter. (SPIDER)

Casinos

All of Babylon 5's casinos are situated in Red Sector. They accept all currencies and offer games from seven systems. Station personnel are allowed to play in the casino off-duty, but have a weekly gambling limit of 50 credits. (SKY, VOICE I)

Telepaths are allowed access to the casino but, unsurprisingly, are forbidden from gambling. (GATHERING)

Centauri, The

One of the five major races aboard Babylon 5, famed for its hedonism and former glory.

The Centauri homeworld, Centauri Prime, was originally inhabited by two sentient species, the Centauri and the Xon, until the Centauri annihilated the Xon. Ever since, the Centauri have held an annual religious celebration at the end of each year during which they count the number of dead Xon and thank the gods for their good fortune. They have approximately 50 gods, including Li, the god of passion, Venzann, the god of food, and Mogath, god of the underworld. (CHRYSALIS, PARLIAMENT)

Family is everything to the Centauri. A Centauri's honor and status comes from his or her family, and marriages are normally arranged to meld the Republic's leading houses (PRAYER). The Centauri build Purple Files, consisting of scandalous pieces of information about each other, which they then use to increase their status (PURPLE). Centauri males' outlandish hairstyles are a status symbol, while women shave their heads (SIGNS, SHADOWS). Apart from their hairstyles, the Centauri also enjoy decorating themselves with jewelry and medallions. Until the 23rd century, almost all Centauri held such traditions as sacred. However, as the Centauri Republic declined, many of its people abandoned its traditions.

Although the Centauri look human and claimed that Earth was a lost colony on their first encounter, biologically the two races are worlds apart. For example, the Centauri have no major arteries in their wrists and their sexual organs are completely different than those of humans (MIDNIGHT, MERCY). Ambassador Mollari later claimed that his people were not trying to deceive the human race but had merely made a clerical error and thought that Earth was Beta 9 rather than Beta 12 (MIDNIGHT).

The Centauri believe that they can predict their own deaths and many have claimed to have had visions of their deaths in their dreams. (MIDNIGHT) (See also **Centauri Republic, The**)

Centauri Emperor, The
Leader of the Centauri Republic. Before the first emperor took the throne of the Republic, he consulted three Technomages who gave him their blessing. This remains a very important symbol to those who believe in the old days of the Republic, including Ambassador Mollari. (GEOMETRY)

The emperor is accompanied by four telepaths who are raised together from birth and mentally linked 24 hours a day, regardless of the distance between them. Thus, what one sees, all see. When the emperor leaves Centauri Prime, two of the telepaths remain at the royal court to keep him informed of what is happening at home. (SHADOWS)

Centauri Prime
The homeworld of the Centauri, situated 75 light years from Babylon 5. Centauri Prime was originally home to two races, the Xon and the Centauri, who battled constantly until the Xon were annihilated. (PRAYER)

Centauri Republic, The

Title for the Centauri Empire. The Republic is a monarchy, led by the emperor, followed by the prime minister (SHADOWS). At the height of its power, the Centauri Republic spanned the galaxy and successfully conquered many worlds, including Narn.

However, by the mid-22nd century, the Republic had begun to decline, due to a combination of laziness and overstretching itself. Bit by bit, the Centauri had to withdraw from many of the worlds they had conquered, including Narn, whose people drove them out of their world by a bloody war of attrition.

When the Centauri made contact with Earth in the mid-22nd century, they claimed that they still had a huge empire and gave the Earth Alliance access to their technology, in return for various trade agreements. Thus, as the Centauri continued to decline, the Alliance went from strength to strength. (LONG)

The Centauri Republic sent several expeditions to Vorlon space over the centuries, none of which returned (SHADOWS). It is widely believed to have collaborated with the Dilgar and consequently didn't want the war criminal Jha'dur tried in case it corroborated this claim (DEATHWALKER).

By the mid-23rd century, the Centauri Republic comprised a mere 12 worlds and many memories of glory. It contributed money to Babylon 5 in the hope that it might one day lead to an Earth–Centauri alliance. (GATHERING, VOICE I)

The Centauri once had a diplomatic mission on Minbar which was closed for several years when the Centauri envoy misbehaved. The mission was reopened in 2260, when Ambassador Mollari's aide Vir Kotto was assigned to Minbar. (STRIFE)

During the early years of the Babylon Project, the Centauri Republic made every effort to make amends to the Narn Regime. However, this policy angered many within the Republic, including Londo Mollari. Together with his allies, Mollari took the Centauri into war against the Narn, strictly against the wishes of the dying emperor, Turhan.

The Centauri Republic, together with Mollari's allies, the Shadows, defeated the Narn in 2259 after only six months. They ignored protests from many organizations, including the

Earth Alliance and Minbari Federation, by using mass drivers on the Narn homeworld. When the Narn surrendered, their homeworld became a Centauri colony and the Kha'Ri was replaced by a ruling body appointed by the Centauri (TWILIGHT). The Republic then began to expand into Drazi and Pak'ma'ra territory (FALL, MATTERS).

Central Corridor, The
Circular passage which runs through each major sector of Babylon 5.

Centarum
The Centauri ruling body, much like the Earth Senate.

Chakan
The provisional governor of the Mars Colony in 2258. (VOICE I)

Chang, Doctor
Scientist aboard the *Icarus* who discovered the ruins of an ancient civilization on a planet out on the Rim. Unfortunately for him and the crew of the *Icarus*, it was the Shadows' homeworld, Z'ha'dum. (REVELATIONS, Z'HA'DUM)

Changeling Net
An expensive and dangerous device used to project a holographic image around an individual, thus providing the perfect disguise. Changeling Nets are outlawed in every civilized sector and constant exposure to such an intense and unstable energy field can be fatal. In 2257, a Changeling Net was used by a Minbari assassin to pose as Commander Sinclair when he attempted to kill Ambassador Kosh. (GATHERING)

Chase
An associate of the bounty hunter Max, Chase helped hold Dr. Everett Jacobs hostage before being overcome by Security Chief Garibaldi and Dr. Franklin. (HUNTER)

Chase, Mr.
Arms dealer who sold weapons to Ambassador G'Kar's underground resistance movement in 2259. G'Kar realized that

many of the weapons had originally been sold by the Narns to Earth Alliance during the Earth–Minbari War. Played by Jack Kehler. (INQUISITOR)

Chit
See **Credit Chit**

Chiyoda-Ku, The
A luxury starliner. (TREASON)

Children of Time
Members of an alien religion, who refer to themselves as The Chosen and are said to be "born of the egg." They do not have an ambassador aboard Babylon 5.

The Children of Time's religious covenant is outlined in the Scrolls. It states that they cannot talk about their religion to nonmembers and that they must avoid exposure to alternative belief systems. It also forbids its members from undergoing surgical procedures of any kind; if one does, an individual is said to lose his or her soul. Animals, on the other hand, can be operated upon because they supposedly have no souls to lose. (BELIEVERS)

Chudomo, Third Fain of
Noble and honored Minbari sect within the religious caste which has served with honor for more than 500 years (PARLIAMENT). Its members include Lennier, Ashan and Lovell (PARLIAMENT, HONOR).

Many members of the Third Fain of Chu'Domo were aboard the *Black Star* when it was destroyed by Captain Sheridan in the Earth–Minbari War. Consequently, when Sheridan assumed command of Babylon 5 in 2259, the clan decided to act against him, without the approval of the Grey Council, and ordered Lovell and Ashan to frame him for murder. When their plan was exposed, Sheridan decided to keep the clan's motives a secret in order to save Lennier's honor. (HONOR)

Cirrus, Will
Together with his wife, Mariah, Will Cirrus volunteered for a long-term deep space mission in the mid-22nd century and

left Earth on the *Copernicus.* Will was murdered while in cryogenic suspension by a Soldier of Darkness, who removed his organs without leaving any entry or exit wound. When his body was examined aboard Babylon 5, it should have weighed 180 lbs, but was actually a mere 90 lbs. According to Mariah, he wouldn't have liked the future. (LONG)

Cirrus, Mariah

The wife of Will Cirrus, Mariah accompanied her husband on a long-term deep space mission and spent more than 100 years in cryogenic suspension aboard the *Copernicus* until she was revived aboard Babylon 5 in 2259.

Mariah was surprised that the *Copernicus* was found by humans in space and was disappointed that her race hadn't outgrown violence. When she learned that the Earth Alliance gained jumpgate technology shortly after the *Copernicus* embarked on its journey, Mariah began to feel that she and Will should never have signed up for the mission.

While aboard Babylon 5, she became close to Dr. Franklin and told him that her marriage to Will was far from perfect; they had broken up half a dozen times before they left Earth, and all they had in common was the stars and their dreams. Her last word to Will before he died was "goodnight."

Mariah was also haunted by horrific flashbacks and dreams. Later, she learned that a Soldier of Darkness had shared her cryogenic tube and used her to stay alive until it could find more food.

Once the Soldier had been destroyed, Mariah decided to return to Earth to mourn for her husband and catch up on the 100 years she had lost. She told Dr. Franklin that she might return to Babylon 5 one day to see him again, if he was still interested. Played by Anne-Marie Johnson. (LONG)

Clark, William Morgan (Vice-President/President)

Morgan Clark served as Luis Santiago's vice-president before being appointed as Earth Alliance president in 2259, following Santiago's death.

Clark's career has been far from uncontroversial. He first hit the headlines when the Psi Corps broke their charter to endorse his electoral campaign (REVELATIONS). Then, at the end of 2258, he disembarked from *Earthforce 1* for medical tests 24 hours before it exploded, killing President Santiago in the process (CHRYSALIS). Although Clark claimed to be suffering from a viral infection, an examination proved that he was perfectly healthy. Thus the evidence clearly suggests that Clark is in league with the Psi Corps and knew that the president's ship would be destroyed (HUNTER).

Clark was sworn in as Earth Alliance president aboard *Earthforce* 2 and promised to place more emphasis on Alliance interests (CHRYSALIS). Shortly after taking office, Clark was told the reason why the Minbari surrendered during the Earth–Minbari War. He doesn't believe that Minbari souls are being reborn into humans (DEPARTURE, DARKNESS).

When Captain Sheridan told Clark that they had arrested Jack, a member of a "new order on Earth," Clark ordered the captain to send the traitor and all evidence relating to the case back to Earth. While en route to Earth, Jack conveniently disappeared without a trace (REVELATIONS). Evidence proving Santiago's complicity was unearthed by Ivanova in 2260 (VOICES).

Played by Gary McGurk.

Cobra Bay

Cobra-like port for Babylon 5's Starfuries. To launch a Starfury from a cobra bay, the vessel is tilted down on a pair of arms, the bay door is opened, and the ship is thrust out into space by the centrifugal force of the station's spinning. Starfuries return to the station via the main docking bay and are then transferred back to the cobra bays.

Cole, Marcus

A human Ranger, Marcus Cole became involved with the army of light when his brother joined the covert organization. Marcus initially thought that his brother was a fool who was merely chasing legends and playing hero. Marcus was working at a mining colony when his Ranger brother warned him about an impending Shadow attack; he didn't listen. However, his attitude changed when he saw his brother die during the attack. Just as the Ranger died, Marcus promised his brother to continue what he had started and joined the Rangers shortly after.

At the beginning of 2260, Marcus arrived on Babylon 5 to ask Captain Sheridan to rescue the Rangers blockaded at Zagros 7. He always keeps his promises, stopped believing in miracles a long time ago, and has seen the effect alcohol has on the Minbari. He isn't a great believer in small talk but instead prefers to speak only when he has something to say. He uses a Minbari fighting pike for defense. Played by Jason Carter. (MATTERS)

Comac 4
Planet destroyed by Jha'dur in 2231. (DEATHWALKER)

Command and Control
See **Observation Dome**

Connally, Neeoma
The leading representative of the Dockers' Guild aboard the Babylon 5, Neeoma Connally decided to dedicate her life to protecting workers' rights following the murder of her father during the miners' strikes on Ganymede.

Between 2256 and 2258, Connally repeatedly stated that the workers were underpaid, overworked and ill-equipped. In 2257, a negotiator promised her that the dockers would receive a pay raise the following year. Consequently, she was furious when the extra money didn't materialize and led the dockers into an illegal strike when a computer malfunction cost one of the dockers, Alberto Delvientos, his life. Connally was convinced that the Senate would not invoke the Rush Act and was delighted when Commander Sinclair manipulated the act to reallocate 1.3 million credits from the station's military budget to meet the dockers' demands. (MEANS)

When the station was overrun by GROPOS in 2259, Connally again complained that the dockers were being overworked. Captain Sheridan instructed Commander Ivanova to try to arrange time off with pay for the dockers. (GROPOS)

Played by Katy Boyer.

Conspiracy of Light
Term first used by Draal to describe Sheridan's stand against corruption within the Earth Alliance. (TWILIGHT)

Copernicus, The
A deep range exploration craft built before Earth Alliance received jumpgate technology from the Centauri Republic, the *Copernicus* took its two cryogenically-frozen passengers, Mariah and Will Cirrus, on a mission which lasted more than a hundred years. The ship was programmed to home in on any signal that it came across and revive its passengers upon arrival.

During the Earth–Minbari War, the *Copernicus* was passing by a moon in Sector 18,70,59 when a Soldier of Darkness came aboard. The Soldier changed the ship's course to take it to Z'ha'dum, unaware that it was programmed to make contact with any signal it received. The creature then killed Will Cirrus and used Mariah to keep him alive during the journey.

In 2259, the *Copernicus* responded to a signal from Babylon 5. Upon landing on the station, it revived its remaining passengers. (LONG)

Copernicus, The
A shuttle which docked in Babylon 5 shortly before the accidental destruction of the *Talquith*. (MEANS)

Core Shuttle
Low gravity transport vehicle which runs through Babylon 5's central core.

Corey, Guinevere
An ambitious Earthforce lawyer assigned to Captain Sheridan when he was accused of callously murdering a Minbari, Lovell, Guinevere Corey was confident that Sheridan wouldn't be found guilty beyond a reasonable doubt. When Sheridan cleared his name but decided to protect the honor of the Third Fain of Chu'Domo, she felt that his solution was "ill-advised." Corey believes that only the "legally ignorant" say that truth is the only thing that matters. She also said that all clients say that they "don't believe it" when accused of a crime. Played by Julie Caitlin Brown. (HONOR)

Correlilmurzon
A delegate of Lumati sent to Babylon 5 in 2259 to see if humanity would be a worthy ally. Correlilmurzon was accom-

panied by a translator, Taq, so that there was no chance that he would speak to a member of an "inferior species." When he visited Down Below, Correlilmurzon believed that it was designed to keep inferior members of the human race away from the superior members topside, and consequently decided that humanity was a superior race.

When she learned that sex was required to seal the alliance, Commander Ivanova performed a silly dance around Correlilmurzon, which she claimed was a human technique for sexual intercourse. Before leaving the station, the Lumati delegate left her a present and a note saying, "Next time, my way." Played by Ian Abecrombie. (SACRIFICE)

Cortez, The

An explorer ship, assigned to patrol the Rim under the command of Captain Jack Maynard.

Between 2254 and 2259, the ship mapped Sector 900. In 2259, the ship left the Rim to repair the Euphrates jumpgate and became the first explorer ship to visit Babylon 5, where it restocked its supplies.

Shortly after leaving the station, its tracking system was destroyed as the result of an accident, and the Cortez became trapped in hyperspace. When Babylon 5 partly received the ship's distress signal, the station's Starfuries formed a line just inside the jumpgate in order to track the Cortez and show it the exit from hyperspace. When Lieutenant Keffer found the ship, he fired in the direction of the exit and the Cortez made history by becoming the only ship ever rescued in hyperspace. (STAR)

Corwin, David (Second Lieutenant)

A Babylon 5 dome technician. When interviewed in September 2259 by ISN, Corwin said that working on Babylon 5 was "a valuable experience" and claimed that his colleagues rarely became irate! Unfortunately, he's not a very good liar. Played by Joshua Cox. (WORD)

Cotto, Vir

As Ambassador Mollari's diplomatic attaché, Vir Cotto has witnessed both his master's and the Centauri Republic's descent into darkness.

Vir once admitted that there had been one constant in his life: either he didn't fit in or he was asked to leave. He was sent to Babylon 5 because his family didn't want him around and was appointed as Londo's aide because it was a joke job and there were no other willing candidates.

When Ambassador Mollari's influence dramatically increased in 2259, Vir was deemed to be an inappropriate assistant by Centauri Prime, who despatched a replacement attaché who had been groomed for the role. Vir only kept his position when Londo insisted that the young Centauri was "absolutely invaluable" to him and was the most skilled assistant he had ever had. According to the ambassador, Vir's family were "absolutely astonished" by the news and were ready to nominate him for godhood! Although Vir was pleased to remain on the station, he was less impressed when he learned that Londo had invited his family to stay on Babylon 5 for an entire month. (HONOR)

When asked if he believed in fate, Vir said that he believed there are certain degrees of fate and an individual's choices can make a difference within certain constraints. (GEOMETRY)

Unlike his master, Vir never had any desire to recapture the glory of the Centauri Republic. He believes that every generation mourns for the previous one, while failing to learn the lessons of history (KNIVES). When his cousin, Kiron Maray, was being pressured to abandon his girlfriend and agree to an arranged marriage, Vir revealed that he detested the way the Centauri Empire places wealth and power over love (PRAYER). Contrary to the traditions of the Republic, he also believes that disgrace is better than death (KNIVES).

Vir repeatedly warned Ambassador Mollari about the consequences of his actions, but his master refused to listen. When Londo decided to ask Morden to destroy Quadrant 14, thus taking the Centauri into war against the Narn, Vir told him not to do it. When it is clear that Londo had no intention of changing his course of action, Vir told him that one day he would remind him of his decision and he might understand. (SHADOWS)

While Vir continued to work as the ambassador's aide, he felt increasingly haunted by his lack of action. When Morden asked him what he wanted, Vir replied that he would like to see his head on a pike as a warning to the next ten generations that some favors come at too high a price. (Z'HA'DUM)

Near the end of 2259, Vir told G'Kar that he was sorry for what his people had done, but the Narn refused to accept his apology. (INQUISITOR)

Although he is timid, Vir does not scare easily and refused to be chased away by a Techno-mage demon (GEOMETRY). He has a fondness for games and gadgets (PURPLE) and doesn't require much alcohol to become drunk (HONOR). Vir once told his cousin, Kiron Maray, that he was Centauri ambassador aboard Babylon 5 (PRAYER). In 2260, Vir was reassigned to the Minbari homeworld (STRIFE).

Played by Stephen Furst.

Couro Prido

A Centauri dueling society. Its name means "proud knives" and its members included Londo Mollari and Urza Jaddo. (KNIVES)

Cramer, Mary Ann

An ISN reporter assigned to Babylon 5 in 2258, Mary Ann Cramer interviewed Commander Sinclair on the second anniversary of Babylon 5 going on-line (INFECTION). She later tried and failed to talk to him in the middle of the dockers' strike (MEANS). She has little interest in Security Chief Garibaldi's charms (INFECTION). Played by Patricia Healy.

Crane, Marie

A candidate in the 2258 Earth Alliance presidential election, Maria Crane lost to Luis Santiago. Played by Anne Bruice. (MIDNIGHT)

Cranston, Derek

Earthforce special agent assigned to Babylon in 2259 to track down Dr. Everett Jacobs. Captain Sheridan made his life as difficult as possible and eventually convinced him that Jacobs was never aboard the station. Played by Bernie Casey. (HUNTER)

Crawler

A surface vehicle used on Mars. (GRAIL)

Credit Chit
Futuristic variant of the credit card, used by the Earth Alliance. (HONOR)

Cup of the Goddess
See **Holy Grail, The**

Custodian
Title given to the guardian of Epsilon 3. The custodian is linked to the Great Machine within the planet and the pair share a symbiotic relationship. In 2258, Draal succeeded Varn as custodian. (VOICE II)

Cutter
Presidential Security Officer Cutter served as assistant to Lianna Kemmer. He was also a member of Homeguard. In 2258, he framed Garibaldi for the death of his associate, Nolan, by placing schematics of the cobra bay and 100,000 Centauri credits in the security chief's quarters. Cutter then intended to sabotage President Santiago's visit to the station, but was stopped at the last minute by Garibaldi and Kemmer. Played by Tom Donaldson. (SURVIVORS)

D

Daffy Duck
Twentieth-century cartoon character. Security Chief Garibaldi loves Daffy's cartoons, particularly "Duck Dodgers in the 24th and a ½ Century."

Daggair
One of Ambassador Mollari's three wives. While she had little time for Londo, Daggair was happy to play the dutiful and loving wife, as it helped her social-climbing. When Londo was given permission to divorce two of his three wives in 2259, Daggair was willing to do anything to keep her title and share of his money. Despite her efforts, Londo could see right through the pretense and divorced her. Played by Lois Nettleson. (MATES)

Dagool
A Brakiri thug, Dagool was caught by Security Chief Garibaldi stealing credits three times in one month. Played by Mark Ginther. (SURVIVORS)

Da'Kal
Ambassador G'Kar's mate. Da'Kal and G'Kar have an open relationship and consequently have different lovers. Unsurprisingly, therefore, Da'Kal offered no objection when G'Kar told her that he might have to mate with Lyta Alexander in

order to create Narn's first telepath (GATHERING). Prior to the Narn–Centauri War, Da'Kal lived in Hebka (BLOOD).

Damocles Sector, The

The rare poison florazyne is found exclusively in this sector. Caroline Sykes visited the Damocles Sector before arriving on Babylon 5 in 2257, thus allowing Ambassador G'Kar to claim that she provided Commander Sinclair with the florazyne used in the assassination attempt on Ambassador Kosh. (GATHERING)

Darabuto, Xavier

Shopkeeper who had criticized new import regulations in 2259 and had his shop closed by the Nightwatch as a result. (FALL)

D'arc

A Tuchanq ambassador, D'arc was revealed to be a mass murderer and sentenced to death by President Clark while visiting Babylon 5 in 2259. As she evaded arrest, D'arc was effectively brainwiped during an accident and lost all knowledge of her crimes. Her execution was later faked by Captain Sheridan. (LAW)

Dark Star, The

Seedy dance club aboard Babylon 5. Unsurprisingly, it is one of Ambassador Mollari's favorite haunts. The Centauri met the dancer Adira Tyree at the Dark Star (PURPLE) and also took Lennier there to teach him about dancers and poker. When Mollari was caught cheating during a card game, it led to a massive brawl in the club. The station's security subsequently arrested 30 humans and aliens, including the ambassador and Lennier (MERCY).

Data Crystals

The most common means of information storage used on Babylon 5. The Minbari provide a great many of them to other races. They utilize a holographic-based 3-dimensional system. (BLOOD)

"Datya"
Term used by Shonto to describe his father. (BELIEVERS)

Davo
Planet in the Centauri Republic. The homeworld of Adira
Tyree, Davo is famous for its starlaces. (PURPLE)

Defense Grid
Babylon 5's in-built defense system comprising laser cannons
and guns as well as a tracking device. Revamped in 2259 with
the very latest weapons from Earthforce Research and Development, including pulse cannons, interceptors and a tracking
system which was three times faster than the original. With
the new defense grid, Babylon 5 was capable of defending
itself against a warship. (GROPOS)

Deeron
Kalain's first officer aboard the *Trigati*. At the beginning of
2259, Deeron led the ship's final, suicidal assault on Babylon
5, prior to its destruction at the hands of the Minbari. Played
by Jennifer Gatti. (DEPARTURE)

"De Farhurst"
A Minbari phrase which means, "I yield to your authority."
When Sheridan was attacked by the Minbari Lovell, he
claimed that the Minbari had shouted "death first." However,
the sole witness, Ashan, claimed that Lovell had said "de
farhurst." It was later discovered that Ashan was lying.
(HONOR)

Delenn (Ambassador)
The Minbari ambassador aboard Babylon 5 and a former
member of the Grey Council.
   Delenn was raised as a member of the religious caste.
When she was young, she was visiting the city with her family
when she became separated from her parents. She was afraid
until she found herself in an old temple. Inside the temple
she felt safe, and decided to stay there until her parents arrived for her. After a while, she fell asleep for a few hours, and
when she woke up she saw the vision of a figure, possibly
Valen, standing over her, smiling. He told Delenn that she

would be alright and that if she believed her parents would come, they would. Shortly after, her parents arrived. Ever since then, Delenn has believed that "faith manages." (CONFESSIONS)

Delenn was appointed as a member of the Grey Council and witnessed firsthand the death of the Minbari leader Dukhat in 2242. She also helped save him from a Soul Hunter assigned to steal his spirit. (SOUL)

Delenn was with the Grey Council during the Battle of the Line and suggested that they bring one of the human fighters aboard their warcruiser to learn more about Earth's defenses and the human race. When she was asked to pick a subject, she chose Jeffrey Sinclair's Starfury. Delenn was shocked when examinations showed that Sinclair had a Minbari soul and that Minbari souls had been reborn, either in part or in full, into humans. As a result, she supported the decision to surrender. (DEPARTURE)

In 2256, she was assigned to Babylon 5 to study the human race and determine whether they were the race referred to by Valen in an important prophecy (SQUARED). She decided that she could perform her mission better if she kept her position on the Council a secret (SOUL). In order to learn more about humanity, Delenn joined Garibaldi to watch a 20th-century cartoon, "Duck Dodgers in the 24th and a $1/2$ Century," and learned one of the security chief's limericks (MIDNIGHT, GATHERING).

Delenn felt that humans were a mass of contradictions but, with time, one could learn to live with them (VOICE I, PRAYER). She also believed that only humans would have built Babylon 5 because, unlike all other races, they build communities, even out of diverse and sometimes hostile people. She claimed that if the Narns or Centauri had built the station, it would not be open to all aliens (WORD).

When summoned before the Grey Council in 2258, Delenn told them that humans had a unique capacity to fight against impossible odds and that their passions propelled them to the stars and toward their destiny. She then claimed that humanity's main weakness was that they did not appreciate their own strength and nobility. Delenn then concluded that the human race represented the future and the Minbari could learn a great deal from them. (SQUARED)

Delenn enjoyed a close relationship with Commander Sinclair. In 2256 she gave him classified Minbari information on the Vorlon Empire and details of the Minbari assassin who attempted to poison Ambassador Kosh (GATHERING). Two years later, Delenn avoided telling the commander that her old friend and mentor Draal intended to become custodian of Epsilon 3, because she was convinced that Sinclair wouldn't allow Draal to sacrifice himself to the machine but would do it himself (VOICE II). However, she was under orders to kill the commander if he remembered the secret of his missing 24 hours during the Battle of the Line (SKY). After Sinclair was interrogated in a Virtual Reality Cybernet, Delenn suspected that he knew at least some of the events that had occurred (CHRYSALIS). When Sinclair asked Delenn why she visited the Zen Garden almost every other day, she told him that nothing expresses the idea that one mind can change the universe more clearly than a Japanese stone garden (GATHERING).

Delenn has always sought to keep out of the circle of hatred between the Centauri and Narns. She has always refused to consider a military alliance with either power, and once used a special ring to inflict potentially bone-crushing gravities against Ambassador G'Kar until he swore never to mock or even mention the Grey Council again (GATHERING). When Neroon ignored Branmer's wishes for a quiet funeral and widely displayed his body as a monument to war, Delenn felt obliged to steal Branmer's body and, as per his instructions, had it cremated and his ashes scattered in Minbari space near Minbar. When Sinclair and Neroon began a heated discussion about the Earth–Minbari War, she said that debating old wars should be left to historians and is not a fit topic of discussion for their participants (LEGACIES).

Delenn told Shall Mayan that she sometimes regretted some of the decisions she had made during the course of her life, and was outraged when the poet was the victim of a Homeguard attack aboard Babylon 5 (PRAYER). When Delenn and Draal needed to travel to the surface of Epsilon 3 to avert the planet's destruction in 2258, she enlisted the help of Ambassador Mollari. Once they returned to Babylon 5, Delenn told him that she owed him a favor. Two years later, Delenn repaid the debt when she arranged for the Centauri diplomatic attaché Vir Kotto to be reassigned to Minbar (STRIFE).

Delenn had her first direct encounter with the Shadows when the mysterious human emissary, Morden, met with the ambassador to ask her what she wanted. Within minutes of their meeting, she sensed that he was an agent of darkness and a triangle on her head suddenly appeared without explanation. (SIGNS)

Of all the members of the Grey Council, Delenn has traveled the most, and has visited many worlds and encountered many life-forms. As a result, she was offered the role of Minbari leader in 2258. Delenn became the first Minbari ever to decline the position when she told the Council that she had to stay on Babylon 5 because she had a part to play in the upcoming events which had been prophesied. The offer was then withdrawn and the Council was forced to choose another leader. (SQUARED)

At the end of 2258, Delenn asked Ambassador Kosh (via Lennier) whether the Shadows had returned to Z'ha'dum. The Vorlon replied, "Yes" (CHRYSALIS, Z'HA'DUM). She then went to Kosh and told him that she had her doubts and needed to be sure about her course of action. When the Vorlon left his encounter suit to reveal his true self, Delenn told him that she would keep her promise and entered a chrysalis in which she began a radical and extremely painful transformation (CHRYSALIS). Delenn subsequently emerged from her cocoon as a half-human, half-Minbari hybrid and told the Babylon 5 Advisory Council that she had undergone her transformation to become a bridge of understanding between humans and Minbari, so that the two races would never fight each other again. She then began the long process of trying to understand what it is to be human. Delenn began to dress more like a human and had to learn about hair care and the facts of female life from Ivanova (MATES). She had many problems trying to master the human art of swearing (TWILIGHT).

Despite her good intentions, Delenn found that her transformation was criticized by both humans and Minbari alike. The Minbari aboard the station began to question her authority as their ambassador, while many bigoted humans perceived her actions as an affront to mankind (WORD). Delenn felt increasingly alone and began to question her own actions when she was removed from the Grey Council and replaced by Neroon. The fact that she was allowed to continue to serve as the Minbari ambassador aboard Babylon 5 offered little consolation (ALONE).

Delenn became close friends with Captain Sheridan and comforted him when he questioned his worth as the commander of Babylon 5. She told him that the universe makes sure that everyone is in the right place at the right time because they are "star-stuff": part of the universe made flesh (DISTANT). A few weeks later, she asked Sheridan to dinner wearing a dress that, she had been told, would "turn heads" (RACE). When Sheridan was accused of murdering an innocent Minbari, she refused to believe he would commit such a crime (HONOR). Their relationship became more intense when Delenn asked him to allow her into the Markab isolation zone to help those dying of Drafa. Before she left for the zone, she told him that if she caught the disease she hoped to see Sheridan in another place where "shadows do not fall." The captain then told her to call him "John" when they next met (CONFESSIONS).

In September 2259, Delenn was reluctantly interviewed for the ISN documentary "36 Hours Aboard Babylon 5." After the interview, she started to read The Universe Today and found the "Eye on Minbari" section to be particularly interesting because it often included a lot of information about her people that she had not been told. (DIVIDED)

Delenn first learned that the Army of Light known as the Rangers had been re-formed during a message from Ambassador Sinclair. Following the end of the Narn–Centauri War, Delenn gave Sheridan joint authority as leader of all Rangers in the area. (TWILIGHT)

As the year drew to a close, Delenn faced Sebastian, an inquisitor summoned by Ambassador Kosh. She was tortured and humiliated, but passed the test when she showed that she was willing to give her life for another, alone and uncelebrated. As a result, the test helped Delenn believe in herself and her destiny once again. (INQUISITOR)

When Delenn was shown footage of a Shadow ship in 2260, she recognized it from the descriptions from the last Great War. However, when she was asked about the vessel by

Earthforce Special Intelligence agent David Endawi, she could not give him any information and later explained to Sheridan that their only chance of survival was to allow the Shadows to believe that no one knew anything about them or what they were doing. Delenn didn't believe that a Shadow ship could be defeated until Sheridan destroyed one using the Bonehead Maneuver. (MATTERS)

Played by Mira Furlan.

Delta Gamma Nine
United Spaceways transport upon which Lyta Alexander first arrived on Babylon 5 in 2257. (GATHERING)

Delta Squad
One of Babylon 5's Starfury squadrons. Also known as Delta Wing.

Delta Wing
See **Delta Squad**

Delvientos, Alberto
Dock worker killed in 2258 when the *Talquith* was destroyed in bay as the result of a computer malfunction. The brother of Eduardo. (MEANS)

Delvientos, Eduardo
A senior foreman in Babylon 5's docks, Eduardo Delvientos had worked in space docks for 40 years and came from a family of dockers. Eduardo claimed to have worked in all of Babylon 5's worst locations.

Following the death of his brother, Alberto, in 2258, Eduardo became a keen advocate of strike action—at any cost. Although he was not a violent man, he felt that workers had suffered more than enough and threw the first punch against Security Chief Garibaldi when the Rush Act was invoked (MEANS). Delvientos was pleased with the peaceful resolution to the dockers' strike and was interviewed for the ISN documentary "36 Hours Aboard Babylon 5" in 2259 (WORD). Played by Jose Rey.

Deneb Sector

Sector of space surveyed by Catherine Sakai, following her reconciliation with Commander Sinclair in 2259. (PARLIA-MENT)

Deuce

A vicious extortionist aboard Babylon 5, Deuce brought a Na'ka'leen feeder aboard the station to brainwipe his opponents, including Miriam Runningdear. He pretended that the feeder was actually Ambassador Kosh to make people believe that the all-powerful Vorlons worked for him. When Deuce attempted to feed his "pet" with Ombuds Wellington and Aldous Gajic, his lair was stormed by a Security team. During the ensuing shoot-out, Deuce shot Gajic, who sacrificed his life to save Jordan. The killer was then brought to justice. Deuce's real name was Desmond Mosechenko. Played by William Sanderson. (GRAIL)

Devalera

Drug used to revive people in cardiac arrest. If it fails, a cardial stimulator might be required. (LONG)

Devereaux

Operative of the movement responsible for the assassination of Earth Alliance President Santiago. In mid-December 2258, Devereaux hired a number of lurkers, including Stephen Petrov, to load an unspecified cargo. Two weeks later, Garibaldi investigated Petrov's mysterious death and discovered Devereaux's cargo consisted of transmitters set to jam all communication to the president's personal cruiser, *Earthforce 1*. When the security chief arrested Devereaux and his two associates, he found that their PPGs were unmarked, thus suggesting that they were Earthforce special agents. Shortly after, the three men were freed by their associate, Jack, who then shot his superior, Garibaldi, in the back. Devereaux and his associates were subsequently attacked and killed by Jack. Played by Edward Conery. (CHRYSALIS)

Dilgar, The

An extinct and brutal race which attacked and conquered the non-aligned worlds in 2230. The Dilgar were defeated two years later by a coalition of the Earth Alliance and non-aligned worlds. All its war leaders were caught and tried for war crimes with the exception of Jha'dur, who disappeared without a trace. Both the Centauri and the Narn are believed to have collaborated with the Dilgar.

Almost all of the Dilgar who survived the war were killed a few years later when their homeworld's sun went nova, destroying the planet in the process. When Jha'dur boarded Babylon 5 in 2258, she was believed to be the last surviving member of her race. As she left the station, her ship was destroyed by the Vorlons. (DEATHWALKER)

Dilgar Invasion, The
Abbreviation for the Dilgar invasion of the non-aligned worlds in 2230. (DEATHWALKER)

Dockers' Guild, The
Trade union which represents the Earth Alliance's dock workers. Neeoma Connally is the Guild's leading representative aboard Babylon 5 and speaks for the station's 1500 dockers.

During the station's first two years of operation, the Dockers' Guild argued that its members were overworked, underpaid and ill-equipped. When computer failure led to the death of a docker, Alberto Delvientos, the Guild led its members into industrial action. Although the Senate claimed that the dockers were bound by government contract and could not quit nor strike, the Guild continued with the legitimate dispute. When the Senate invoked the Rush Act, the Guild was pleasantly surprised when Commander Sinclair offered to use 1.3 million credits from Babylon 5's military budget to meet the dock workers' demands. (MEANS)

Dodger (Private)
A GROPOS with the 356th squadron, Elizabeth Durman was known to everyone around her as Dodger. Her Earthforce serial number was 56927. During her time aboard Babylon 5, Dodger defended Ambassador Delenn from a racist attack by Private Kleist and was attracted to the station's security chief, Garibaldi. She thought he had a "nice butt" and offered him a no-strings-attached night of passion. He explained that he would prefer to take things more slowly and arranged to have

a drink when she next visited the station. Unfortunately for both of them, shortly after leaving Babylon 5 Dodger was killed during Operation : Sudden Death. Played by Marie Marshall. (GROPOS)

Down Below

Name of the station's undeveloped areas and home of lurkers. Security Chief Garibaldi believes that Down Below accounts for nine-tenths of the station's crime (GRAIL). Down Below mainly operates through barter (RACE).

Downtown

Captain Sheridan's nickname for the area between the hull and the water reclamation system, downtown is said to be the most unpleasant area in Babylon 5, except for the methane toilets. Situated in levels 50 and 51 between the Blue and Gray Sectors, downtown is full of machinery, lead walls and pipes. It was welded shut when the station went on-line.

During the search for Dr. Everett Jacobs in 2259, Sheridan advised Earthforce special agent Cranston to search downtown for the fugitive physician. Cranston's team had to burn through 49 pressure doors to gain access to the area, including two big doors on either side of the waste recycling plant. Naturally, the only thing this staff found in downtown was an unpleasant smell. (HUNTER)

Draal

Delenn's mentor and close personal friend, Draal lived his entire life on Minbar until 2258, when he decided that his life no longer had meaning. Draal felt that Minbar was changing for the worse and that his people had lost direction in the years since the death of Dukhat, and sensed growing dissatisfaction and selfishness. Consequently, he visited Delenn on Babylon 5 to say goodbye to his old friend. (VOICE I)

While aboard the station, Draal heard someone calling for his help and later discovered that it was Varn, the dying custodian of Epsilon 3. Draal realized that Varn was looking for a successor and decided to take his place to save the lives of all those aboard Babylon 5. In doing so, Draal found a new purpose in life. Draal then told the crew of Babylon 5 that he would not show his face again until the time was right and warned that anyone who attempted to land on Epsilon 3 would be destroyed. (VOICE II)

When Draal reappeared to Captain Sheridan in 2259, he explained that the machine had revitalized him. Delenn said that he looked 30 years younger. Draal then offered Sheridan an alliance and placed Epsilon 3's impressive power at his disposal. (TWILIGHT)

Draal revealed that he was not alone inside the surface of Epsilon. His colleagues included Zathras (TWILIGHT). He also once told Ambassador Mollari that he liked the Hokey-Pokey (VOICE I). Played by Louis Turenne (VOICE I and II) and John Schuck (TWILIGHT).

Drafa

A terminal and highly contagious disease which wiped out the Markab race in 2259. Drafa was named after the island the disease was first found on, centuries before it eradicated the Markab race. The island was noted for its excesses and immorality, so when its entire population was wiped out by a plague, most Markabs believed that it was a punishment from God. Over the years, the island's story became the stuff of legend; Markab children were warned if they were immoral, the Dark Angel of Drafa would bring them disease and death.

When Drafa claimed a new victim in 2258, the family lied about it to avoid scandal. They were convinced that they couldn't contract the disease because they were moral, so they happily went into the population, spreading Drafa wherever they went. Each case was hushed up by the Markab authorities, who did not want to be blamed for allowing the spread of immorality which supposedly caused Drafa. As word of the disease began to spread, many Markabs tried to leave the homeworld for outer colonies, including Babylon 5. Instead of leaving Drafa behind them, however, they merely took the disease with them to Markab outposts.

The incubation period of Drafa lasts between a week and a few days and its symptoms included chronic dizziness, acute sore throat, swelling lymph and surface glands, and low blood pressure. Once a patient develops the symptoms, death is guaranteed within 24 hours.

While trying to find a cure, Doctors Franklin and Lazarenn discovered that Drafa is an airborne disease which attacks the yellow cells in Markabs as well as the green cells in Pak'ma'ra. It slowly erodes the synaptic gaps, which eventually shuts down heart activity and respiration. Although Dr. Franklin discovered a cure for the disease, it was too late for the Markabs. (CONFESSIONS)

Drake, Nelson

As Dr. Vance Hendricks' ruthless assistant, Nelson Drake killed a customs guard using a cardial stimulator to bring an Ikaaran artifact aboard Babylon 5. The relic was, in fact, a bio-organic weapon which transformed him into a living killing machine programmed to kill anything that wasn't pure Ikaaran. When Sinclair made the machine's personality matrix realize that Ikaara 7 had been destroyed by others of its own kind, it released Nelson Drake. Played by Marshall Teague. (INFECTION)

Drazi

Alien race aboard Babylon 5 and a leading member of the League of Non-Aligned Worlds, Drazi prefer to fight first and think later.

A Drazi cycle refers to a Drazi year, which is the equivalent of 1.2 human years. Every five human years, the Drazi divide into two groups—one green, one purple—by randomly choosing a colored sash from a barrel. The Drazi who chooses the leader's sash becomes the group's leader. The green and purple Drazi then attempt to beat each other into surrender. The group that wins the fight by the end of the cycle then becomes dominant until the next struggle. In 2259, the struggle escalated when green Drazi started killing their purple opponents. On Babylon 5, Commander Ivanova resolved the crisis when she unintentionally became the leader of the greens and made them dye their sashes purple. One of her subordinates explained that the Drazi leadership were still in the process of changing the rules so that aliens wearing the leader's sash could not command the group. (GEOMETRY)

Droshalla

A Drazi higher being which is said to "light the way" (MATTERS). Ambassador Kosh appeared to all nearby Drazi as

Droshalla when he left his encounter suit to rescue Captain Sheridan (FALL).

Drozac
Drazi ranger killed while helping Marcus Cole escape from the Centauri blockade of Zagros 7 in 2260. (MATTERS)

Dubai
An alien race aboard Babylon 5. Swapped quarters with the Tukati, who didn't like being quartered next to the Pak'ma'ra. (DISTANT)

Ducats
Centauri currency. Also known as "ducks." (SURVIVORS)

"Duck Dodgers in the 24th and a ½ Century"
A classic Daffy Duck cartoon and Security Chief Garibaldi's "second favorite thing" in the whole universe. (MIDNIGHT)

Dug Out, The
Sports bar aboard Babylon 5, situated near the Zocalo. Its specialities include Zoon Burgers, Jovian Tubers and Attraxion Ale. (TKO)

Dukhat
The former Minbari leader, Dukhat was killed in 2242 when an Earth ship, the *Amundsen*, misunderstood the Minbari's intentions and opened fire. Dukhat's death provided the basis of the Earth–Minbari War. A Soul Hunter attempted to steal Dukhat's soul, but was prevented by the other Minbari on the ship, including Satai Delenn. (SOUL)

Du'Rog
An old enemy of G'Kar who claimed the ambassador had ruined his family name and humiliated him in front of the Kha'Ri. When he learned that he was dying, Du'Rog spent all of his remaining funds on hiring an assassin from the Thenta Makur to terrify and then kill G'Kar. G'Kar suspected that Na'Toth was the assassin, but she pointed out that she had never met the Narn. (PARLIAMENT)

Du'Rog died leaving a wife, Ka'Het, a son, T'Kog, and a

daughter, Mi'Ra. When they learned that the assassin had failed in his task, Du'Rog's family took a Chon-Kar against G'Kar. They subsequently abandoned it when the ambassador financially compensated the family and they received evidence which cleared Du'Rog's name. (BLOOD)

Played by Mark Hendrickson.

Duridium
A chemical by-product of Quantium 40. (MIND)

Duridium Nitrate
A concentrated explosive, available from several commercial manufacturers. Each batch of duridium nitrate has a molecular coding system which can be traced. (CONVICTIONS)

Durman, Elizabeth
See **Dodger**

Durza
Arguably a giant of Centauri opera, Durza was one of Ambassador Mollari's favorite singers. (KNIVES)

Dust
An illegal drug which allows the user to enter the minds of others and relive memories of the past. (DUST)

E

Earharts

Officers' lounge aboard Babylon 5 named after American avi-
ator, Amelia Earhart. Anyone who brings official business into
the bar must buy everyone a drink, as Security Chief Garibaldi once found out to his cost. (RACE)

Earth Alliance, The

A commonwealth of independent states which comprises
more than two dozen worlds in fourteen solar systems
(WORD). Besides Earth, members of the Alliance include
the colonies on the Moon and Mars, as well as a number of
bronze-tech worlds. In general, the Alliance determines the
foreign policies of its member worlds and leaves them to determine their own domestic policies.

In the mid-22nd century, the Earth Alliance made contact
with the Centauri Republic. In return for various trade agreements the Centauri gave the Earth Alliance access to their
technology (MIDNIGHT). The Alliance initially used Centauri jumpgates but soon learned to build its own (LONG). As
the Earth Alliance became increasingly powerful, the declining Centauri Republic became more and more desperate to
forge a military or political alliance (GATHERING).

The Alliance sent several expeditions into Vorlon space,
but none returned. When EarthGov enquired about their
fates, the Vorlon Empire told them that the ships had been

lost and advised the Alliance not to mount any further explorations into Vorlon space.

In 2230, the Earth Alliance joined forces with the non-aligned worlds to fight the Dilgar. At first, the Alliance was more interested in building its reputation as a major galactic empire, but became morally involved when it witnessed first-hand the atrocities which had been committed by the Dilgar. (DEATHWALKER)

The Earth–Minbari War represented the first time Earth Alliance was faced with invasion and extinction. It was brought to its knees by the Minbari, who suddenly surrendered on the verge of victory. In 2249, Earth Alliance President Santiago launched the Babylon Project in the hope that the Alliance would never again fight based on a misunderstanding. Although the majority of the Alliance's population initially supported the program, they swiftly began to grow disillusioned with it.

The only issue which proved more controversial than the Babylon Project was the Mars Colony (WORD). After the Earth–Minbari War, the population of the colony demanded independence from Earth with added vigor, while many of those on Earth resented that their taxes were paying for the "Marsies" to have the best atmosphere reprocessors and water reclamation technology (VOICE I). Although the Earth Senate used shock troops to quell the Mars Rebellion in 2258, it has failed to offer any viable long-term solution to the growing crisis.

When Morgan Clark succeeded Luis Santiago as Earth Alliance president in January 2259, he promised to place greater emphasis on Earth interests and combat growing alien influence. One of his first actions was to appoint Captain Sheridan as commander of Babylon 5 against the wishes of the Minbari. (DEPARTURE) (See also **Earth–Minbari War, The; Babylon Project, The** and **Mars Colony, The**)

Earth–Centauri Non-Aggression Treaty

Non-aggression pact signed by the Earth Alliance and the Centauri Republic in 2259 which guaranteed their areas of influence (FALL). The treaty also outlawed members of the Alliance from officially speaking to any Narn leaders without the permission of the Centauri (MATTERS).

EarthDome
Situated in Geneva, Switzerland, EarthDome is the home of EarthGov. All EarthDome personnel have coded identification crystal implants which emit a low-level, short range signal. Thus the implant can be used to prevent kidnapping. (HUNTER)

Earthforce
The Earth Alliance's military division. Officers of Earthforce's different branches can be distinguished by the color of their uniforms: command staff wear blue, marines wear olive/brown, and security staff wear gray. They can also be distinguished by their stetbar: gold for command, silver for command staff, green for security, red for medical and yellow for science division. Ever since the Earth–Minbari War, Earthforce has been obsessed with gaining new technology. (VOICE I)

Earthforce 1
Earth Alliance presidential space cruiser. In 2258, President Santiago traveled on *Earthforce 1* to Babylon 5, where he officially gave Zeta Squad to the station (SURVIVORS). On January 1st 2259, *Earthforce 1* exploded as a result of a malfunction in its fusion reactor. It was destroyed near the transfer point at Io while en route to Jupiter, and was carrying President Santiago at the time. Its gold channel frequency was 1010105 (CHRYSALIS).

Earthforce 2
Earth Alliance presidential space cruiser. Former Vice-President Morgan Clark was sworn in as president aboard this ship following the death of Luis Santiago aboard *Earthforce 1*. (CHRYSALIS)

Earthforce Bureau of Internal Investigations
Internal affairs unit, also known as "eyes" (short for I.I.). The Bureau ran a series of investigations into senior command staff on all outposts in 2258. The investigations were exploited by Colonel Ari Ben Zayne, who used them to assume control of Babylon 5 before his true motives were exposed. (EYES)

Earthforce Defense Bio-Weapons Division

Earth Alliance military unit in charge of the development of bio-organic weaponry. In 2258, the Division confiscated the Ikaaran bio-organic weaponry aboard Babylon 5 for "reasons of planetary security." (INFECTION)

Earthforce Special Intelligence

The Earth Alliance's equivalent of the USA's FBI, the Special Intelligence agency falls under the direct control of the president. President Clark used the organization to track down Dr. Everett Jacobs in 2259. Also known as ESI. (HUNTER)

EarthGov

Abbreviation for Earth Government.

Earth History Exhibition

Historical display aboard Babylon 5. Exhibits include a 20th-century electric guitar. (MATES)

Earth–Minbari War, The

A brutal conflict between the Earth Alliance and the Minbari Federation during which the human race faced annihilation.

The Earth–Minbari War was based on a misunderstanding that occurred when the two species made contact in 2242. Captain Ellasai Ferdinand VI of the Earthforce warship *Amundsen* misinterpreted the intentions of the Minbari ship and opened fire, killing their leader, Dukhat. He then claimed that they had fired first, thus precipitating war.

The Earth Alliance offered little opposition to the Minbari, who used a stealth technology which the humans were unable to overcome. The Alliance's only real victory during the entire conflict came when Captain John Sheridan destroyed the Minbari flagship, the *Black Star*, and three heavy cruisers (DEPARTURE). The Alliance's forces were depleted rapidly, so it was forced to buy weapons from the Narn (MID-NIGHT).

It only took a few years for the Minbari to penetrate Earth Alliance territory and they bypassed several human outposts and colonies, including the Mars Colony, to attack Earth (TWILIGHT). The Alliance mounted a desperate (and suicidal) bid to save the Earth from invasion, known as the Battle of the Line. Once again, the Alliance could not stop its enemy and 19,800 pilots were killed during the offensive.

However, on the verge of defeat, the Minbari surrendered on the orders of the Grey Council. Although their reason was not made public, the leaders of the Earth Alliance were told that the Minbari had discovered that their souls were being reborn, either in part or in full, into human beings. While many of the Alliance leaders thought that the Minbari had gone insane, they were in no position to argue and accepted the Minbari's conditional surrender in 2248 (DARKNESS). The Minbari made it absolutely clear that they would not pay any reparations to the Alliance.

In the years following the war, the Minbari's decision to surrender on the verge of victory was widely debated both on Earth and on Minbar. Some believed that the Battle of the Line convinced the Minbari that they could not conquer Earth or beat the Alliance (GATHERING). Others, including some members of Bureau 13, speculated that the Minbari decided to destroy Earth from within using human spies (SKY). On Minbar, rumors suggested that the Grey Council had experienced some kind of religious vision.

Over a quarter of a million humans were killed during the Earth–Minbari War. The Babylon Project was conceived to avoid a similar catastrophe. (See also **Battle of the Line, The**)

Eclipse Cafe
Cafe situated along the Zocalo.

Ellison
A GROPOS, Ellison was a member of 356th Squadron's Green Squad. (GROPOS)

Ellison, Harlan
A renowned and notoriously outspoken 20th-century author, Harlan Ellison's treatises include "Working Without a Diet." Ellison's work makes Commander Ivanova laugh. (TKO)

Elric
human leader of a group of Techno-mages who boarded Babylon 5 in 2259. Elric revealed that they were heading for the Rim and had nothing to say to anyone in the known galaxy.

Elric refused to grant private audiences and had little interest in meeting Ambassador Mollari, regardless of how much money the Centauri offered him. When Mollari annoyed him, the Techno-mage possessed his data system with a holodemon and later created some winged demons to keep him busy. Before he left the station, Elric told Mollari that he was touched by darkness and that he could hear the cries of billions—his victims. Played by Michael Ansara. (GEOMETRY)

Encounter Suit

Large apparel which protects aliens from hostile environments. Normally worn by Ambassador Kosh when he is in the presence of others, although he uses his encounter suit more for disguise than protection (PRAYER, FALL). Kosh's encounter suit also shields him from telepath scan (GATHERING). Also known as an Environment Suit.

Endawi, David

Member of Earthforce Special Intelligence sent to Babylon 5 at the beginning of 2260 to investigate the film taken by Lieutenant Keffer of a Shadow ship. Endawi met with the senior command staff, Ambassador Delenn, Ambassador Mollari and G'Kar, but found no concrete evidence about the ship. Upon returning to Earth, his report suggested that nobody on the station knew about the ship and only provided him with legends and interesting stories. Endawi doesn't drink on duty. Played by Tucker Smallwood. (MATTERS)

Energy Cap

The power source of Phased Plaser Guns. (STRIFE)

Energy Pod

A portable energy source. Knights One and Two used an energy pod to power a Virtual Reality Cybernet. (SKY)

Environment Suit

See **Encounter Suit**

Eronium Radiation
A benign form of radiation. All subjects of Project : Lazarus
were known to emit this. (SPIDER)

Epsilon 3
The planet around which Babylon 5 orbits, also known as
Euphrates. All surveys prior to the station's construction
showed that no forms of life were present on the surface of
Epsilon 3 or up to two miles beneath the planet's surface.

In 2258, Epsilon 3 became the site of a great deal of seismic activity. Then something or someone five miles beneath
the planet's surface began to send a series of regular signals
which were repeated at specific intervals. Commander Sinclair and Lieutenant-Commander Ivanova traveled beneath
the surface to investigate and discovered that the planet was
once the home of a highly advanced civilization which built a
Great Machine inside Epsilon 3. The custodian of the machine, Varn, controlled the planet and shared a symbiotic
relationship with it. Thus, as Varn began to die, he lost control of its seismic activity. (VOICE I)

When Sinclair and Ivanova took Varn to Babylon 5 for
medical treatment, the Great Machine's fusion reactors began
to build toward critical mass. Aware that if Epsilon 3 exploded
it would destroy Babylon 5, Draal assumed Varn's place as the
custodian of Epsilon 3. According to Varn, the Great Machine would allow Draal to see all tomorrows, hear all songs
and touch the edge of the universe with thoughts. Once installed inside the Great Machine, Draal warned all the alien
races who attempted to claim the advanced technology inside
Epsilon 3 that the planet belonged to no one and that anyone
attempting to land would be destroyed by its powerful defense
system. He then told Commander Sinclair that he would
communicate with the station again when the time was right
(VOICE II). The following year, Draal contacted Sinclair's
successor, Captain Sheridan, to offer him an alliance (TWI-
LIGHT).

As well as Draal, Epsilon 3 is home to some others, including Zathras. (TWILIGHT)

ESI
See **Earthforce Special Intelligence**

Estevez (Doctor)
Physician aboard Babylon 5. (STRIFE)

Euphrates
See **Epsilon 3**

Euphrates Treaty, The
A settlement between the Centauri Republic and the Narn Regime, signed in 2258. Commander Sinclair was particularly keen for the two parties to sign the agreement, as it represented Babylon 5's first success as a peacekeeping body. While the settlement favored the Narns more than the Centauri, Ambassador Mollari was happy to sign it after Sinclair had saved both the honor of the Centauri Republic and his career by helping him retrieve his Purple Files. (PURPLE)

Europa
A Jovian moon. Europa was once the site of a series of illegal strikes which were resolved when the Earth Senate invoked the Rush Act and killed many of the striking workers, including Neeoma Connally's father. (MEANS)

Exchange Machines
Credit exchange facilities situated on Babylon 5. (GRAIL)

Eye, The
The oldest symbol of Centauri power and nobility, the Eye belonged to the first Centauri emperor. It was lost during the 22nd century at the Battle of Na'Shok, and was recovered more than a hundred years later by Reno, who sold it for a huge price to Ambassador Mollari. Lord Kiro planned to use the Eye to become the Centauri emperor, but his plans were cut short when he was killed by a Shadow ship instructed to return the Eye to Ambassador Mollari. (SIGNS)

Eyes
See **Earthforce Bureau of Internal Investigations**

F

Fashar (Ambassador)
The Markab ambassador aboard Babylon 5. In 2259, Fashar objected to the tests for Drafa Plague performed on all the station's Markabs and said that they questioned his people's morality. As a result, he decided to gather his people in the isolation zone to pray, repent and escape from the immorality of humans and other races. Fashar subsequently died in the isolation zone along with all the station's Markabs. (CONFESSIONS)

Feeder
See **Na'ka'leen Feeders**

Ferdinand, Ellasai, VI (Captain)
An explorer and a man of peace, Earth Alliance Captain Ellasai Ferdinand VI misunderstood the intentions of a Minbari cruiser during first contact between the two worlds, and gave orders to open fire on the ship. In the process, he killed the Minbari leader, Dukhat. When the ship's flight recorder information was erased as a result of the explosions during its attack on the Minbari, Captain Ferdinand claimed that the Minbari had fired first, thus justifying the Earth–Minbari War. (LAW)

Finagle's Place
Shop on Zocalo.

Fingal Eggs
An alien delicacy. The Shakespeare Corporation wanted to import fingal eggs to Babylon 5 but were stopped by Garibaldi, who ruled that they were a serious hazard to station security. (BELIEVERS)

Fireflies Incorporated
An interstellar corporation. Ambassador Mollari inadvertently purchased 500,000 shares in Fireflies Incorporated when his data system was possessed by Elric's holodemon. (GEOMETRY)

Firestorm
See **Franklin, Richard (General)**

First Ones, The
Name given to vast and timeless beings which predate humanity by billions of years. They explored beyond the Rim, built empires and taught the majority of the younger races as they emerged. They also fought the Shadows, a race that existed even earlier than the First Ones.

Slowly, over a million years, the First Ones went away: some passed beyond the stars, never to return, while others just disappeared. In the mid-13th century, the remaining First Ones joined a coalition of worlds, including Minbari, to defeat the Shadows in a Great War. After the war, all the remaining First Ones disappeared—all except the Vorlons, who waited for the Shadows to return. (Z'HA'DUM)

Flak Jacket
Futuristic equivalent of a bulletproof vest, worn by members of Babylon 5's staff when they face a clear and present danger. The jacket is lined with an outer layer of material able to refract or absorb some of the impact of energy weapons.

Flarn
Minbari food. (CONFESSIONS)

Flinn, Mr.
Human who claimed that his grandfather, Amos, was kidnapped by aliens and subjected to 48 hours worth of experi-

ments aboard their ship. Mr. Flinn traced the descendants of his grandfather's captors and tried to sue them for damages aboard Babylon 5. Ombuds Zimmerman was hardly delighted to be assigned to the case. Played by Babylon 5's Director of Photography, John Flinn. (GRAIL)

Florazyne
An extremely rare chemical, florazyne is only found in one system, the Damocles Sector. In 2257, it was used by a Minbari assassin to poison Ambassador Kosh. (GATHERING)

Flyer
Minbari shuttle.

Flying Dutchman, The
An ancient sailing vessel that disappeared while trying to sail the Cape of Good Hope. Legend claims that the ship has been seen over the centuries trying to find its way home. Commander Sinclair and Security Chief Garibaldi both likened Babylon 4 to the *Flying Dutchman*. (SQUARED)

Foam Protect
A form of shock-absorbing foam which is used to protect passengers during crashes. (PRESENT)

Fortress of Light
Term first used by Delenn to describe Babylon 5's role in the Shadow War. (TWILIGHT)

Fosaro
A boxer supported by SportCorps. (TKO)

Foster
A junior Earthforce officer assigned to Lieutenant-Commander Sinclair during his search for covert human–alien activity on Mars, Foster was killed when their shuttle crashed as the result of a systems malfunction. (AGAINST)

Fosterage
The Centauri practice of surrogate parenting and instruction, fosterage was extremely common in the early days of the Republic. Although the custom had virtually died out by the mid-23rd century, it was still allowed by Centauri law and to reject fosterage would be seen as an act of defiance against tradition. In 2258, Ambassador Mollari arranged for Kiron Maray and Aria Tensus to be fostered by his second cousin, Andilo. (PRAYER)

Foundation, The
A multi-alien religion started in the mid-22nd century which believes in the concept of God, but does not attempt to define it. Dr. Franklin is a Foundationalist. (Z'HA'DUM)

Franklin, Richard (General)
An Earth Alliance war hero, also known as "Firestorm," General Richard Franklin fought in almost all of Earthforce's major offensives in the mid-23rd century, including the Dilgar Invasion and the Earth–Minbari War.

As a military career officer, Richard Franklin spent most of his time away from his home and family on Earth. When he was home, he would treat his five children (Stephen, Juanita, Maria, Celia and Kathy) like soldiers and used to tell Stephen that "You should be intelligent enough to let someone else tell you what to do." Richard believed that a man who didn't stand by his principles wasn't a man at all, and didn't raise his son to say things he didn't mean. All of his life, Richard Franklin lived according to the demands of duty rather than his wishes and desires. Consequently, he was horrified when his son left Earth to hitchhike across the galaxy on a sightseeing tour. The general felt that Stephen was running away from his duty and refused to talk to him until he joined Earthforce in the Earth–Minbari War.

General Franklin arrived on Babylon 5 in 2259 with 25,000 troops required for Operation : Sudden Death. Once aboard the station, Franklin made up his differences with his son, Stephen. He told the young man that he loved him and apologized to him for the first time in his life. He then led the 356th Platoon to victory in Matok. Played by Paul Winfield. (GROPOS) (See also **Operation : Sudden Death**)

Franklin, Stephen (Doctor)
Babylon 5's chief medical officer, Dr. Stephen Franklin was
assigned to the station in 2258 following the departure of Dr.
Benjamin Kyle. The son of General Richard Franklin, Stephen Franklin always had a difficult relationship with his father. Stephen believed that "Firestorm" always put Earthforce
first and everything else, including his children, second. As a
result, the general was nearly always away on some Earthforce
mission, leaving his wife, his son and his four daughters,
Juanita, Maria, Celia and Kathy, to worry about him. When
he was home, Richard treated his children like soldiers and
taught them to tidy their rooms with military precision. His
son later revealed that he was scared that if he didn't follow
orders, he would be expelled from the platoon! As the years
went by, Stephen Franklin became increasingly resentful of
having to wait for and worry about his father. He also criticized him for killing aliens, saying that he should at least try
to build a relationship with them. (GROPOS)

Franklin was 17 years old when he traveled on his first
transport, which was on the Moon–Mars run. While aboard
the ship, one of his friends started to fool around in one of its
airlocks and accidentlly opened the doorway into space.
Franklin was powerless to help and watched his dying friend
floating around the transport, looking like "a puppet with his
strings all tangled up." When the young man's body was
brought back on to the ship, his eyes looked frozen. Ever
since then, Franklin has never found spacing jokes funny.
(WORD)

While studying at Harvard University, Franklin said that he
wanted his name to go down in history (INFECTION). His
teachers included Dr. Vance Hendricks (INFECTION) and
Dr. Everett Jacobs (HUNTER). Hendricks said that Franklin
was his favorite student and that he excelled in alien history,
anatomy and culture (INFECTION), while Jacobs helped the
young student when he had problems with xeno-biology.
Franklin was marked 3.7 in Jacobs' first aid class, although he
always seemed to think it was 4. In between classes, Jacobs
would tell Franklin about all the things he had seen in his
travels across the galaxies, thus encouraging him to leave
Earth and explore the galaxy (HUNTER).

Desperate to leave home and inspired by Jacobs' tales,

Franklin spent several years hitchhiking across the galaxy, trading his medical skills for passage (SKY). During his travels, he visited Markab and became friends with Dr. Lazarenn. The Markab physician later recalled that Franklin believed that everything was a test to be passed and a problem to be solved (CONFESSIONS).

When the Earth–Minbari War broke out, Franklin ended his hitchhiking voyage and joined Earthforce. Toward the end of the conflict, he was asked to hand in his notes on the Minbari for use in genetic and biological weapons, but instead chose to destroy them. As a doctor, he swore an oath to save life, not take it, and refused to cooperate in killing. (SKY)

Thus, Dr. Franklin will break any rule to save life or soothe pain. He believes that all forms of life are equal and has always been fascinated by aliens (SACRIFICE, GROPOS). Unsurprisingly, therefore, he loves serving on Babylon 5 because of the variety of aliens he encounters aboard the station (GROPOS). He quickly becomes excited at the prospect of discovering new alien life (KNIVES). Franklin is an idealist. He believes that there's always hope and feels that Babylon 5 is worthwhile for the simple reason that it saves lives (WORD). He doesn't believe in the process of brainwiping (MERCY) and was willing to accept that the infamous war criminal Jha'dur intended to give the galaxy her universal anti-agapic to make amends for her earlier evil actions. Franklin always opposed corporation expeditions to dead alien worlds because they reminded him of grave-robbing (INFECTION), and strongly dislikes frauds and con-artists (MERCY).

He was convinced that the M'ola and Tharg would abandon their religious beliefs and ask him to perform the operation necessary to save their son's life. When they refused, the doctor risked his career to perform the operation illegally. (BELIEVERS)

Franklin doesn't like it when his patients lie to him (REVELATIONS) and feels that a doctor and his patient form a team with one common goal: the patient's recovery (STAR). He makes it a rule never to sleep with his patients (LONG). Toward the end of 2258, he was given custody of the Alien Healing Device and hoped to use it to save lives when all other traditional medical means failed (MERCY). The following year, he put his theory to the test when he donated some of his life energy to Security Chief Garibaldi (REVELATIONS). Naturally, he hates to lose a patient and feels haunted by all those he couldn't save (CONFESSIONS). Sometimes when he goes to bed, he closes his eyes and sees the faces of every patient he has lost (Z'HA'DUM).

As far as Franklin is concerned, work always comes first. Consequently, his romantic relationships have always been strained because he couldn't find someone who accepted his commitment to his work. If he ever did find his ideal woman and decided to have children with her, he felt that they would have to leave Babylon 5 because the station was not the ideal place to start a family (LONG). In his first two years as Babylon 5's chief medical officer, Franklin found himself briefly involved with Janice Rosen (MERCY) and Mariah Cirrus (LONG). Although Mariah returned to Earth, she told him she might see him again some time if he was interested (LONG).

During the latter part of 2258, the doctor started an illegal clinic in Down Below for those who could not afford to pay for medical treatment in the station's medlabs (MERCY). Captain Sheridan later discovered that Franklin was one of a group of doctors who had started an underground railroad of unregistered telepaths. Thus Franklin had set up the clinic Down Below to process the telepaths and change their records without Babylon 5's medlab staff knowing anything about it. Following Psi Cop Bester's investigation into the railroad in 2259, Franklin reallocated the telepaths away from the station (RACE).

When his father visited Babylon 5 in 2259, Franklin took the advice of Commander Ivanova and tried to make peace with him before it was too late. During a heart-to-heart talk with "Firestorm," Franklin admitted that he had always respected his father, but had said many things that he shouldn't have said. The doctor then said that his father gave him strength, independence and courage and stated that his life wouldn't have been the same without him. Franklin then told him that he had always loved him and always would (GROPOS). Later in the year, Dr. Franklin was flattered when Captain Sheridan compared him with the general (KNIVES).

Franklin is a Foundationalist. He once revealed that he had a problem believing in God because he wondered if God had stopped believing in its people (Z'HA'DUM). He doesn't believe that Soul Hunters have the ability to steal a soul and feels that the Minbari stories about the mysterious aliens were nothing more than superstition (SOUL).

When he was asked about mankind's growing disillusionment and cynicism in 2259, Franklin said that he believed that the human race had lost interest in the future when it got all the things that it wanted. He felt that mankind was like a child who desperately wanted a Christmas present, only to be disappointed when he or she finally got it. (HUNTER)

Driven and obsessive, Dr. Franklin became increasingly dependent on stims during the course of 2259. When Garibaldi tried to inquire about his growing addiction to the drugs at the beginning of 2260, Franklin initially rebuked the security chief, but later explained to him that he didn't have a problem but would cut down on using them. Unfortunately for Franklin, he couldn't keep his promise. (STRIFE) (See also **Children of Time** and **Foundation, The**).

Played by Richard Biggs.

Franks, Aaron
Pseudonym used by Colonel Ari Ben Zayne while visiting Babylon 5. According to Zayne, Franks was a member of the Quartermaster Corporation and was hoping to win a military supply contract with the station. (EYES)

Frazi
Class of Narn heavy fighter. (MIND)

Free Mars
Free Mars was originally a peaceful movement which was established to win Mars independence through the use of political pressure and peaceful protests. However, in the years leading up to the Earth–Minbari War, its members decided that Free Mars could only reach its goal through the use of violence. In 2258, the movement led the Mars Rebellion against the Earth-appointed government. (SPIDER)

Fresh Air
The finest restaurant on Babylon 5.

Full Torso Stimulation
A desperate procedure used to save a patient's life by stimulating the entire body. (SOUL)

FutureCorp
Earth-based company established by Taro Isogi. Shortly before his death in 2259, Isogi proposed a deal between FutureCorp and the Mars Conglomerate which, he claimed, would not only prove to be extremely lucrative but would also bring a lasting peace to the Mars Colony. (SPIDER)

G

Gajic, Aldous

Aldous Gajic worked as an accountant for one of the major corporations on Earth, during which time he lived "in a world of numbers." One year, he took his family on a vacation to the Mars Colony. While visiting the Amazonis Planitia, an accident claimed the lives of his wife, Sarah, and their children.

Aldous spent a long time grieving for his family and decided to leave his job as an accountant to search for a purpose in his life. Then he met a man, the last member of a holy order that had been searching for the Holy Grail for the last millennium. The man told Aldous that he had "infinite promise and goodness," and when he died he gave Aldous his staff. Upon assuming the quest for the Holy Grail, Gajic found meaning in his life once again.

Having completed the search across Earth, Aldous decided to take the search outward to the stars and traveled to Babylon 5 to ask the alien ambassadors for help with his quest. While on the station, he befriended Thomas Jordan and sacrificed his life to save him. Jordan continued Aldous' quest upon his death. Played by David Warner. (GRAIL)

Galactic Boutique, The

Shop along the Zocalo. Adira Tyree said that she would meet Trakis there before she decided to betray him. (PURPLE)

Galus, Ray

The former leader of Zeta Squad, Ray Galus was killed during a mission to rescue the *Cortez* from hyperspace in 2259. Although Galus was killed when his Starfury was hit by a passing Shadow ship, Lieutenant Keffer's superiors didn't believe his report and instead concluded that Galus was killed by some kind of hyperspace shock wave. Played by Art Kimbro. (STAR)

Garesh 7

A heavily fortified Centauri world, used as a supply base during the Narn–Centauri War. When the Narns mounted a desperate attack on Garesh 7, they were defeated by Shadow forces while the Centauri launched a surprise and utterly brutal attack on the Narn homeworld. (TWILIGHT)

Garibaldi, Alfredo

Alfredo Garibaldi worked all his life as a security officer and taught his son, Michael, everything he knew. He was a first class cook and would make *bagna cauda* for his son every year, as a birthday present. It was his way of telling his son that he loved him (SPIDER, LONG). He always said that laughter was better than pills for any ailment and was famed for "colorful" language (SPIDER).

Alfredo Garibaldi fought in the Dilgar Invasion under General Richard Franklin, who later referred to him as "an excellent soldier" (GROPOS). He was still working in security when he died of Torgs Syndrome, aged 75 (SPIDER).

Garibaldi, Michael Alfredo (Security Chief)

Born on Earth in 2221, Michael Alfredo Garibaldi had law enforcement in the blood. Garibaldi's grandmother was a Boston cop and, among other things, told him about the "blue flu," a fictitious illness that some workers used to block sanctions on work stoppages (MEANS). His father, Alfredo, worked in security all of his life and taught his son everything he knew (SPIDER).

Every year, Garibaldi's father would cook *bagna cauda* for him as a birthday present. Although his father never told him that he loved him, Garibaldi would watch his father cook and know that he was doing it because he loved him. Ever since his father's death, Garibaldi has cooked himself *bagna cauda* on his birthday as a tribute to his memory. He believes that it is vital to cook *bagna cauda* with the real ingredients and refuses to use any substitutes. (STAR)

Garibaldi has spent most of his life working in security and nearly as much time fighting his alcoholism. By his own admission, he tends to hit the bottle when life gets too tough (SURVIVORS). As a result of one of his drinking sessions, he saw a chorus line of purple wombats doing showtunes in his bathroom (KNIVES).

In 2241, Garibaldi worked as a security officer on the ice-mining operation at Europa. Corruption was rife at Europa; half the staff accepted bribes, while the rest just didn't care. As the only officer who tried to do his job properly, the pressure on Garibaldi was tremendous and he inevitably sought solace in a bottle. Things changed when he met Frank Kemmer, a pilot on the Jovian Moon Run. Garibaldi became close friends with Frank and spent a great deal of time with his family. His daughter, Lianna, called him "Uncle Mike." Frank kept the security chief sane and sober and Garibaldi loved him like a brother. When Garibaldi came close to exposing the racket schemes on Europa, the criminals rigged a shuttle pad to explode and killed Frank Kemmer. They then framed Garibaldi for his death. The security officer was blamed for negligence and blackballed through the entire system. Garibaldi couldn't face Frank's family to tell the truth about what happened and he drowned his sorrows for "a long, long time." (SURVIVORS)

Garibaldi's other postings included Orion 4 and Fortune City. While serving at Fortune City, he used a shock stick on a drunk fighter, Walker Smith. The pair subsequently became great friends. (SURVIVORS, TKO)

During the Earth–Minbari War, Garibaldi served as a GROPOS. It was some time before he saw any action and, while they waited, one soldier in the unit repeatedly warned them that their perimeter was weak. Everyone would check the perimeter, judge it to be secure and mock the man, saying that he was mad. Then, one night, the Minbari came through the perimeter like it was paper and the soldier who had warned the unit about it was the first to die. According to Garibaldi, "He was a nut but he was right." After the war, he was haunted by dreams and saw some good counselors (LONG). He worked in a string of jobs and continued his love–hate relationship with the bottle.

In 2255, he ran a "no-questions-asked" shuttle transport service on the Mars Colony. During that time, he was hired by Lieutenant-Commander Sinclair to take him and his two junior officers, Foster and Sanchez. When Sinclair arrived on the first day of the assignment, he found Garibaldi asleep in the passenger compartment of his ship. Once he had been woken up, Garibaldi flew the group across the surface of Mars while they looked for something. Sinclair refused to tell him what they were looking for and filed fake flight plans. Garibaldi knew that Sinclair was a hero of the Battle of the Line and wasn't what he expected. On the fifth day of the search, a systems malfunction forced Garibaldi to crash-land the ship. Foster was killed during the crash and Sanchez broke his leg. Garibaldi and Sinclair were then forced to start a 50-mile hike out of the desert. When the pair took shelter in a cave during a dust storm, Garibaldi became bored of listening to Sinclair's conversation with Sanchez over the link and wandered out of the cave. He then started to drink. Shortly after, he reactivated his link and learned from Sanchez that Sinclair had been trapped in the cave. Sanchez then told him that if Sinclair died, it would be his fault. Garibaldi managed to reach Sinclair and save his life. When he recovered, Sinclair said that he would kill him if he did anything like that again. Some time later, Garibaldi and Sinclair discovered a huge spider-like ship (actually a Shadow ship) excavating a similar craft. They then entered a top-secret operation involving the Psi Corps and the Shadows, where they saw some kind of medical experiment. When they were discovered, Sinclair and Garibaldi used grenades to destroy the operation and escaped. A subsequent Earthforce search found no evidence of the base. In any case, Garibaldi and Sinclair's experience on Mars proved to be the basis of a close and lasting friendship. Garibaldi would always be Sinclair's friend. (CHRYSALIS)

Later in the year, Garibaldi began working for Mars Colony Security. It was a tough job and the only thing that made it worthwhile for Garibaldi was Lise Hampton, a young woman whom he met a few days after he started work. They built a serious relationship together and even talked about marriage a few times. Lise became the one woman who really meant something to Garibaldi. However, as the couple became closer and closer, Garibaldi became more and more afraid: afraid of commitment, afraid that she would leave him, afraid she loved him, and afraid that he loved her. Then, when Sinclair offered him the post of chief security officer aboard Babylon 5 in 2256, he saw it as a chance to redeem himself and accepted the job. Lise refused to leave her life on Mars behind and the couple had a massive argument which ended with him taking the first transport to Babylon 5 (VOICE). Garibaldi had only met Sinclair on two occasions when he was offered the post on Babylon 5 (SQUARED).

He didn't speak to Lise again until 2258, when he contacted her after the Mars riot. He apologized for what he had done and told her that he still loved her and wanted to resume their relationship. He then learned that she had married a man named Franz and that they were expecting their first child. (VOICE I)

Garibaldi was an unpopular choice for the position and was appointed because Sinclair insisted on it. Prior to working on the Mars Colony, he had been fired from his five previous posts for "unspecified personal problems" and he had his own doubts about his ability (GATHERING). When his aide, Jack, tried to kill him at the end of 2258, he questioned his worth as a security officer and looked set to leave Babylon 5. He reconsidered his decision when he saved Ivanova from the green Drazi and decided to return to duty because he had two unique qualifications for the job: he knew everything and everyone on Babylon 5 intimately and didn't trust anyone (GEOMETRY). In 2260, his confidence had increased further and he told Franklin that they were both perfectionists who annoy the hell out of Earth but are good (STRIFE).

Although Commander Sinclair once assured Talia Winters that Garibaldi wasn't omnipotent, there's very little he doesn't know about the station and its inhabitants (VOICE). He once told G'Kar that he never started a conversation without knowing the outcome (INQUISITOR). During his time on the station, Garibaldi made a series of diverse discoveries. For example, he learned that Ivanova was using the Gold Channel to speak to her dying father and also knew that she was growing coffee beans in the hydroponics garden (PURPLE).

He learned that a sixth major alien race was on the prowl from the Rangers and subsequently became their liaison on the station (SHADOWS). He was also aware that Dr. Franklin was becoming increasingly addicted to stims (STRIFE). Besides knowing everything, Garibaldi also never forgets a face (Z'HA'DUM).

As security chief on Babylon 5, Garibaldi's life is seldom quiet. In fact, he's normally rushed off his feet. Every day he gets up and hopes that nothing will happen and would love to be bored out of his skull for just 24 hours (WORD). Garibaldi also likes quiet (VOICE II).

Garibaldi doesn't break rules. He considers himself personally responsible for all prisoners aboard the station and resigned when Sheridan illegally detained Morden. He only agreed to return to work when Sheridan told him he was right and that it wouldn't happen again (Z'HA'DUM). During the search for Branmer's corpse, the first place he searched was Sinclair's quarters and he did so in the presence of Ambassador Delenn (LEGACIES). Although he dislikes the Psi Corps, he knew that he had to help the organization track down any unregistered telepaths on the station (RACE). He was also reluctant to delay telling Ambassador Mollari about a Centauri who was killed by a Narn on the station during the Narn–Centauri War (SACRIFICE).

However, the security chief always gave himself wide discretionary powers. As far as he was concerned, both he and Sinclair had to rewrite the rulebook to make Babylon 5 work (EYES). Garibaldi occasionally monitors ambassadorial communications and went through Captain Sheridan's personal log to see what kind of man he was when he first arrived on the station (STRIFE). Before Earthforce confiscated all records of the station's encounter with Babylon 4, Garibaldi made a copy of all the data on the grounds that he never knew when he would need it for his memoirs (KNIVES).

Despite the serious and frequently unpleasant nature of his job, Garibaldi always maintained a healthily irreverent sense of humor. When he was scanned to see if he was a Psi Corps mole, he couldn't resist pretending that an alternate personality was taking him over, while his computer password was "Peek-a-boo." (DIVIDED, EYES)

When he met Talia Winters, Garibaldi was attracted to her

immediately. He saw her as "the kind of girl a guy like me doesn't have a chance with" (MATES, GROPOS). Shortly after she arrived on the station, he offered to share his favorite and then his second favorite things in the universe with her. When she declined, Ambassador Delenn joined him for his second favorite thing, "Duck Dodgers in the 24th and a ½ Century" (MIDNIGHT). Talia provided Garibaldi with his third favorite thing in the universe, tea (SPIDER). Talia was never comfortable with Garibaldi's attention, but they eventually became good friends. Garibaldi suggested to Sheridan that Talia should join their fight against the new order on Earth, but she was exposed as a Psi Corps traitor just before they could make their offer (DIVIDED).

In 2259, Garibaldi turned down a no-strings-attached night of passion with a female GROPOS, Dodger. He explained to her that he wanted to take things slowly and didn't want to make any more mistakes, and they arranged to go on a date when she returned from Operation : Sudden Death. Unfortunately for both of them, she was killed during the mission. According to Dodger, he was a bad liar. (GROPOS)

Garibaldi's hobbies included the construction of an antique Kawasaki Ninja ZX-11 motorcycle. He began building it 2253 and was slowly bringing it together when Lennier offered to help, and finished the job within a matter of days. Although Garibaldi was initially annoyed with the Minbari, they subsequently went for a ride down the station's central corridor. (EYES)

Besides Sinclair, Garibaldi's closest friends include Sheridan, Ivanova, Franklin and Londo. When he was framed for conspiracy and needed help, he turned to Londo (MIDNIGHT). Garibaldi has a lot of enemies on the station (SURVIVORS). When he needs a disguise, he wears casual clothes and a hat (HUNTER). He doesn't like being irritated because it gives him wind (EYES). He would never consider betraying Earth or his people, but he is never surprised by anything EarthGov does (SURVIVORS).

In 2260, Garibaldi faced legal charges of threatening a Brakiri, his family and his water clan when he showed him a passing comet to distract him. The comet happened to be a Brakiri symbol of death (STRIFE). He is agnostic, but normally refers to God as "she" (EYES).

As Ivanova once pointed out, Garibaldi eats "like a starving man" (MIDNIGHT). He was willing to steal her breakfast (SQUARED). Every morning, Garibaldi fastens and then zips his trousers. He hates waiting (SQUARED).

Garibaldi thinks that if he says what he wants, he won't get it. He once revealed that his ultimate desire was to make a difference somehow, somewhere and redeem himself for his past actions (WORD). If Sinclair's vision aboard Babylon 4 is anything to go by, Garibaldi's wish will be fulfilled when he sets Babylon 5 to self-destruct and mounts a desperate defense of the station while Sinclair leaves (SQUARED).

Played by Jerry Doyle.

G'Drog

Narn captain who saved Catherine Sakai in Sigma 957, on the orders of Ambassador G'Kar. (MIND)

Geegil

A Narn who traveled to Babylon 5 to assassinate G'Kar when the ambassador refused to seal the alliance between their two clans by making love to his wife. (DUET, CODA)

General Order 47

Earthforce regulation which states that Earthforce personnel are required to respond to a distress call from any vessel not currently in hostilities against Earth. Captain Sheridan used General Order 47 to justify his decision to give a Narn cruiser sanctuary in Babylon 5 space at the end of 2259. (FALL)

Geneva

The capital of Earth, Geneva is the location of EarthDome and headquarters of ISN.

G'kamazad

A city on the Narn homeworld. G'Kar and his family spent the final years of the Narn rebellion against the Centauri here. (WORD)

G'Kar (Ambassador)

As a young Narn, G'Kar lived with his family in G'kamazad, one of the biggest cities on Narn, where they served under a

Centauri family during the final years of the rebellion. Due to his mother's illness, the family were unable to escape through the underground and all stayed with their Centauri masters.

Life in the household was tense, and one day G'Kar's father spilt hot Jhala on the mistress of the house. The Centauri had him hung from a Jhawa tree for three days before he died. On his last night, G'Kar disobeyed his mother and went out to see his dying father. He told him that he was proud of G'Kar and told him to fight and be all the things he never was. G'Kar then watched him die. The next morning, G'Kar ran away and killed his first Centauri. (WORD)

G'Kar dedicated his life to advancing the cause of his people and was widely recognized as a clever and strong resistance leader during the Narns' war of attrition (DEATHWALKER). When the Narns achieved freedom, he became obsessed with the desire that they would never be conquered again. Above everything else, G'Kar has always wanted to guarantee the safety of the Narn. He felt that the Narn would never be safe while the Centauri were alive, and so considered their annihilation as a prerequisite of Narn security (SIGNS).

In 2253, G'Kar became a member of the third circle of the Kha'Ri and was sent to Babylon 5 in 2256. He initially believed in the Babylon Project, as he hoped it would strengthen Narn security and lead to the Narn gaining new alliances (WORD). When he traveled to the station, G'Kar left his mate, Da'Kal, in Hebka city on the Narn homeworld (GATHERING, BLOOD).

The following year, G'Kar became involved in the assassination attempt on Ambassador Kosh. He hoped to implicate the Earth Alliance and the Centauri Republic in the attack, thus providing the basis for a Narn alliance with either the Vorlons or the Minbari. However, both Commander Sinclair and Ambassador Mollari emerged unscathed from the attempt to blacken their names, and Sinclair later told G'Kar that he had placed a nano–homing beacon into his drink which would attach itself to his intestinal tract. Sinclair then warned him that if he endangered Babylon 5 again, the results would be "unpleasant." (GATHERING)

G'Kar is a follower of G'Quan. As senior Narn on station, it is his duty to provide a G'Quan Eth for the Holy Days of

G'Quan. When his G'Quan Eth was destroyed shortly before the ceremony in 2258, he desperately struggled to convince Londo Mollari to sell him his plant. Finally he received the Centauri's plant when Sinclair confiscated it (MEANS). The ambassador always hoped that Na'Toth would become a follower of G'Quan and left his book of G'Quan to her in his will (SHADOWS).

G'Kar believes that the universe is run by the complex interweaving of three elements: energy, matter and enlightened self-interest (SURVIVORS). Consequently, he feels that everything and everyone could be bought and sold. G'Kar approached Lyta Alexander about the Narns' lack of telepaths and asked her if she would prefer to mate with him or provide DNA cells for cloning (GATHERING). He later tried to enlist Garibaldi as an analyst, security expert and/or cryptographer (SURVIVORS). G'Kar also believes that the advanced exploit the weak mainly because they can (WORD).

When Catherine Sakai needed his approval to survey Sigma 957, G'Kar told her that he once passed the planet and warned her that strange things happen there. When she decided to ignore his warning, he arranged for a Narn ship to rescue her. After she had been rescued from the area, she asked him why he had saved her and he suggested that Narns, humans and all sentient beings do things that seem like a good idea at the time and that they often make decisions on the basis of "Why Not?" (MIND)

G'Kar feels that all Narns must make sacrifices for their people (DEATHWALKER). When he was hunted down by a member of the Thenta Makur, he risked his life by not informing the Earth Alliance officers, in case it weakened the Narns' position in negotiations (PARLIAMENT). However, when Jha'dur told him that she would only sell the Narns her anti-agapic if she was provided with the head of Na'Toth, he was outraged and gave up on the negotiations (DEATHWALKER).

Inevitably, G'Kar's staunch defense of Narns' rights meant that he was always at Ambassador Mollari's throat, both metaphorically and literally. Although he enjoyed making the Centauri diplomat suffer during the invasion of Ragesh 3, when his nephew Carn was forced to claim that Narns had liberated the colony, he later found himself under constant attack from Londo as the tide began to turn in his favor.

When he learned of the total and utter destruction of the Narn military base in Quadrant 37 at the end of 2258, G'Kar doubted that the Centauri alone were responsible. He suspected that it was the work of either a new race or a very old race and traveled to Narn straight after to investigate (CHRYSALIS). G'Kar subsequently returned to Babylon 5 with news that an ancient enemy was dwelling in the Rim, but nobody aboard the station chose to listen to his warnings (REVELATIONS).

G'Kar felt that Emperor Turhan's visit to Babylon 5 was an outrage and, with the Kha'Ri's permission, decided to assassinate him. G'Kar was robbed of his opportunity to strike when Turhan was taken ill, but was overwhelmed when Dr. Franklin told him that the Centauri emperor had traveled to Babylon 5 to publicly apologize to the Narns about what his people and his family had done to them. For the first time in his life, the Narn ambassador believed that there was a spark of decency in Centauri. He immediately set out to find Londo Mollari, shook hands with him and bought him a drink with which they toasted the emperor. Twenty-four hours later, they were at war following the attack on Quadrant 14. G'Kar initially tried to kill Mollari but was stopped by Sheridan, who told him that it wasn't the best way to serve his people. (SHADOWS)

During the Narn–Centauri War, G'Kar struggled to stop Narn violence against the Centauri on Babylon 5 in the hope that he would win military aid from the Earth Alliance or Minbari. Ultimately, he had to fight for his authority with the leader of the Narn extremists. Although he defeated his challenger, he stabbed him in the back with a poisoned Drazi sword as he walked away. However, he refused to show weakness in front of his people. After everything he had done to prevent violence on the station, G'Kar was brutally disappointed when Sheridan and Delenn could only provide the Narn with unofficial civilian aid. (SACRIFICE)

As the Narn–Centauri War drew to an end, G'Kar wanted to join the Narn military forces, but was asked to stay on Babylon 5 by his uncle, G'Sten. Although G'Kar began to suspect that the Centauri had learned about the Narns' war plans and intended to attack the Narn homeworld, he was powerless to stop the Centauri.

Following the decimation of the Narn homeworld and the Narn surrender, G'Kar was ordered by the Kha'Ri to swallow his pride and request sanctuary from Captain Sheridan aboard Babylon 5. He was stripped of ambassadorial status by Londo, but swore that the Narn would be free of the Centauri again, even if it took a thousand years. Londo demanded that G'Kar was sent to the Narn homeworld to stand trial according to the Narn–Centauri Agreement, but was overruled by Sheridan and Delenn. (TWILIGHT)

As a civilian, G'Kar started an underground resistance movement aboard Babylon 5 and smuggled weapons to the Narn homeworld. He proved his authority to the Narns on the station by providing a message from the homeworld, which was arranged by Sheridan and the Rangers. When Vir Kotto said that he was sorry for what his people had done, G'Kar refused to accept his apology. (INQUISITOR)

In 2260, G'Kar found himself stuck in a lift with Londo Mollari and would die unless he cooperated with the Centauri. However, G'Kar made it clear that he would happily sacrifice his own life to see Londo dead. (CONVICTIONS)

When Na'Far was sent to replace him by the Centauri, G'Kar agreed to return to Narn to stand trial in order to save the lives of the families of all the Narns stationed aboard Babylon 5. He remained determined to protect the unity of the Narn, which he felt was essential if they were ever to defeat the Centauri. However, he was later convinced to stay on Babylon 5 by the Narns aboard the station, who told him that their families would rather die than live as slaves. (STRIFE)

G'Kar believes that females are the finest thing in life and has a fascination with human women (PURPLE, PARLIAMENT, CHRYSALIS). He also studies human literature and believes in the human phrase "Keep your friends close and your enemies closer" (PARLIAMENT, REVELATIONS).

He has taken several Chon-Kar and has survived three assassination attempts, including that of Du'Rog and his family (DEATHWALKER, PARLIAMENT, BLOOD). G'Kar gets headaches when bizarre things happen (MATES).

Played by Andreas Katsulas.

G'Lan
Narn religious figure. Na'Toth's father was a follower of
G'Lan. (MEANS)

Gloppit Egg
Name given to a piece of industrial "goo" by Dr. Franklin.
The physician told his patient, Shon, that the egg contained a
very rare creature from the planet Placibo and needed to be
talked to and patted. The egg glowed when it was rubbed.
(BELIEVERS)

Glory Shop
Store on the Zocalo.

Goks
Minbari equivalent of cats. Delenn felt that such creatures are
the universe's way of making sure that people don't take themselves too seriously. (RACE)

Gold Channel, The
Priority access communication channel which provides in-
stantaneous transmission by means of tachyon particles. The
Gold Channel requires Commander Sinclair's personal permission to use. Only the ambassadors and senior officers know
it exists. Used by Ivanova to contact her dying father. (PUR-
PLE)

Golian
An alien race aboard Babylon 5. Many Golians have a passionate hatred for the Centauri. (PURPLE)

G'Quan
One of Narn's greatest spiritual leaders. Disciples of G'Quan
adhere to his teachings outlined in the Book of G'Quan.
Drinking alcohol is forbidden during Holy Days of G'Quan.
As a symbol of their faith, all disciples (wherever they may be)
must burn a G'Quan Eth plant once a year when the sun rises
precisely behind the G'Quan mountains on the Narn
homeworld. (MEANS) (See also **Book of G'Quan, The**)

G'Quan Eth

A plant indigenous to Narn, the G'Quan Eth is difficult to grow, hard to transport and very expensive to own. It is used to burn incense during the Holy Days of G'Quan. Many Centauri, including Ambassador Mollari, use its seeds to enhance alcoholic beverages.

The G'Quan Eth ("Eth" is Narnish for "plant") has an illegal chemical composition and is therefore a controlled botanical substance on Babylon 5. It is a crime to possess the plant unless for legitimate medical or religious purposes. Sinclair used these grounds to confiscate Londo's G'Quan Eth and give it to G'Kar on the condition that the Narn compensated the original owner. (MEANS)

G'Quan Mountains

Mountains situated on the Narn homeworld. (MEANS)

Gray 19

Area of the alien sector in which Sebastian tortured Ambassador Delenn and Captain Sheridan. (INQUISITOR)

Gray, Harriman

A Psi Corps military specialist. As a boy, Harriman Gray dreamed of being a combat pilot. He built models of every space fighter available, collected squadron patches and all he ever wanted was to be a space fighter. At the age of 16, he was accepted into AirDome, but during his first month there his telepathic power manifested itself. As telepaths are not allowed in regular military service, he was expelled, thus bringing his dream to an end.

When the Corps said he could serve in Earthforce as a Psi Corps liaison, he felt that his life had purpose again. Although he didn't know Bester personally, the Psi Cop assigned him to Colonel Ari Ben Zayne. Gray thought that Zayne was efficient but lacked compassion. When Zayne conducted an internal investigation on Babylon 5 in 2258, Gray scanned the colonel and found that he was crazed and deranged. He then helped overpower him by telepathically projecting pain into his mind. Played by Jeffrey Combs. (EYES)

Gray Sector

Shortly after the station went on-line in 2256, the industrial Gray Sector was dubbed the "Babylon 5 Triangle" by the station's maintenance staff, many of whom claimed to have seen strange lights and heard unusual noises. There are always problems with scans and communications in Gray Sector, and several missing people were last seen there before they disappeared. (KNIVES)

Great Machine, The

Title for the extremely advanced technology at the heart of Epsilon 3 which is controlled by the custodian. (See also **Epsilon 3** and **Custodian**)

Great Maker

Much-used term to describe God, particularly by Londo.

Green Sector

The area of Babylon 5 that plays host to the alien ambassadors' quarters and is the focus of the station's diplomatic activities, Green can be accessed by station personnel only. (DEPARTURE)

Green Tiger, The

Store on the Zocalo.

Green 2

Location of Babylon 5's Ambassadorial Wing.

Grey Council

The Minbari ruling body, also known as "The Nine." The Grey Council was established by Valen and comprises nine members: three from the religious caste; three from the warrior caste; and three from the worker caste. The religious caste normally takes precedence on most domestic matters, leaving the warrior caste to deal with external threats.

Tradition dictates that when a member joins a Council meeting, he or she must say, "I am Grey. I stand between the candle and the star. We are Grey. We stand between the darkness and the light." (SQUARED)

The Grey Council normally stays in the great hall, which is

open to members only. They are shrouded in mystery and the identity of members is kept a secret to avoid the cult of personality arising.

In 2248, the Grey Council watched the Battle of the Line from their warship and decided to interrogate a human about the planet's defenses. When they discovered that the specimen, Jeffrey Sinclair, had a Minbari soul, they examined other pilots and learned that Minbari souls were being reborn, either in part or in full, into human beings. It then ordered the war against the humans to end, without explanation. They subsequently erased Sinclair's memory with the permission of EarthGov, and released him. (DARKNESS)

Six years later, the Council agreed to co-fund the construction of Babylon 5 with the Earth Alliance provided that they could have approval of its commander. They insisted on Sinclair. (SIGNS)

In 2258, the Council summoned Delenn to return and revealed that they had chosen her to be their next leader. When she heard the news, she became the first person in a thousand years to reject the position (SQUARED). The following year, Delenn was removed from the Council and replaced by a member of the Star Riders, Neroon, thus giving the warrior caste unprecedented power within the Council (ALONE).

GroundPounders
Earth Alliance infantry troops, commonly abbreviated to GROPOS. (GROPOS)

GROPOS
See **GroundPounders.** (GROPOS)

G'Sten
A Narn military leader, G'Sten was killed during the Narn assault on Garesh 7 at the end of the Narn–Centauri War. Prior to his death, he visited his nephew, Ambassador G'Kar, on Babylon 5. He told G'Kar that his father would be very proud of him and asked the Narn diplomat not to join the assault and stay aboard Babylon 5. Played by W. Morgan Sheppard. (TWILIGHT)

Guerra

Command and Control officer aboard Babylon 5 in 2257.
Played by Ed Wasser. (GATHERING)

Gyor

A former Sho'Rin, Gyor lost his title to Walker Smith in 2258.
Played by James Courtney. (TKO)

H

Hague (General)

A member of the Joint Chiefs of Staff, General Hague ordered Captain Sheridan to assume command of Babylon 5 on January 2259 (DEPARTURE) and instructed him to assess the loyalty of the station's senior command staff. He then told Sheridan to invite his colleagues to join their Conspiracy of Light aimed at the forces that were trying to destroy Earth from within (ALONE).

Hague's operatives include Sarah, who instructed Sheridan to prevent Earthforce Intelligence from capturing Dr. Everett Jacobs. The fugitive physician possessed a data crystal containing evidence that President Morgan Clark was not ill when he disembarked from *Earthforce 1*, thus corroborating the theory that Clark knew that his predecessor would be killed. When Sheridan saved both Jacobs and his data crystal from their opponents, he scored the first victory for Hague and his associates. (HUNTER)

General Hague doesn't care for protocol and prefers not to be greeted by honor guards. (ALONE)

Played by Robert Foxworth.

Hampton, Lise

A former girlfriend of Michael Garibaldi. The couple first met each other a few days after Garibaldi had been stationed on Mars and had spent a year together when he was offered the post of chief security officer aboard Babylon 5. Lise had a life, a job and some friends on Mars and didn't want to leave. The couple argued and Garibaldi took the first shuttle to the station. (VOICE I)

During the Mars Rebellion in 2258, Lise was caught in a crossfire while trying to get food. When Garibaldi contacted her to try to restart their relationship, he learned that she was married to Franz and was expecting their first child. (VOICE II)

Played by Denise Gentile.

Hanson
A security officer stationed on Babylon 5. (SPIDER)

Happy Daze
A rough and ready bar in Down Below. When he was framed by the Homeguard, Security Chief Garibaldi hid in Happy Daze and succumbed to having an alcoholic drink there. As he left the bar, Garibaldi said that he liked its decor, ambience and clientele. He was captured leaving the bar in a drunken haze by Major Lianna Kremmer and her security staff. (SURVIVORS)

Ha'Rok
Narn councilor sent to Babylon 5 on the *Callisto* to meet with Jha'dur and arrange a deal for her anti-agapic. Na'Toth was waiting for him to arrive on the station when she saw Jha'dur and tried to kill her. When Ha'Rok learned what had happened, he immediately returned to Narn, leaving Ambassador G'Kar to deal with the negotiations. (DEATHWALKER)

Hazeltine, Eric
An environment technician aboard Babylon 5, Eric Hazeltine was killed in 2257 by the Minbari assassin posing as his old friend, Del Varner. Security found Hazeltine's body in a transport tube access panel. Played by Steven Barnett. (GATHERING)

HazMat
Abbreviation used on Babylon 5 to describe any hazardous materials.

Hebka
City on the Narn homeworld. Da'Kal lived there prior to the Narn–Centauri War. (BLOOD)

Hedronn
A member of the Minbari Grey Council, Hedronn was present at the Battle of the Line. He claimed to be a member of the Minbari Ministry of Culture, and didn't accept Sheridan's authority on Babylon 5. Played by Robin Sachs. (DEPARTURE)

Hendricks, Vance (Doctor)
A respected teacher and researcher who decided to pursue a career as an interplanetary archeologist. Hendricks' expedition to the ruins of Ikaara 7 was funded by Interplanetary Expeditions (IPX), which he later revealed was a front for an important bio-organic weapons supplier. He ignored the standard quarantine procedures to bring Ikaaran artifacts aboard Babylon 5 and didn't care what his assistant, Nelson Drake, did as long as he got them onto the station. Hendricks then met his former pupil, Dr. Stephen Franklin, and together the pair studied the Ikaaran relics. Hendricks was pleased that one of the artifacts assimilated Drake and transformed him into an Ikaaran killing machine, as it proved that the bio-organic weapons still worked, thus increasing their financial value. However, Dr. Franklin ignored a very lucrative offer from his former teacher and turned him in. Played by David McCallum. (INFECTION)

Hernandez, Maya (Doctor)
Physician in charge of one of Babylon 5's medlabs. In 2258, Dr. Franklin bet her a steak dinner that he would save Shon. When Shon's parents refused to allow him to operate on their son, Dr. Hernandez assisted Franklin to perform the operation illegally. Played by Silvana Gallardo. (BELIEVERS)

Heyerdahl, The
An Earth transport named after Thor Heyerdahl, the noted explorer. The *Heyerdahl* brought Cynthia Torqueman and an ISN crew to Babylon 5 in 2259 just in time to witness the *N'Ton's* attack on the *Malios*. (WORD)

Hidoshi (Senator)

Senator Hidoshi acted as a liaison between the Senate and Babylon 5 during 2258 and the early part of 2259. Among other things, he ordered Commander Sinclair to send Jha'dur to Earth immediately (DEATHWALKER), instructed him to find a quick and decisive solution to the dock workers' illegal strike (MEANS), and confirmed that President Santiago had given Commander Sinclair jurisdiction over Babylon 5's entire sector (VOICE II).

Hidoshi's grandfather worked in space docks and, as a result, he had a great deal of sympathy for the dockers aboard Babylon 5 in 2258. When Sinclair used the Rush Act to give them a pay raise, Hidoshi enjoyed the way he had beaten his colleagues and warned the commander that he had made several new enemies as a result. (MEANS)

When asked about the numerous management changes on the station, Hidoshi suggested that they might have occurred because Babylon 5 was "too big for anybody to ride." By September 2259, he was no longer a member of the Senate. (WORDS)

Played by Aki Aleong.

Hokey-Pokey

Classic human song and dance. Ambassador Mollari couldn't understand why, out of all of humanity's musical compositions, the Hokey-Pokey remained the most popular. He studied it for seven days and had it analyzed by computer, only to conclude that it had no meaning. Despite Londo's rendition, Draal quite liked the song. (VOICE I)

Holy Grail, The

The legendary cup which promises the regeneration and redemption of its owner. Also known as the Sacred Vessel of Regeneration and the Cup of the Goddess. In 2258, Aldous Gajic traveled to Babylon 5 in search of the Grail. Upon his death, his quest was assumed by Thomas Jordan. (GRAIL)

Homeguard

A radical pro-Earth movement, the Homeguard has members and sympathizers across the galaxy. The organization's goals are to prevent alien races from setting human policy, to stop aliens from stealing human jobs and to resist growing alien social and cultural influence on Earth and its colonies.

In 2258, the Homeguard launched a series of vicious anti-alien attacks on Babylon 5. The local Homeguard cell, under the command of Malcolm Biggs, planned to assassinate the station's four alien ambassadors, but they were brought to justice by Commander Sinclair and Lieutenant-Commander Ivanova. Had they succeeded, the ambassadors' deaths would have acted as a signal to the other members of the Homeguard to terminate the other alien emissaries on Earth. (PRAYER)

A few months later, the Homeguard attempted to sabotage President Santiago's visit to Babylon 5, but once again their plans were thwarted at the last minute. (SURVIVORS)

Members of the Homeguard were pleased when Santiago was killed on January 1st 2259, although it is a mystery whether or not they were involved in his murder. A Homeguard faction known as the Homers blamed the president's death on aliens. (TREASON)

Horn, Abel

Abel Horn became involved with the Free Mars movement before the Earth–Minbari War and stayed with the organization when it abandoned the use of peaceful protest and turned to violence as the only means of winning independence from Earth.

In the years leading up to the 2258 Mars Rebellion, Abel Horn became known as one of the most dangerous leaders of Free Mars. He was responsible for countless acts of violence and devastation, including the destruction of the Ritchie Station. However, during the rebellion the Earthforce cruiser *Pournelle* destroyed his ship over Phobos and killed Abel Horn.

Horn's body was recovered by Bureau 13 operatives who used him as a subject of Project : Lazarus. Telepathic scanning focused the former revolutionary on the moment of his death, which he then relived over and over again while his thought processes and actions were controlled by a computer implant.

In 2259, Abel Horn was sent to Babylon 5 to kill FutureCorp executive Taro Isogi and discredit Amanda Carter, a member of the Mars Conglomerate and Horn's former lover. Horn killed Isogi with a massive electrical charge produced by his prosthetic arm which disrupted every cell in the executive's body. However, on the two occasions he tried to kill the witness to the murder, Talia Winters, she entered his mind and undermined his program. The cyber-organic killer became confused and unfocused, and demanded to know what he had become.

Horn was killed for a second time by Captain Sheridan when he tried to shoot Security Chief Garibaldi. His body then self-destructed to eliminate all pieces of evidence. Played by Michael Beck. (SPIDER)

Hyach
An alien race aboard Babylon 5. (ACCUSATIONS)

Hyach 7
A Narn colony once conquered by the Dilgar. (DEATH-WALKER)

Hydroponics
Used to grow fruit and vegetables. (GATHERING, PRAYER)

Hyperion, The
An Earth Alliance heavy cruiser, the *Hyperion* was one of the few Earth Alliance ships which survived the Earth–Minbari War. In 2258, the ship was sent to Babylon 5 following the discovery of advanced alien technology beneath the surface of Epsilon 3. Under the command of Captain Ellis Pierce, the *Hyperion*'s mission was to stake the Earth Alliance's claim to the technology and protect Babylon 5 from possible attack. (VOICE II)

Hyperspace
A different dimension in space which allows shorter travel between points in the galaxy. Entered through a jumppoint, many of which are generated by jumpgates.

No ship lost in hyperspace had ever been rescued before 2259. Sheridan made history by recovering the *Cortez*, using a line of Starfuries (DISTANT). There is some speculation as to whether or not it is possible for anything to live in hyperspace.

I

Icarus, The
Scientific vessel destroyed when it landed on the Shadow stronghold, Z'ha'dum. Members of the crew who would not serve the Shadows were killed. Captain Sheridan's wife, Anna, was also on board. (KNIVES)

ICE
See **Intruder Countermeasure Electronics**

ICE-breaker
Computer program used to override Intruder Countermeasure Electronics. Security Chief Garibaldi employed an ICE-breaker to trace the individual who was illegally using the Gold Channel. (PURPLE)

Identicard
A personal identification card.

Ikaara 7
Ikaara 7 was the home of an advanced, space-faring society which was annihilated some time around the 13th century.

After their homeworld had suffered half a dozen invasions, the Ikaaran leaders decided that they needed to create the perfect weapon to defend themselves: a bio-organic weapon which could adapt to any situation and was capable of intelligent thought. Using the brainwaves of a researcher, Tu'Lar, to form its personality matrix, Ikaara's leading scientists created eleven machines which were programmed to meld with a living being and then kill anything that wasn't pure Ikaaran. However, when the warriors saved the planet from yet another invasion, they then turned on their creators and wiped out the entire population of Ikaara 7. (INFECTION)

Ilarus
The Centauri goddess of luck and patron of gamblers. (SUR-VIVORS)

Indonesian Consortium, The
A commonwealth located on Earth. (VOICE I)

Ingata, The
The Minbari war cruiser upon which Branmer's body was transported on its journey to the homeworld in 2258. (LEGA-CIES)

Inquisitor, The
See **Sebastian**

Interplanetary Expeditions (IPX)
The corporation that sponsored the controversial ISN documentary "36 Hours Aboard Babylon 5" in September 2259. Its catchphrase was, "Exploring the past to create a better future" (WORD). According to Dr. Vance Hendricks, IPX was a front for the important bio-weapons supplier who funded his trip to Ikaara 7 (INFECTION).

Interstellar News Network (ISN)
The galaxy's leading news network, based in Geneva. All its broadcasts are hypertext captioned. In 2260, ISN itself hit the headlines when it broadcast Lieutenant Keffer's footage of a Shadow ship in hyperspace. It was immediately taken off the air by Earthforce. (MATTERS)

InterWeb
An Earth Alliance computer network. (EYES)

"In the Light of Two Moons"
A poem written by Shall Mayan. "In the Light of Two Moons" took many years to write, and made its debut in 2258 on Babylon 5. (PRAYER)

Intruder Countermeasure Electronics (ICE)
Computer program which protects the user from external tracking. Lieutenant-Commander Ivanova used ICE to prevent Security Chief Garibaldi from tracing her when she used the Gold Channel to contact her dying father. (PURPLE)

Io
A moon of Jupiter, Io is the site of an Earth Alliance outpost, jumpgate and transfer point. Prior to their appointments to Babylon 5, John Sheridan and Ivanova served together at Io (DEPARTURE), while Dr. Kyle met his successor, Dr. Franklin, at the Io transfer point (SOUL).

Ipsha
A non-aligned alien race, the Ipsha fought the Dilgar during the Dilgar Invasion. (DEATHWALKER)

Ironheart, Jason
Jason Ironheart worked as an instructor at the Psi Corps Training Academy and gave high-level training to P5–P10 telepaths. Among other things, Ironheart taught about jamming, long-range scans and fringe skills.

Ironheart was a P10 when he volunteered for a covert Earthforce Military Intelligence genetic experiment aimed at increasing his telepathic and telekinetic abilities. According to Ironheart, the ultimate aim of the experiment was to create a telekinetic assassin who was capable of killing with just a thought.

Ironheart took between five and fifteen injections a day for months. Then, one day, he woke up and could "see everything." Ironheart knew that he had to escape from the Psi Corps, otherwise it would have him killed and dissected to discover the drugs that had transformed him. Before he left the Corps' base, he killed the researcher who had created him, so that he could not manufacture another telepath/telekinetic like him.

As his abilities continued to grow, Ironheart traveled to Babylon 5 to say farewell to his old lover, Talia Winters, and prepare for the final stage of his transformation. While he was aboard the station, his abilities increased beyond his control. As a result, he found it increasingly difficult to control his mindquakes.

Ironheart was programmed with a telepathic password to shut him down and put him to sleep. When Psi Cops Bester and Kelsey tried to use the password, he killed Kelsey in an act of self-defense.

Shortly after he left the station, Ironheart's ship exploded. Although official records state he was killed during the explosion, in reality he moved onto a higher plane of existence. Ironheart said farewell to the station's command staff and gave Talia Winters an unspecified gift which, he told her, was in memory of their love. Played by William Allen Young. (MIND)

Isogi, Taro

As the chief executive of FutureCorp, Taro Isogi dedicated his business and his life to improving the lives of others. During his career, he developed a close friendship with Talia Winters, whom he considered to be the finest commercial telepath he had ever worked with.

In 2259, Isogi traveled to Babylon 5 to meet Amanda Carter of the Mars Conglomerate. He proposed a solution to the Mars crisis which would bring freedom and peace to the colony and a healthy profit to FutureCorp. Although this was risky and extremely expensive in the short term, Isogi felt that the Mars Colony could be self-sufficient by 2269 if alien trade agreements were finalized.

Shortly after his first meeting with Amanda Carter, Isogi was murdered by Bureau 13 operative Abel Horn. Carter later agreed to pursue Isogi's plan as a tribute to his memory. Played by James Shigeta. (SPIDER)

Isolab

Self-contained, hermetically sealed isolation chamber in medlab. Isolabs are used for biological research and to identify hazardous microorganisms, and also create nonhumanoid atmospheres. They are accessed through their own airlock. (SACRIFICE)

Itagi

Boxer beaten by Walker Smith. Some spectators referred to their fight as "World War 4." (TKO)

Ivanov, Andrei

The husband of Sofie Ivanova and father of Susan Ivanova and Gayna Ivanov, Andrei Ivanov was a Russian Jew and a scholar who devoted his life to logic, reason and peace. A typical Russian realist, Ivanov used to say that "If regret could be harvested, then Russia would be the world's food basket."

Ivanova called Susan "dushenkanyia," which means "little soul." Following the death of his wife and son, he became too wrapped up in his own grief to give his daughter the love and support she needed. When she joined Earthforce, he opposed her decision because he was afraid of losing her. Susan invited him to visit Babylon 5 several times but he never took her up on the offer. He always declined because he believed that mankind had no right to travel across the stars until it had learned to live peacefully on Earth. Rabbi Koslov thought that Andrei would have liked the station.

Andrei Ivanov died in 2258 after a long illness. When Susan contacted him on his deathbed, he apologized to her for not giving her the love she needed and asked for her forgiveness. Played by Robert Phalen. (PURPLE)

Ivanov, Gayna

The son of Andrei and Sofie Ivanov and brother of Susan, Gayna Ivanov was killed in the Earth–Minbari War, a year after his mother committed suicide. (TKO)

Ivanova, Sofie

The wife of Andrei Ivanov and mother of Susan and Gayna, Sofie Ivanova always kept her telepathic abilities a secret. On her 35th birthday, the Psi Corps caught her. Given the choice between joining the organization, life imprisonment and a telepathic suppressant, Sofie decided to accept the last option and she was treated with weekly injections which slowly eroded her spirit. Sofie wanted to make sure that Susan would not share her fate. She taught her how to fail the Psi Corps telepathic tests and kept transferring her from school to school in order to stay one step ahead of the Corps. After ten years of the Psi Corps treatment, Sofie Ivanova committed suicide. (MIDNIGHT, LEGACIES, EYES)

Played by Marie Chambers.

Ivanova, Susan (Lieutenant-Commander/Commander)

As Babylon 5's first officer, Susan Ivanova supervises everyday operations aboard the station.

Born August 30th, 2230, in St. Petersburg, the Russian Consortium, Earth, Susan Ivanova was educated largely abroad to prevent the Psi Corps from learning that she was a latent telepath (WORD, DIVIDED). Sofie taught Susan how to avoid being discovered by the Psi Corps and convinced her that she must never be scanned (DIVIDED). When her mother was discovered by the Corps and slowly pushed toward suicide by it, Susan built up a deep resentment for the organization (MIDNIGHT).

When she was 13 years old, Susan became obsessed with the radical neo-communist Kushoyev and persuaded her father to take her to one of his readings. Although Andrei thought that Kushoyev's work would destroy Russian culture and didn't want to go, she sulked until he relented.

After the reading, father and daughter attended a question and answer session, during which Susan asked her idol a question she had worked on for weeks. When Kushoyev said that it was the stupidest thing he had ever heard and called her "a bourgeois little twit barely out of diapers," her father was not impressed. He stood up, pointed out that she was not a bourgeois or a twit and had been out of diapers for many years, while his writing had to rise above the contents of diapers. He then added that if he wasn't a man of peace, he would have horsewhipped him through the streets of St. Petersburg just like his father should have done many years earlier! Susan was mortified, but felt better when her father told her, "It was a good question, dushenkanyia."

After the death of her mother, Susan became estranged from her father, who buried himself in his own grief. The following year, when her brother Gayna was killed in the Earth–Minbari War, she ignored Andrei's wishes and joined

Earthforce in 2247. Susan felt that she had to finish what her brother had started and graduated from the OTC in 2249, just after the end of the war. (WORD)

Ivanova embarked on a passionate affair with Malcolm Biggs, whom she left in 2250 when she accepted a transfer to Io. While she thought the transfer was a big and exciting career move, she cried herself to sleep for her first few months (PRAYER). At Io, Ivanova served under John Sheridan for the first time. He got a taste of her dislike of telepaths when she threw a telepath out of a third story window into an "ample" pool (SPIDER). Ivanova worked her way up the ranks without connections or patrons and was appointed Babylon 5's first officer in January 2258 (FALL). Her record was exemplary (EYES).

Like her father, Ivanova tried hard to keep her feelings to herself. When he passed away in 2258, she chose not to tell anyone and didn't attend his funeral due to work commitments. She was later convinced by Rabbi Koslov to let go of the pain, guilt and anguish surrounding her father's death and sat shivah for him on Babylon 5 (TKO). Enlightened by her experience, Ivanova later urged Dr. Franklin to make peace with his father before it was too late (GROPOS). Raised a Jew, Ivanova said that she believed in God most of the time (Z'HA'DUM).

Ivanova shares her father's typically Russian realism and she became famous aboard the station for her sharp one-liners. As a result, many of the staff on Babylon 5 consider her to be a pessimist (SOUL). She once said that a good leader should have a strong chin. Consequently, she voted for Marie Crane in the 2258 Earth Alliance presidential election because her opponent, Luis Santiago, didn't have a strong chin, but several weak ones (MIDNIGHT). Ivanova subsequently became a strong supporter of Santiago and felt shattered when he was killed in January 2259 (DEPARTURE).

According to Ivanova, the hardest thing about serving on Babylon 5 was getting out of bed. She always had a problem waking up when it was dark outside, so she found mornings on Babylon 5 to be particularly difficult. Ivanova also wondered why her mouth always tastes like old carpet every morning. (SIGNS)

Ivanova is an experienced combat officer. She has over 100 hours flight experience and occasionally yearns to leave Babylon 5 and take a Starfury into action (BELIEVERS). When she was described as being cute by an amorous male in the casino, she acquitted herself admirably in a fight with everyone in the building (EYES).

Despite her spotless record, Ivanova has been known to break rules. For example, in 2258 she used the Gold Channel to contact her dying father and confronted a Raiders squadron without backup to give the *Asimov* a chance to escape. (PURPLE, BELIEVERS)

When her ex-lover Malcolm Biggs returned to Babylon 5, she was willing to consider rekindling their romance. However, when Biggs was revealed to be a leading member of the Homeguard, she was horrified and agreed to help Sinclair bring him to justice if she could be there for his capture. She couldn't believe how much Biggs had changed and said that she had known many aliens who were more human than he was. (PRAYER)

Sinclair depended on Ivanova and said she was the finest officer he ever served with (TKO). Unsurprisingly, therefore, she was promoted to the rank of commander in January 2259 by Captain Sheridan the day after he assumed command of Babylon 5 (GEOMETRY).

Ivanova's first assignment as a commander was to stop the green and purple Drazi aboard the station from fighting each other during their battle of supremacy. She first tried to find a peaceful solution to their dispute, but when she learned that they were fighting a war out of tradition, she decided her only option was to structure the fighting so that no one was seriously hurt or killed. Ivanova paid the price of peace when she found herself caught between the warring factions in one fight and broke her foot. She was then kidnapped by the purple Drazi who intended to use her to lure their green opponents into a trap. Finally, she managed to stop the fighting when she unintentionally assumed the leadership of the purple Drazi and ordered them to dye their sashes green, thus ending the war on the station. (GEOMETRY)

Her next significant diplomatic mission was to convince the Lumati to join the Babylon project. Sheridan told her to do whatever it took to forge an alliance with the advanced aliens. When they agreed to sign on to the program, Ivanova was shocked to learn that the Lumati finalize all agreements through sexual intercourse and found herself caught in a moral dilemma. When Dr. Franklin pointed out that the Lumati were probably quite ignorant of human biology, she performed a manic dance for Correlilmurzon which, she told him, was human-style mating. Before he left the station, the Lumati sent her a present and a message saying, "Next time, my way!" (SACRIFICE)

Ivanova always remembered how John Sheridan once told her not to fear answers but only running out of questions. When Sheridan revealed that he had never told her that, she was left trying to recall who she had confused him with. (HONOR)

When she goes off-duty, Ivanova normally winds down at the casino (MIDNIGHT). She exercises vigorously once a day and fights to keep her figure, but her diet is low in iron and calcium (DISTANT). The commander would sometimes visit Bay 13 late at night to look at Ambassador Kosh's ship (PREY).

During her first two years aboard Babylon 5, Ivanova refused to be scanned on several occasions so that she could keep her latent telepathic ability a secret. She initially dismissed the possibility that she could ever be friends with Psi Corps telepath Talia Winters, but their relationship slowly changed. The unlikely pair developed a respect for each other when they clashed over the fate of the unregistered telepath Alisa Beldon and became much closer when Talia confided in Susan that she had learned the true nature of Psi Corps and no longer wanted to be a part of it (RACE). However, their intimate relationship was destroyed when Talia was revealed to be an unwitting Psi Corps mole (DIVIDED).

During the unofficial internal investigation which unveiled Talia's alternate personality, Ivanova confided in Sheridan about her latent telepathic power. She explained that even though she was probably not even a P1, she would be forced into the same situation that her mother faced if the Corps caught up with her (DIVIDED).

In the long term, Susan Ivanova hopes to command a starship one day. When Nightwatch representative Mr. Welles told her that his organization could find her a command faster than she could imagine, she refused the bribe. (FALL)

Played by Claudia Christian.

J

Jack

Security officer aboard Babylon 5 who worked as Security Chief Garibaldi's aide during 2258. Garibaldi trusted and relied upon Jack: he taught him everything he knew and treated him like a brother (REVELATIONS). Unfortunately, Jack was a member of the new order on Earth and was involved in the assassination of President Santiago in 2259. When Garibaldi came too close to exposing the plan, Jack shot him in the back. Shortly after, he killed several of his associates aboard the station, including Devereaux.

While Garibaldi was in a coma, Jack watched and waited for him to recover and was ready to strike if the security chief could identify him (CHRYSALIS). Jack was relieved when Garibaldi couldn't remember who had shot him, but was unaware that he intended to ask Talia Winters to perform a scan on him in the hope that they might learn something. As a result, Garibaldi realized that his assistant had pulled the trigger. When Garibaldi asked Jack why he had betrayed him, he boasted that he was part of the "winning side." He seemed unafraid when Garibaldi pointed out that shooting a superior officer was an act of mutiny and that he could be spaced.

Before Jack could stand trial, President Clark instructed Commander Sheridan to send the traitor and all the evidence on the case to Earth. While en route to Earth, Jack was transferred from his prison transport to another vessel which had all the correct Earthforce security markers, authorization papers and access codes, but was not an Earthforce ship. As a result, he disappeared without a trace. (REVELATIONS)

Played by Macaulay Burton.

Jackson
Security officer aboard Babylon 5. (SPIDER)

Jacobs, Everett (Doctor)
A former teacher at Harvard University, Dr. Everett Jacobs later joined Earthforce and served as Earth Alliance Vice-President Morgan Clark's personal physician in 2258.

Jacobs examined Clark when he disembarked from *Earthforce 1* a mere 24 hours before its destruction, claiming to have a viral infection. His tests showed that the vice-president was perfectly fit, thus suggesting that he had pretended to be ill in order to leave the ship before it exploded.

As far as Clark was concerned, Jacobs knew too much, but he couldn't have him killed straight away in case it aroused suspicion. Clark waited a few months and was preparing an accident for the physician when General Hague's operatives learned what was happening and helped Jacobs escape. He was sent to Io where he was supposed to meet one of Hague's contacts, but couldn't find him and fled to Babylon 5.

Earthforce Special Intelligence alerted the station that Jacobs was wanted dead or alive and despatched Derek Cranston to coordinate the search for the doctor. ESI claimed that the doctor had misused his security clearance to gain access to classified information, including details of technology and covert operations, which could ruin EarthGov and embarrass half a dozen non-aligned worlds. It then suggested that he had arrived on Babylon 5 to meet a buyer or arrange transport to an alien world.

However, Captain Sheridan learned the truth about Jacobs from one of Hague's associates and instructed Security Chief Garibaldi and Dr. Franklin to find the doctor before ESI.

While on the station, Jacobs continued to record a diary for his beloved wife, Mary, and used stims to stay awake to avoid capture. He was taken hostage by an amoral bounty hunter, Max, and held for ransom until Garibaldi and Franklin came to the rescue. He then gave them a data crystal containing details of Clark's examination.

In order to escape being detected by an intensive station-wide scan, Jacobs was placed in an artificial coma and was hidden inside Ambassador Kosh's ship. While he was asleep, he could hear the ship singing to him. Jacobs was taken away from the station by General Hague's associates. Played by Tony Steedman. (HUNTER)

Jaddo, Urza

"The hero of the Battle of Gorash" and the finest swordsman in the Couro Prido, Urza Jaddo was a lifelong friend and ally of Londo Mollari. Urza's capacity for Brivare was almost legendary and he had never been beaten in a duel by Mollari. He was comfortably married to Maruelia and always knew how to throw a banquet.

As he grew older, Jaddo became disillusioned with the Centauri Republic. He tired of its quest for bloodshed and war as well as all of the accompanying political deceit. He felt haunted by what he had seen on Garesh and felt more like a murderer than a killer.

In 2259, Urza Jaddo and his entire family were named as traitors to the Centauri Republic by Lord Refa and his associates. When Urza asked Mollari to help him save his family honor, he initially agreed to help. However, the ambassador withdrew his support shortly after Refa told him that an alliance could not save the Jaddo household and would only destroy the Mollari family. Urza then challenged Londo to a morrargo and allowed his friend to kill him. Later, Londo realized that he had sacrificed his life to save the honor of his family, who under the rules of the morrargo, became part of the Mollari household. Played by Carmen Argenziano. (KNIVES)

Ja'Doc

Narn aboard Babylon 5 who begged G'Kar not to leave the station in 2260. Although his family knew that they would be persecuted by the Centauri until G'Kar surrendered to them, Ja'Doc told the former ambassador that his family would rather die in the cause of freedom than live as slaves. (STRIFE)

Ja'Dog
Narn captain sent by Ambassador G'Kar to save Catherine Sakai from Sigma 957. Played by Michael McKenzie. (MIND)

Japote
A Centauri food, best served fresh. Ambassador Mollari is particularly fond of Japote. (KNIVES)

Jarheads
Common insult. (GROPOS)

Ja'Toth, Councilor
The father of Na'Toth, Ja'Toth was a follower of G'Lan. (PARLIAMENT, MEANS)

Jensen
A former member of the Psi Corps who joined forces with the underground railroad of unregistered telepaths. Jensen was killed by Bester during a deep scan and revealed in his dying thought that most of the unregistered telepaths were aboard Babylon 5. (RACE)

Jha'dur
The infamous Dilgar war-criminal, also known as "Deathwalker." Born in 2195, Jha'dur believed that it was natural for the superior to control the inferior. As a Dilgar warmaster, she was personally responsible for countless deaths. She wiped out races, destroyed whole planets and experimented on living beings.

Jha'dur led the Dilgar invasion of the non-aligned sectors in 2230. She also conquered Hilak 7 before experimenting on its population. Following the defeat of the Dilgar in 2232, Jha'dur disappeared and was sheltered by the Wind Swords for more than 25 years. She provided them with weapons technology later used in the Earth–Minbari War and developed her anti-agapic.

In 2258, Jha'dur arrived on Babylon 5 posing as a free trader, Gila Lobos, intending to negotiate a settlement for her anti-agapic. When her true identity was revealed, the League of Non-Aligned Worlds threatened to attack Babylon 5 unless she stood trial for crimes against sentients. Eventually it was agreed that Jha'dur would be sent to Earth to develop her anti-agapic with scientists from the Earth Alliance and League of Non-Aligned Worlds.

Jha'dur claimed that she wanted to give the universe the gift of immortality as a monument to her extinct race. She later revealed that one of the key ingredients of her serum had to come from living tissues, which meant that a person could only live forever at the expense of another. Thus Jha'dur hoped that her anti-agapic would lead to a bloody battle for eternal life across the universe.

Just as her ship left the station for Earth, it was destroyed by the Vorlons. Played by Sarah Douglas. (DEATHWALKER)

Jhala
Non-alcoholic Centauri drink, best served hot. Ambassador Mollari mainly drinks Jhala to recover from a hangover. (PURPLE, VOICE I)

Jinxo
See **Jordan, Thomas**

Jordan, Thomas
Thomas Jordan became a space construction worker during the Earth–Minbari War because he was too young to fight in the conflict. He subsequently worked as a grade 10 zero-gravity construction worker on all five of the Babylon stations.

Thomas said that the day he started work on the Babylon Station was the happiest day of his life. However, when the first three Babylon stations were all destroyed when he took days off, he was nicknamed "Jinxo" by his colleagues and also referred to as the Babylon Curse.

During the construction of Babylon 4, Thomas didn't take any leave until the station was finished. Twenty-four hours after it had become operational, he decided he could leave the station. As his shuttle disappeared, Thomas looked out of his window and saw the station disappear into a time warp.

Unsurprisingly, therefore, Thomas vowed to stay aboard Babylon 5. Once the station was complete, he could have found a good job elsewhere, but Thomas refused to leave Babylon 5 and became a lurker. While living Down Below, he borrowed money from the extortionist Deuce, who later gave Thomas 300 cycles to provide him with information about the supply corridors across the station or pay him a staggering 100,000 credits. When Thomas questioned the size of his debt, Deuce blamed the radical increase on inflation.

Jinxo was unwilling to aid Deuce's smuggling racket and decided to try to pickpocket the money from visitors to the station. Unfortunately, he made an incompetent thief and was arrested twice. As a result, when Thomas was caught trying to steal Aldous Gajic's credits by Garibaldi he was taken before the Ombuds.

Ombuds Wellington initially barred Thomas from the station for five years, but changed his sentence when Gajic asked to take the young man into his custody. While spending time with Aldous he was touched when his benefactor told him that he was a man of "infinite promise and goodness." When Aldous sacrificed his life to save Thomas from Deuce, the former construction worker decided to take up the quest for the Holy Grail. Played by Tom Booker. (GRAIL)

Jovian Sunspot
An exotic drink. Both Abbut and Captain Sheridan enjoy the occasional Jovian Sunspot. (DEATHWALKER, SPIDER)

J'Quoth'Tiel
The first Narn leader following the declaration of Narn independence in 2228. (LAW)

Jumpgates
Huge, stationary constructions in space which create jumppoints into hyperspace, also known as Vortex Generators. When a ship enters a jumpgate, the gate registers its ID code and the ship thus becomes liable to a fee. A jumpgate can be programmed to reject a ship's ID code, and during the Earth–Minbari War, all gates were programmed not to transport Minbari ships. (SIGNS)

Jumpgates also create dampening fields which slow ships down as they leave hyperspace and enter normal space (GATHERING). Almost all gates have a five-minute recharge time. (See **Jumppoints** and **Hyperspace** for further details)

Jumppoints
Portals into hyperspace, normally generated by jumpgates. Larger ships can create their own jumppoints, as can the *White Star*. (See **Jumpgates** and **Hyperspace** for further details)

K

Ka'Het

The wife of Du'Rog, mother of Mi'Ra and T'Kog. Following Du'Rog's death, Ka'Het took a Chon-Kar against Ambassador G'Kar, which the family later abandoned when the Narn financially compensated them and it received evidence clearing Du'Rog's name. (BLOOD)

Kalain

Kalain was the *Trigati*'s first officer during the Earth–Minbari War and led the Minbari warship and its crew into self-imposed exile following the suicide of the *Trigati*'s captain, Sineval. Like his former commander, Kalain believed that the Grey Council had betrayed the Minbari and could not give the order to surrender.

In 2259, he boarded Babylon 5 and was arrested for the attempted murder of Ambassador Delenn. However, Kalain had no intention of killing anyone aboard the station and committed suicide as part of an elaborate plan to justify the *Trigati*'s final offensive against Babylon 5. Played by Richard Grove. (DEPARTURE)

Kalika, Ambassador

An Abbai representative of the League of Non-Aligned Worlds. When Kalika learned that Jha'dur was aboard Babylon 5 and about to be sent to Earth, she traveled to the station and insisted that Deathwalker should be tried for crimes against sentients. When the Babylon 5 Advisory Council voted against a trial, she warned Commander Sinclair that the League of Non-Aligned Worlds would leave the Babylon Project. Later, she accepted Sinclair's compromise that Jha'dur would stand trial after she had helped scientists from Earthforce and non-aligned worlds develop her anti-agapic. Played by Robin Curtis. (DEATHWALKER)

Ka'Pul

A city on the Narn homeworld. (BLOOD)

Kat

A female bartender on the Zocalo. Played by Kathryn Cresside. (VOICE I)

Ka'Ti

Title given to Mutari aides. Caliban and Security Chief Garibaldi stood Ka"Ti to Walker Smith in 2258. (TKO)

Ka'Toc

A Narn sword. Once drawn, a Ka"Toc must not be sheathed again until it has blood upon it. (STRIFE)

Kawasaki Ninja ZX-11

A 20th-century Earth motorcycle. According to Security Chief Garibaldi, the Kawasaki Ninja ZX-11 was the best performance bike of its time. Garibaldi began building a 1992 1052cc model, complete with six valves and six-speed gearbox, in 2253. He acquired all the parts over a five-year period, including a Japanese manual, when Lennier offered to help build it in 2258. While the security chief tried to protect Commander Sinclair during Colonel Ari Ben Zayne's internal investigation, Lennier not only constructed it but managed to make the bike fully operational, although he did choose to replace the poisonous fuel system with a Minbari power source which was clean and efficient. Garibaldi had hoped to build the bike himself one day and was initially disappointed that Lennier had completed it all by himself, but complimented the good-hearted Minbari for doing such a good job shortly after. The unlikely duo then took the bike for a ride through the station's central corridor. (EYES)

Keffer, Warren (Lieutenant)

An easygoing hot-shot Starfury pilot stationed aboard Babylon 5 in 2259, Warren Keffer became the commander of Zeta Squad following the death of Ray Galus.

At the beginning of 2259, Lieutenant Keffer revealed that he needed explanations and logic (DEPARTURE). Consequently, when he encountered a Shadow ship in hyperspace which killed his superior officer, Commander Galus, and temporarily immobilized his own Starfury, he became determined to find out what it was and prove its existence. Shortly after, he began to search for Shadow ships during his spare time (LONG).

For Keffer, fear was part of his job. Fortunately, he would not be intimidated easily and would happily confront a superior opponent (GROPOS). Keffer was not trained in First Contact Protocol and was essentially a combat pilot (MATTERS). He was shocked when he was ordered to investigate an unidentified flying object near Babylon 5 which turned out to be a Ba-Bear-Lon 5 Teddy Bear spaced by Captain Sheridan (HONOR).

Keffer lived in Blue 47. When the station was overrun by GROPOS, he had to share with Yang and Large. Much to his surprise, he became friends with both GROPOS and was dejected when they were both killed in Operation : Sudden Death.

Toward the end of 2259, Keffer was ordered to stop his search for the Shadow ship (CONFESSIONS). However, he refused to forget about the "ghost" which had killed Galus and when he learned that Delta Squad pilot Mitch had encountered a similar vessel, Keffer begged for his assistance. Eventually, Mitch provided him with the means to track a Shadow ship.

While escorting a Narn warcruiser away from Babylon 5 territory, Keffer's Starfury detected a Shadow ship and broke formation to pursue it. Keffer then filmed the Shadow vessel and ejected his vessel's gun camera record just before his Starfury was destroyed. Keffer was later declared missing in action and widely presumed to be dead. (FALL)

Played by Robert Russler.

Kelsey

Female Psi Cop who, together with Bester, was sent to Babylon 5 in 2258 to track down the rogue telepath Jason Ironheart. Kelsey was later killed by Ironheart in an act of self-defense. Played by Felicity Waterman. (MIND)

Kemmer, Frank

A pilot on the Jovian moon run who befriended Michael Garibaldi in 2241. When Garibaldi was close to uncovering a racket scheme, the criminals rigged Kemmer's shuttle pad to explode and framed Garibaldi for negligence. As a result, Garibaldi was blamed for Kemmer's death. (SURVIVORS)

Kemmer, Lianna (Major)

The daughter of Frank Kemmer, Lianna Kemmer "died inside" when her father was killed in 2241. She blamed Garibaldi for his death and was convinced of his guilt when he hit the bottle and ran away immediately away after the incident.

In 2258, Lianna arrived on Babylon 5 as a member of Presidential Security to prepare the station for President Santiago's visit. When Nolan accused Garibaldi of placing the explosive which destroyed Cobra Bay 12 shortly before his death, Lianna seized the opportunity to discredit her father's "killer" and tried to have him arrested for conspiracy. Ultimately, however, Garibaldi convinced her that he was innocent and the pair managed to stop Cutter from destroying the cobra bays. Lianna later thanked Garibaldi for covering for her in his report. Played by Robin Wake (in flashback) and Elaine Thomas. (SURVIVORS)

Kha'Mak

A representative of the Narn council, Kha'Mak informed Ambassador G'Kar that the Kha'Ri endorsed his plan to kill Emperor Turhan in 2259. Played by Neil Bradley. (SHADOWS)

Kha'Ri

The Narn ruling council. Following the Narn–Centauri War, all members of the Kha'Ri stood trial for atrocities against the Centauri except for G'Kar, who had been granted sanctuary aboard Babylon 5. (TWILIGHT)

Khatib (Lieutenant)

Earthforce officer sent to Babylon 5 in 2259 to investigate the murder of J. D. Ortega. Lieutenant Khatib killed Ortega's murderer, Yang, as part of an elaborate cover-up and was then killed by his commanding officer, Wallace. (ACCUSATIONS)

Kiro, Lord

A descendant of the first Centauri emperor, Lord Kiro planned to use the Eye to become emperor of the Republic.

On his first birthday, Lady Ladira predicted that Kiro would be killed by Shadows. He thought that she was wrong and took her role as the family's prophetess and seer far too seriously. Kiro's family had been waiting for the Eye to return for more than 100 years and when Ambassador Mollari retrieved it for the Centauri noble, he had no intention of giving it to Emperor Turhan. Kiro hired the Raiders to steal the Eye and take him hostage, before they could begin their plan to seize control of the Centauri Republic. However, once aboard the Raiders' battle wagon, Kiro was double-crossed by his employees, who intended to hold both him and the Eye for ransom. The Raiders' plans were cut short when a Shadow ship destroyed their vessel and reclaimed the Eye for Ambassador Mollari. Played by Gerrit Graham. (SIGNS)

Kleist (Private)

A GROPOS who, in the words of Lieutenant Keffer, had an "attitude problem." While aboard Babylon 5 in 2259, Private Kleist called Ambassador Delenn a "freak" and accused her of being an insult to all the human beings who died during the Earth–Minbari War, before mindlessly starting a fight with Keffer which quickly spread throughout one of the station's casinos. Kleist was killed during Operation : Sudden Death. Played by Morgan Hunter. (GROPOS)

Knight One

A member of the covert organization within EarthGov known as Bureau 13 (SKY, SPIDER). In 2258, Knight One met with Knight Two aboard Babylon 5 and kidnapped Commander Sinclair. Knight One then monitored Sinclair's body while he was placed inside a Virtual Reality Cybernet. Knight One casually killed Benson when the security officer discovered that he was holding Sinclair captive, and was later killed by the commander in an act of self-defense. Played by Judson Scott (SKY).

Knight Two

A member of a covert organization within EarthGov (SKY, SPIDER). Knight Two joined Knight One aboard Babylon 5 in 2258 and the pair kidnapped Commander Sinclair. Knight Two then entered Sinclair's mind using a Virtual Reality Cybernet and interrogated the Earth Alliance war hero about his missing 24 hours during the Battle of the Line. When Sinclair remembered that he had been taken aboard a Minbari war cruiser and met the Grey Council, Knight Two became convinced that he offered to collaborate with the Minbari during the course of the meeting.

Before Knight Two could find any further information, Sinclair made a violent escape from the Cybernet. In the process, he caused a neural feedback which "fried" Knight Two's memory. Knight Two was sent back to Earth with little memory of what had happened. Played by Christopher Neame. (SKY)

Knives

Members of the Couro Prido. (KNIVES)

Kobya (Doctor)

A medlab physician. (STRIFE)

Ko'Dath

Ko'Dath was Ambassador G'Kar's first diplomatic attaché. She was eager to take her post on Babylon 5 and arrived early. When she tried to report to the ambassador, she learned that he was in the Dark Star and was unimpressed by the seedy dance club. Although G'Kar was actually trying to find Ambassador Mollari in the club, Ko'Dath was unconvinced by his claims. A tough, no-nonsense Narn, Ko'Dath had little time for small-talk and was proud to serve her world (PURPLE). She was later killed as a result of an accident with an airlock (PARLIAMENT). Played by Mary Woronov.

Kolee
The Centauri household goddess of passion. (PARLIA-MENT)

Kosh
See **Naranek, Kosh (Ambassador)**

Koslov (Rabbi)
Rabbi Koslov was a lifelong friend of the Ivanov family. Fol-lowing the death of Andrei Ivanov in 2258, Koslov left Earth for the first time to visit Susan Ivanova on Babylon 5. He traveled to the station on the Earth transport ship the *White Star* and, while en route, enjoyed an interesting conversation with the boxer Walker Smith.

Once aboard the station, the Rabbi insisted that Susan sat shivah for her late father. When the lieutenant-commander said that she was too busy, Koslov visited Commander Sinclair and arranged for her to take time off. He was delighted when she finally decided to sit shivah.

Koslov was extremely impressed by the Earth Alliance space station and referred to it as "a great miracle." Played by Theodore Bikel. (TKO)

Kozorr
A member of the Minbari warrior caste. In 2259, Kozorr ac-cused Ambassador Sinclair of conspiring to kill the new Minbari leader. (TREASON)

Krantz, Lewis (Major)
Earth Alliance officer assigned to supervise the final stages of Babylon 4's construction. When Babylon 4 was evacuated in 2258, Major Krantz was determined to take Zathras off the station, despite the mysterious alien's warning that he would die if he entered another timeframe. As far as Krantz was concerned, however, he needed Zathras to prove his story that Babylon 4 had somehow become unstuck in time. Ironically, just as Krantz's group were leaving the station, Zathras be-came trapped under a piece of masonry and had to be left behind. Played by Kent Broadhurst. (SQUARED)

K'sha Na'vas

A Narn cruiser. Captained by Vin'Tok. (BLOOD)

Kushoyev

A radical neo-communist writer. (TKO)

Kutai

A Centauri war sword.

Kyle, Benjamin (Doctor)

Babylon 5's original chief medical officer, Dr. Kyle was re-called to Earth following the assassination attempt on Ambas-sador Kosh.

When Kosh was found dying outside Bay 11, Commander Sinclair disobeyed the requests of the Vorlon Empire and ordered Kyle to open the ambassador's encounter suit and do what he could to save his life. Kyle was worried about the legend which claimed that the only human who ever saw a Vorlon turned to stone, but obeyed the order and managed to temporarily stabilize Kosh's condition.

As Kosh's life signs slowly continued to deteriorate, Kyle realized that the only way to save the Vorlon was to find the poison that was killing him and analyze it. After discussing the situation with Sinclair, Kyle and Lieutenant-Commander Takashima asked Lyta Alexander to perform an illegal tele-pathic scan on Kosh. As a result of the scan, the doctor lo-cated and analyzed the poison and altered the molecular structure of a compound to create a counteragent. As a result, he saved Kosh's life with just hours to spare. (GATHERING)

Dr. Kyle kept his hippocratic oath and never discussed what he saw (PRAYER). All he ever revealed was that Kosh was a very unusual alien (GATHERING). A week after the assassi-nation attempt, Dr. Kyle was reassigned to Earth to work di-rectly with President Santiago (PRAYER). Kyle met his successor, Dr. Stephen Franklin, at the transfer point at Io (SOUL).

Played by Johnny Sekka.

L

Ladira, Lady

A Centauri seer and prophetess, Lady Ladira was the aunt of Lord Kiro. On Kiro's first birthday, she predicted that he would be killed by Shadows. Upon boarding Babylon 5 in 2258, she was haunted by visions of fire, death and pain which culminated in the destruction of the station. She later shared the vision with Commander Sinclair, who saw a lone ship leaving Babylon 5 just before it exploded. According to Ladira, Sinclair could find a way to avoid this prophecy. Played by Fredi Olster. (SIGNS)

LaGrange 2

Outpost near the Mars Colony. Colonel Ari Ben Zayne stayed at LaGrange 2 prior to his arrival on Babylon 5 in 2258. (EYES)

Lakes Syndrome

Lakes Syndrome is an extremely painful and fatal condition, the symptoms of which include arthritis, blurred vision, burning intestines and inflamed veins. Dr. Laura Rosen contracted the syndrome, but transferred it to Karl Mueller in an act of self-defense in 2258. (MERCY)

Lantz, Frederick

Frederick Lantz was an idealist who joined the Ministry of Peace in the hope of building a better world for his grandchil-

dren. Like British Prime Minister Neville Chamberlain some
300 years before him, he desired peace in his time. In 2259,
he traveled to Babylon 5 to finalize the Earth–Centauri Non-
Aggression Pact. Presumably, Lantz was unaware of the
Minipax's more sinister motives. Played by Roy Dotrice.
(FALL)

Lardec 4
A colony wiped out by Jha'dur, who infected its entire population with Stafford's Disease in an experiment to see how long
they took to die. (DEATHWALKER)

Large (Private)
A loud, tough but friendly GROPOS, famed for endless war
stories. Large was a GROPOS for over 30 years, and served
with his best friend Buffer for more than 25 years, until Buffer
was killed during the Mars Rebellion in 2258. The following
year, Large took Private Yang under his wing and befriended
Lieutenant Keffer while aboard Babylon 5. Shortly after, Private Large was killed during Operation : Sudden Death.
Played by Ken Foree. (GROPOS)

Laser-Mirror-Starweb
Futuristic variant on Earth's rock-paper-scissors game.
(DUET)

Lazarenn (Doctor)
A Markab physician stationed on Babylon 5 when his race was
wiped out by the Drafa plague. Dr. Lazarenn first met the
station's chief medical officer, Dr. Franklin, before the Earth–
Minbari War, when the human visited the Markab
homeworld and the pair became good friends.

When new cases of Drafa were found on the Markab
homeworld, Dr. Lazarenn was ordered to keep the situation a
secret and, because the disease officially didn't exist, he was
given very little money to find a cure. When Franklin became
suspicious about a series of unexplained Markab deaths in
2259, Lazarenn told him the truth and tried to help him find
a cure. He then volunteered to conduct the autopsy on one of
the disease's victims in the isolab, during which he began to
show the symptoms of Drafa. From his deathbed, Lazarenn

helped Dr. Franklin find a cure, but it was too late to save his
people. (CONFESSIONS)

Played by Jim Norton.

League of Non-Aligned Worlds, The

An alliance of non-aligned races which includes the Drazi,
the Abbai, the Pak'ma'ra, the Vree and the Llort. The League
had a good relationship with the Earth Alliance ever since the
Alliance helped the non-aligned worlds defeat the Dilgar in
2232. While they do not have a seat on the Babylon 5 Advisory Council, the League of Non-Aligned Worlds casts the
deciding vote when the Council is deadlocked, and Commander Sinclair was keen for it to play a major role aboard
the station.

In 2258, the League was disgusted when the Advisory
Council voted against making the infamous war criminal
Jha'dur stand trial for crimes against sentients and threatened
to withdraw from the assembly. Fortunately, it chose not to
when Sinclair, as representative of the Earth Alliance, offered
to make Jha'dur stand trial after she had developed her anti-
agapic. Ambassador Kalika accepted the agreement on behalf
of the League. (DEATHWALKER)

Lennier

Born into the Minbari religious caste and a member of the
Third Fain of Chu'Domo, Lennier traveled to Babylon 5 in
2258 to assume his position as Ambassador Delenn's diplomatic attaché.

Lennier was raised in a Minbari monastery from birth.
Among other things, he read extensively about alien cultures,
considered the 97 Minbari dialects and subtongues and developed a passion for history (MERCY, DEATHWALKER). He
excelled in areas of probability, and was ranked Master Adept
by his math teachers. This makes him a natural poker player,
although as Ambassador Mollari discovered, he has yet to
learn the finer points of strategy and bluffing. For self-defense,
Lennier learned Minbari martial arts (MERCY).

The young Minbari left the temple for the first time in his
life to serve on Babylon 5 and was highly recommended to
Ambassador Delenn by his teachers. When he arrived on the
station, he wouldn't look Satai Delenn in the eye until he was

ordered to. However, Delenn could sense that even when he was looking at her, in his heart Lennier was still looking down (ALONE). When she instructed him only to refer to her as Satai when he was specifically told to do so, Lennier didn't understand but followed her order anyway, quoting the Minbari proverb, "Understanding is not required, only obedience" (PARLIAMENT).

Lennier developed a close relationship with his master and refused to abandon her when she faced the wrath of the Grey Council in 2259. When she lost her position as Satai, Lennier dismissed the possibility of returning to Minbar but instead reminded Delenn that he had sworn himself to her side and would serve her for the rest of her life (ALONE). A few months later, Lennier accompanied Delenn when she entered the Markab isolation zone to comfort the Markabs as they died of Drafa. At the time, there was no way of knowing whether or not the Minbari could contract the disease (CONFESSIONS).

Ambassador Mollari once convinced Lennier to join him for a tour of Babylon 5, which culminated in a brawl in the Dark Star when the Centauri was caught cheating at cards. When Commander Sinclair questioned them about what had happened, Lennier claimed that his unfamiliarity with the club's rules and customs caused offense and consequently led to the brawl, thus saving the Centauri from embarrassment. When Lennier learned that the ambassador had cheated using one of his sexual organs, he decided to take a vow of silence on the matter (MERCY). On the 30th anniversary of Mollari's Day of Ascension, Lennier gave him a pack of cards marked precisely in the way he liked (MATES).

Although he lost members of his clan and his family when the *Black Star* was destroyed during the Earth–Minbari War, Lennier had little interest in framing the "Starkiller," John Sheridan, for a crime he did not commit. He chose to believe the word of Delenn rather than that of his clansman, Ashan, because Lennier knew that she was "honorable" and was willing to dishonor the Fain of Chu'Domo to reveal the truth about its plot to discredit Sheridan. (HONOR)

Lennier serves as Sheridan's first officer aboard the *White Star*. After the ship's first battle with a Shadow vessel, he said his monastery didn't prepare him for such events and considered asking them to incorporate them into their program. (MATTERS)

Lennier believes that all life is sacred and would willingly sacrifice his life for another. During the series of bombings in 2260, he was almost killed saving Delenn and Londo from an explosion (CONVICTIONS). As the Minbari ambassador's diplomatic attaché, Lennier has a small allowance (MERCY).

Played by Bill Mumy.

Li
As the Centauri goddess of passion, Li represents a synthesis of male and female Centauri. (MERCY)

Liati
A wild Centauri animal. (KNIVES)

Li'Dac
A member of the Narn Fifth Circle, Li'Dac sponsored Na'Toth as Ambassador G'Kar's diplomatic attaché. (PARLIA-MENT)

Lifegiver
See **Alien Healing Device**

Link
Personal communication device used by the staff of Babylon 5 which is also capable of accessing the station's mainframe computer. A link is worn on the outside of the hand by means of an adhesive.

Llamuda
Traveling robe worn by the Children of Time for "great journeys," including the voyage into the afterlife. (BELIEVERS)

Llort
Alien race and member of the League of Non-Aligned Worlds, the Llort collect souvenirs just for the sake of doing so. They claim to have little interest in dead bodies. (LEGA-CIES)

Lobos, Gila
See **Jha'dur**

Lovell
A member of Third Fain of Chu'Domo, Lovell came from a highly respected family. When his clan ordered him to discredit Captain Sheridan in 2259, Lovell sacrificed his life to frame the "Starkiller" for murder. (HONOR)

Lu'Kor
A Drazi Mutari beaten by the Sho'Ri, Gyor, in 2258. (TKO)

Lumati
An advanced alien race which prizes evolution and believes that it is morally right for strong races to survive and grow, leaving the weaker races to die, the Lumati dislike intervening in the affairs of others and prefer to let nature take its course. They also believe that alliances are built not just on tactical advantage but on similarities in culture, and claim that only an "inferior" race would argue that all species are equal. The Lumati, as a "superior" race, refused to speak to any race which has not proven itself to be superior, in case it is actually an inferior race. In much the same way that humans use a handshake to seal an agreement, the Lumati use sexual intercourse to seal a deal!

The Earth Alliance was always keen for the Lumati to join the Babylon Project. Consequently, when they sent a delegation to Babylon 5 in 2259, Captain Sheridan instructed Commander Ivanova to do whatever it took to get them to sign on to the program. Although the Lumati delegate Corre-lilmurzon was initially unimpressed by what he saw aboard the station, he was convinced that humanity was a superior race when he visited Down Below, which he believed was designed to separate inferior humans from the superior humans aboard the station. He was extremely impressed by this process of dividing the superior from the inferior and hoped that the Lumati would try such a scheme on their homeworld. It was then left to Commander Ivanova to seal the deal with a manic dance which, she told the delegate, was the human race's style of intercourse. (SACRIFICE)

Lurker

A member of the Psi Corps who volunteered for a series of experiments which transformed him into a P12 or possibly a P13. Lurker knew Jason Ironheart and escaped with him from the Psi Corps to set up an underground railroad of unregistered telepaths (RACE). In December 2258, he was hired to load cargo for Devereaux. He later saw Stephen Petrov just before he was killed by Devereaux and pointed Security Chief Garibaldi to his killer (CHRYSALIS). When Bester came aboard Babylon 5 searching for the unregistered telepaths, Lurker reluctantly gave the order to kill the Psi Cop and had Talia Winters kidnapped. Although Bester survived the attempt on his life, he managed to convince Talia to join their cause and seemed to know about the gift Jason Ironheart had given her. When Bester discovered the group, Lurker joined forces with Talia and the other unregistered telepaths to trick the Psi Cop into believing that he had killed all of the group with Talia's help (RACE).

Played by Gianin Loffler.

Lurkers

Term for the inhabitants of Down Below who arrive on Babylon 5 looking for new jobs and new lives and become stranded on the station when they run out of money and can't find work. Some lurkers take menial jobs, most of which are illegal. (CHRYSALIS, SACRIFICE)

M

Macabee, Pierce
A regional director of the Ministry of Peace, Pierce Macabee visited Babylon 5 in 2259 to give a series of speeches to gain support for the Ministry's programs, including the Nightwatch. Macabee was particularly keen to enlist the support of Talia Winters. Played by Alex Hyde-White. (Z'HA'DUM)

Maintenance 'Bot
Robot used to monitor and repair the exterior of Babylon 5's hull. (GATHERING)

Malachi (Prime Minister)
The Centauri prime minister under Emperor Turhan. Malachi served Turhan well and is believed to have committed suicide when the emperor died. However, he was actually assassinated by Lord Refa and his associates during their coup d'état. Played by Malachi Throne. (SHADOWS)

Malax
A non-aligned planet destroyed by Jha'dur in 2231. (DEATH-WALKER)

Malios
Centauri cruiser attacked and destroyed by the N'Ton in September 2259. The *Malios* was later discovered to have been carrying weapons for the Narn–Centauri War. (WORD)

Malten, Arthur
Former head of the Association of Commercial Telepaths, Arthur Malten was later exposed as the leader of a revolutionary movement which had planted a number of bombs in an effort to discredit Free Mars. Malten himself was subsequently killed by Free Mars terrorists. (VOICES)

"Manya"
Word for mother used by Shon. (BELIEVERS)

Maray, Kiron
A Centauri youth and cousin of Vir Kotto. When Kiron Maray arrived on Babylon 5 with stolen credit chips, he was immediately arrested by Security and subsequently placed into Ambassador Mollari's custody. He told the ambassador that he had fallen in love with Aria Tensus, but was supposed to marry the "ugliest woman on Centauri Prime."

Kiron was shot with a PPG during a Homeguard attack and was left for dead. When he recovered, he learned that both he and his girlfriend would be fostered by Andilo Mollari until they came of adult age, when they could decide for themselves who they wanted to marry. Played by Rodney Eastman. (PRAYER)

Markabs
Non-aligned race aboard Babylon 5, wiped out by Drafa in 2259 (CONFESSIONS). The Markabs were known for their religious rituals in which they used psychotropics to lose control of themselves (KNIVES). Although some Markabs on isolated colonies may have survived the Drafa plague, the race is effectively dead (CONFESSIONS).

Marie Celeste, The
An Earth Alliance transport.

Mariel

The youngest of Londo Mollari's three wives. According to the ambassador, she was attracted to men of power like moths are to light. However, while the moths were burned by the light, Mariel burns the men! Mariel claimed to be a giving, passionate and faithful wife just before she bought a Narn booby trap disguised as a Centauri artifact in an effort to kill her husband. When Londo survived, she was divorced. Played by Blair Valk. (SOUL)

Mars Colony, The

The Mars Colony was the most controversial issue on Earth (MIDNIGHT). Many members of Earth's population felt that they were being taxed so that the "Marsies" could get the best atmosphere reprocessors and water reclamation technology (VOICE I).

In 2258, the Mars Colony was the site of a bloody revolt against the Earth-appointed provisional government. Rebels, many of whom were part of the Free Mars movement, threatened that the "sands will run red with Earther blood" unless Mars was given its independence from Earth (VOICE I). Eventually, President Santiago bowed to pressure from the Earth Senate and used elite shock troops to quell the riot (VOICE II).

In 2259, FutureCorp chief executive Taro Isogi proposed a peaceful settlement to the Mars crisis, but was assassinated shortly after. Amanda Carter of the Mars Conglomerate later decided to pursue Isogi's plan as a tribute to his memory. (SPIDER)

The first colony was destroyed by a surprise terrorist attack. (See also **Free Mars, Mars Rebellion**)

Mars Conglomerate, The

Mars' leading and monopolistic corporation. (SPIDER)

Mars Rebellion

Revolt against the Earth-appointed government on Mars which took place in 2258. The Mars Rebellion was quelled when Earth Alliance President Santiago authorized the use of shock troops (VOICE I, II). There have been other insurrections prior to this, such as the Mars food riots, triggered by an Earth supply embargo.

Mass Drivers
Powerful weapon of mass destruction outlawed by virtually every civilized race. Used by the Centauri Republic in 2259 to decimate the Narn homeworld. (TWILIGHT)

Matok
Rebel stronghold during the civil war on Akdor. Conquered by Earth Alliance forces during Operation : Sudden Death in 2259. (GROPOS) (See also **Operation : Sudden Death**)

Max
A vicious bounty hunter, Max said that everything interested him. He took the fugitive physician Dr. Everett Jacobs hostage in 2259 and wanted a 10,000 credits "finder's fee" for his safe return to Earthforce Special Intelligence. Sadly for him, his plans were thwarted by Garibaldi and Franklin. Played by Richard Moll. (HUNTER)

Mayan, Shal
A highly respected Minbari poet and writer of Ti'Lar. Shal Mayan had traveled widely and believed that all sentient beings are best defined by their capacity and need for love. She had no regrets.

While aboard Babylon 5 in 2258, Mayan was brutally attacked and branded by a vicious pro-Earth group, the Homeguard. She had declined the offer of a bodyguard or a security escort because she had never been attacked before and couldn't see why she would be. Her work had sometimes caused lively and heated discussion, but nothing more.

Shal Mayan found the Homeguard's hatred incomprehensible (PRAYER). She later returned to Babylon 5 from Earth and was given a full security escort while aboard the station (EYES).

Played by Nancy Grahn.

Maynard, Jack (Captain)
Captain Jack Maynard became John Sheridan's first commanding officer when he worked on the Moon–Mars Patrol.

They became great friends and Maynard once quoted him an ancient Egyptian blessing: "God be between you and harm in all the empty places where you must walk." Maynard is known as "Stinky" to Sheridan.

Maynard saw Sheridan on ISN when he was posted to Babylon 5 and was surprised that he had accepted the post. However, he was extremely grateful when Sheridan and the station's crew rescued his ship, the *Cortez*, from hyperspace.

Something embarrassing happened to Maynard when he took leave on Mars, but he refuses to allow anyone to talk about it.

While in Sector 857, Maynard caught sight of a Shadow ship. Played by Russ Tamblyn. (DISTANT)

Maze, The
Labyrinth situated in Babylon 5's Red Sector.

Medbracelet
Device worn around the wrist for a doctor to monitor a patient's condition. (KNIVES)

Medlabs
Babylon 5's medical facilities. As chief medical officer aboard Babylon 5, Dr. Franklin works in the primary medlab and supervises the activities of all the other doctors on the station, many of whom are based in the other medlabs. Although patients have to pay for treatment, the medlab facilities are undermanned and lack sufficient resources (MERCY, STRIFE). Medlab One was redesigned and refitted in 2260 (MATTERS).

Melori
A Centauri liner. Returned Timov, Daggair and Mariel to Centauri Prime following the 30th anniversary of Londo Mollari's Ascension Day. (MATES)

Mess Hall
Officers' food hall, located in Blue Sector. (Z'HA'DUM)

Metana
A waitress at the Dark Star. (MERCY)

Metazine

A drug administered to Commander Sinclair while he was in a Virtual Reality Cybernet. (SKY)

Minbar

The Minbari homeworld. Almost a quarter of Minbar is covered by its north polar ice cap. The planet is rich in crystalline deposits and many of its cities are cut directly from crystal formations. During the spring, they create some breathtaking patterns of light. Minbar is the seventh planet from its sun. (WORD)

Minbari, The

The Minbari are divided into three castes: the religious caste, the warrior caste and the worker caste, each of which is represented equally on the Grey Council. The religious caste takes precedence over the warrior caste, which is concerned mainly with external threats, while the worker caste is the least influential sector of their society and its interests are normally represented by the other castes. Religious and warrior castes rarely agree, but did on war against Earth. (DARKNESS)

Each caste is subdivided into clans and the main five warrior clans are the Star Riders, the Moon Shields, the Wind Swords, the Night Walkers and the Fire Wings. No single clan should dictate the policy of the caste or the Minbari (LEGACIES). Members of a clan are considered to be responsible for the actions of others within their clan (HONOR).

There are three basic Minbari languages—Lenann, Feek and Adronato (the language of the religious caste)—and a further 97 Minbari dialects and subtongues (WORD). The Minbari use base eleven.

The Minbari have a strict code of honor and no Minbari has killed another since Valen brought their society together, over a thousand years ago (DEPARTURE). They are taught that it is an honor to help another to save face (MERCY). Minbari do not lie, because to do so would be an affront to the honor and soul. They must speak the truth or say nothing. If a Minbari is accused of lying, it requires an immediate and fatal response. However, Minbari have been known to fudge the facts in order to help others save face (HONOR).

The Minbari believe in reincarnation and every generation of Minbari is said to be reborn into another. During the last 1000–2000 years, fewer Minbari have been born and many of those who are born lack the greatness of those born before. Originally, the Minbari thought that the Soul Hunters were responsible for depleting their souls, but learned during the Battle of the Line that Minbari souls were being reborn, either in full or in part, into human beings. Once their discovery had been confirmed, the Grey Council knew that it could not continue the war because Minbari do not kill Minbari. (DEPARTURE)

According to the Minbari, some groups of souls travel with each other; some are drawn together to relive good relationships or correct failed ones (MATES). Everyone will come together at the end of time (CONFESSIONS).

For the Minbari, all religious matters are considered private and must not be interfered with (BELIEVERS). Holy men, or "true seekers," are revered for their faith and their quest for the perfection of soul and the redemption of the race. When a "true seeker" dies, they have a chemical compound crushed into the ground where they rest. The compound then glows every night for a hundred years (GRAIL).

The Minbari are taught that the dying and people in pain or fear should be comforted and ministered to (CONFESSIONS). They view love as a potent healing force and also feel that no race can be truly intelligent without laughter. Consequently, members of the religious caste spend a year in the temple learning how to appreciate humor (PRAYER, RACE).

Physically, the Minbari have a much stronger constitution than humans, which enabled them to fight harder and longer than their opponents during the Earth–Minbari War (SOUL). Minbari do not sweat in the same way that humans do. Consequently, they do not bathe, but instead use a chemical compound which strips the outer layer of the epidermal tissue in an act which is symbolic of rebirth (MATES). They react badly to alcohol, and a small quantity can turn a Minbari psychotic (MERCY).

The Minbari have no press and are told only what they need to know and nothing more (DIVIDED). Many Minbari books consider the power of one mind to change the universe (GATHERING).

Members of a Minbari warrior caste would not carry an alien weapon because it would be considered an affront to their pride (HONOR). When traveling with honored members of the dead, a Minbari warcruiser will keep its gunports open as a symbol of respect (LEGACIES).

It takes two days to prepare a meal for an honored guest. There are 15 stages of preparation and the spices are blessed with a specific prayer at each stage. Each spice is used only once. If the chef commits an error, he or she must start again. The chef must stay up for two days to oversee the process in case of error and can only drink water and eat bread in order to remain pure.

When it comes to eating the meal, similar rituals are to be observed or the chef must start again. First, the host and the guest must swap bowls as a gesture of welcome. Then, the chef is offered a portion of food as a gesture of thanks. A place is left for Valen, together with a piece of flarn. The host and guest must use their right hands and meditate at various intervals during the meal. (CONFESSIONS) (See also **Grey Council, The; Earth–Minbari War, The; Battle of the Line, The;** and **Valen**)

Minbari Assassin

A member of a radical faction of the Minbari warrior caste. The Minbari assassin was supposed to meet Del Varner in Tigris Sector to collect a Changeling Net, with which he intended to pose as a Narn so that he could board Babylon 5 on a Narn supply ship. When he missed Varner, he arrived on Babylon 5 on a short-range ship which attached itself to the outside on Blue 5, Level B, and allowed the assassin to burn his way in. Later, the assassin met and killed Del Varner aboard the station and stole his Changeling Net.

The Minbari assassin then posed as Del Varner to support Londo's gambling, thus stopping him from arriving at the reception for Ambassador Kosh. He later pulled out of paying the Centauri's gambling debts. He subsequently posed as Commander Sinclair when he tried to poison Kosh.

When Kosh was recovering in medlab, the Minbari assassin posed as Lyta Alexander to sabotage his recovery. He also attacked an environment technician, Eric Hazeltine, who thought that he was his old friend, Del Varner.

The Minbari assassin was finally overcome by Sinclair during a bitter struggle for survival. He referred to the "hole" in Sinclair's mind and activated a self-destruct device which almost destroyed the entire sector. (GATHERING)

Mind Burst
A sudden explosion of telepathic power. (LEGACIES)

Mind Probe
Device used by Adira Tyree to extract Londo's access code to his Purple Files. (PURPLE)

Mindquake
A sudden explosion of extraordinary amounts of telekinetic power. Jason Ironheart suffered from mindquakes while aboard Babylon 5 in 2258. (MIND)

Ministry of Peace, The
Established in 2259 to establish peace between all humans across the cosmos as an essential precursor to interstellar peace. The Ministry of Peace launched a series of programs, including the Nightwatch, and was responsible for the Earth–Centauri Non-Aggression Pact. (Z'HA'DUM)

Mi'Ra
Daughter of Du'Rog and Ka'Het, sister of T'Kog. Mi'Ra was keen for vengeance against G'Kar following the death of her father and took a Chon-Kar. She later abandoned it when her family's name was cleared and they were compensated by G'Kar. (BLOOD)

Missionary License
Permit required by all missionaries and preachers on Babylon 5. (LONG)

Mitch
Member of Delta Squad who saw a "ghost" (actually a Shadow ship) in hyperspace. Mitch provided Lieutenant Kef-

fer with the means of tracking the ships. Played by Rick Hamilton. (FALL)

Mitchell, Bill
Member of Alpha Squad, commanded by Jeffrey Sinclair during the Battle of the Line. Bill Mitchell never listened to orders and broke formation during the Battle of the Line to attack a Minbari ship on Sinclair's tail. Shortly after, his Starfury was destroyed along with Mitchell's lifepod. Played by Justin Williams. (SKY)

Miyoshi (Lieutenant)
Earthforce investigator sent to Babylon 5 in 2259 to investigate the murder of J. D. Ortega and Susan Ivanova's involvement with the Free Mars movement. When her colleagues, Commander Wallace and Lieutenant Khatib, were exposed as murderers, Miyoshi violently tried to steal the evidence of supermorbidium from Ivanova in a desperate effort to save her career. During the attack, Miyoshi was killed by a security officer in an act of self-defense. (ACCUSATIONS)

Mobotabwe, Derek
ISN reporter on Mars during the 2258 riot. Played by Langdon Bensing. (VOICE I)

Mogath
Centauri god of the underworld and protector of front doors! (PARLIAMENT)

M'ola
Mother of Shon, wife of Tharg, M'ola couldn't sleep, eat or meditate while her son slowly headed toward death, but she could not bring herself to allow a surgical procedure to be performed on him. When Dr. Franklin performed the operation illegally, she and her husband killed Shon. Played by Tricia O'Neil. (BELIEVERS)

Mollari, Andilo
The second cousin of Londo Mollari and a very powerful Centauri. In 2258, he agreed to foster Kiron Maray and his young girlfriend, Aria Tensus. (PRAYER)

Mollari, Carn

The nephew of Ambassador Mollari. Carn wanted to join the Centauri armed forces until Londo told him it would be a waste of his talents and arranged for him to become the head researcher and project director at Ragesh 3. During the Narn invasion of the agricultural colony in 2258, Carn was forced to claim that the colony had requested Narn intervention. Played by Peter Trencher. (MIDNIGHT)

Mollari, Londo

As Centauri ambassador on Babylon 5, Londo Mollari's lust for the glory days of the Centauri Republic unleashed the force of the darkness known as the Shadows.

When his father was old and dying, Londo found him sitting in his room, alone, in the dark and crying. His father then told him, "My shoes are too tight, but I have forgotten how to dance." Londo never understood what he meant until many years later, when he found himself faced with two love-struck Centauri who wished to defy tradition and marry for love rather than the honor of their houses. When the boy, Kiron Maray, was almost killed, Londo arranged for both Kiron and his girlfriend, Aria Tensus, to be fostered by his second cousin, Andilo Mollari. (PRAYER)

As a young member of the Couro Prido, Londo was hungry to prove himself to the world and his colleagues. His best friends included Urza Jaddo, a fellow Knife (KNIVES). Mollari swore that he would die on his feet doing something noble and brave and led the raid on Phalos 12 as a young and foolish Centauri (VOICE I).

During the early part of his life, Londo also became preoccupied with Centauri females and went to the finest clubs to watch the most exotic dancers. One day he was angry and upset and went to a club. He sat there, gazing into nothingness, until he looked up and saw a dancer looking at him. She said, "Whatever it is, it can't be that bad" and then kissed him. He married her, but the next day, when he was away from the club and heard her voice, he decided to make a quick getaway. The couple were soon divorced, and Londo was left to face his three arranged marriages. (VOICE II)

Londo couldn't remember his first hangover because, as he

once pointed out, it wouldn't have been a hangover if he could remember it. (HONOR)

Like most Centauri, Londo believes that he has seen his own death in a dream, in which he was killed strangling a one-eyed Narn. When he first saw Ambassador G'Kar, he recognized him as the Narn from his dream (MIDNIGHT). Londo also had dreams of becoming the Centauri emperor, and of a fleet of Shadow ships flying around Centauri Prime (SHADOWS).

As the years went by, Londo could only watch as the great Centauri Republic continued its slow but steady decline and became a tourist attraction. When he was assigned to Babylon 5 in 2256, his orders were to create alliances (particularly with Earth Alliance and, perhaps, the Minbari) and make sure no one got the "upper hand" in agreements.

When he first boarded the station, Londo seized the opportunity to demonstrate his love for casinos. He had developed a winning scheme to 15 decimal places and was always looking for investors to fund his gambling (GATHERING). Despite his system, Londo has yet to make his fortune and admits to having a long and dubious relationship with Ilarus, the goddess of luck and patron of gamblers (SURVIVORS). However, he does have a highly unusual way of cheating at poker (MERCY).

Londo studied humans to try to make sense of them. One thing he couldn't understand was why, out of 6000 years worth of composers, one song, the Hokey-Pokey, remained so popular. He studied it for seven days and had it analyzed by computer, only to learn that it has no meaning. (VOICE I)

For Londo, the Narns represented a permanent reminder that the Centauri Republic's star had fallen. He viewed them as a barbaric, pagan people, who had been civilized by Centauri and were only fit to be their slaves. (MEANS)

Most of the Centauri's anger was vented at the Narn ambassador, G'Kar. In 2257, G'Kar blackmailed him with evidence of atrocities committed by his grandfather during the Centauri occupation of Narn and, the following year, gloated when his nephew, Carn Mollari, was forced to claim that Ragesh 3 had been liberated, rather than invaded, by the Narns. Londo felt responsible for what happened to Carn because he had personally arranged his posting on the colony, and tried to assassinate G'Kar. When Garibaldi stopped him, he said he would have to wait for his dream to come true in some 20 years' time. (MIDNIGHT)

A few months after the Ragesh 3 invasion, Londo refused to give G'Kar his G'Quan Eth plant for a Narn religious ceremony as an act of retaliation for the Narns' treatment of his nephew. It would be the first of many blows against the Narn ambassador dealt by Londo Mollari. (MEANS)

Londo always considered Garibaldi a good friend because he listened and was kind to him when he had nothing to gain (SACRIFICE). He was less enamored of his attaché, Vir Cotto, whom he initially found to be little more than a nuisance.

Londo maintained that love had nothing to do with marriage, which instead represented tradition and the melding of great Centauri houses (PRAYER). He referred to his three wives, Timov, Daggair and Mariel, as "Famine, Pestilence and Death," and repeatedly spoke of the sacrifice he had made by marrying them. Consequently, he was delighted when Emperor Turhan gave him permission to divorce two of his three wives in 2259 and chose to keep Timov, the only one who made no pretense of her lack of feeling for him, on the grounds that she was honest and he knew where he stood with her (MATES).

Although Londo claims to be cynical about love, he still pines for true love. In 2258, he thought that he might have found what he was yearning for with Adira Tyree, but was heartbroken to discover that she was a slave on a mission to steal his Purple Files. (PURPLE)

In September 2258, Londo acquired the Eye, the oldest symbol of Centauri nobility, which had been missing for more than 100 years. As he prepared for it to be returned to Centauri Prime, he was approached by Morden, the mysterious emissary of the Shadows, who asked him what he wanted. When Londo realized that he was serious, he replied: "I want my people to reclaim their rightful place in the galaxy. I want to see the Centauri stretch out their hand again and command the stars. I want a rebirth of glory, a renaissance of power. I want to stop running through my life like a man late for an appointment, afraid to look back or look forward. I want us to be what we used to be. I want it all back, the way that it was." After the meeting, the Eye was stolen by the Raiders and Londo believed that his career was finished. Then he received a visit from Morden, who returned the Eye to him. Londo was overjoyed, but when he tried to buy Morden a drink to celebrate the Eye's recovery, he saw that he had disappeared. (SIGNS)

Toward the end of the year, Londo was disgusted when he was ordered to give Quadrant 37 to the Narns, and met with Morden to discuss the situation. Morden instructed him to tell his government that he would personally deal with the situation. While Londo expected the Shadows to cripple the Narn forces or protect the passage of Centauri ships in the quadrant, he was shocked by the destruction of the Narn military outpost housing 10,000 Narns. However, he soon got over the shock as the Centauri Republic started to express its gratitude. (CHRYSALIS)

A few weeks after the attack, Morden asked Londo to tell him if he heard anything about happenings in the Rim. When he learned that the Narns were sending a warcruiser to Z'ha'dum, Londo told Morden, who arranged a short reception party for the ship. (REVELATIONS)

Londo then joined forces with Lord Refa, a scheming Centauri noble who shared his lust for Centauri glory. Shortly after, he sought an audience with the group of Techno-mages visiting the station, which would have provided an important sign of support for his rise to power to those who believed in the old days of the Republic. Although they refused, Elric told the ambassador before he left the station that he was touched by darkness and that he could hear the screams of billions—his victims. (GEOMETRY)

Although he was uncomfortable with Refa's plans to seize power from Emperor Turhan, when he was told that it was time to do something to make his associates stand out from the other factions, Londo asked Morden to attack the Narn colony on Quadrant 14, thus plunging the Centauri into war with the Narns. Emperor Turhan told Londo with his last breath that "We are both damned," but Londo then claimed that he endorsed the war effort with the words, "Continue. Take my people back to the stars."

Following the ascension of Refa's puppet emperor, Cartagia, Londo could have been named to the royal court, which would have been the first step toward becoming emperor. However, he claimed that he had no ambitions in that direction and told Vir that he preferred to work behind the scenes, where the rewards were nearly as great while the risks were far smaller. (SHADOWS)

As the war continued, Londo found that his influence grew with every day. He felt that he was becoming a "wishing well with legs" but had lost his only true friend on the station, Garibaldi. When Londo told him that everyone acted like they were afraid of him, Garibaldi replied that they were afraid. As a favor to his "good friend," he allowed the murder of a loudmouthed Centauri thug by a Narn to be resolved quietly. (SACRIFICE)

However, Londo's increased influence couldn't save him from the humiliation of being merchandised. The ambassador was particularly annoyed that the Londo Mollari doll didn't have "attributes." (HONOR)

In an increasingly rare act of kindness, Londo stopped Vir from being reassigned, when Centauri Prime attempted to send a replacement diplomatic attaché. (HONOR)

Londo was shocked to learn that his old friend and ally, Urza Jaddo, had been named a traitor by the Republic and that Refa was leading a coup d'état against his enemies. When Londo outlined his plan to save the Jaddo House through an alliance, Refa told him that it would be unfortunate because it would only serve to destroy the Mollari House. Upon hearing this, Londo decided to withdraw his support for the Jaddo House and Urza challenged him to a morrargo, a duel to the death. At the end of the fight, Urza sacrificed himself to save the honor of his family. Under the rules of the morrargo, Londo accepted the Jaddo family as his own. (KNIVES)

Londo was hailed as the architect of the Centauri victory over the Narn and witnessed the decimation of the Narn homeworld firsthand, from the *Valerius*. When Refa asked him to enlist the help of the Shadows, he swore that it would be the last time. He later returned to Babylon 5 to announce that Narn had unconditionally surrendered and revealed details of the Narn–Centauri Agreement (TWILIGHT). Afterward, he seized every opportunity to humiliate the Narns because he didn't want them to get out of their place again

(STRIFE). When Kosh revealed himself as a creature of light at the end of 2259, Londo saw nothing (FALL).

The following year, he told Morden that it was time for the Centauri to seek their destiny without his help. Morden showed him a map of the galaxy which he divided into Shadow and Centauri areas of influence. During an Earthforce investigation, Londo saw a Shadow ship for the first time and recognized it from his dreams. (MATTERS)

During the series of bombings aboard the station, Lennier became the only person who ever saved Londo's life (CONVICTIONS). Shortly after, Londo had Vir reassigned to the Minbari homeworld and became free to pursue his own evil destiny (STRIFE).

The passwords to Londo's Purple Files were "wine, women and song." (PURPLE)

Played by Peter Jurasik.

Molios, The
A Centauri transport. In September 2259, it was carrying fusion bombs and support equipment for ion cannons, mass drivers and heavy energy weapons destined for the Narn–Centauri War when it was destroyed by a Narn vessel, the *Na'Ton*. (WORD)

Morbidium
A metal used in the production of phased plaser weapons. (ACCUSATIONS)

Morden
The human emissary of the Shadows. Morden was aboard the *Icarus* when it landed on Z'ha'dum and agreed to serve the Shadows in return for his life. He subsequently became the Shadows' emissary and is always accompanied by them. (Z'HA'DUM)

In September 2258, he traveled to Babylon 5 to ask each of the alien ambassadors what they wanted. Kosh and Delenn sent him away before he could even ask his question, while G'Kar told him that he wanted the Centauri destroyed and justice for his people. When Londo told him of his lust for past Centauri glories and his yearning for things to be the way they were, Morden told his associates that Londo was perfect for their needs and gained his trust by retrieving the Eye for him from the Raiders. (SIGNS)

Morden and his associates then took the Centauri into war with the Narns and helped speed up their victory (CHRYSALIS, SHADOWS, TWILIGHT). When Londo warned him that a Narn warcruiser would be visiting Z'ha'dum, Morden made sure the Shadows were waiting (REVELATIONS).

Morden was illegally questioned by Sheridan until Delenn and Kosh asked him to release him. They explained that they didn't want the Shadows to know that they were preparing to face them, and explained that if Morden revealed anything he would be killed.

When Londo ended their alliance in 2260, Morden outlined the Centauri and Shadow areas of influence across the galaxy. Morden then told his former ally that he had already enlisted Lord Refa's aid to secure a world within Centauri jurisdiction, Zagros 7. Morden had also forged relations between the Shadows and the Psi Corps and EarthGov. (MATTERS)

Played by Ed Wasser.

Morishi

A security officer aboard Babylon 5. Morishi only had one week's leave between 2257 and 2260. Played by Cary Hiroyuki Tagawa. (CONVICTIONS)

Morph Gas

Nonlethal gas used to put people to sleep. Garibaldi suggested it be used on the dock workers so they could be arrested when the Rush Act was invoked. (MEANS)

Morrargo

A Centauri duel to the death. To reject a morrargo brings disgrace not only to the individual, but to his entire house. The victor of the morrargo must accept the family of the victim as his own. (KNIVES)

Morrell (Doctor)

A medlab physician. (STRIFE)

Mosechenko, Desmond
See **Deuce**

Motorcycle, The
Extinct form of transport used on Earth. The last gasoline motorcycle was built in 2035 as they were harmful to both living creatures and the environment. (EYES)

Mueller (Doctor)
An expert on molecular biology. In 2260, Dr. Mueller had his holiday interrupted to answer two questions set by the Alien Science Probe encountered by Babylon 5. (STRIFE)

Mueller, Karl Edward
In 2258, Karl Edward Mueller was tried for the calculated and unprovoked murder of two residents of Babylon 5 plus the brutal and the senseless slaying of a security officer. When he was found guilty of murder in the first degree, Ombuds Wellington sentenced him to brainwipe. Security Chief Garibaldi suspected that he had killed many more than three times. His theories were proved correct during a comparative scan conducted by Talia Winters, who learned that he had murdered on many worlds in order to build a choir of victims who would sing him into Heaven when he died.

Just before he was brainwiped, Mueller escaped from Security and was shot in the arm as he fled. He then held Janice Rosen and Dr. Franklin hostage and forced Laura Rosen to heal him. When she realized that Mueller would kill all of them once he had recovered, she reversed the energy flow and he died as a result of the sudden exposure to the tremendous pain of Lakes Syndrome. Played by Mark Rolston. (QUALITY)

Muta-Do, The
Referee of the Mutai, also known as The Sayer, the Muta-Do is over 90 years old and has fought in over a thousand Mutai. Initially refused Walker Smith entry. After his victory, declared that all humans can fight in the Mutai. Played by Soon-Tek Oh. (TKO)

Captain John J. Sheridan (Bruce Boxleitner) assumes command of Babylon 5 in "Points of Departure."

Earth Alliance space station Babylon 5

The *White Star* is attacked by a Shadow ship in
"Matters of Honor."

Babylon 5's no-nonsense First Officer, Commander
Susan Ivanova (Claudia Christian)

The various diplomats and attachés aboard Babylon 5 in 2260.
(Top row, left–right) Ambassador Kosh Naranek, Vir Cotto,
Ambassador G'Kar, and Lennier. (Bottom row, left–right)
Ambassador Londo Mollari, Captain John Sheridan, and
Ambassador Delenn.

Babylon 5's commanding staff in 2258. Security Chief Michael
Garibaldi, Commander Jeffrey Sinclair, and Lieutenant
Commander Susan Ivanova.

Ranger Marcus Cole (Jason Carter) visits Babylon 5
to enlist Captain Sheridan's assistance.

Captain Sheridan chairs a meeting of the Babylon 5
Advisory Council in "Revelations."

Lyta Alexander accuses Commander Sinclair of attempting
to murder Ambassador Kosh Naranek in "The Gathering."

Security Officer Zack Allan (Jeffrey Conaway)

A standard, single pilot Starfury

The Shadows patrol the Rim of known space.

Mutai, The

An alien combat event for the "bravest of their race." The object is to take your opponent down. There are no rounds, no rules and no gloves. Many fighters are killed or crippled. The fighting ring is known as the Sands of Blood. In 2258, Walker Smith became first human to fight in the Mutai. It means "trial of blood." (TKO)

Mutari

Fighters in the Mutai, also known as the "bravest of their race." Fighters must show respect for the Mutai at all times. (TKO)

N

Na'Far (Councilor)
Member of the Centauri-appointed Narn government sent to Babylon 5 in 2260 to replace citizen G'Kar as the Narn representative aboard the station. He asked G'Kar, as the only remaining member of the Kha'Ri, to return to the Narn homeworld to stand trial. He then told the former ambassador that if he didn't return, the families of all the Narns aboard Babylon 5 would be harassed, tortured and possibly killed.

Na'Far felt that Narns would achieve freedom one day, but needed time to rebuild their forces and lull the Centauri into a false sense of security. In the meantime, Narns were suffering needlessly. because of G'Kar's resistance efforts. Na'Far wanted his world rebuilt and his people fed, clothed and safe. Played by Stephen Macht. (STRIFE)

Na'Kal
Narn warship commander who sought sanctuary at Babylon 5. Captain Sheridan had to destroy a Centauri battle cruiser to allow Na'Kal's ship to escape. Played by Robin Sachs. (FALL)

Na'ka'leen Feeders
Quasi-sentient beings that feed on brainwaves, the Na'ka'leen feeders were first discovered by the Centauri when they colonized their homeworld. The feeders attacked every Centauri on the planet until the Republic quarantined it.

Na'ka'leen feeders can move extremely fast and become

quiet before they attack. They prefer to feed on older minds. Deuce brought a feeder to Babylon 5 in 2258. The creature was later destroyed by a Security team. (GRAIL)

Nano-Technology

Micro-machines that are too small for the human eye to see. In 2257, Commander Sinclair claimed he had placed a nano-beacon in Ambassador G'Kar's intestinal tract as a homing device. He could, therefore, be tracked down if he ever endangered Babylon 5. Sinclair, of course, was bluffing—but G'Kar didn't know that. (GATHERING)

Naranek, Kosh (Ambassador)

As the Vorlon Ambassador on Babylon 5, Kosh Naranek has revealed little about himself to those on Babylon 5.

Kosh nearly always appears wearing his encounter suit. While the suit supposedly provides the Vorlon with his required environment (which contained a high level of methane, sulfur and carbon dioxide), it became clear that Kosh was actually using it as a disguise when he was poisoned through the hand of his suit in 2257 (GATHERING). Delenn later revealed that Kosh was hiding his true nature because, as a First One, everyone would recognize him (Z'HA'DUM).

Ambassador Kosh rarely speaks and on the rare occasions he does, he tends to give short, concise and seemingly meaningless answers. When Captain Sheridan and Talia Winters complained that they couldn't understand him, he wasn't bothered (DEATHWALKER, MATTERS). However, he did advise Talia not to listen to the song but the music (DEATHWALKER).

He rarely attended meetings of the Advisory Council prior to Captain Sheridan's arrival and his daily activities were shrouded in mystery. All that was known for certain was that he often returned to the Vorlon homeworlds (MATTERS). He once explained that, as a Vorlon, he was uninterested in the affairs of others. Nevertheless, he does study alien worlds, including Earth (PRAYER). He also likes the fact that people are scared of both him and his people (GRAIL).

In 2258, Ambassador Kosh hired Talia Winters for "important business" involving a strange man named Abbut. Although the negotiations made absolutely no sense to the telepath, she later realized that Abbut had been hired by Kosh to scan her mind. (DEATHWALKER)

When he was approached by the Shadow emissary Morden, Kosh told him, "Leave this place. They are not for you." (SIGNS). He later advised Captain Sheridan that he should never ask him what he wants (HUNTER).

At the end of 2258, Kosh confirmed Delenn's fears that the Shadows had returned to Z'ha'dum. He then appeared to her outside his encounter suit, which convinced her to undergo her transformation into a half-human, half-Minbari hybrid. (Z'HA'DUM)

When Sheridan was held captive by the Streibs in the following year, the Vorlon made contact with his mind in a dream (ALONE). According to Kosh, Sheridan's thoughts became a song and he listened to it. Kosh later told him that he was the second person he had made contact with in that manner (HUNTER).

As a result of their mental encounter, Kosh agreed to take Sheridan for a series of lessons. Although the human hoped that he would learn more about the Vorlon, Kosh told him that he was trying to teach the human more about himself and was preparing him to fight legends (HUNTER). Later in the year, Kosh agreed to help Sheridan prepare for his journey to Z'ha'dum (Z'HA'DUM).

Kosh also agreed to help Sheridan and his staff hide the fugitive physician Dr. Everett Jacobs and allowed him to be placed in his ship on the condition that he was unconscious. (HUNTER)

At the end of 2259, Kosh left his encounter suit to fly to Captain Sheridan's aid as he was plunging to his death from a core shuttle. As a First One, he was revealed to be a creature of light and appeared as different beings to different aliens; for example, the humans who saw Kosh perceived him as an angel, while the Drazi witnesses saw him as Droshalla (FALL). Kosh later admitted that it was a great strain to be seen by so many at once and had to spend a week resting in his ship (MATTERS).

Voiced by Ardwright Chamberlain.

Narn

The Narn homeworld. Narn was a lush, forest planet before the Centauri invasion at the beginning of the 21st century. When they left some 130 years later, it was a bleak and barren world. Narn was left subject to drastic extremes of temperature and only managed to restore a few areas of forestry. (BLOOD)

The Centauri were not the first alien race to invade Narn. During the first Great War, one of the Narn's southern continents was used as a base of operations by the Shadows. (MATTERS)

Narn is 12.2 light years (or a little over 10 Narn light years) away from Babylon 5. (MEANS)

In 2259, Narn was decimated by a brutal Centauri attack (TWILIGHT). Following the Narn surrender, the homeworld could only be reached through official Centauri channels (INQUISITOR).

Narn, The

The Narn were an agrarian and peaceful people until they encountered the Centauri (CHRYSALIS). They greeted the Centauri in peace and were promptly enslaved by them at the beginning of the 21st century. The Narn then fought a war of attrition until the Centauri left their world in 2228.

Once the Narn won their freedom, they swore that they would never be conquered again. They became obsessed with gaining new technology and were keen to establish an alliance with either the Minbari Federation or the Vorlon Empire. (GATHERING)

Many Narn became arms dealers and sold weapons to Earth during the Earth–Minbari War (MIDNIGHT, INQUISITOR). When they sold weapons, they generally provided an adviser who not only demonstrated how to use them but also made sure that they were not resold (MIDNIGHT).

Narn aristocrats believe that education is beneath them and, consequently, their servants tend to be better educated. Narns are taught the art of negotiation from an early age and can hibernate for six days at a time.

Narn–Centauri Agreement, The

Following the Narn Regime's unconditional surrender at the end of the Narn–Centauri War, the Narn homeworld became a Centauri colony and accepted a three-point plan:

1. The Kha'Ri was disbanded and its members were arrested to stand trial for war crimes against the Centauri.

2. If any Centauri was killed by a Narn, 500 Narns, including the murderer and his or her family, would be executed.

3. The Centauri would appoint a ruling body to replace the Kha'Ri. (TWILIGHT)

Narn–Centauri War

Following the invasion of Quadrant 14 in 2259, the Narn Regime declared war on the Centauri Republic (SHADOWS). However, the Narn were unprepared for a direct war, having previously fought a war of attrition against the Centauri. The war escalated when the Centauri began to attack civilian targets, claiming that the Narn had placed military targets inside civilian populations, thus using their people as shields (SACRIFICE).

In a bid to turn their fortune around, the Narns mounted an attack on the Centauri supply world of Garesh 7. They were unaware that the Centauri knew of their intentions and had arranged a reception of Shadow ships, while they led a full assault on the Narn homeworld. After a few days, the Narn unconditionally surrendered. (TWILIGHT)

Narn Regime

Title for the Narn federation.

Narn Supply Ship

The vessel that brought the Minbari assassin to Babylon 5 space in 2257. (GATHERING)

Na'Toth

G'Kar's diplomatic attaché following the death of Ko'Dath. Unfortunately for Na'Toth, she arrived on Babylon 5 shortly after G'Kar had received a death threat, and he immediately suspected her.

Several members of Na'Toth's family, including her grandfather, were on Hilak 7 when it was conquered by Jha'dur.

Na'Toth's grandfather was experimented upon by the infamous Dilgar, and when he escaped to Narn he had a device placed in his brain which slowly destroyed his mind, spirit and body while his family could only watch. When he died, Na'Toth's family took a Chon-Kar against Jha'dur.

In 2258, Na'Toth tried to fulfill her blood oath when she saw Jha'dur on Babylon 5. She was subsequently placed under house arrest. (DEATHWALKER)

Na'Toth's father was a disciple of Ji'Lan while her mother didn't believe in anything. Na'Toth believed in herself as a warrior because "chance favors the warrior." (MEANS)

Although Na'Toth initially thought that Ambassador G'Kar was something of a buffoon, the pair became firm allies as she realized how dedicated he was to his world and his people.

Na'Toth is believed to have died during the Centauri attack on the Narn homeworld. (TWILIGHT)

Played by Caitlin Brown (season one) and Mary Kay Adams (season two).

Nazeem

A GROPOS assigned to the 356th Squadron during Operation : Sudden Death. Nazeem's serial number was 87953. (GROPOS)

Needler

A gunlike device which fires a thin needle coated with a toxin. (TKO)

Neroon

A member of the Star Riders clan, Neroon served as Branmer's aide and executive officer between 2243 and 2258. He was always loyal to the Minbari war hero and would have sacrificed his life for him.

When Branmer died in 2258, Neroon ignored his request for a quiet cremation and displayed his body to the Minbari across the galaxy. When his body was stolen by Ambassador Delenn, Neroon was ordered to support her story that it had disappeared as part of a true religious mystery. (LEGACIES)

In 2259, Neroon was appointed a member of the Grey Council and replaced the half-human Delenn, whom he felt was an affront to the Minbari. When he learned why the

Minbari had surrendered to Earth, he said that he didn't
know whether to laugh or weep and admitted that he would
not have stopped fighting if he had heard the truth. (ALONE)

On Minbar, Neroon led the prosecution of Ambassador
Sinclair for conspiring to kill the Minbari leader. (HARM)

Played by John Vickery.

Netter (General)

The head of Earth Alliance President Santiago's security staff.
General Netter was stationed aboard *Earthforce 1* during the
president's visit to Babylon 5 and ordered Sinclair to give his
staff full cooperation. Played by Rod Perry. (SURVIVORS)

Netter's Syndrome

Lennier once claimed to have this fatal disease in an effort to
get rid of an obnoxious man who was annoying him in the
passenger lounge. (CONVICTIONS)

N'Grath

Babylon 5's resident enforcer, N'Grath is an insectoid alien
who can sell, provide and fix things for individuals provided
they have sufficient funds at their disposal. N'Grath provided
the rogue Soul Hunter (#1) with a plan of the station and
complete (Level 5) access (SOUL). Shortly after, his staff
stalled Sinclair and Londo long enough for Trakis to get to
Adira Tyree (PURPLE). N'Grath then provided Ambassador
G'Kar with a short-lived bodyguard (PARLIAMENT). However, he wouldn't help Garibaldi when the security chief was
on the run and told him that he only did legitimate business
(SURVIVORS).

Nightwatch, The

A program launched by the Ministry of Peace in 2259, the
Nightwatch was devised as an early warning system to warn
against breaches of the peace. It was named after the brave
citizens who stood in the dark watching for enemies and endorsed by EarthDome. Members of Nightwatch were paid 50
credits a week to wear their Nightwatch band and find people
who were working against the "public good." It was also
Nightwatch's duty to protect society from "misinformation,"

"harmful ideas" and "its own worst instinct." (Z'HA'DUM, FALL)

"Ni sec schlect slem wa"

Minbari phrase which means, "I'm your friend, in peace." (WORD)

N'Kai

A word which appears in all 97 Minbari subtongues and dialects, but never means the same thing twice. Its meanings include sand, father and boot. (MERCY)

Nolan

Homeguard sympathizer killed by his own explosive device, which he planted in one of Babylon 5's cobra bays in 2258. With his dying breath, Nolan said that the bomb had been placed in the bay by Security Chief Garibaldi. (SURVIVORS)

N'Ton

The Narn vessel that attacked and destroyed the *Malios* in September 2259. (WORD)

O

Observation Dome

Situated in Babylon 5's Blue Sector, the Observation Dome is the focus of all station operations. Civilians are not allowed in the Dome without the permission of the station's commander (EYES). Commander Sinclair used to turn off his link and spend ten minutes of every day in the Dome, gazing at the stars (MIDNIGHT). Also known as Command and Control, or C&C for short (WORD).

Ock

The Brakiri manager of the Dark Star dance club. Played by Jim Giannini. (PURPLE)

O'Connor

A member of Major Liana Kemmer's presidential security staff. Assigned to Babylon 5 in 2258 to supervise President Santiago's visit. (SURVIVORS)

Office of Planetary Security, The

A division of the Earth Alliance government. In 2258, the Office of Planetary Security was keen to secure Epsilon 3's advanced technology for the Earth Alliance. (VOICE II)

Ombuds, The

Magistrates aboard Babylon 5. The Ombuds can sentence convicted murderers to imprisonment or brainwipe, while individuals found guilty of committing an act of mutiny or treason can be sentenced to death by spacing (MERCY). The station's Ombuds include Wellington and Zimmerman (MERCY, GRAIL).

Omega, The
Earthforce ship. (MEANS)

Omelos
Planet situated in the Caliban sector. The birthplace of Jha'dur. (DEATHWALKER)

One, The
Name used by Zathras to refer to the galaxy's "great hope" during a terrible war against the forces of darkness. Zathras revealed that The One had risked his life to stop Babylon 4 in 2258 in order to allow the crew to disembark and was willing to sacrifice himself for others. When Zathras was trapped beneath a falling piece of masonry and left to die, he knew that The One would come to his aid. The One appeared to be none other than a war-weary Jeffrey Sinclair, but this may not be the entire story. (SQUARED)

Operation : Sudden Death
Name of the Earthforce offensive on the rebel stronghold in Matok in 2259. Operation : Sudden Death was the brainchild of General Richard Franklin, who devised the plan with the help of Captain Sheridan, and was a top-secret operation; even the general's own troops were unaware of the offensive and thought that they were headed for Io until they left Babylon 5 and found themselves on Akdor.

   As a result of Operation : Sudden Death, the Earth Alliance seized control of Matok, but the 356th Squadron suffered an enormous number of casualties. (GROPOS)

Orca
A Markab fruit juice. Both Stephen and Richard Franklin liked it. (GROPOS)

Orion
Planet. A member of the Earth Alliance.

Ortega, J. D.
An Earthforce flight instructor whose pupils included Susan Ivanova, J. D. Ortega always said that Starfuries and their pilots should be "hardwired" to each other, meaning that they should work together as one. (ACCUSATIONS)

Orwell, Mr.
Freelance retailer based on Babylon 5. In 2259, Mr. Orwell had to call in some favors to get Security Chief Garibaldi the ingredients of *bagna cauda*. Played by Miguel A. Nunez, Jr. (STAR)

Oxy Pills
Oxygen pills. Can be used for many purposes, including sobering people up. (SURVIVORS, EYES)

P

Paingivers
Necklaces and bracelets used to inflict searing pain. Ambassador G'Kar sampled their effectiveness at the hands of the Narn assassin Tu'Pari in 2258. (PARLIAMENT)

Pak'ma'ra
An alien race aboard Babylon 5 and part of the League of Non-Aligned Worlds, the Pak'ma'ra are carrion eaters. During the search for Branmer's body in 2258, all the station's Pak'ma'ra had their stomachs pumped. Although they were innocent of the crime, this did not make Dr. Franklin feel any better after he had performed the procedure. (LEGACIES)

In 2259, the Pak'ma'ra began to contract the fatal Markab disease, Drafa. Fortunately, Franklin found a cure before it could claim many Pak'ma'ra victims. (CONFESSIONS)

Paso Liati
The Couro Prido's nickname for Londo Mollari. It means "crazed Liati." (KNIVES)

Passenger Lounge
Waiting area near Babylon 5's docking bays.

Patrick
Executive officer aboard the *Cortez*, Patrick was with Captain Maynard when he saw a Shadow ship, but didn't see the vessel himself. Played by Daniel Beer. (STAR)

Petrov, Stephen

A lurker who had a habit of getting involved with the wrong kind of people. In June 2258, Stephen Petrov was arrested for petty theft by Security Chief Garibaldi, who subsequently enlisted him as an informant.

In December 2258, Petrov was hired to load cargo for Devereaux and learned that his employer was involved in a plot to assassinate Earth Alliance President Santiago. When he was killed on December 30th, 2258, his dying words to Garibaldi were, "They're going to kill him." This pointed the security chief in the direction of the conspirators. Played by David Anthony Marshall. (CHRYSALIS)

Phased Plaser Gun (PPG)

A standard Earthforce weapon, PPGs are produced as both rifles and pistols. They are powered by a removable energy cap and fire superheated gas known as plasma (STRIFE). A PPG can be used to stun or kill and, at full power, can burn right through the body and most objects. They get extremely hot when fired.

Each PPG can be traced through a serial number stamped on its inner coil. The coil is made of a morbidium alloy which is harder than diamond and cannot be removed. Only Earthforce special agents have unnumbered PPGs. (CHRYSALIS)

Phobos Station

An Earth Alliance outpost. When Phobos Station was attacked in 2258, it was believed to be the work of Free Mars. (EYES)

Phroomis

A Narn delicacy. (DUET)

Pierce, Ellis (Captain)

Commanding officer aboard the Earth Alliance heavy cruiser, the *Hyperion*. Following the discovery of advanced alien technology beneath the surface of Epsilon 3 in 2258, Captain Pierce was dispatched to the Tigris Sector to make sure that Earth would have first refusal of the planet's technology and was happy to use force to fulfill its mission. When Commander Sinclair resisted his heavy-handed tactics, Pierce tried to assume control of the situation on the authority of the Office of Planetary Security. He also told the commander that he felt that Babylon 5 was an easy posting. When Sinclair's authority over the system was confirmed by President Santiago, Ellis expressed his "regrets" for exceeding his authority during the crisis. Played by Ron Canada. (VOICE II)

Placibo
Fictitious homeworld of the equally imaginary Gloppit egg given to Shon by Dr. Franklin. (BELIEVERS)

Plug (Sergeant-Major)
No-nonsense Earthforce soldier, a member of the 356th Squadron. Played by Ryan Cutrona. (GROPOS)

Poison Tab
See **Skin Tab**

Poker
Human card game, exported to Centauri during trade. Poker was one of Ambassador Mollari's favorite pastimes. When he learned that Lennier excelled at studying mathematical probability, he introduced him to the game. Although the Minbari played poker well, he had a lot to learn about strategy and the art of bluffing. (MERCY)

Pournelle, The
An Earth Alliance heavy cruiser. The *Pournelle* destroyed Abel Horn's ship during the 2258 Mars Rebellion. (SPIDER)

PPG
See **Phased Plaser Gun**

Preslecomp
A drug used to fight blood iron deficiency. Dr. Franklin prescribed preslecomp to Michael Garibaldi while he recovered from an assassination attempt in 2259. (DISTANT)

Priority 1 Alert

A Priority 1 Alert is involved when Babylon 5 is under attack. If declared, the station's population must head to the shelters immediately. (WORD)

Project : Lazarus

Project : Lazarus marked the culmination of the Earthforce cyber experiments during the 2230s.

After numerous attempts to find a way of incorporating computers into the minds of healthy human beings failed, Earthforce scientists decided to use subjects on the verge of death. Accident victims, wounded soldiers and comatose individuals all had their brains hardwired with a computer intelligence while a deep telepathic scan focused the subject on the moment of death. Thus, the computer took control while the individual subconsciously died over and over again and was left devoid of conscious thought.

Although the cyber experiments were officially abandoned before the Earth–Minbari War, Bureau 13 used Project : Lazarus to provide some of its operatives. Its subjects included Abel Horn. (SPIDER)

Proxima System

Del Varner was wanted for smuggling illegal technology from this sector. (GATHERING)

Proxima 3

Earth Alliance outpost Proxima 3 was the site of a series of bombings by Robert J. Carlsen in 2259 (CONVICTIONS). In the previous year, Dr. Vance Hendricks claimed to have quarantined the Ikaaran bio-organic devices at Proxima 3's local jumpgate (INFECTION).

Psi Cops

The Psi Corps' internal investigations division. All Psi Cops are rated P12 and have a great deal of discretionary power in regard to Psi Corps rules and regulations. For example, they can order members of the Psi Corps to submit to telepathic scans and have been known to use unauthorized scans. (MIND)

Psi Corps, The

When telepaths were discovered on Earth at the beginning of the 21st century, the government decided that it had to take action to protect the general public's privacy from telepathic intrusion. EarthGov created several supervisory bodies and made several attempts at legislation, all of which either failed or were overturned in the various courts of law. Then, in the middle of the century, all of the government agencies that oversaw and regulated telepaths were merged into one body: the Psi Corps. Telepaths who refused to join the Corps could choose between life imprisonment and regular treatment with telepathic suppressants known as sleepers.

Young telepaths stay at Psi Corps centers before they attend a Psi Corps Training Academy. During a telepath's first year at each institution, he or she is assigned a senior student for support. As well as regulation telepaths, the Psi Corps is also in charge of telekinetics. Within the Corps, telepaths are known as "teeps" while telekinetics are dubbed "teeks." (DIVIDED)

One of the first things the Psi Corps teachers its members is the ability to block out the thoughts of others. Telepaths wear gloves to prevent them from unintentionally performing any casual scans. (LEGACIES)

All telepaths are rated from P1 to P11. It takes years of training to qualify as a P5 and half the candidates burn out or end up vegetables (GATHERING). P12 telepaths are eligible to join the Psi Cops.

The Psi Corps is divided into commercial and political branches (GATHERING, PURPLE). In general, commercial telepaths require clearance, payment and details of the business transaction before they will mediate in a deal (DEATHWALKER). Few telepaths train to work in criminal cases because they are considered very stressful and have a high burn-out rate (MERCY).

There are strict Psi Corps regulations about the use of scans. Unauthorized scans can only be performed with a court order or with the permission of the subject's next of kin (GATHERING). Any evidence discovered while scanning a defendant is considered inadmissable in court. Only deathbed scans, with permission, are admissable, and then, only if there is corroborative evidence. (MERCY). In 2258, a new

Earthforce regulation allowed command-level members of staff facing specific charges to be scanned (EYES). This regulation was challenged successfully by Sinclair.

Most telepaths like to feel the acoustics of a room before they conduct a scan. As well as reading minds, many members of Psi Corps can also project sensations and images into the minds of others. (EYES)

In the years following the Earth–Minbari War, the Psi Corps became an increasingly influential and much more sinister organization. The Corps started to kill its opponents and place them in relocation camps that were no better than concentration camps. In its drive to create stronger telepaths, the Psi Corps began to conduct dangerous experiments on its members and impregnated some of them against their will. (MIND, RACE)

One of Psi Corps' most successful experiments was its sleeper spy program, which allowed the organization to place moles in several government agencies, including Babylon 5. Psi Corps researchers would use a combination of drugs and scans to create a new personality in Psi Corps agents. The artificial personality was then submerged into the subconscious of the operative so that it wouldn't be detected in deep scans. The Psi Corps–induced personality would then listen and watch everything until it received a telepathically transmitted password. Once that occurred, the real personality was killed and the new program took over. Each agent was codenamed "Control." The artificial personalities were programmed for self-preservation and would act on any threat they perceived. In 2259, Talia Winters was exposed as the Psi Corps mole stationed aboard Babylon 5.

The Psi Corps' Charter prohibits the organization from recommending political candidates to its members. Consequently, the Corps was heavily rebuked when it endorsed Vice-President Morgan Clark's electoral campaign. (REVELATIONS)

The Psi Corps uses propaganda and subliminal messages in its adverts to gain support. (CORPS, WORD)

Purple Files

Purple Files contain scandalous pieces of information about individuals and families within the Centauri Republic. The

Centauri use their Purple Files to increase their status and power. The Mollari household's significant power is a result of their members' extensive Purple Files. When Londo's files were temporarily stolen, they contained enough information to destroy the Centauri Republic. (PURPLE)

Q

Quadrant 14

Formerly a Narn colony on the border of Centauri space and home to a quarter of a million Narns, Quadrant 14 was attacked without warning by Shadow ships in 2259. When the Narns investigated and detected Centauri ships in the area, the Kha'Ri decided that it had no choice but to declare war against the Centauri.

Thanks to the Shadows, the Centauri conquered the colony with ease and planned to find a "productive" use for the survivors. However, when Captain Sheridan threatened to send Earth Alliance observers to the area to check that the Narns were not being mistreated and investigate how the Centauri managed to defeat them so easily, Ambassador Mollari decided to release the survivors as a "gesture of goodwill." (SHADOWS)

Quadrant 37

Region of space declared neutral territory between the Narns and Centauris in 2228, when the Centauri withdrew from the Narn homeworld. Quadrant 37 later became the site of a heavily armed Narn military outpost, and toward the end of 2258 the Narns launched a series of attacks on Centauri ships in the area. When asked why his people were risking war, Ambassador G'Kar informed the Babylon 5 Advisory Council that his people would no longer accept a neutrality agreement which had been imposed upon them by force more than thirty years earlier.

When the Centauri leadership reluctantly decided to give Quadrant 37 to the Narns, Ambassador Mollari asked for Morden's help with the matter. Morden told him that he would take care of the situation and instructed the ambassador to inform the Centauri government that he would take personal responsibility for the area. The Shadows then completely destroyed the Narn outpost in the area, killing 10,000 of Narn's finest warriors in the process. When the Narn ships sent to investigate the attack scanned Centauri ships that had been sent to survey the outpost, the Centauri were blamed for the attack and the Republic's leaders became much more interested in the architect of their victory, Londo Mollari. (CHRYSALIS)

However, Ambassador G'Kar doubted that the Centauri were capable of such a vicious and powerful assault, and decided to visit the sector to survey the damage himself. While there, his ship narrowly escaped being destroyed by the Shadows. (REVELATIONS)

Quantium 40

A mineral used in the construction of jumpgates. By 2258, Quantium 40 had become so scarce that it had drastically curtailed the Earth Alliance's construction of jumpgates (MIND). Luckily for Catherine Sakai, she surveyed a planet rich in Quantium 40 just prior to her arrival on Babylon 5 and received a percentage of the profits (PARLIAMENT). A few weeks later, Sakai surveyed Sigma 957 for Quantium 40, but was unable to complete her mission and barely returned with her life (MIND).

Quantrell, Ronald (Senator)

Earth Alliance senator interviewed for the ISN documentary "36 Hours Aboard Babylon 5" in 2259. Although he stated that the Senate should pursue the Babylon Project as a tribute to the memory of President Santiago, he went on to suggest that Babylon 5's peacekeeping mission had lost its appeal; the Alliance's military forces were restored and had nothing to fear from the Minbari. Senator Quantrell also claimed that the station merely served as a place of commerce and contributed to the Earth Alliance's intergalactic prominence. Played by Christopher Curry. (WORD)

Quartermaster Corporation

A huge supplier of military goods. Colonel Ari Ben Zayne posed as a representative of the Quartermaster Corporation when he arrived on Babylon 5 in 2258. (EYES)

Quat, Pol

A senator for the Indonesian Consortium. In 2258, Pol Quat criticized the fact that Earth's less affluent nations had to pay an equal share of planetary costs for a smaller share of the benefits. (VOICE I)

R

Racine
A member of the Minbari Grey Council. (TREASON)

Ragesh 3
Ragesh 3 was situated in Narn territory prior to the Centauri invasion of their world. However, when the Centauri withdrew from the Narn homeworld, they failed to return sovereignty of Ragesh 3 to the Narns. Thus it remained the site of a Centauri agricultural colony and was home to 5,000 Centauri.

In January 2258, Ragesh 3 was attacked, without warning or provocation, by Narn forces. When asked why the Narns had committed this act of aggression, Ambassador G'Kar claimed that the colonists wanted independence from the Centauri Republic and had sought Narn intervention. He then displayed a message from the colony's head researcher and project director, Carn Mollari, corroborating his story. However, Commander Sinclair later gained evidence that the Narns had really attacked and conquered the colony after all and told G'Kar that he would bring it before the Babylon 5 Advisory Council if his people failed to withdraw. The Narns complied. (MIDNIGHT)

During the occupation of Ragesh 3, many pieces of important Centauri scientific material were "lost" by the Narn. The Narn government informed the Centauri that all the equip-

ment could be recovered in return for hard currency. (SUR-
VIVORS)

Raider #1

Raider leader hired by Lord Kiro to steal the Eye and help
him become the Centauri emperor. However, the Raider had
no intention of following Kiro's orders and instead planned to
ransom the Eye and Lord Kiro, who would make regular pay-
ments to the Raiders in return for their silence regarding his
scheme. Sadly for him, Raider #1 was killed before he could
set his plan in motion when the Shadows attacked and destroyed his vessel. Played by Whip Hubley. (SIGNS)

Raiders, The

A group of interstellar pirates, many of whom worked in the
region of space around Babylon 5. The station was an obvious
target because of all the vessels traveling to and from it. (MID-
NIGHT)

   The Raiders' combat vessels were extremely vulnerable to
attack because they were designed to enter planetary atmospheres as well as to function in space, resulting in compro-
mised zero-gravity maneuvering ability.

   During the course of 2258, Raider attacks drew nearer and
nearer to Babylon 5, until they mounted a full assault on the
station in August of that year. Their small craft were virtually
wiped out by Babylon 5's Starfuries and defense grid, while
their battle wagon was destroyed just hours later by a Shadow
ship. The few Raiders who were captured during the attack on
Babylon 5 were sent to Earth to stand trial (SIGNS). After
August 2258, the Raiders were practically out of business
(ALONE).

Raiders' Battle Wagon, The

A large vessel capable of creating its own jumpgate, the battle
wagon enabled the Raiders to attack almost anywhere. It took
the Raiders five years to save enough credits to buy the ship. It
was destroyed by the Shadows shortly after the Raiders bought
it. (SIGNS)

Ramirez (Lieutenant)

Lieutenant Ramirez served aboard Babylon 5 as a Starfury pilot. He was a fan of the Mars baseball team and bet thirty credits with Dr. Franklin that the Dodgers wouldn't make it into the World Series. Ramirez died as the result of radiation poisoning following a Streib attack. Played by Nick Corri. (ALONE)

Ranger

In 2259, this soldier of light delivered a message from Ambassador Sinclair to Security Chief Garibaldi and Ambassador Delenn. He had sworn to deliver the message at any cost, even his own life, and was a frequent traveler to Babylon 5. (SHADOWS)

Ranger Pin

A special brooch worn by each and every Ranger, with a central stone called Isil-zha by the Minbari. When it is made, a Ranger pin is forged in the white of a flame and then cooled in three bowls: one containing ancient holy water, another filled with Minbari blood, and a final bowl of human blood. When a Ranger dies, the figures on both sides are said to shed three tears: one of water and two of blood. Unsurprisingly, the pins are treasured by their owners. (MATTERS)

Rangers, The

An Army of Light established by Jeffrey Sinclair in 2259 to fight the forces of darkness in the Great War.

Each Ranger has sworn his or her life, fortune and blood to their cause. During their first year, the Rangers' mission was to patrol the frontier and transfer reports that were too sensitive for normal channels (SHADOWS). They were trained in camps on Minbar and several other worlds, including Zagros 7 (MATTERS).

Ambassador Delenn and Security Chief Garibaldi were the first people aboard Babylon 5 to learn about the Rangers, thanks to a cryptic message from Ambassador Sinclair (SHADOWS). On Draal's advice, Delenn later introduced Captain Sheridan to the private army and gave him equal authority over all Rangers in the area (TWILIGHT). When Sheridan instructed the Rangers to provide a message from a

Narn family on the Centauri-occupied Narn homeworld, somehow they managed to succeed. As a result, they saved G'Kar's position as leader of the Narns on Babylon 5 (IN-QUISITOR).

At the beginning of 2260, the Shadows attempted to strike against the Rangers' training camp in Zagros 7 and asked the Centauri to secure the area for them. Captain Sheridan led a mission to break the Centauri blockade long enough for the Rangers trapped on the colony to escape. (MATTERS)

Ra'Pak

A member of the second circle of the Kha'Ri prior to the Narn–Centauri War, Ra'Pak had a strong dislike of Ambassador G'Kar. (BLOOD)

Rathenn

A member of the Minbari Grey Council (DARKNESS) and a mutual acquaintance of Delenn and Draal (VOICE I). In January 2259, Rathenn was sent to EarthDome to restore Jeffrey Sinclair's memory of his encounter with the Grey Council during the Battle of the Line and invite him to serve as the Earth Alliance's ambassador on Minbar (DARKNESS).

Recorders

Small spherical video/audio recording devices, capable of flight. (GATHERING, INFECTION)

Red-Level Surveillance

Classification for top-level surveillance of a suspect. In 2258, the Homeguard sympathizer Robert was placed under red-level surveillance while security investigated the series of anti-alien attacks aboard Babylon 5. (PRAYER)

Red Sector

The focus of commercial and leisure activities on Babylon 5. The Zocalo, the Zen Garden, the maze and the hydroponic gardens are situated in Red Sector, as well as various hotel suites, casinos and bars.

Refa, Lord

A scheming Centauri noble, Lord Refa found that he and Ambassador Mollari had something in common: they both wanted to restore the Centauri Republic's "rightful place in the galaxy." Mollari came to Refa's attention following his unexplained (but extremely impressive) destruction of Quadrant 14. (GEOMETRY)

As Emperor Turhan's health deteriorated, Refa and his associates prepared to seize power. They ordered the assassination of Prime Minister Malachi and maneuvered Cartagia onto the throne following the death of Turhan. (SHADOWS)

When Refa declared Urza Jaddo a traitor to the Centauri, he refused to help Mollari clear his name and warned that if the ambassador associated himself with Jaddo, he too would be destroyed (KNIVES). A few months later, Refa secured Zagros 7 for Morden behind Mollari's back, thus proving that Refa has no abiding loyalty to the "architect" of the Centauri victory against the Narn (MATTERS, TWILIGHT).

Played by William Forward.

Reno

Shady "businessman" who specializes in finding objects and people. Once paid, Reno always keeps his side of the bargain.

In 2258, Reno provided Ambassador Mollari with the Eye, for which he received enough money to buy a small planet. When Mollari asked how he acquired it, Reno told the ambassador that he didn't want to know. Played by Robert Silver. (SIGNS)

Rhoner (Doctor)

A medical officer aboard the *Cortez*. (LONG)

Rick

A member of the underground railroad of unregistered telepaths, Rick told the group's leader, Lurker, that they should kill Bester when he arrived on Babylon 5 in 2259. Played by Brian Cousins. (RACE)

Rim, The

The boundary of known space. The Shadows slowly began to rebuild their forces in the Rim during the mid-23rd century. (Z'HA'DUM)

Ritchie Station

A Mars station destroyed by Free Mars terrorist Abel Horn. John and Anna Sheridan had close friends at the Ritchie Station at the time of its destruction. (SPIDER)

Roberts

Homeguard sympathizer questioned during the string of anti-alien attacks on Babylon 5 in 2258. Roberts brought an illegal weapon aboard the station to defend himself and was placed under red-level surveillance in the hope that he was either a member of Homeguard or would be recruited. He was subsequently attacked by two Drazi and was saved by the security officers who had been following him. While Roberts was recovering in medlab, Malcolm Biggs was caught inviting him to become a member of the Homeguard. Played by Michael Chan. (PRAYER)

Rose

Rose worked as Dr. Franklin's assistant in his illegal clinic Down Below. She thought that Laura Rosen was a con-artist. Played by Lynn Anderson. (MERCY)

Rosen, Janice

The daughter of Laura Rosen, Janice was delighted by the way the Alien Healing Device allowed her mother to become a healer once again. Janice didn't care if she worked or not; seeing her mother happy was enough. When her mother set up an illegal clinic aboard Babylon 5 in 2258, Janice didn't tell her that they had money to go back to Earth because she wanted Laura to stay on the station as a healer rather than returning home to risk further humiliation and pain.

While her mother ran her illegal clinic, Janice Rosen worked in a jewelry boutique on the Zocalo where she had a quota of goods to sell. If she failed to reach her quota, her boss took the money out of her salary.

Janice was angry at Dr. Franklin when he accused her

mother of being a fraud, but they became close friends when
he admitted that he was wrong. She was later held hostage
with the doctor by the psychotic killer Karl Edward Mueller,
who forced her mother to heal his wounds. Laura realized
that her only chance of saving her daughter was to reverse the
energy flow and Mueller was killed as a result.

When Laura decided to return to Earth after the incident,
Janice chose to stay on Babylon 5. Played by Kate McNeil.
(MERCY)

Rosen, Laura (Doctor)

As a doctor, Laura Rosen became obsessed with her role as a
healer. She worked days, nights and weekends and relied on
stims to keep her going. She soon became addicted to stims,
but wouldn't listen to everyone's warnings. Then she inevitably made a mistake and one of her patients died as a result.
Deprived of her doctor's license, Laura Rosen not only lost
her job but also her reason for living.

A few years later, the disgraced doctor decided that she
could redeem herself if she found an alien technology capable of healing. In 2256, Laura found what she was looking for
when she bought the Alien Healing Device from a trader. At
the time, she had no idea what it was and spent several
months trying to learn how it functioned. Eventually, she realized that the machine was designed as a form of corporal
punishment whereby criminals sentenced to death would
have their life energy removed, which would then be used to
heal those dying with terminal diseases. Laura learned how
to use it at a low setting without killing people and decided to
dedicate her remaining years to healing others before she died
of Lakes Syndrome. Using the device, she began donating
some of her life energy to others to help overcome illness. She
didn't tell her daughter, Janice, how the device worked in
case she stopped her from using it.

While working as a healer on Babylon 5 in 2258, Laura
Rosen was described as "a cross between a faith healer and a
sideshow medicine woman." She made a living by accepting
donations from her patients. When Dr. Franklin heard about
what she was doing, he initially believed that she was a fraud.
Once he discovered the truth, however, he began to respect

and admire her and allowed her to continue to run the clinic, provided he could monitor her medical condition every week.

Laura Rosen was forced to drain the life energy of Karl Edward Mueller when the psychotic killer threatened to kill her daughter as well as Dr. Franklin unless she healed his wounded arm. Realizing that Mueller would probably kill all three of them once his arm was reinvigorated, she reversed the flow of life energy and the murderer died as a result of the sudden exposure to Lakes Syndrome. Rosen felt that she had done what was necessary rather than what was right and felt guilty about taking another man's life. Ombuds Wellington ruled that she had acted in self-defense, but ordered her to surrender the Alien Healing Device to Dr. Franklin.

Free of Lakes Syndrome, Laura Rosen decided to go back to Earth to begin a new life. Babylon 5's doctors said that she would probably live for another 20–30 years. Played by June Lockhart. (MERCY)

Ru'Dac

A Narn courier who died as the result of an accident on the day he was leaving Narn with a message for Ambassador G'Kar in 2258. Presumably, Ru'Dac was killed by Tu'Pari, who then posed as the courier to deliver Du'Rog's death threat. (PARLIAMENT)

Runningdear, Mirriam

Mirriam Runningdear managed a shop on Babylon 5 located in Red 26 and was the only person willing to testify against the evil extortionist Deuce. Before she could go before an Ombuds, Mirriam was abducted by Deuce and attacked by his Na'ka'leen feeder, which completely erased her mind. As a result, she lost her entire life experience and had to be completely retrained. (GRAIL)

Rush Act, The

The Rush Act is used to combat illegal strike action and allows the commanding officer of the site of the strike to use "any means necessary" to end the dispute. Once the Act has been invoked by the Senate, most commanding officers attempt to end the strike action through the use of force.

During the 2258 dock workers' strike, Commander Sinclair

used the Rush Act to reallocate 1.3 million credits from the station's military budgets to meet the strikers' demands. Before 2258, the Rush Act was last invoked during the Europa strike. (MEANS)

Russian Consortium
A commonwealth located on Earth, the Russian Consortium spent many years trying to create an anti-agapic, and was also the birthplace of Commander Ivanova. (DEATHWALKER)

Rutarian
A Centauri god. In 2258, Na'Toth stole the statue of Rutarian aboard Babylon 5 in the hope that G'Kar could swap it for Ambassador Mollari's G'Quan Eth plant. (MEANS)

S

Sacred Vessel of Regeneration, The
See **Holy Grail, The**

Sakai, Catherine
Occasional girlfriend of Jeffrey Sinclair. A Buddhist, Catherine Sakai first met Sinclair at the Academy and lived with him for a year, during which time she became well versed in Tennyson.

After the Academy, they began their cycle of breaking up and reconciliation and were reunited every two or three years. Half the time, one of them had another partner, while the other half, they talked about old times at the Academy, Sinclair asked about her aunt, she asked him about his brother, they spent the night together and one of them left.

They could never agree on anything. Sakai always thought about Sinclair in the summer, while he thought about her in the autumn. According to Sinclair, their relationship was always "three parts passion, two parts tease."

Prior to meeting Babylon 5 in 2258, Sakai left Sinclair and promised him that she would stay away from Sinclair. When they were reunited, they decided to give their relationship one last chance. (PARLIAMENT)

She always thought that Sinclair worried too much, while he thought she didn't worry enough. According to Sakai, it was the "perfect combination."

Sakai ignored G'Kar's warning and was almost killed while

surveying Sigma 957. She was rescued from death by a Narn cruiser sent by Ambassador G'Kar. (MIND)

At the end of the year, Sakai accepted Sinclair's marriage proposal and asked Ivanova to be her maid of honor. However, their plans had to be changed when Sinclair was reassigned to the Minbari homeworld. (CHRYSALIS, DARK-NESS)

Played by Julia Nickson.

Sanchez
A junior Earthforce officer assigned to Lieutenant-Commander Sinclair during his search for covert human–alien activity on Mars. Sanchez's leg was broken when their shuttle crashed and, consequently, the young officer was left behind while Sinclair and Garibaldi made a 50-mile trek across Mars to find help. (AGAINST)

Sanchez (Doctor)
Medlab physician. (MATTERS)

San Diego
Subject of an unprovoked terrorist nuclear attack (MID-NIGHT). The San Diego wastelands are the base of operations of Bureau 13 (SPIDER).

Sands of Blood, The
See **Mutai, The**

Santiago, Luis (President)
Luis Santiago served as Earth Alliance vice-president before and during the Earth–Minbari War before assuming the post of president.

Santiago launched the Babylon Project in 2249 to avoid another war based on a misunderstanding (LAW). He won a third term in office in January 2258, and his election promises were to cut spending, keep Earth out of war, resolve the problem with the Mars Colony, and place greater emphasis on the preservation of Earth cultures (MIDNIGHT).

Later in the year, Santiago visited Babylon 5 to present its new fighter wing, Zeta Squad. At the time, he was trying to gain support for his new alien immigration and trade agreements which allowed greater alien trade and immigration, and faced strong opposition from the Earth Senate. Despite all the criticism and controversy, he remained a strong supporter of Babylon 5. (SURVIVORS)

At the end of 2258, Santiago embarked on the Five-Planet Goodwill Tour of the outer planet colonies. He was expected to make a major policy speech on New Year's Day, 2259, which would outline his plans to build better human–alien relations. Santiago was killed with *Earthforce 1* exploded just before arriving at Jupiter and was succeeded by his vice-president, Morgan Clark. (CHRYSALIS)

Played by Douglas Netter.

Sarah

An operative of General Hague's, Sarah told Sheridan that Dr. Everett Jacobs was loyal to Earth and ordered the commander to find him and his data crystal before Earthforce Special Intelligence. When she was given the crystal, she told Sheridan that he had scored a major victory for the good guys. Played by Wanda De Jesus. (HUNTER)

Satai

Honorary title given to members of the Minbari Grey Council.

Sayer, The
See **Muta-Do, The**

Scotura

Urzo Jaddo's nickname in the Couro Prido. It means "the silent beast." (KNIVES)

Sebastian

Sebastian believed he was a chosen one, a messenger on a crusade from God until the Vorlons taught him "the terrible depth" of his mistakes.

Sebastian lived in 14B Heresford Lane and committed a series of killings in London's East End, until he was abducted by the Vorlons on November 11, 1888. He paid 400 years of penance by serving the Vorlons as an inquisitor who tests "chosen ones." Prior to 2259, everyone he had confronted had failed the test. Sebastian was kept in stasis when he was not required.

When he boarded Babylon 5 to test Delenn, he noted how little humanity had changed or improved. When Delenn and Sheridan show that they are both willing to die for each other, alone and uncelebrated, they pass the inquisition. Before leaving the station, Sebastian tells Sheridan that he hopes that the Vorlons will now allow him to die and acknowledges the fact that he will always be remembered on Earth as Jack the Ripper. (INQUISITOR)

[Author's note: A mistake in this script meant that Sheridan referred to Sebastian's killings in London's *West* End. This has subsequently been corrected in a dialogue loop.]

Sector 7
Region located extremely close to Babylon 5. The site where a Centauri war cruiser materialized to blockade crafts in order to demand the return of Centauri imprisoned aboard the station on the charge of shipping weapons in September 2259. (WORD)

Sector 14
Location of Babylon 4 and a spatial anomaly. (SQUARED, KNIVES)

Sector 15
Jason Ironheart was last sighted here before visiting Babylon 5. (MIND)

Sector 29
Site of heavy fighting during the Narn–Centauri War. (Z'HA'DUM)

Sector 45
Formerly the Markab system, stripped bare by aliens following their deaths. The local jumpgate was destroyed by Captain Sheridan during the Bonehard Maneuver, which he performed to destroy a Shadow ship and stop alien grave-robbing. (MATTERS)

Sector 90
Site of a transfer station where an old friend of Garibaldi's smuggled illegal goods and helped move weapons for the Narn resistance as a favor to Garibaldi. (INQUISITOR)

Sector 92
A region relatively close to Babylon 5. In 2259, Captain Sheridan investigated a series of unusual sightings and the disappearance of a transport ship in the area, and was attacked and kidnapped by the Streibs. (ALONE)

Sector 119
A Minbari-controlled area. In 2258, the Minbari allowed the Centauri to use trade routes provided they could use the nearby Centauri jumpgate. (VOICE I)

Sector 127
Home of an abandoned Centauri colony, liberated and booby-trapped by the Narns. (MATES)

Sector 900
Region on the Rim, mapped by the *Cortez* between 2257 and 2259. (DISTANT)

Secure Code
Ever since the Earth–Minbari War, every Earthforce command and control center has been configured to broadcast its ID Secure Code on a subchannel. Thus, it acts as a form of electronic tagging to prevent counterfeit orders. (SQUARED)

Security 'Bot
Robot used for surveillance. (STRIFE)

Senate, The
The Earth Alliance's governing body.

Sentauro
Arguably a giant of Centauri opera and one of Vir Kotto's favorite singers. (KNIVES)

Shadows, The

The oldest race, the Shadows predate even the First Ones. They fought the First Ones from the dawn of time until they were defeated in a Great War, which took place in the middle of the 13th century. A thousand years later, they began to rebuild their forces.

The Shadows are four-legged, spidery creatures. They have many servants, including the Soldiers of Darkness. The Shadows cannot be seen by humans and most aliens, because the creatures are beyond their normal range of perception. However, they can be detected by telepaths. They are based on the Rim and inhabit such worlds as Z'ha'dum. (REVELATIONS, Z'HA'DUM)

Unsurprisingly, their technology is extremely advanced. Shadow ships are huge, bio-organic, spidery vessels and their larger craft can separate into two vessels during attacks. Their ships are equipped with a cloaking device and a powerful beam that can slice through other ships with ease. (TWILIGHT)

Once a Shadow ship targets an opponent, it never stops, slows down or gives up until it has caught or destroyed the ship. When the Shadows don't recognize an opponent, they will try to disable ships and board them. (MATTERS)

The Shadows are aware that they lost the Great War because they moved too quickly. Consequently, they began to rebuild their forces slowly and quietly during the mid-23rd century. (Z'HA'DUM)

The Shadows prefer to work behind the scenes and manipulate others into fighting and destroying their enemies, rather than joining the battle themselves (SURVIVAL). As a result, they have forged ties with such groups as the Psi Corps and the Centauri Republic while they continue to pursue their own plans (SIGNS, CHRYSALIS, SHADOWS, MATTERS).

Shag Toth

Minbari name for a Soul Hunter. (SOUL)

Shai Alyt

Title given to Minbari captains. (LEGACIES, DEPARTURE)

Shakespeare Corporation

When it wanted to bring fingal eggs to Babylon 5 in 2258, they were stopped by Garibaldi as a "serious hazard" to station security. (BELIEVERS)

Shar, Mila

Head of agricultural delegation from Abbai 4. She was keen to see Babylon 5's acclaimed hydroponics system, but was also worried about the series of Homeguard attacks against aliens. She was subsequently captured by Homeguard, but saved by Commander Sinclair and Lieutenant-Commander Ivanova. Played by Diane Adair. (PRAYER)

Shedraks

Alien race aboard Babylon 5. (VOICES)

Sheridan, Anna

Wife of John J. Sheridan, Anna Sheridan is believed to have died in 2257, when the *Icarus* exploded above Z'ha'dum. Although she saw little of her husband and relied on subspace communication to keep their love alive, she always said that "love knows no borders" and considered herself very happy and lucky (REVELATIONS). In 2259, John Sheridan learned that the crew of the *Icarus* had been captured by the Shadows, and those who would not serve were killed (Z'HA'DUM). Played by Beth Toussaint.

Sheridan, Elizabeth

Younger sister of John Sheridan, Elizabeth had children with her partner, Danny. She knew John's wife Anna before he did. In 2259, she visited Babylon 5 and was annoyed he hadn't got on with his own life. Played by Beverly Leech. (REVELATIONS)

Sheridan, John J. (Captain)

Captain John J. Sheridan assumed command of Babylon 5 on 8th January 2259, following the reassignment of Commander Sinclair. (DEPARTURE)

A descendant of General Philip John Sheridan of the Union Army, John Sheridan was the son of a diplomatic envoy (DEPARTURE). His father taught him to live each mo-

ment like it was his last, to love without reservation and fight
without fear (SHADOWS). They used to argue a lot over their
principles, until they agreed to accept their differences. During all their fights, they never stopped talking to or loving
each other (GROPOS).

As a child, Sheridan enjoyed wandering around creepy
places, including haunted houses, forbidden paths and Indian
burial grounds. He always felt that being alone was part of the
fun and maintained his curiosity as he grew older (KNIVES).
He ran away on his 21st birthday to see the new Dalai Lama
being installed (DEPARTURE).

Sheridan joined Earthforce before the planetary draft. He
wanted to serve something bigger than himself and to make a
difference somehow and somewhere (SHADOWS). The first
thing he learned at the Academy was that a lack of knowledge
would kill you (MATTERS). Sheridan was proud when he
wore an Earthforce outfit for the first time (FALL).

He began his career working on the Moon–Mars Patrol
under the command of Captain Jack Maynard. Sheridan
thought Maynard knew everything and was nicknamed
Swamp Rat by his commanding officer. Maynard also once
quoted him an ancient Egyptian blessing, "God be between
you and harm in all the empty places where you must walk."
(STAR)

Sheridan admits to having served at so many places that he
can't remember half of them. Among other things, he spent
time at Matok during the Karanie expedition, served with Susan Ivanova at Io and was stalked by a Grylor on Janos 7.
(KNIVES)

As captain of the *Agamemnon*, Sheridan scored Earth's only
real victory in the Earth–Minbari War when he destroyed the
Minbari flagship, the *Black Star*, and three heavy cruisers in
2247. However, when the Minbari learned that he had defeated the ships by mining an asteroid field between Jupiter
and Mars and sending a distress signal, they felt he had won a
dishonorable victory and named him "Starkiller" (DEPAR-
TURE, HONOR). Sheridan received the Earthforce Silver
Star for Valor in the Earth–Minbari War (WORD).

At another point during the war, Sheridan's fighter was disabled and he lost all power and contact with his ship. All he
could do was sit there for eight hours, which seemed like

eight years. Before he was rescued, he began to think that he would never see another living being again. Sheridan never forgot the feeling of helplessness he experienced when he was all alone in the night. (HONOR)

Following the war, Sheridan's mission aboard the *Agamemnon* was part military and part diplomatic. He visited many non-aligned worlds to maintain an Earth Alliance presence (WORD). He also made first contact with the Ti Kar and, after his crew had deciphered their advanced language, was invited onto their ship. He spent two days with them, during which time he was reminded how wondrous the galaxy really is (SPIDER).

In 2249, Sheridan married Anna, a scientist. Although his career kept them apart most of the time, the two enjoyed their long-distance relationship (REVELATIONS). Apparently, she even liked his corny jokes—or at least pretended to (RACE).

Something embarrassing happened to Sheridan on July 12, 2253. Captain Maynard is sworn to secrecy about the matter. (DISTANT)

In 2257, Sheridan had arranged to meet his wife on Centauri Prime for their anniversary. However, when the time came, Sheridan was too busy and canceled their date, even though they hadn't seen much of each other in 2256. She then left on a two-week scientific survey on the *Icarus* from which she didn't return. Sheridan blamed himself for her death and was haunted by the fact that he forgot to tell her that he loved her the last time they spoke. Two years later, he learned that Anna had accepted the assignment before he had canceled their arranged meeting, and the burden of guilt was eased. (REVELATIONS)

Following the death of his wife Anna in 2257, Sheridan took the *Agamemnon* on an exploratory mission out on the Rim. (DEPARTURE)

Sheridan was President Santiago's first choice to replace Sinclair if the need arose (DEPARTURE). His appointment took place in spite of the protests of the Grey Council, who refused to accept the Starkiller's authority on the station (DEPARTURE). Sheridan later learned that President Clark wanted him on the station because he believed he was a "hardnosed" warrior, who would use the station for the good of Earth and at the expense of its alien inhabitants (ALONE).

Upon taking command, Sheridan started to make his good luck speech, which he always delivers within 24 hours of assuming a new command. When the speech was interrupted, he had to abandon it until late at night, when he successfully gave it to an empty Observation Dome. He was left with five minutes to spare. (DEPARTURE)

One of his first actions aboard the station was to promote Ivanova to the rank of commander and he filled in the paperwork the day after he arrived. He also decided that he wanted to keep Garibaldi in the post of chief security officer because he knew the station and its personnel better than anyone. (GEOMETRY)

Sheridan had his doubts about serving on Babylon 5. Although he initially saw it as a great opportunity, he found that the attitude of many Minbari was hard to get used to (DEPARTURE, HONOR). Furthermore, he remembered how he always wanted to command an explorer ship and started to worry that he would become a glorified bureaucrat on the station. Ultimately, however, Sheridan was comforted by Ambassador Delenn, who assured him that he was in the right place at the right time. As a result, Sheridan became intrigued by her "special relationship" with the universe and the pair developed a close, and possibly romantic, relationship (DISTANT).

It was Sheridan's belief that Babylon 5 should create the peace rather than enforce it, as the station was built upon the assumption that people would be able to come together and work out their problems. He also felt that it represented an opportunity to build a better galaxy for mankind and its descendants, thus making the hard work of its ancestors worthwhile. (WORD)

According to his record, Sheridan is a patriot who will fight to protect Earth from both internal and external threats. Consequently, when General Hague informed him of the growing conspiracy on Earth, he decided to join the fight against the new order and enlisted the support of Ivanova, Garibaldi and Franklin. (ALONE)

Sheridan also collects secrets about conspiracies, black projects and covert organizations. In 2253, he first heard about a dirty tricks squad within EarthGov dealing in starchamber justice and black projects. Three years later, he learned its name, Bureau 13, from a man who died shortly after telling him it. Sheridan referred to the organization as a "spider in the web" and said that he intended to find it and kill it. (SPIDER)

The captain is a celebrated tactical thinker who is particularly good at fighting a superior enemy and overcoming adverse odds. His record commends his strategies during the Earth–Minbari War and the Mars Riots (STRIFE). Sheridan himself believes that no ship is invincible and everything has a weakness (MATTERS).

First and foremost, Sheridan considers himself to be a soldier and is fully aware of the true nature of his duty. He knows that the one truth about war is that people die and that killing is part of a soldier's job. All a soldier can do is live with it and hope the cause is justified (GROPOS). He is well aware of the fact that change is part of military life and that he can be stationed elsewhere within 24 hours (WORD). He also knows that the first casualty of war is the truth (SACRIFICE).

From the moment he arrived on the station, Sheridan had a strange feeling that Ambassador Kosh was watching him. Before he had assumed command, Kosh rarely attended Advisory Council meetings, but now he suddenly started to show an interest. (HUNTER)

When Sheridan was held captive on the Streib ship, his mind was entered by the Vorlon ambassador in a cryptic dream (ALONE). Once he was back on board the station, he decided to make it his pet project to learn more about Kosh, the Vorlons and his ship. When he asked Kosh to teach him about the Vorlons, he told Sheridan that instead he would teach him about himself until he was ready to "fight legends" (HUNTER).

The intent of Kosh's lessons changed later in the year when Sheridan illegally questioned the Shadow emissary Morden and realized that his wife, Anna, had been captured and possibly killed by the Shadows of Z'ha'dum. As he drew closer to breaking Morden, Delenn and Kosh asked Sheridan to release him immediately. They then explained that if Morden revealed the whole truth, the Shadows would start to attack before the Vorlons, Rangers and other soldiers of light were ready for them. As Sheridan considered his course of action, he was reminded of a showreel depicting Churchill after the bombing of Coventry. History later revealed that the British prime minister had to sacrifice the town so the Germans would not realize that British intelligence had cracked their top-secret Enigma code. He then decided to release the Shadow emissary, Morden, on the condition that Kosh prepared him for an offensive strike against Z'ha'dum. (Z'HA'DUM)

During his first year on the station, Sheridan grew closer and closer to Delenn. He was touched by her bravery when she risked her life to enter the Markab isolation zone, and told her to call him John the next time they met (CONFESSIONS). A few weeks later, they demonstrated that they were both willing to die for each other when faced by the Vorlon inquisitor, Sebastian. They were then declared to be chosen ones (INQUISITOR).

Delenn and Sheridan both traveled to Epsilon 3 to see Draal, who proposed an alliance and placed the planet's technology at Sheridan's disposal. Delenn then introduced Sheridan to the Rangers and gave him equal authority over all the Rangers in the area. (TWILIGHT)

Sheridan felt increasingly sympathetic toward the Narns as they headed for defeat in the war against the Centauri. He had hoped that Earth would ally itself with the Regime to curb Centauri aggression, but his superiors were reluctant to become involved in another war. Instead, he and Delenn joined forces to provide civilian aid to the Narns.

When the Narns surrendered to the Centauri, Sheridan granted G'Kar sanctuary aboard the station and refused to hand him over to the Centauri. Via the Rangers, he later provided G'Kar with a message which he used to assert his authority as the Narns' leader on the station.

At the end of the year, Sheridan sheltered a Narn warship and was forced to destroy a Centauri warship while the Narn ship fled. He was then shocked to learn that Earth had successfully negotiated a non-aggression pact with the Centauri. To make matters worse, two Centauri on the station tried to assassinate him and he was left plunging to his death from the station central corridor until Kosh left his encounter suit to fly to his rescue.

At the beginning of 2260, Sheridan decided that the time to react was over and it was time to take the offensive. He then assumed command of the *White Star* and scored his first victory in the Shadow War when he defeated a Shadow ship using the Bonehard Maneuver (MATTERS). According to Garibaldi, he was Babylon 5's only chance to survive the Shadow War (STRIFE).

According to Lennier, Sheridan is the only person who can defy Kosh (INQUISITOR). Sheridan initially liked the idea of Babylon 5 merchandise but subsequently had it outlawed when he saw a teddy that was supposed to be him. He then spaced the bear (HONOR).

His personal authorization code is gamma-six-six-z-niner (KNIVES). He speaks a few words of Drazi and knows Morse Code (ALONE).

Sheridan had never seen a Techno-mage prior to 2259 and was unsure if they existed until then. (GEOMETRY)

Sheridan's Rule Number 29: "Always let your enemy think you know more than you know." (SHADOWS)

In his spare time, Sheridan plays baseball in Babylon Park (KNIVES). He is partial to an occasional Jovian Sunspot and his personal edition of the *Universe Today* normally contains extra baseball news (DIVIDED, SPIDER). Sheridan likes fresh fruit, particularly oranges, grapes, nectarines and black plums (not the red ones!) (DEPARTURE). He hasn't seen a real tree, like a redwood or a pine tree, since 2254 (DIVIDED).

John Sheridan snores, but adamantly denies it. (RACE)

Played by Bruce Boxleitner.

Shi-Ki
Installation ceremony of the Minbari leader. (TREASON)

Shinar
A Markab girl aboard Babylon 5. She found her father dead of Drafa and became separated from her mother inside the Markab isolation zone. She was then befriended by Delenn, while Lennier helped find her mother. (CONFESSIONS)

Shioshnic
A Markab trader who ignored restrictions and passed through Sector 14 before boarding Babylon 5. He spent three days on the station before committing suicide by beating himself to

death. Sheridan later learned that Shioshnic had been possessed by a noncorporeal entity. (KNIVES)

Shivah

A Jewish tradition to mourn the death of a loved one, during which family, friends and members of the Jewish community gather at the home of the bereaved to offer comfort and prayer for the departed. After much debate, Susan Ivanova sat shivah for her father, Andrei, aboard Babylon 5 in 2258. (TKO)

Sh'lassans

Alien race, a member of the League of Non-Aligned Worlds. (GROPOS)

Sh'lassan Triumvirate

In 2259, the Sh'lassan Triumvirate turned to the Earth Alliance for assistance during the civil war on Akdor. Officially, Earth refused their request but, in reality, were preparing a top-secret attack plan, Operation : Sudden Death, which was implemented immediately after Earth Alliance support was announced. In return for their involvement, the Alliance was allowed to have a permanent presence in the sector, which was strategically close to the Centauri and Narns. (GROPOS)

Shock Stick

Rod which conducts electricity to incapacitate but not kill.

Shon

The son of Tharg and M'ola, Shon was suffering from a congestive blockage in the upper air passage when he came aboard Babylon 5 looking for a cure. After an examination, Dr. Franklin decided that a straightforward surgical procedure could cure his condition.

However, when Shon's parents refused to allow the operation on religious grounds, Franklin treated him with microbeams and mineral oil and tried to convince his parents to allow him to have the operation. The doctor also gave him a Gloppit egg to care for, which was actually a piece of industrial goo.

When Franklin asked Sinclair to suspend M'ola and Tharg's parental authority, he spoke to Shon and the boy told him that he wanted to live but didn't want to lose his soul in an operation. When Sinclair asked him about the Gloppit egg, Shon explained that it was a piece of industrial goo but asked him not to tell Franklin, because he thought it was an alien life-form.

Following his discussion with Shon, Sinclair decided not to give Franklin permission to operate on Shon. However, he had become obsessed with saving the child and performed the operation anyway. Although it was a success, Shon was then killed by his parents, who believed his soul had moved on and there was only a shell left. Played by Jonathan Charles Kaplan. (BELIEVERS)

Shon-Kar

A Narn blood oath. Na'Toth took a Chon-Kar against Jha'dur when the infamous Dilgar war-criminal experimented upon her grandfather (DEATHWALKER) and Du'Rog's family also took one against G'Kar, but later abandoned it when they were financially compensated and gained evidence which cleared Du'Rog's name (BLOOD). G'Kar has taken many blood oaths (DEATHWALKER).

Sho'Rin

Champion of the Mutai. Means "Bravest of the Brave." (TKO)

Sigma 957

An uninhabited Class 4 world in a contested area of space. The planet has a nitrogen and oxygen atmosphere and contains traces of duridium, a by-product of Quantium 40.

In 2248, Catherine Sakai was sent to survey the planet by Universal Terraform. She needed Ambassador G'Kar's approval to survey the planet and ignored his warning that strange things happened there. While orbiting the planet, Sakai's ship was almost destroyed by an advanced alien life-form and had to be rescued by a Narn ship dispatched by G'Kar. (MIND)

Sinclair, Jeffrey (Commander/Ambassador)

The first commander of Babylon 5, subsequently reassigned to Minbar where he became the first human ambassador.

Born on Mars on May 3rd, 2218, 9:15 a.m. Earth Standard Time, Jeffrey Sinclair came from a long line of fighter pilots that can be traced back to World War II (SKY). His father taught Sinclair everything he knew and always told him that the best way to understand someone is to fight them (MIDNIGHT). His father flew for Earthforce during the Dilgar Invasion and was there when it retook Balus. He never forgot what he saw (DEATHWALKER).

Sinclair was raised a Catholic and spent three years being taught by Jesuits. During that time, he learned that morning was the best part of the day and would get up at 5 a.m. every day for sunrise Mass. (SQUARED)

He enlisted in Earthforce Defense in 2237, became a fighter pilot in 2240 and was promoted to squad leader the following year. He looked set to become an admiral one day. (SKY)

While studying at the Academy, Sinclair began his long-standing relationship with Catherine Sakai. They lived together for a year and would repeatedly get together and break up until 2258 (PARLIAMENT). Sinclair also found another love of his life at the Academy: the works of Tennyson. "Ulysses" is Sinclair's very favorite poem and he once told a Minbari that he might understand him better if he read it (MIND, DARKNESS).

Sinclair commanded Alpha Squad during the Battle of the Line. Prior to the conflict, his squadron swore that they would go down together (GATHERING). Earthforce was outgunned and outmanned, and Sinclair knew it was a suicide mission (SKY). He later told Catherine Sakai that "the sky was full of stars and every one of them an exploding ship—one of ours."

Alpha Squad was destroyed in less than a minute. Sinclair managed to destroy a Minbari fighter before his stabilizers took a hit. He then used his remaining power to try to ram a Minbari cruiser. The next thing Sinclair remembered was waking up in his Starfury 24 hours later, checking in and learning that the Minbari had surrendered. Sinclair was amazed: he knew Earthforce had lost the war and couldn't imagine why they had surrendered. (GATHERING)

Sinclair spent several years convincing himself that he had blacked out because of acceleration and nothing happened during the missing 24 hours of his life (GATHERING). He also had to resist the urge to strangle any Minbari he saw (SKY). Following the Earth–Minbari War, Sinclair was given a number of missions by Earthforce to keep him busy and out of their way (ODDS).

In 2255, he was sent to investigate covert human–alien activities on Mars. Seeing that previous missions had found nothing, Sinclair suspected a leak and decided to hire a private shuttle for the mission (PRESENT, SILENT). As a result, Sinclair hired Michael Garibaldi as a shuttle pilot and was accompanied by two junior officers, Sanchez and Foster. On the fifth day of their search, a systems malfunction forced Garibaldi to crash-land the ship. The crash claimed Foster's life and Sanchez broke his leg during impact. Garibaldi and Sinclair were then forced to start a 50-mile hike out of the desert (ODDS).

The pair took shelter in a cave during a dust storm, and Sinclair began talking to Sanchez when he saw Garibaldi wandering out of the cave. Just as he tried to stop him, a cave wall collapsed on Sinclair. When Garibaldi rescued him, Sinclair told him that he would kill him if he did anything like that again. (SURVIVAL)

Sinclair and Garibaldi continued their journey and discovered a huge spider-like ship (actually a Shadow ship) excavating a similar craft, and a top-secret operation involving the Psi Corps and the Shadows. Posing as telepaths, the pair entered the base and witnessed some kind of medical experiment. When they were discovered, Sinclair and Garibaldi used grenades to destroy the operation, and escaped. An Earthforce search found no evidence of the base. For Sinclair and Garibaldi, it was the start of a close friendship and Sinclair insisted that he was appointed security chief of Babylon 5 in 2256. (SILENT)

It was around this time that Sinclair met Laurel Takashima and promised her that she would be promoted if she didn't break the rules. Sinclair later requested that she served as his first officer.

In 2256, Sinclair was surprised to be offered the post of commander of Babylon 5. He was aware of how prestigious the post was, despite its problems. He later learned that he wasn't in Earthforce's top ten and that the Minbari would not accept anyone else but him. Before he assumed command of the station, he was assured by Santiago that he had final authority over the station and the entire sector. (VOICE I)

Sinclair was a hands-on commander and liked to do everything himself. He had a tendency to put himself in the line of fire too often, until Garibaldi warned him about his obsessive hero syndrome (INFECTION). Sinclair liked to know everything about Babylon 5 and kept up to date with Garibaldi's files (PURPLE).

The commander believed strongly in Babylon 5's peacekeeping mission and he was extremely proud of the station (PARLIAMENT). He was also proud of his senior staff. He had faith in Garibaldi and believed that Ivanova was the finest officer he had ever served with (GATHERING, EYES). He admired Dr. Franklin's drive to save lives and desire to put an end to suffering, but occasionally got annoyed with it.

Sinclair had to reevaluate the missing 24 hours of his life following the assassination attempt on Ambassador Kosh, when the killer referred to the "hole" in his mind. His suspicions were later confirmed when he was kidnapped by Knights One and Two and placed in a cybernet, where he learned that he had been aboard a Minbari ship and tortured, interrogated and scanned by the Minbari Grey Council. He was shocked to learn that Delenn was one of his interrogators. (SKY)

During his time on the station, Sinclair frequently had to bend and rewrite the rules. In 2257, he risked war with the all-powerful Vorlons when he disobeyed their requests and ordered Dr. Kyle to open Kosh's encounter suit and do whatever he could to save his life. The following year, during the illegal dock workers' strike, he deliberately manipulated the Senate when they invoked the Rush Act, and used it to solve the dispute through a pay increase rather than through force. (MEANS)

Sinclair always maintained a respect for all human and alien religions. During the station's religious festival, he decided that Earth would be represented by all religious and spiritual groups as well as by an atheist (PARLIAMENT). Sinclair believed that life was nothing without the things people hold sacred. He also felt that all religions must be right because God doesn't care how you say your prayers as long as you say them. Sinclair refused to overrule alien religious beliefs, even when they looked set to cost a young boy his life (BELIEVERS).

Sinclair disliked giving interviews. Prior to working on Babylon 5, the last time he had been interviewed someone told him to relax and say what he felt. He was reassigned to a distant outpost in less than ten minutes after the interview (INFECTION). When he was convinced to face the cameras on Babylon 5, he expressed his belief that man must leave Earth if it is to survive the planet's inevitable destruction (INFECTION).

When Catherine Sakai boarded the station, she and Sinclair once again rekindled their romance. He admitted that even through all the arguments and separations, he never stopped thinking about or loving her. At the end of 2258, they decided that they had finally got the relationship right and Sinclair proposed to Sakai. When she accepted, they started to plan their wedding for the next year. (CHRYSALIS)

Sinclair had a taste of things to come during the evacuation of Babylon 4. While aboard the station, he experienced a flashforward in time in which Garibaldi had set Babylon 5 to self-destruct and mounted a suicidal defense against an invading force. The vision concluded with Garibaldi telling Sinclair to leave the station and that he wanted to lead the defense because it was the moment he was born for. (SQUARED)

He later learns from a mysterious alien named Zathras that Babylon 4 will be used as a base of operations in a great war against the forces of darkness. Zathras tells Sinclair about his great leader, The One, and tells him that he has a destiny. Sinclair is unaware that The One is actually a future version of himself.

At the end of 2258, Sinclair sensed that the galaxy had reached a crossroads and he didn't like where everyone was heading. He was unable to stop the conspiracy to kill President Santiago and predicted that nothing would be the same again. (CHRYSALIS)

On January 3rd, 2259, Sinclair was recalled to Earth without explanation (DEPARTURE). Three days later, he was summoned before President Clark and Rathenn, a member of the Minbari Grey Council, who returned his memory of events during the Battle of the Line and offered him a chance to become the first human ambassador allowed permanent residence on the planet (DARKNESS). Although Delenn claimed that he was offered the post as an act of good faith in the hope that it would create a greater understanding between humans and Minbari, the real purpose of his posting on the planet remained something of a mystery (REVELATIONS, SHADOWS).

Shortly after arriving on the planet, he was linked with a plot to kill the new Minbari leader and stood trial for treason. When he was found guilty, Sinclair invoked an ancient Minbari law which allowed him to exchange his life for war. The new leader then personally pardoned Sinclair because he would not allow his Minbari soul to be executed. (PEACE)

A few months later, Sinclair sent a message to Garibaldi and Delenn in which he revealed that he was building a secret army of light known as the Rangers and warned them about the coming darkness. (SHADOWS)

Sinclair takes milk and two sugars in his coffee (GATHER-ING). He prizes knowledge and honesty, and fastens then zips his trousers every morning (SQUARED, EYES). He admits to becoming "cranky" when he is deprived of sleep (MEANS).

Played by Michael O'Hare.

Sineval

A Minbari warleader, captain of the *Trigati* during the Earth–Minbari War. When the Grey Council ordered the Minbari to surrender, he refused to pass the order to his crew and committed suicide. Consequently, Sineval became a martyr to the cause of war, while his first officer, Kalain, led the *Trigati* into self-imposed exile. (LEGACIES, DEPARTURE)

Singer

A friend of Amanda Carter. Abel Horn claimed that Singer found him after he had died and took him to a doctor who managed to save his life during the 2258 Mars Rebellion. (SPIDER)

Skin Tab

Used to administer drugs into a body. Used to poison Kosh (GATHERING) and to administer stims to Walker Smith

(TKO). Also known as a poison tab (GATHERING). (See also **Slappers**.)

Skydancer, The
Catherine Sakai's survey ship. The *Skydancer* was almost destroyed while orbiting Sigma 957, but was saved by a Narn vessel. (MIND)

Slappers
Slang for Skin Tabs, usually via the back of the wrist. Garibaldi caught a Llort buying one just prior to Walker Smith's arrival on the station. (TKO)

Slaver's Glove
Used to give painful electrical shocks. Not designed to inflict permanent damage or to kill. (PURPLE, SPIDER)

Slitch
Animal native to Orion. (EYES)

Smith, Walker
An ex-SportCorp boxer who visited Babylon 5 to fight in the Mutai. Walker Smith first met Michael Garibaldi in Fortune City. He was in a drunken fight when the security officer knocked him out with a shock stick. According to Smith, it was the start of a "beautiful friendship." Prior to 2258, they last saw each other on Orion 4.

Smith traveled to Io, Mars and the Arain station before getting passage to Earth, where he fought a SportCorp boxing match with Itagi. Some called the match "World War 4." Smith won the fight and became the number one contender for the title.

However, SportCorp had invested money in Fosaro and told Smith to "retire" for a few years. When he refused, SportCorp tampered with his blood test to make it look as if he was using adrinos and said he was working for the Syndis. As a result, he lost his boxing license in 2256 and spent the next two years fighting illegally.

In 2258, he traveled to Babylon 5 on an Earth transport ship, the *White Star*, and befriended Rabbi Koslov. Once aboard the station, he met Garibaldi and told him that he intended to make history by becoming the first human to ever fight in the Mutai. Smith was convinced that if he won, SportCorp would have to let him have a shot at the title.

Smith was initially rejected by the Muta-Do for being disrespectful, but was tutored by a former Mutari, Caliban, and learned how to make a proper challenge. He then fought the Sho'Rin, Gyor, and scored a points victory over him. Smith then left the station for Earth and his title fight. Played by Greg McKinney. (TKO)

Soldier of Darkness

A Shadow warrior which appears beyond the normal range of perception of humans and aliens. Requires an exceptional amount of PPG shots to be hurt or killed. It is smart, patient and deadly, and is known to feed on human internal organs. (LONG)

Solis Planum

Site on Mars. (VOICE I)

Soul Hunters

Little is known about this mysterious alien race. Nobody knows who they are or where they came from, but they are believed to be immortal. They are drawn to death in much the same way that moths are attracted by light, and can sense the moment of death.

Soul Hunters believe that the soul ends when the body dies. Consequently, they believe that they are preserving life and collect souls for the greater good. Soul Hunters worship their collections of souls and never travel without them.

Many alien races know of their existence. Most are scared of them and almost none cooperate with their soul-snatching. The Minbari know them as Jhak'tot and are brought up to be scared of them. Soul Hunters are said to be particularly interested in certain Minbari castes.

Although it is not their normal atmosphere, they can breathe oxygen. Commander Sinclair told Soul Hunter #2 that he and his brothers were not welcome aboard Babylon 5. (SOUL)

Soul Hunter #1

A Soul Hunter who had traveled widely and visited many worlds, including Earth. Soul Hunter #1 was a collector of "the greatest souls" and had been ordered by his people to save several souls, including that of the Minbari leader Dukhat. On each occasion, he was either prevented or stopped by others.

The Soul Hunter's failure brought shame upon his order and made him become obsessed with the danger of losing souls. Then he suddenly declared that he had found a solution to his problem, and left them. When the order learned that he had started to kill people and was then stealing their souls, they tried to track him down. Prior to his arrival on Babylon 5, the Soul Hunters nearly succeeded in capturing him, and damaged his ship.

On Babylon 5, he attempted to kill Ambassador Delenn and steal her soul but was stopped by Commander Sinclair, who turned the soul-stealing device on the Soul Hunter. His collection of souls was later released by Delenn. Played by W. Morgan Sheppard. (SOUL)

Soul Hunter #2

The second Soul Hunter to visit Babylon 5, Soul Hunter #2 arrived on the trail of the rogue Soul Hunter (#1). He later helped Commander Sinclair track the rogue before he could kill Ambassador Delenn. Played by John Snyder. (SOUL)

Spacing

Term used to describe execution by exposure to the vacuum of space. The Ombuds can sentence a criminal to spacing for mutiny or treason. (WORD)

Spoo

Alien delicacy. G'Kar enjoys fresh spoo but Londo doesn't seem to share his enthusiasm (MIDNIGHT). Londo bought 200,000 shares in a Spoo Ranch when his data system was possessed by Elric's holodemon (GEOMETRY).

SportCorp
The governing body of sporting activity in Earth Alliance. According to Walker Smith, SportCorp is corrupt and supports fighters such as Fosaro. (TKO)

Stafford's Disease
Fatal condition. Jha'dur infected the entire population of Lardec 4 with Stafford's Disease to see how quickly it took for them to die (DEATHWALKER). Dr. Rosen said the Alien Healing Device could treat the disease (MERCY).

Starfuries
High performance Earth Alliance space combat/reconnaissance fighters. Babylon 5 predominantly uses SA-23E Mitchell-Hyundyne single-seat Starfuries, designed for combat in space. Other kinds of Starfuries include a two-person craft which has cockpits fore and aft, and the Black Omega interceptors, which are used for surveillance missions. Starfuries cannot enter planetary atmospheres. (VOICE I)

Space-suited pilots stand up in the craft to sustain the high g-forces from various maneuvers and fuel is stored in the ships' wings. The Starfuries are equipped with four Copeland JC466/A pulse discharge cannons, two underneath the cockpit and the other two above the pilot. They also have secondary cannons above the cockpit. Four vectoring thrust nozzles/propulsion units on the tip of each wing allow maximum maneuverability with a minimum of power, while the Starfury's direction is determined by fins at the rear. Each Starfury has a grapple which, used either manually or by computer, can grab ships or objects in space (SOUL, KNIVES). Each Starfury is equipped with an on-board Duffy-1018MJS targetting computer and the entire cockpit can eject and act as a lifeboat.

Babylon 5's Starfuries are organized into three squadrons of eight ships: Alpha, Delta and Zeta. They are launched from the station's cobra bays. (See also **Cobra Bays**)

Starkiller
Name given to Sheridan following the destruction of the Minbari warcruiser the *Black Star* and three heavy cruisers. The Minbari thought that Sheridan had won the battle dis-

honorably by mining an asteroid field between Jupiter and Mars and sending a distress signal which lured the ships to their destruction. (See also **Sheridan, John J.**)

Starlaces
A pretty Centauri flower. (PURPLE)

Star Riders Clan
Part of the Minbari warrior caste, the clan's members include Neroon. (LEGACIES)

Starweb
Energy web used to capture individuals and creatures. (DUET, CODA)

Station Phobos
Station located on the largest of Mars' two moons.

StellarCom
Used for external communication outside Babylon 5.

Stetbar
A bar on an individual's Earthforce uniform that illustrates which part of service the member is in. It is color coded so that gold signifies command, red stands for medical and green means security. Captain Sheridan exchanged one of his for a "moment of perfect beauty" during one of his lessons with Ambassador Kosh. (HONOR)

Stims
Used to stimulate physical and mental activity. Stims are perfectly legal when prescribed and used in moderation.

Stoner, Matthew
Talia Winters' ex-husband. Matthew Stoner was assigned to Talia during her first year at Psi Corps Academy and when the pair were found to be genetically compatible, the Corps arranged their marriage.

While at the Academy, Stoner arranged for a Psi Corps experiment. He was exposed to a drug which scrambled his neural pathways and almost killed him. When he recovered, he supposedly had lost his telepathic abilities and left the Corps. He then worked as a freelance navigator and a part-time trader.

In 2259, he visited Babylon 5 and offered to use the same procedure which had erased his Psi abilities on Talia, thus providing her with an exit from the Corps. However, Garibaldi realizes that Stoner is actually an empath and is still working for the Corps. He later admits that he had been sent to the station to convince Talia to join him in the hope that they would have telepathic/empathic children. Before he left the station, he added that he was acting in Talia's best interests. Played by Keith Szarabajka. (MATES)

Streams of Time

Term used by the Children of Time to refer to the future. No one knows what the stream brings until the water surrounds them. (BELIEVERS)

Streibs

Race of aliens who abduct examples of alien life-forms they encounter to investigate their defenses. They analyze their specimens' strength, tolerance to pain and resourcefulness, and study their ships to learn about their race's technology. The Streib once abducted a few members of the Minbari, who tracked them down to their homeworld to make sure that they would never do it again. In 2259, they kidnapped Sheridan and a Narn captain, Ta'Lon, for research, and the pair managed to escape as Ivanova mounted an offensive against the Streibs. (ALONE)

Stroke Off

Common insult. Used by Walker Smith (TKO) and Karl Edward Mueller (MERCY) among others.

Sunhawk

Drazi ship. During the Deathwalker crisis, its captain, Vakar Ashok, demanded the extradition of Jha'dur for war crimes and threatened to attack the station if its staff didn't comply. (DEATHWALKER)

Supermorbidium
The 156th atom, used in the production of phased plaser weapons. (ACCUSATIONS)

Sykes, Carolyn
A human trader, self-made businesswoman and former girl-friend of Commander Sinclair. In 2257, Carolyn arrived on Babylon 5 a mere two minutes before Ambassador Kosh was poisoned. Ambassador G'Kar claimed that she had supplied Sinclair with the poison, florazyne, which she gained from her visit to the Damocles Sector. She had been dealing with the Centauri a week before her visit to the station and told them she would blast the merchandise in space and into the sun unless she was paid (GATHERING). Carolyn wanted Sinclair to quit Earthforce and become a trader. When he refused, they split up (PARLIAMENT). Played by Blaire Baron.

Syria Planum
Location on Mars. Site of a classified Psi Corps intelligence and training operation.

T

Takarn (Captain)

The leader of a group of violent outcasts who were expelled from Epsilon 3 before Varn assumed control of the planet in the mid-18th century. In 2258, Takarn and his crew arrived in the Tigris Sector and attempted to claim Epsilon 3 as their legacy. His ship later engaged Babylon 5 and the *Hyperion* in a battle for the planet. When Draal became custodian of the planet and warned that anyone who tried to land would be destroyed, Takarn ignored him and attempted to seize control of Epsilon 3. As a result, Takarn's ship and his people were destroyed by the planet's defense system. Played by Michelan Sisti. (VOICE II)

Takashima, Laurel (Lieutenant-Commander)

Babylon 5's original first officer, Lieutenant-Commander Laurel Takashima was recalled to Earth following the assassination attempt on Ambassador Kosh in 2257.

Laurel Takashima was born on Earth. Upon the completion of her Earthforce training, Takashima was assigned to work at Mars Colony Security, shortly before the Food Riots. When she learned that officers had to buy promotions from the sector captain, she refused to pay her way through the ranks. As a result, she stopped caring, broke rules and put people at risk.

Things changed when she met Jeffrey Sinclair, who told her that if she promised to start fighting within the rules, he would make sure she was promoted. Takashima obeyed his request and Sinclair kept his promise by making sure that she was assigned to Babylon 5 as his first officer.

In 2257, Dr. Kyle convinced her to break the rules one more time when he wanted her help to convince Lyta Alexander to perform an illegal scan of the dying Vorlon ambassador, Kosh. (GATHERING)

Following the assassination attempt on Kosh, Takashima was recalled to Earth and subsequently reassigned to border patrol on the Rim.

Played by Tamlyn Tomita.

Ta'Lon

Narn captain taken prisoner by the Streibs and forced to fight their other "specimens" by a mechanical device attached to his head. When he started to attack Captain Sheridan, he asked the human to kill him. Sheridan refused and reluctantly incapacitated Ta'Lon (breaking four of his ribs in the process) before removing the alien mechanism. Together, the pair managed to escape from their cell and leave the Streib ship in a rescue pod just as Commander Ivanova and the *Agamemnon* came to their rescue. (ALONE)

Ta'Lon spent time in a hospital on Narn recovering from his ordeal and always wanted to return to Babylon 5 to thank Sheridan for saving his life. In 2260, Ta'Lon was appointed as Na'Far's bodyguard and accompanied the Narn to Babylon 5. Once there, he told Sheridan that he owed him his life and hoped to serve him for the rest of his life. He then decided to stand down as Na'Far's escort and stay on Babylon 5. Played by Marshall Teague. (STRIFE)

Talquith

Narn transport dispatched to Babylon 5 in 2258 with a G'Quan Eth for Ambassador G'Kar. Just as it arrived aboard the station, the *Talquith* was destroyed as the result of a malfunction in the docking computer. (MEANS)

Taq

A translator for Correlilmurzon, Taq spoke on behalf of the Lumati delegate until humanity was judged to be a "superior" species and thus worthy of direct communication. Played by Paul Williams. (SACRIFICE)

Taree
A Narn beverage. (SURVIVORS)

Tasaki (Doctor)
An enthusiastic scientist stationed aboard Babylon 5, Dr. Tasaki led the investigation into the increased seismic activity on Epsilon 3. He told Lieutenant-Commander Ivanova that he would be happy to die while making a scientific discovery. Tasaki's wife was stationed on Proxima and loved mysteries. Played by Jim Ishida. (VOICE I)

Techno-mages
Dreamers, shapers, singers and makers who study the mysteries of laser circuits, crystals and scanners and use them to achieve the effect of magic.

Legends claim that Techno-mages know all the true secrets: they know the 14 words that will make someone fall in love with you forever and the seven words to painlessly say goodbye to a dying friend; they know how to be rich and how to be poor; and they know how to rediscover dreams when the world has taken them away.

Techno-mages prefer to stay at their homes and rarely travel. The Centauri believe that to see a group of Techno-mages is a bad omen.

In 2259, the Techno-mages fled the known galaxy to preserve their knowledge from the "black and terrible storm" that lay ahead. According to one Techno-mage, Elric, they would not return for at least a hundred years. (GEOMETRY)

Tech Runners
Smugglers and couriers of illegal technology, Tech Runners are not known for their generosity. (GATHERING)

Telepaths
Individuals capable of reading minds. According to Earth Alliance records, one in a thousand human beings are telepathic and one in ten thousand telepaths has telekinetic abilities. Half of Earth's telekinetics are clinically insane (MIND). All

human telepaths are registered and by law must join the Psi Corps, take telepathic suppressants, or face lifelong imprisonment (LEGACIES).

On Minbar telepaths are highly respected. Telepathy is considered a gift, and consequently telepaths share their abilities with others in return for clothing and food. (LEGACIES)

The Centauri emperor depends on his telepathic staff, who are raised together from birth and remain in constant telepathic contact with each other. (SHADOWS)

The Narns do not have telepaths and are desperate to either employ them or genetically create a breed of Narn telepaths. (GATHERING, LEGACIES)

Telepaths can sense the presence of Shadows (Z'HA'DUM), while the Vorlons are believed to be wary of telepaths (DEATHWALKER). (See also **Psi Corps, The**)

Tennyson

A renowned human poet, Tennyson wrote one of Jeffrey Sinclair's favorite poems, "Ulysses." (GATHERING, DARKNESS)

Tensus, Aria

A young Centauri female, Aria Tensus was the girlfriend of Kiron Maray. Aria and Kiron arrived on Babylon 5 in 2258 with stolen credit chips. They were arrested by the station's Security on arrival and placed in Ambassador Mollari's custody by Commander Sinclair. Aria explained that her family had arranged for her to marry a man "old enough to be her grandfather" and said that she wouldn't do it because she loved Kiron.

During a vicious Homeguard attack, Aria was stunned by a shock stick and Kiron was almost killed. When he recovered, they learned that they would be fostered by Andilo Mollari until they reached adult age, when they could decide who they wanted to marry for themselves. Played by Danica McKellar. (PRAYER)

Teronn

A Minbari living on Babylon 5, Teronn questioned Delenn's position as the Minbari ambassador following her transformation into a half-human, half-Minbari hybrid. With her permission, he spoke directly to the Grey Council about the matter. Played by Sandey Grinn. (DISTANT)

Tharg

The husband of M'ola and father of Shon. Tharg loved his young son very much and admitted that Shon had brought a great deal of happiness and joy into his life.

However, when Shon was dying of a congestive blockage in his upper air passage, Tharg refused to allow him to undergo a surgical procedure that could save his life. As a member of the Children of Time, Tharg believed that if a surgical procedure was performed on Shon he would lose his soul. Thus, he decided that it was better for Shon to die than for him to lose his soul during an operation.

When Dr. Franklin performed the operation on Shon without his permission, he told the human physician that he understood why he had done it but couldn't forgive him. Tharg and M'ola then killed Shon, saying that he was just a soulless shell after the operation.

Tharg always found the Parable of the Seventh Declamation of the Scroll of Hero to be an inspiring lesson. He disliked showing his emotions to strangers. Played by Stephen Lee. (BELIEVERS)

Thenta Makur

A highly respected guild of Narn assassins. The Thenta Makur leave a black flower known as a Death Blossom before the victims as a warning that they should get their affairs in order before they are killed. If a member of the guild fails to complete his task within the specified deadline or betrays a commission, the Narn becomes a target of the Thenta Makur. (PARLIAMENT)

Theo (Brother)

The leader of a group of monks granted permanent residence aboard Babylon 5 in 2260. Theo's monks intended to learn about God from the alien races and were skilled in computer research, physics, bio-genetics, chemistry and engineering. Shortly after their arrival, they helped Commander Ivanova find a mad bomber, Robert J. Carlsen. Played by Louis Turenne. (CONVICTIONS)

Third Principle of Sentient Life, The
A canon of Minbari beliefs which refers to "the capacity for self-sacrifice: the conscious ability to override evolution and self-preservation for a cause, a friend or a loved one." (VOICE I)

Thirteen
The mysterious controller of Bureau 13, Thirteen was once a Psi Cop who has been officially declared dead. She was also present at Abel Horn's transformation into a cyberorganic lifeform in 2258. Played by Annie Grindlay. (SPIDER)

"36 Hours Aboard Babylon 5"
Controversial ISN documentary broadcast on September 16th, 2259. Hosted by Cynthia Torqueman and funded by Interplanetary Expeditions. (WORD)

Tigris Sector
A system located in neutral space, the Tigris Sector is home to Babylon 5 and Epsilon 3.

Ti Kar, The
A highly unusual alien species. Captain Sheridan made first contact with the Ti Kar while serving as the commander of the *Agamemnon*.

In 2259, the Ti Kar sent a delegation to Babylon 5 to discuss the possibility of joining the Babylon Project. For the talks, Commander Ivanova had to prepare six yarwood chairs placed a meter apart from each other in a star shape. A heloc was then left on the center seat. (SPIDER)

Ti Korvo, The
Title given leader of the Ti Kar delegation sent to Babylon 5 in 2259. (SPIDER)

Ti'Lar
Minbari poem songs that attempt to recall old memories and prompt new ideas. (PRAYER)

Time Stabilizer

Device used by an individual to help survive time jumps. Zathras gave his time stabilizer to The One as he struggled to keep Babylon 4 stable in 2258. (SQUARED)

Timov

The daughter of Algur, Timov married Londo Mollari in 2239. She believed that the secret of their marriage's success was their lack of communication. Unlike Londo's other two wives, Timov had little interest in social climbing or politics and made no pretense of loving her husband, even when she was faced with the threat of divorce in 2259.

The only thing Londo and Timov have in common is their blood. Consequently, when Londo was dying and needed a blood transfusion, she agreed to save his life on the condition that Dr. Franklin did not tell the ambassador that she was the donor. That way, she explained, she was spared his "false gratitude."

When Londo rewarded her honesty by keeping her as his only wife, Timov told him that she could never love him but, at best, could tolerate him. Timov was known to bite people on more than one occasion. Played by Jane Carr. (MATES)

Tirolus

Planet destroyed by Jha'dur in 2231. (DEATHWALKER)

T'Kog

The son of Du'Rog and Ka'Het, brother of Mi'Ra. Following his father's death, T'Kog took a Chon-Kar against Ambassador G'Kar, which the family later abandoned when the Narn financially compensated them and it received evidence clearing Du'Rog's name. (BLOOD)

Torqueman, Cynthia

A leading ISN reporter, Cynthia Torqueman hosted the controversial documentary "36 Hours Aboard Babylon 5" in 2259. She suggested that the first rule of survival aboard the station was "expect the unexpected." Played by Kim Zimmer. (WORD)

Trakis

A Golian slave master with a grudge against the Centauri, Trakis used Adira Tyree to obtain Ambassador Mollari's Purple Files, which he then hoped to sell to the Narn. When Adira tried to run away with the files, he found out where she was by placing a bugging device on Mollari and seized the files from her. Unfortunately, Trakis was caught discussing the files with Ambassador G'Kar shortly after and Londo had them returned to him. Played by Clive Revill. (PURPLE)

Transport Association

Organization that represents freelance pilots, businessmen and couriers traveling to Babylon 5. In 2260, the Transport Association objected to tighter policies on the movement of weapons, which would cause delays of 10–15% and require a 5% increase in inspection staff, whose wages would be paid for by an increase in the docking fee. (STRIFE)

Transport Tubes

Internal elevators aboard Babylon 5. Often referred to as "the tube."

Treel

Centauri fish served on Babylon 5. (TKO)

Trial of Blood

See **Mutai, The**

Trigati, The

Minbari warcruiser commanded by Sineval during the Earth–Minbari War. When the Grey Council gave the order to surrender, Sineval refused to comply and committed suicide. His first officer, Kalain, then led the ship into self-imposed exile. Over the years, the *Trigati* and its crew became a Minbari legend.

In 2259, Kalain boarded Babylon 5 and was arrested for the attempted murder of Ambassador Delenn. However, Kalain had no intention of killing anyone aboard the station and committed suicide to justify the *Trigati's* final offensive against Babylon 5. When Sheridan learned that the *Trigati* wasn't using its stealth technology, he realized that the crew wanted to die and were mounting a suicide strike. When he refused to fire first, the *Trigati* would not take offensive action.

Shortly after, a Minbari warcruiser assigned to track the ship arrived on the scene and blasted the *Trigati*'s engine. The ship was then destroyed trying to jump into hyperspace. (DEPARTURE)

Triluminary

A multipurpose Minbari object. A triluminary scanned Jeffrey Sinclair during the Battle of the Line and later restored his memory of the encounter with the Grey Council, created the cocoon which transformed Delenn into a half-human, half-Minbari hybrid and stunned the Minbari warriors guarding Branmer's body (SKY, DEPARTURE, CHRYSALIS, DARKNESS, LEGACIES). There are only three in existence (SQUARED).

Tu'Bar

While serving as a member of the First Circle of the Kha'Ri in 2258, Tu'Bar authorized Ambassador G'Kar's meeting with the Shadow emissary, Morden. (SIGNS)

Tuchanq

An alien race once conquered by Narns. In 2259, the Tuchanq forged an alliance with the Centauri Republic, which then proceeded to invade the Tuchanq homeworld with the help of the Shadows. (LAW)

Tukati, The

The researcher whose brain patterns were programmed into Ikaara's bio-organic weapons. (INFECTION)

Tu'Pari

A member of the Thenta Makur, Tu'Pari was sent to Babylon 5 to assassinate Ambassador G'Kar in 2258. He posed as a diplomatic courier to deliver Du'Rog's death threat to G'Kar before revealing his true identity.

Just before Tu'Pari killed G'Kar, he was tricked by Na'Toth who managed to free the ambassador from his paingivers. G'Kar and Na'Toth then drugged the assassin and allowed him to wake up after he had missed his deadline. G'Kar also placed a substantial amount of money in Tu'Pari's accounts to make the Thenta Makur believe that he had betrayed his commission and sold out his principles. Tu'Pari left the station a worried Narn. Played by Thomas Kopache. (PARLIAMENT)

Turhan (Emperor)

A former Centauri emperor, Turhan died in 2259 and was succeeded by his nephew, Cartagia. Turhan's ancestors led the Centauri invasion of Narn and his father personally ordered the execution of 100,000 Narns. However, Turhan himself had no hatred for the Narn Regime and felt guilty about what his family and his people had done to them. He made many concessions to the Narn and returned many of their former territories.

He had heard about Babylon 5's work and was moved by the staff's efforts for peace. Consequently, in 2259, he decided to travel to the station to make an important speech. Turhan had become tired with the trappings of status and chose not to wear a wig for his visit.

While aboard the station, Emperor Turhan admitted to Captain Sheridan that he had never before chosen to do anything in his life: he had been born into a role that had been prepared for him and did everything he was asked to do, without ever stopping to think for himself. Consequently, he had traveled to Babylon 5 to pursue a course of action that he had himself chosen.

However, Turhan was robbed of the opportunity to change the course of history when he collapsed from heart failure shortly before he could make his speech. A few hours later, he told Dr. Franklin that he had come to the station because he wanted to stand next to a Narn in neutral territory and apologize to him for what his people and his family had done. Turhan wanted the hatred between the Narn and Centauri to end and hoped to make amends for the crimes they had committed.

Turhan had heard many legends about the Vorlons and was keen to meet Ambassador Kosh, either inside or outside his encounter suit. Kosh visited the emperor on his deathbed. When Turhan learned of the Centauri attack on Quadrant

14, he asked Kosh how it would end. The Vorlon replied, "In fire."

With his last breath, Emperor Turhan whispered into Ambassador Mollari's ear. Although Londo claimed that he had told him, "Continue. Take my people back to the stars," in reality, the emperor had told him, "You are both damned."

Following Turhan's death, Lord Refa and his associates successfully maneuvered the late emperor's nephew, Cartagia, onto the throne. Played by Turhan Bey. (SHADOWS)

Tyree, Adira

Born in Davo, Adira Tyree was a Centauri slave ordered by her master, Trakis, to steal Ambassador Mollari's Purple Files. In return, she was promised her freedom.

Adira began a passionate affair with Londo before stealing his files. She then tried to double-cross Trakis, but was subsequently caught by her master. When he was arrested, Commander Sinclair convinced Trakis to release Adira from her contract, and she left Babylon 5 a free woman. Played by Fabiana Udenio. (PURPLE)

U

Ultra-Violet Priority
Classification for Earthforce's most important missions. (PREY)

Una (Doctor)
The chief medical officer aboard the *Cortez*. (DISTANT)

United Spaceways Transport
Interstellar transport company. (GATHERING)

Universal Terraform
Huge corporation that employed Catherine Sakai to survey Sigma 957 for Quantium 40 in 2258. (MIND)

***Universe Today*, The**
The galaxy's leading newspaper. The *Universe Today* can be personalized to suit the preferences of its reader; for example, while Ambassador Delenn likes extra information on the Minbari, Captain Sheridan prefers to keep up with the latest baseball games (DIVIDED). The paper once ran a controversial story asking if some form of alien life was living in hyperspace (DISTANT). The *Universe Today* is produced on a recycled synthetic material.

"Ulysses"
A classic poem written by the human author, Tennyson. Jeffrey Sinclair first read "Ulysses" at the Academy and it be-

came his favorite poem (GATHERING, PARLIAMENT). He later took it to Minbar and told his hosts that they might understand him better if they read it (DARKNESS).

Ulysses, The
Carolyn Sykes' trading vessel. (GATHERING)

V

Valen

The leading Minbari religious figure, Valen founded modern Minbari society and established the Grey Council. Valen brought Minbari society together and forbade Minbari from killing each other. By the mid-23rd century, it had become their greatest taboo. (DARKNESS)

Valen made a major prophecy referring to a great war against the forces of darkness and an alien race, many members of which had a destiny that the Minbari could not interfere with (SQUARED). In order to defeat the darkness, the Minbari would have to join forces with this race (DEPARTURE).

When the Grey Council discovered that Minbari souls were being reborn in part or in full into human beings, members of the religious caste began to speculate that humanity was the alien race Valen had referred to in his prophecy. Consequently, Satai Delenn was assigned to Babylon 5 to study the species. (SQUARED)

Delenn believed that she too had a part to play in Valen's prophecy and disobeyed the orders of the Grey Council by transforming herself into a half-human, half-Minbari hybrid. (SQUARED, ALONE)

Valerius, The

The Centauri warcruiser from which Ambassador Mollari and Lord Refa witnessed the decimation of the Narn homeworld at the end of the Narn–Centauri War. (TWILIGHT)

Valo (Lord)

A Centauri noble, Lord Valo refused to speak to Londo Mollari until 2259, when the ambassador suddenly became much more important and influential within the Centauri Republic. (KNIVES)

Val Too

A popular Centauri toast. (KNIVES)

Varn

Varn served as custodian of Epsilon 3 for 500 years. He was entrusted to look after the planet and its amazing technology when his people left Epsilon 3 in the mid-18th century.

In 2258, Varn appeared to Commander Sinclair, Draal and Ambassador Mollari and asked for their help. Although he could not say it openly, he required one of them to take his place at the heart of the machine. As his condition deteriorated, Epsilon 3 headed for destruction until Draal took Varn's place as custodian. Varn spent his last days helping Draal become at one with the machine, and told Delenn that the Minbari would experience wonders beyond her imagination as the custodian of Epsilon 3. Played by Curt Lowens. (VOICE I, II)

Varner, Del

A human male, Del Varner was born on Earth on 27 June 2218 and worked as a tech-runner. Among other places, Varner smuggled forbidden technology from the Vega and Proxima systems and was wanted by the Earth Alliance Court. He was known to do a lot of business with the Centauri Republic.

Del Varner had considerable debts when he was hired to provide a radical member of the Minbari warrior caste with a Changeling Net. When the Minbari failed to arrive at their arranged meeting point in the Tigris Sector, Varner traveled to Babylon 5. His client later found him on the station, killed him and stole his Changeling Net. The Minbari then posed as Varner using the device. Del Varner's body was later found in his quarters by Security Chief Garibaldi. Played by John Fleck. (GATHERING)

Vega Colony

The Vega Colony is a five-day voyage through hyperspace from Z'ha'dum. Morden claimed to have spent a few months recovering from the destruction of the *Icarus* at the Vega Colony, but Captain Sheridan knew he was lying. (Z'HA'DUM)

Vega Sector

Home of the Vega Colony (Z'HA'DUM). One of the systems from which Del Varner smuggled forbidden technology (GATHERING).

Venzann

The Centauri god of food. (PARLIAMENT)

Vernon, Al

A human trader married to a Narn, Al Vernon did a great deal of business with the Centauri, including Ambassador Mollari. In 2259, Vernon provided the Du'Rog family with the evidence to restore their family honor. (BLOOD)

Vibe Shower

Shower which cleanses using sonic and antibacterial lighting rather than water. All of Babylon 5's standard quarters are equipped with vibe showers because the station's water reclamation system can only provide enough water for command and executive suites. (MIND, DEPARTURE)

Vibration Detonator

Device used to ignite C5 explosive by vibrating at a certain frequency. (SURVIVORS)

Vickers

Vickers are part-machine, part-sentient living recorders and can record sight, sound, bio-rhythms, thought patterns and just about anything. They are employed by several races and their name is derived from the title of an old piece of Earth technology called the VCR. Vickers cannot be telepathically scanned.

In 2258, Ambassador Kosh hired Babylon 5's resident Vicker, Abbut, to make a recording from Talia Winters' mind. (DEATHWALKER)

Vin'Tok
Narn Captain of the *K'sha Na'vas* and an old friend of Ambassador G'Kar. (BLOOD)

Virtual Reality Cybernet
A device used to simulate virtual reality environments. In 2258, Knight Two probed Commander Sinclair's mind for the secret of his missing 24 hours during the Battle of the Line with a Virtual Reality Cybernet. (SKY)

Vorlon Empire, The
The official title of the Vorlons' dominion. Naturally, little is known about the empire and all fact-finding expeditions into Vorlon space have disappeared without a trace. (See also **Vorlons, The**)

Vorlons, The
The oldest and most powerful race aboard Babylon 5, the Vorlons are shrouded in mystery. Indeed, the station's staff have discovered that the more one knows about the Vorlons, the less one really knows.

The Vorlons are the last remaining First Ones. They helped defeat the Shadows in the Great War during the mid-13th century and waited a thousand years for them to return (Z'HA'DUM). They have traveled widely and, as the new races began to emerge, taught them how to perceive them. As a result, a Vorlon looks different to each race, according to its own beliefs; for example, when a human looks at a Vorlon, the individual sees an angel. As far as the Vorlons are concerned, this guarantees that the younger races will react to them in the correct manner. It is a physical strain for a Vorlon to appear before another race (FALL).

Although the Vorlons have explored the galaxy many times over, they did not appreciate it when the younger races tried to make contact with them or sent expeditions into their territory. Both the Earth Alliance and Centauri Republic sent ships into Vorlon space that disappeared without a trace. The Vorlon government then advised the Centauri and human leaders of the situation and they told them not to send other ships into their space. (SHADOWS, WORD)

Several years later, when Ambassador Kosh was the subject of an assassination attempt, they ordered Commander Sinclair not to open his encounter suit for "security reasons." Thus the Vorlons would sacrifice their lives to protect their secrecy. As a result of their mysterious nature, the Vorlons became the stuff of legends. One such tale suggested that the only human who ever saw a Vorlon was turned to stone. (GATHERING)

The Vorlons use bio-organic technology and their ships register as life-forms. Captain Sheridan once estimated that Vorlon technology must be at least a thousand years ahead of Earth. According to Ambassador Kosh, the Vorlons take no interest in the affairs of others. As a result, it remains a mystery why they joined the Babylon Project. (PRAYER)

Despite their claim, however, the Vorlons do occasionally interfere. The most notable incident occurred in 2258, when they killed the infamous war criminal Jha'dur and, in the process, destroyed the galaxy's chance of finding a universal anti-agapic. When asked about their motive, Ambassador Kosh told Sinclair that the younger races were not ready for immortality. None of the other races made a complaint to the Babylon 5 Advisory Council because they all knew it would be pointless. (DEATHWALKER, EYES)

During one of their visits to Earth in the 19th century, the Vorlons kidnapped a serial killer known as Jack the Ripper. They took him to their homeworld, taught him the error of his ways and then employed him as an inquisitor to test "chosen ones." (INQUISITOR)

Vorlon space is approximately eight days away from Babylon 5. The Vorlons are believed to be wary of telepaths and can be killed by florazyne. (DEATHWALKER, GATHERING)

Vortex Generator
See **Jumpgates**

Voudreau, Elise (Senator)

In 2259, Earth Alliance Senator Elise Voudreau ordered Captain Sheridan to monitor the negotiations between Taro Isogi and Amanda Carter and told him that they were planning another rebellion on Mars. When Sheridan pointed out that Babylon 5 acted as a free port for commerce and was unauthorized to interfere with private negotiations, she told him that practicalities were more important than principles. Played by Jessica Walters. (SPIDER)

Vree

An alien race and member of the League of Non-Aligned Worlds. In 2258, the Vree threatened to attack Babylon 5 unless the station placed Jha'dur into their custody. They are famed for their unsavory eating habits. (DEATHWALKER)

W

Wallace (Commander)
Earthforce investigator sent to Babylon 5 in 2259 to investigate the murder of J. D. Ortega and Susan Ivanova's involvement with the Free Mars movement. Wallace was later arrested for the suspected murder of his colleague, Lieutenant Khatib. (ACCUSATIONS)

Wallace, Tonia
ISN reporter assigned to cover Operation : Sudden Death in 2259. (GROPOS)

War Council
Established in 2260 to allow its members to share information and strategies during the Shadow War. Initially, the War Council comprised Captain Sheridan, Ambassador Delenn, Commander Ivanova, Security Chief Garibaldi and Dr. Franklin. Sheridan also reserved a place for the Ranger stationed on Babylon 5. (MATTERS)

Welch, Lou
Security officer Lou Welch started working on Babylon 5 when it went on-line in 2256. Asked if he enjoyed working there, he once said that it was better than a kick in the teeth. (EYES)

Welch had a lot of time and respect for Security Chief Garibaldi. When he arrested Garibaldi's would-be assassin,

Jack, in 2259, Welch asked Captain Sheridan if he wanted the suspect beaten up before they threw him in the brig. Sheridan declined the offer, but commended Welch for his enthusiasm (REVELATIONS). Welch was keen for Garibaldi to resume his post as the station's security chief and told him that things weren't the same without him. He even resisted the temptation to eat the cake the security staff had bought for Garibaldi until the chief returned to active duty (GEOMETRY).

Later in the year, Welch fell victim to Matt Stoner's empathic powers not once but twice: first, the security officer was convinced to give the prisoner his meal a few hours early; and then he prepared a transport for him to leave the station on. Fortunately, Garibaldi stopped Welch from unwittingly aiding Stoner. (MATES)

Played by David Crowley.

Welles (Mr.)

A senior member of the Nightwatch, Mr. Welles accompanied Frederick Lantz during his visit to Babylon 5 in 2259. During a meeting with the station's Nightwatch members, Welles learned that a shopkeeper, Xavier Darabuto, had been complaining about new import regulations and subsequently had Darabuto's shop on the Zocalo closed by authority of the Nightwatch. He later invited Commander Ivanova to join the organization, claiming that the Nightwatch could help her take command of a starship sooner than she imagined. Although she angrily declined the offer, Welles said that it was still open. When a member of Nightwatch told him that Captain Sheridan was sheltering a Narn cruiser, Welles immediately informed the Centauri. Played by John Vickery. (FALL)

Wellington, Ombuds

One of the magistrates aboard Babylon 5, Ombuds Wellington believed that his colleague, Ombuds Zimmerman, dealt with the more straightforward cases while he was always lumbered with the weird ones. Wellington almost became a victim of Deuce's Na'ka'leen feeder, but was saved by Aldous Gajic and a security squad. Played by Jim Norton. (GRAIL)

White Star, The
Earth-registered liner which brought Rabbi Koslov and Walker Smith to Babylon 5 in 2258. (TKO)

White Star, The
A revolutionary Minbari warship, the *White Star* incorporates both Minbari and Vorlon technology. In 2260, Captain Sheridan took command of the ship in order to fight in the Shadow War.

Neither the Grey Council nor the Earth Alliance were informed about the *White Star*'s construction. It is staffed by members of the religious caste, many of whom helped to design and build the craft. Because the crew cannot speak English, Lennier acts as a liaison between Sheridan and his crew. The *White Star* has artificial gravity and, despite being relatively small, can make its own jumppoint.

The crew enjoyed their first victory when the *White Star* was used to rescue the Rangers on Zagros 7 from the Centauri blockade and also destroyed a Shadow ship. (MATTERS)

Wind Swords, The
The Wind Swords form the most militant Minbari warrior caste. Following the Dilgar Invasion, they sheltered the infamous war criminal Jha'dur in return for her services. As a result, the Wind Swords provided the Grey Council with weapons created by Jha'dur at the beginning of the Earth–Minbari War.

The Wind Swords are aware of the "hole" in Commander Sinclair's mind and tried to frame him for the murder of Ambassador Kosh in 2257. According to Jha'dur, they feared Sinclair but believed that he had a sentimental streak. (DEATHWALKER)

Winters, Talia
A Psi Corps commercial telepath assigned to Babylon 5 in 2258 and recalled to Earth in mysterious circumstances the following year.

Talia Winters was raised by Psi Corps from the age of five and never knew her mother or father (RACE). During her first year at a Psi Corps center, she was cared for by a senior telepath, Abby. Talia cried throughout her first day at the

Academy, until Abby held her and scanned her lightly to create a warm and safe place in the five-year-old's mind. Talia then stopped crying (SPIDER).

During her first year at the Psi Corps Academy, Talia was assigned to a senior trainee, Matt Stoner. She thought that he was charming, sympathetic and made the transition easier. When they were found to be "genetically compatible," Talia and Stoner were married by the Corps. The relationship was short-lived, as Stoner mysteriously left the Corps shortly after the wedding and the marriage was annulled (MATES). While at the Academy, Talia also worked with Lyta Alexander during a six-month intern program, and the pair became friends (DIVIDED). Talia's teachers at the Psi Corps Academy included Jason Ironheart. Ironheart was the perfect model of what Talia wanted to be in the Corps, and he became her lover.

Besides her instruction as a commercial telepath, Talia also trained in criminal cases (MERCY). She was rated a P5 by Psi Corps, but was extremely disappointed when she failed her telekinetic test. She tried for days, but just couldn't move her old penny (MIND).

In 2254, Talia had the most frightening experience of her life when she scanned the mind of a serial killer on the Mars Colony (DEATHWALKER, MERCY). In 2258, her experience was recorded by Abbut for Ambassador Kosh, who wanted to see how her mind functioned and how she reacted to fear (DEATHWALKER).

It was around this time that Talia was experimented upon at the classified Psi Corps intelligence and training operation in Syria Planum and had an alternate personality planted into her subconscious. (SILENT)

When Talia first arrived on Babylon 5 in 2258, she was upset by the way Lieutenant-Commander Ivanova took an instant dislike to her. After the pair clashed over the future of an unregistered telepath, Alisa Beldon, they slowly began to build a friendship (LEGACIES). Talia was also briefly involved sexually with Ivanova.

Talia was initially uncomfortable with Security Chief Garibaldi's amorous intentions (MIND, MIDNIGHT). She once claimed that he was always waiting in the transport tube for her. However, as time went on, the relationship between the pair slowly improved (VOICE I).

As a member of the Psi Corps, Talia refused to break the organization's rules or to even twist the letter of the law to change their intent (Z'HA'DUM). Consequently, when the Corps was unable to provide a substitute telepath, she had to scan the mind of a psychotic killer, Karl Edward Mueller. Talia later said he was the most inhuman being she had ever scanned (MERCY).

During her two years aboard the station, a series of events made Talia reconsider her allegiance to Psi Corps. When the rogue telepath Jason Ironheart visited Talia on the station in 2258, he warned her that the Corps was performing illegal experiments and had seized control of Earth from within. As he transformed into a higher being, Ironheart gave her an unspecified gift. At first, it involved telekinetic powers and allowed her to move a penny, but continued to develop over time. (MIND)

The following year, Talia was kidnapped by members of an underground railroad of unregistered telepaths who convinced her that it was time to start resisting the Corps. She then joined forces with the group to send a telepathic projection into Bester's mind which convinced the Psi Cop that he had killed all the members of the group with Talia's help. The leader of the group later told Talia that they shouldn't have been able to fool a Psi Cop with such a projection and that it only worked because of her gift from Jason Ironheart. When Talia asked him what she was becoming, he replied, "the future." She also realized that Bester was no longer able to scan her.

Once Bester had left the station, Talia told Ivanova that she was right about the Corps and the pair developed a close and intimate relationship. (RACE)

Shortly after, Talia's ex-husband Matt Stoner visited Babylon 5 and claimed that he had lost his telepathic powers and been expelled by the Corps. When Stoner said that he knew how to erase Talia's telepathic abilities, she decided to accept his offer of a new life together. However, thanks to Garibaldi, she later learned that Stoner had been transformed into an empath and had actually been sent by the Corps to win Talia over in the hope that they would one day have empathic children together. (MATES)

During an official internal investigation led by Captain

Sheridan and rogue telepath Lyta Alexander, Talia Winters'
Psi Corps-induced alternate personality was activated. It killed
a security guard and tried to murder Lyta Alexander twice.
Once her secret was exposed, Talia Winters was sent back to
Earth. (DIVIDED)

   Talia always drank tea to soothe her nerves. (SPIDER)

   Played by Andrea Thompson.

"Working Without a Diet"
A treatise written by the renowned 20th-century author
Harlan Ellison. Commander Ivanova thought that it was hilar-
ious. (TKO)

X

XB7 Tracking Unit
Scanning device used by the Earth Alliance during the Earth–Minbari War and by Babylon 5. The XB7 Tracking Unit is unable to overcome Minbari stealth technology. (DEPARTURE)

Xon
A sentient race that once coexisted on Centauri Prime with the Centauri. The two races constantly battled each other until the Xon were annihilated. The Xon are remembered at the end of every year by the Centauri, who hold an annual religious celebration in which they count the number of dead Xon and thank the gods for their good fortune. (PARLIAMENT)

Y

Yang
An enforcer for AreTech who murdered J. D. Ortega, Yang was killed by Lieutenant Khatib to keep the existence of supermorbidium a secret. (ACCUSATIONS)

Yang (Private)
A young GROPOS befriended by Private Large. Yang had only been with the service for a few months when he was killed during Operation : Sudden Death in 2259. Played by Art Chudabala. (GROPOS)

Yedor
The capital of Minbar and site of an Earth Alliance embassy. (TREASON)

Yellow Sector
Yellow Sector encompasses all of Babylon 5's nonrotating sectors. It houses the station's zero-gravity cargo bays and its fusion engines.

Yogtree
Fried tree worm, served as a delicacy. Walker Smith seemed to enjoy it until he learned what it was made of. (TKO)

Z

Zagros 7

A Drazi colony situated on the edge of Centauri space. In 2259, Zagros 7 became the site of a Ranger training camp. The following year, it was blockaded by the Centauri in preparation for the Shadows' arrival. Marcus Cole managed to break the blockade to travel to Babylon 5, where he sought the assistance of Captain Sheridan and Ambassador Delenn. Sheridan then used the *White Star* to break the blockade long enough for the Rangers to escape from the colony. They did so just as the first Shadow ship entered the area. (MATTERS)

Zathras

An alien of unknown origin who suddenly appeared in Babylon 4's conference room in a flash of light, just as the station became lost in time. Zathras told the station's staff that his comrades needed Babylon 4 to use as a base of operations in a Great War against the forces of darkness.

When Babylon 4 temporarily became stable in 2258, Zathras explained that his leader, The One, had stopped the station to allow its crew to disembark. Zathras warned The One about the pain, but he was willing to risk his life for the crew. When The One appeared on the station, Zathras gave him his time stabilizer to allow him to survive the time shifts.

Although Zathras didn't want to die, he said that he would sacrifice himself if it was necessary. He hoped that if he died for his cause or for The One, he would become a hero and that his comrades would build a statue of Zathras.

When Major Krantz demanded to know what year he came from, Zathras revealed that his year is 4993. Unfortunately, he didn't know how to convert this to a human time scale and admitted that mathematics were not one of his skills.

Despite Zathras' warnings that he would die if he left Babylon 4 in 2258, Major Krantz insisted that he accompany them. However, just as the group were leaving, the alien became trapped under a piece of falling masonry. When Commander Sinclair tried to rescue him, Zathras told him to leave the station while he could because he had a destiny to fulfill. Zathras was unsurprised when The One (apparently a warweary Jeffrey Sinclair) came to his aid. (SQUARED)

Prior to, or perhaps after, his experience on Babylon 4, Zathras lived on Epsilon 3. (TWILIGHT)

Played by Tim Choate.

Zen Garden, The

Small Japanese stone garden situated in Red Sector. (GATHERING)

Zento, Orin

Earth's finest labor negotiator, Orin Zento had successfully prevented and stopped a number of strikes on many Earth Alliance worlds and outposts.

In 2258, Zento was dispatched to Babylon 5 to settle the dock workers' illegal strike. He blamed Commander Sinclair for letting their dispute escalate and, with the Senate's approval, invoked the Rush Act when the dockers refused to go back to work. Believing that Sinclair intended to settle the dispute by force, Zento promised to give him full support in any action he took. Thus he was humiliated when Sinclair chose to reallocate 1.3 million credits from Babylon 5's military budget to meet the dockers' demands. Played by John Snyder. (MEANS)

Zestus

Planet renowned for its waitresses. (TKO)

Zeta Squad
Babylon 5's newest Starfury squadron, Zeta Squad was personally delivered by President Santiago in 2258. A number of the
station's crew felt that Zeta Squad should have been provided
two years earlier. Also known as Zeta Wing. (SURVIVORS)

Zeta Wing
See **Zeta Squad**

Z'ha'dum
A dead planet situated on the Rim, Z'ha'dum was once the
base of operations for the Shadows. However, the planet's ancient population was not extinct, but lay dormant following
the Great War in the mid-13th century. A thousand years
later, the Shadows began to rebuild their forces on Z'ha'dum.

In 2257, the *Icarus* landed on the planet and its crew encountered the Shadows. The ship was destroyed and those
who would not serve them were killed. In this way, the Shadows enlisted some new slaves, including Morden. Two years
later, a Narn military ship sent to investigate the planet was
destroyed by the Shadows, who had been warned of its arrival
by Ambassador Mollari, via Morden. (REVELATIONS)

When Captain Sheridan learned that his wife Anna had
been killed by the Shadows, he told Ambassador Kosh that he
would one day go to Z'ha'dum. Although the Vorlon warned
him that if he did travel there, he would not live to tell the
tale, Sheridan replied that he would go down fighting.
(Z'HA'DUM)

Zhalan
Delenn's flyer. (ALONE)

Zimmerman (Ombuds)
One of Babylon 5's magistrates. According to Ombuds Wellington, Zimmerman always managed to escape the station's
more unusual cases. (GRAIL)

Zocalo, The
Babylon 5's marketplace, situated in Red Sector.

Zoful
A Minbari liner. (CONVICTIONS)

Zoog
A Centauri god whose divinity is highly debatable. While Ambassador Mollari believes that Zoog should be a god, his diplomatic attaché, Vir Kotto, disagrees entirely. (CHRYSALIS)

APPENDIX I
Timeline of Important Events in the Babylon 5 Universe

10,000,000 BC +
The Shadows are alone in the universe.

The First Ones evolve. They explore the universe, build great empires and "help" the younger races who emerge.

Several battles take place between the First Ones and the Shadows.

1250 (Approx)
An alliance of worlds, including the last remaining First Ones and the Minbari, defeats the Shadows in the Great War. After the war, the last remaining First Ones disappear—all except the Vorlons.

1750 (Approx)
Varn becomes custodian of Epsilon 3.

2100 (Approx)
Mars is colonized by Earth.

EarthGov proves the existence of telepaths and starts to regulate their activities. The Psi Corps is subsequently established to implement government policy.

Narn is conquered by the Centauri Republic.

2150 (Approx)
Earth makes contact with the Centauri and learns that their Republic is rapidly declining.

2228
The Centauri withdraw from Narn.

2230
The Earth Alliance joins the non-aligned worlds' war with the Dilgar.

2242
The Minbari make first contact with Earth. The human captain misinterprets their intentions and opens fire. Consequently, war breaks out between the two worlds.

2248
On the verge of victory, the Minbari surrender to Earth.

2249
Earth Alliance President Luis Santiago launches the Babylon Project to avoid another war based on misunderstanding. The first three stations are sabotaged during construction and have to be abandoned.

2250 (Approx)
The Shadows slowly reawaken and begin to build their forces on Z'ha'dum.

2254
Babylon 4 goes on-line. It mysteriously disappears exactly 24 hours later.

2256
Babylon 5 goes on-line.

2257

The Vorlons almost declare war on Earth when Babylon 5's commander, Jeffrey Sinclair, is accused of attempting to kill their ambassador. When Sinclair proves his innocence, all hostilities cease.

2258

The crew of Babylon 5 discovers that Epsilon 3 was once the home of a highly advanced civilization.

Free Mars leads a rebellion against the Earth-appointed government which is later quelled by Earth troops.

2259

War breaks out between the Narn and Centauri. The Narn are defeated and the Centauri begin to seize control of Drazi and Pak'ma'ra territories.

Earth signs a non-aggression treaty with the Centauri.

APPENDIX II
Story Guide

Story arc follows the series' overarching storyline.
Points of interest include continuity references, unanswered
questions and conjecture about the meaning and significance
of certain events.

PILOT

The Gathering
(GATHERING)
Written by J. Michael Straczynski

Babylon 5's command crew eagerly await the arrival of the
Vorlon ambassador, Kosh Naranek. However, Kosh is almost
killed by an unknown assailant shortly after boarding the station and is found dying after the attack.

Commander Sinclair disobeys the requests of the Vorlon
Empire and orders Dr. Kyle to open Kosh's encounter suit
and do whatever he can to save his life. Things go from bad to
worse when Dr. Kyle and Lieutenant-Commander Takashima
convince Lyta Alexander to perform an unauthorized scan on
Kosh to learn more about the assault. During the scan, she
learns that Sinclair had attacked Kosh and, as a result, the
commander faces extradition to the Vorlon homeworld for
trial.

Security Chief Garibaldi fights to clear Sinclair's name and eventually discovers that the real assassin was a member of a militant Minbari warrior clan, who posed as the station's commander using a Changeling Net. When they learn the truth, the Vorlons drop all charges against Sinclair while Kosh is saved by the information gained by Lyta.

Thanks to Ambassador Delenn, Sinclair learns that Ambassador G'Kar was involved in the conspiracy against Kosh. The Narn had hoped to frame the Earth Alliance and the Centauri Republic for the attack in the hope that it would lead to a Narn–Vorlon or a Narn–Minbari alliance. Sinclair warns G'Kar not to endanger the safety of the station again.

Story arc: Babylon 5 becomes fully operational with the arrival of the mysterious Vorlon Ambassador Kosh Naranek. But what does he look like inside his encounter suit? What exactly are the Vorlons hiding?

Sinclair becomes suspicious about his missing 24 hours during the Battle of the Line when the Minbari assassin refers to the "hole" in his mind. What happened to Sinclair? And why did the Minbari surrender during the Earth–Minbari War when they were on the verge of victory?

SEASON ONE

Signs and Portents

Commander Sinclair fights to protect interstellar peace and begins a more personal search to unlock the secret of his missing 24 hours during the Battle of the Line. Ambassador Mollari joins forces with a mysterious race known as the Shadows and decides that the time has come for the Centauri Republic to reclaim its lost empire, while Ambassador Delenn prepares the cataclysmic events that lie ahead.

Midnight on the Firing Line
(MIDNIGHT)
Written by J. Michael Straczynski

The Narn Regime attacks and conquers Ragesh 3, a Centauri agricultural colony. When Ambassador Mollari is told that the

Centauri are unwilling to retaliate, he attempts to rally the support of the Babylon 5 Advisory Council. However, his case is undermined when Ambassador G'Kar displays a message recorded by the Centauri Ambassador's nephew, Carn Mollari, who claims that the colony asked the Narns to liberate them from Centauri rule. When the Council refuses to intervene, Mollari attempts to kill G'Kar, but is stopped by Security Chief Garibaldi.

Garibaldi investigates a series of Raider attacks on supply ships and successfully manages to predict what their next target will be. When Commander Sinclair mounts a rescue effort, he captures the leaders of the Raiders group and their Narn liaison, who has evidence that Ragesh 3 was invaded, rather than liberated, by the Narn Regime. Faced with the prospect of intervention by the Babylon 5 Advisory Council, Ambassador G'Kar tells his people that they must withdraw from the colony.

Psi Corps telepath Talia Winters assumes her position on the station and tries to learn why Lieutenant-Commander Susan Ivanova seems to have taken an instant dislike to her. Ivanova later tells her that she doubts they could ever be friends.

Story arc: "Midnight on the Firing Line" establishes the hatred between the Narn and Centauri. Each race would love to annihilate the other. Alone, the present Centauri leadership are both unwilling and unable to stand up to growing Narn aggression.

Earth Alliance President Luis Santiago wins his third term in office while Talia and Ivanova's friendship gets off to a bad start. Ambassador Mollari tells Sinclair about a vision of his own death, in which he and G'Kar kill each other in 2278.

Soul Hunter
(SOUL)
Written by J. Michael Straczynski

The arrival of a Soul Hunter on Babylon 5 strikes terror into the hearts of its alien population. However, unlike the other members of his species, the Soul Hunter is no longer content to wait for death and actually kills his victims in order to steal their souls. When he sees Ambassador Delenn, he decides that she will be his next victim.

With the help of a second Soul Hunter who arrives on Babylon 5 on the trail of his "deranged" brother, Commander Sinclair saves Delenn's life and is forced to kill the Soul Hunter in an act of self-defense. Later, Delenn releases his collection of souls.

Story arc: The Minbari believe that souls of each generation are reincarnated into the next. Delenn is revealed to be a member of the Minbari Grey Council and later tells Sinclair that "we were right about you."

Points of interest: The Soul Hunter looks into Delenn's soul and is shocked by what she is planning to do. He also learns that Sinclair is being used by the Minbari.

Born to the Purple
(PURPLE)
Written by Lawrence G. DiTillio

Ambassador Mollari falls in love with a Centauri dancer, Adira Tyree, unaware that she has been ordered by her master, Trakis, to steal his Purple Files. When she claims the files but betrays Trakis, Mollari teams up with Commander Sinclair to find her. Unfortunately, Londo is unaware that he has been bugged and Trakis gets to Adira before they do. However, he is caught and arrested when he tries to sell the files to Ambassador G'Kar. Adira expresses her regrets to the Centauri ambassador and leaves Babylon 5 for Davo.

As Mollari fights to save his Republic and career, Security Chief Garibaldi tries to discover who is making illegal use of the Gold Channel. When he learns that Commander Ivanova is using the top-priority channel to communicate with her dying father, Garibaldi decides to turn a blind eye and invites her to join him for a drink.

Points of interest: Ivanova declines Garibaldi's offer of a drink, but later takes it up in "Eyes."

Infection
(INFECTION)
Written by J. Michael Straczynski

Dr. Vance Hendricks, a former teacher of Dr. Franklin, arrives on Babylon 5 with artifacts from Ikaara 7. One of them is unintentionally activated by his assistant, Nelson Drake, who is assimilated by the device and becomes a bio-organic killing machine programmed to kill anything that isn't pure Ikaaran. Commander Sinclair tries to reason with his machine's central programming and forces it to accept that Ikaara 7 is an extinct world. Then the machine releases Drake. Later, both he and Hendricks are brought to justice.

Following his encounter with the Ikaaran killing machine, Sinclair feels confident enough to face the camera for an ISN interview.

Points of interest: At the end of the episode, Earthforce Defense Bio-Weapons Division confiscates the Ikaaran weapons.

The Parliament of Dreams
(PARLIAMENT)
Written by J. Michael Straczynski

To help promote peace and understanding, Babylon 5 holds a week-long religious festival. During the festivities, Commander Sinclair rekindles his romance with Catherine Sakai and Ambassador G'Kar is stalked by Tu'Pari of the Thenta Makur. With the help of his new aide, Na'Toth, G'Kar manages to overcome the assassin and sets him up for his colleagues.

Points of interest: According to Catherine Sakai, the Minbari religious ceremony held on the station is a rebirth ceremony which can double as a wedding. While most viewers wondered if Sinclair had married Delenn, they missed the reference to her impending rebirth.

Mind War
(MIND)
Written by J. Michael Straczynski

Psi Cops Bester and Kelsey arrive on Babylon 5 in pursuit of Jason Ironheart. Ironheart later meets with his ex-lover, Talia Winters, and tells her that he is moving toward a higher plane of existence as the result of Psi Corps experiments.

Talia and Commander Sinclair help Ironheart leave the station before he transforms into a noncorporeal being. When Kelsey is killed in the escape, Bester is persuaded to support Sinclair's official explanation that Ironheart was killed when his ship exploded as he left the station.

Catherine Sakai ignores Ambassador G'Kar's warning and travels to Sigma 957 on a survey mission. Her ship is disabled when she encounters an unidentified ship above the planet, but she is subsequently saved from certain death by a Narn cruiser dispatched by G'Kar.

Story arc: Jason Ironheart reveals that the Psi Corps is taking over Earth and gives Talia Winters an unspecified gift, which initially gives her telekinetic powers. Catherine Sakai encounters an advanced form of life in Sigma 957.

The War Prayer
(PRAYER)
Written by D.C. Fontana

A series of anti-alien attacks organized by a pro-Earth group, the Homeguard, take place on Babylon 5. Lieutenant-Commander Ivanova is shocked to learn that her ex-lover, Malcolm Biggs, is the leader of the Homeguard cell on the station and helps Commander Sinclair infiltrate the group. The pair learn that they intend to assassinate the four alien ambassadors, which will act as a signal to their colleagues to kill all alien emissaries on Earth. They have the cell arrested and returned to Earth for trial.

Ambassador Mollari and Vir Kotto argue over the future of two love-struck Centauri, Kiron Maray and Aria Tensus, who refuse to participate in their arranged marriages. When Kiron is almost killed during a Homeguard attack, Mollari arranges for them to be fostered by his cousin, Andilo, until they reach adult age and can choose whom they marry.

Story arc: "The War Prayer" introduces the Homeguard, a fanatical pro-Earth group, and illustrates the anti-alien feeling which is growing on Earth.

And the Sky Full of Stars
(SKY)
Written by J. Michael Straczynski

Commander Sinclair is kidnapped and placed into a Virtual Reality Cybernet by Knight One and Knight Two. Knight Two reveals that they are members of a secret organization on Earth and have been sent to Babylon 5 to prove that Sinclair betrayed Earth during the Battle of the Line. As Security Chief Garibaldi and his security staff search for the missing commander, Sinclair remembers that he was taken aboard a Minbari warship during the battle and interrogated, tortured and scanned by the Grey Council.

Eventually, he manages to escape from the Cybernet and overloads Knight Two's brain in the process. In a drug-induced frenzy, Sinclair runs amok on the station until he is calmed down by Ambassador Delenn. As he recovers from the experience, Sinclair becomes determined to solve the mystery of what happened to him when he faced the Grey Council.

Story arc: Sinclair learns that he was kidnapped, interrogated and scanned by the Grey Council (including Delenn) during the Battle of the Line. He becomes determined to discover what exactly happened when he was aboard their cruiser and why they decided to free him. Ambassador Delenn is under orders to kill Sinclair if he remembers what happened to him.

Deathwalker
(DEATHWALKER)
Written by Lawrence G. DiTillio

Jha'dur, the notorious war criminal also known as Death-walker, comes aboard Babylon 5 to sell her universal anti-agapic to the highest bidder. When she is discovered, Commander Sinclair is ordered to return her to Earth, but is stopped by the League of Non-Aligned Worlds, who demand that she stands trial for war crimes.

Babylon 5 looks set to erupt into a war-zone when the Advisory Council votes against making Jha'dur stand trial, until Sinclair and the League agree to send her to Earth to develop her serum with human and Non-Aligned World scientists. Once she has completed her task, Jha'dur will then stand trial.

Before she leaves the station, Jha'dur tells Sinclair that the key ingredient of her serum must come from another living being and that it cannot be synthesized. Thus her monument to the galaxy will be a bloodlust for immortality. As her ship heads for Earth, it is destroyed by the Vorlons. When he is asked why they did it, Ambassador Kosh replies, "You are not ready for immortality."

Kosh also hires Talia Winters to supervise some seemingly nonsensical negotiations with a strange man named Abbut. Talia later learns that Abbut is a Vicker hired by Kosh to probe her mind and record what scares her and how she reacts to surprise.

Story arc: Ambassador Kosh gains a recording of Talia's mind for "the future."

Points of interest: When the Vorlons attack Jha'dur's ship, they destroy it with their second shot. Did they miss first time or were they aiming for something else—like a cloaked Shadow vessel? If they were, does that mean that the Shadows are in league with the militant Minbari warrior caste that sheltered Jha'dur, the Wind Swords?

Believers
(BELIEVERS)
Written by David Gerrold

Dr. Franklin is asked to examine a young alien, Shon, dying of a congestive blockage in the upper air passage, and tells the boy's parents, M'ola and Tharg, that their son can be cured by a straightforward surgical procedure. However, his proposal outrages the parents, who believe that if Shon is operated on he will lose his soul.

As the boy draws closer to death, Franklin becomes convinced that they will abandon their religious beliefs and ask him to perform the operation. When it becomes clear that they won't, Franklin asks Commander Sinclair to suspend their parental authority. When Shon tells Sinclair that he wants to live but doesn't want to lose his soul in the operation, he decides he cannot support the doctor. Shon will be allowed to die.

However, Franklin cannot watch as the boy's condition deteriorates and decides to perform the operation anyway. Although it cures Shon, his parents believe that their son has lost his soul, and kill him.

Meanwhile, Commander Ivanova successfully saves a starliner, the *Asimov*, from a Raiders attack.

Survivors
(SURVIVORS)
Written by Mark Scott Zicree

Major Lianna Kemmer arrives on Babylon 5 to supervise security arrangements for the president's visit. Kemmer blames Garibaldi for the death of her father, Frank, and seizes the opportunity to disgrace the station's security chief when he is framed for planting a bomb which claimed the life of a member of staff.

Garibaldi evades arrest and becomes a fugitive to try to find out who the real culprit was. As the pressure mounts, Garibaldi finds solace in a bottle until he eventually realizes that Kemmer's assistant, Cutter, is a member of the Homeguard and had framed him so that he could sabotage the president's visit. With just seconds to spare, Kemmer and Garibaldi stop Cutter from destroying the station's cobra bays and make up their differences.

Story arc: President Santiago's support for Babylon 5 and desire to forge greater ties between Earth and alien races undermine his popularity at home, especially with the Homeguard.

By Any Means Necessary
(MEANS)
Written by Kathryn Drennan

An accident in one of Babylon 5's docking bays claims the life of a docker, Alberto Delvientos, and pushes the station's dock workers toward starting an illegal strike. When Sinclair's negotiation attempts fail, the Senate sends one of their finest negotiators, Orin Zento, to mediate the dispute. When he fails to convince the dockers to return to work, Zento invokes the Rush Act, empowering the station's commanding officer to use "any means necessary" to end the strike. However, Sinclair chooses not to use force to end the strike and instead reallocates 1.3 million credits from the station's military budget to meet the dockers' demands.

Meanwhile, Ambassador G'Kar fights to find a G'Quan Eth plant to replace the one that was destroyed in the accident. G'Kar desperately needs the plant for an imminent religious ceremony which is supposed to take place when the sun touches the G'Quan Mountains on the Narn homeworld, and is shocked to learn that the only other one aboard the station is owned by Ambassador Mollari. The Centauri gloats as G'Kar attempts to negotiate for the plant and refuses to give it to him until an hour after the religious ceremony was due to take place. However, Sinclair convinces G'Kar that he can still hold the ceremony because of the time it takes for sunlight to travel through space.

Points of interest: Londo refuses to give G'Kar his G'Quan Eth plant as an act of revenge for the Narns' treatment of Carn Mollari in "Midnight on the Firing Line."

Signs and Portents
(SIGNS)
Written by J. Michael Straczynski

As Raiders attacks draw closer to Babylon 5, the command staff prepares for defensive action. Commander Sinclair, still troubled by the mystery surrounding what happened to him during the Battle of the Line, also asks Security Chief Garibaldi to see if he can shed any light on the matter.

Ambassador Mollari gains possession of the Eye, the oldest symbol of Centauri nobility. Lord Kiro, a descendant of the first emperor, arrives on the station to reclaim the artifact and is accompanied by his aunt, Lady Ladira, who has a vision of the destruction of Babylon 5.

A mysterious human named Morden meets each of the four alien ambassadors on the station to ask them a single question: "What do you want?" G'Kar replies that he would like to see the Centauri defeated and would ultimately desire justice for his people, while Delenn and Kosh both dismiss him without answering his question. Only Mollari's desire to reclaim the glory of the past strikes a chord with Morden.

Later, the leader of the Raiders arrives on Babylon 5 and ambushes Ambassador Mollari, Lord Kiro and Lady Ladira. He then steals the Eye and uses Kiro as a hostage to leave the station. In the battle which follows, most of the Raiders' craft are destroyed but their main vessel, the Raiders' wagon, manages to escape with both Kiro and the Eye. Although Kiro had planned the theft with the Raiders and intended to use the Eye to seize the Centauri throne, he finds that he has been double-crossed by the Raiders. Just as he learns of their treachery, the Raiders' wagon is attacked and destroyed by the Shadows. Shortly after, the Shadows' emissary, Morden, meets Londo and returns the Eye to him.

Later, Sinclair learns from Garibaldi that the Minbari insisted that he was appointed as commander of Babylon 5. Before leaving, he is shown a vision of the station's destruction by Lady Ladira.

Story arc: "Signs and Portents" introduces the Shadows and their human emissary, Morden, who befriends Ambassador Londo by saving him from disgrace. Sinclair learns that the Minbari insisted he was appointed as commander of Babylon 5 and that the station is doomed to destruction.

TKO
(TKO)
Written by Lawrence G. DiTillio

Two very different visitors board Babylon 5: professional boxer-turned-prizefighter Walker Smith and Rabbi Yossel Koslov. Smith intends to become the first human to compete in the Mutai, a no-rules alien combat contest, while Koslov hopes to convince Commander Ivanova to sit shivah for her late father.

Smith is initially refused entry into the Mutai by the Muta-Do, but successfully challenges the champion of the Mutai, Sho'Rin Gyor, with the help of Caliban, a weary Mutari. Smith and Gyor fight a bloody match and Smith wins on points. The Muta-Do declares that humans are now welcome to fight in the Mutai.

After a great deal of persuasion, Ivanova agrees to sit shivah for her father and releases her anger and grief over his life and death.

Grail
(GRAIL)
Written by Christy Marx

Aldous Gajic, the sole member of a holy order committed to finding the Holy Grail, arrives on Babylon 5 to discuss his quest with the alien ambassadors. Shortly after arriving, he is pickpocketed by Jinxo, a petty thief and former construction worker who has run into heavy debt with the crimelord Deuce, who is using a Na'ka'leen feeder to brainwipe his enemies.

When Security Chief Garibaldi catches Jinxo pick-pocketing Aldous, he is sent before Ombuds Wellington, who bans him from the station. However, Jinxo tells the Ombuds that he can't leave the station and begs for another punishment. Upon hearing his pleas, Aldous takes the man into his custody.

Aldous and Jinxo develop a close friendship while they interview the alien ambassadors about the Holy Grail. Consequently, when Deuce's henchmen abduct Aldous and

Ombuds Wellington to give them to the feeder, Jinxo seeks
Commander Sinclair's assistance. Together with a security
team, Sinclair and Garibaldi mount an assault on Deuce's
lair. During the shoot-out, Aldous sacrifices his life to save
Jinxo. Just before the holy man dies, Jinxo agrees to take up
his quest for the Holy Grail.

Eyes
(EYES)
Written by Lawrence G. DiTillio

Colonel Ari Ben Zayne and Psi Corps military specialist Harriman Gray arrive on Babylon 5 to evaluate the loyalty of the
station's command staff. Ben Zayne appoints Security Chief
Garibaldi as his assistant and says that each of the command
staff will be telepathically scanned. Lieutenant-Commander
Ivanova refuses to be scanned and offers to resign, but Sinclair
studies Earthforce regulations and learns that Ben Zayne cannot order scans on an officer unless he or she faces specific
charges. When Sinclair uses this against the colonel, Ben
Zayne accuses him of working against the interests of Earth
and assumes command of Babylon 5.

Garibaldi learns that Zayne is a close friend of the Psi Cop
Bester and is jealous of Sinclair's appointment as commander
of the station. When Sinclair faces interrogation, he tells
Gray to scan Ben Zayne and the telepath learns that he is deranged
and acting out of vengeance. Garibaldi arrests him and Sinclair resumes command of the station.

Meanwhile, Lennier offers to help Garibaldi with one of
his pet projects, the construction of an antique Kawasaki
Ninja ZX-11 motorcycle. Garibaldi is initially annoyed when
he discovers that the good-hearted Minbari has managed to
build the bike on his own, but then offers to take him on a
ride down the station's central corridor.

Points of interest: The tension between Earth and the Mars
Colony is reaching breaking point. Ivanova asks for the drink
that Garibaldi offered her in "Born to the Purple." Harriman
Gray is shocked when Ivanova senses that he is lightly scanning her and suspects, just for a second, that she might have
telepathic ability.

Legacies
(LEGACIES)

Written by D.C. Fontana

A Minbari warcruiser arrives at Babylon 5, carrying the body of the war hero Branmer. When his body goes missing, Neroon threatens to launch another war against Earth. Commander Sinclair and Security Chief Garibaldi lead a desperate search for the body before Neroon's threats lead to bloodshed.

Meanwhile, Talia Winters and Lieutenant-Commander Ivanova argue over the future of a 14-year-old telepath, Alisa Beldon. While Talia wants her to join the Psi Corps, Ivanova is determined to find another option. First she arranges a meeting between Alisa and the Narn diplomatic attaché Na'Toth. When Alisa turns down her offer to live on Narn, she then discusses her situation with Ambassador Delenn. As the diplomat outlines how the Minbari treat their telepaths, Alisa accidentally scans her mind and learns that she was involved in stealing Branmer's body.

Sinclair confronts Delenn, who tells him that Branmer was a member of the religious caste and did not want his body to be displayed as a monument to war. Consequently, she stole and cremated his corpse. Delenn then tells Neroon the truth and orders him to support her explanation that Branmer's body was transformed to allow him to take his place with the gods.

Alisa Beldon decides to work as a telepath on Minbar. Before she leaves, Sinclair asks her if she saw anything else in Delenn's mind and she reveals that she sensed a word—"chrysalis."

Story arc: Many members of the Minbari warrior caste did not support the decision to end the war against Earth, and would love to participate in a rematch.

Points of interest: Alisa Beldon hints at Delenn's upcoming transformation. Ivanova and Talia agree to accept their differences and look set to become friends.

A Voice in the Wilderness, Part I
(VOICE I)
Written by J. Michael Straczynski

Epsilon 3 suddenly begins to show signs of life. When a shuttle sent to investigate comes under attack from a highly advanced defense system, the command staff begins to suspect that the supposedly uninhabited planet was once the home of a highly advanced civilization based five miles beneath the surface.

Meanwhile, Garibaldi desperately tries to contact his old girlfriend, Lise Hampton, to see if she has survived the Mars Rebellion and Ambassador Delenn is visited by her old friend and mentor, Draal. While aboard the station, Draal has a vision of a dying alien asking for help and later learns that Ambassador Mollari and Commander Sinclair both had a similar experience.

Sinclair and Lieutenant-Commander Ivanova travel to the planet while the Starfuries protect their craft from its defense system. Once inside the planet, the pair successfully overcome its booby traps and discover the incredibly advanced technology which controls the planet. They then find the planet's custodian, Varn. Varn asks for help and they take him back to the station . . .

A Voice in the Wilderness, Part II
(VOICE II)
Written by J. Michael Straczynski

Garibaldi is surprised by the arrival of the *Hyperion,* an Earthforce heavy cruiser commanded by Captain Ellis Pierce. Pierce tells Sinclair that the Earth Alliance wants first refusal of Epsilon 3's technology and has been sent to protect both the planet and Babylon 5 from any other alien race which intends to make a claim. When Pierce tries to send ships to the surface, they begin a chain reaction in the reactor core of the planet. Scans of the planet show that it will explode in 48 hours. In the process, it will destroy Babylon 5.

Varn is lying unconscious in a medlab when Draal hears his plea and rushes to his aid. Varn reveals that he is the last of a long-lost race and was entrusted to protect the planet's technology some 500 years ago.

Suddenly an alien warship appears. When the craft's captain, Takarn, claims the planet as the property of his people, Pierce threatens to fight them for control of the planet.

Londo meets with Delenn and Draal and the three realize that Varn is seeking a successor. They abduct him from the medlab and take a shuttle to the surface, with Garibaldi in pursuit. When Takarn opens fire at the craft, Pierce decides to strike against the ship and Sinclair orders Babylon 5 to aid the *Hyperion*.

Once on the surface, Draal assumes Varn's place as custodian of Epsilon 3. He orders Babylon 5 and the two warships to cease hostilities and warns them that any ship that tries to land on the planet will be destroyed. When Takarn ignores his warning and heads for the planet's surface, Draal fulfills his claim.

With Sinclair's help, Garibaldi communicates with Lise Hampton. He tells her that he still loves her, but is heartbroken to discover that she is married and expecting her first child.

Story arc: Epsilon 3 is revealed to be the home of a highly advanced technology.

Points of interest: Delenn says that she owes Londo a favor after the Centauri helped her and Draal travel to Epsilon 3. He takes her offer two years later in "A Day in the Strife."

Draal speculates that Varn chose the three people aboard Babylon 5 who best understood the principle of self-sacrifice. While Draal was willing to assume the role of custodian to save lives and Sinclair has repeatedly demonstrated his willingness to sacrifice his life for others, we have yet to see Londo Mollari make a truly noble sacrifice. Perhaps that is his only chance for redemption.

Babylon Squared
(SQUARED)
Written by J. Michael Straczynski

Babylon 5 responds to a distress signal from its predecessor, Babylon 4. Commander Sinclair leads an attempt to evacuate the station before it disappears again.

Once aboard the station, Sinclair learns that it has been trapped in a violent timewarp. He then has a vision of his own future, in which Babylon 5 is under attack from a seemingly invisible enemy. He learns that Garibaldi will put the station on self-destruct and lead its defense while he escapes. Later, Garibaldi has a similar experience when he recalls leaving Lise Hampton on the Mars Colony to assume his role as Babylon 5's security chief.

Sinclair is introduced to Zathras, an alien who has traveled from another time to help "The One" steal Babylon 4. The station will then be used by the forces of light in a catastrophic war against evil. Zathras also reveals that The One is stabilizing Babylon 4's movement through time long enough for the crew to leave. When Sinclair sees The One, he tries to aid the space-suited hero, but is thrust away from him by an unknown force.

Meanwhile, Delenn meets the Grey Council and learns that they have chosen her as the new Minbari leader. After a great deal of deliberation, she declines the offer. She tells them that she wishes to continue studying humanity and has a part to play in a prophecy.

As the final crewmembers leave the station, Zathras is caught under a piece of falling masonry. Sinclair tries to help him, but the alien tells him to leave the station while he can. Once Sinclair is gone, The One comes to Zathras' aid.

Babylon 4 reaches its destruction in time and The One removes his mask—and is none other than a war-scarred Sinclair. He tells Delenn that he failed to warn the others about the coming darkness.

Story arc: Babylon 4 is/will be stolen by Sinclair in the future to use as a base of operations in a war against the forces of darkness. Sinclair's allies will include Delenn. Sinclair also has a flash-forward in which Babylon 5 is set to self-destruct and Garibaldi mounts a suicidal defense of the station while he is led to safety.

In the present, Delenn rejects the offer to lead the Minbari in order to play her part in a prophecy.

Points of interest: Garibaldi's flashback takes him two years into his past. Does that mean that Sinclair went forward in time by two years?

The Quality of Mercy
(MERCY)
Written by J. Michael Straczynski

When he is ordered to build better relations and alliances with the alien races aboard the station, Ambassador Londo Mollari offers to take Lennier on a tour of Babylon 5. Inevitably, things end in disaster when the ambassador is caught cheating at cards and the pair become involved in a huge fight inside the Dark Star.

Dr. Franklin learns that a disgraced doctor, Laura Rosen, is illegally treating lurkers with an alien healing machine. When he investigates, he is shocked to discover that the device actually works by transferring some of its user's life energy to the sick. For Rosen, the device allows her to work as a healer again and provides her with a chance of redemption before she dies of Lakes Syndrome. Franklin commends Laura for her actions, and the pair become friends.

Meanwhile, a psychopathic killer named Karl Edward Mueller is sentenced to brainwipe. Shortly before the procedure is carried out, Mueller manages to escape from security and is shot in the arm as he flees. He then takes Janice Rosen hostage and orders her mother to heal his arm. When Franklin finds them and is also taken hostage, Laura realizes that Mueller will kill them all as soon as he is healed, and reverses the energy flow to overcome Mueller. The killer is exposed to the incredible pain of Lakes Syndrome and dies.

Ombuds Wellington rules that Laura acted in self-defense and she leaves Babylon 5 to start a new life on Earth.

Points of interest: The Alien Healing Device is left with Dr. Franklin, who wonders if one day it may be used to save a life when all other means have failed. Franklin runs an illegal clinic in Down Below and its real purpose is revealed a few months later in "A Race Through Dark Places."

Chrysalis
(CHRYSALIS)
Written by J. Michael Straczynski

Ambassadors Mollari and G'Kar are deadlocked over a border dispute in Quadrant 37, a sector of space which separates their two empires. When Mollari is ordered to surrender the territory to the Narn Regime, he seeks Morden's advice. Morden instructs him to tell the Centauri government that he will deal with the situation personally. The Shadows then destroy the Narn military outpost in the Quadrant, killing 10,000 Narns in the process. Although Londo is shocked by the attack, Morden tells him to savor the praise of his people.

When G'Kar learns of the attack, he finds it hard to believe that the Centauri alone were responsible and begins to suspect that it was the work of either a new race or an ancient race. He then leaves Babylon 5 to investigate.

As Commander Sinclair and Catherine Sakai contemplate marriage, Security Chief Garibaldi uncovers a plot to kill Earth Alliance President Luis Santiago. Before he can tell Sinclair about his findings, Garibaldi is shot in the back by his own aide, Jack. Just before Dr. Franklin begins a desperate operation to save his life, Garibaldi warns Sinclair, but he is too late to stop the destruction of *Earthforce 1*. Santiago's vice president, Morgan Clark, is sworn in as the new president of Earth Alliance.

After a solemn consultation with Ambassador Kosh, Delenn enters a Chrysalis.

Story arc: The Shadows demonstrate their power by wiping out the Narn military outpost in Quadrant 37 with ease. Although Londo is initially shocked by their actions, he is happy to continue his alliance with the Shadows in order to regain Centauri glory. President Santiago is assassinated and Delenn begins her transformation as part of an ancient prophecy.

Points of interest: During his investigation, Garibaldi enlists the help of a lurker who is revealed to be the leader of the underground railroad of unregistered telepaths in "A Race Through Dark Places."

SEASON TWO

The Coming of Shadows

Sinclair learns that Minbari souls are being reborn, either in part or in full, into human beings and that he has a Minbari soul. He is reassigned to Minbar, where he begins to build an army of light known as the Rangers.

His successor, Captain John J. Sheridan, learns that President Santiago was the victim of a conspiracy on Earth involving his successor, President Clark, and a new order on Earth.

Delenn transforms herself into a half-human, half-Minbari hybrid as a bridge on understanding between humans and Minbari and begins to prepare for her role in the coming battle against the forces of darkness. She is evicted from the Grey Council and replaced by a member of the warrior caste, thus giving it unprecedented power. As a result, the Minbari seemed destined for war once again.

With the help of the Shadows, Londo Mollari takes the Centauri into war against the Narn. When the Narn are defeated, the Republic looks for other worlds for conquest.

Points of Departure
(DEPARTURE)
Written by J. Michael Straczynski

When Jeffrey Sinclair is reassigned and becomes the first human ambassador allowed permanent residence on Minbar, Captain John J. Sheridan assumes command of Babylon 5. The Earth Alliance appoints Sheridan without consulting the Minbari, who know the war hero as the "Starkiller," and ignore their protests.

Sheridan's first task is to find the *Trigati*, a rogue Minbari warship which had been sighted near Babylon 5. When the ship's commander, Kalain, is seen aboard the station, Sheridan has him found and detained. However, shortly after his arrest, Kalain commits suicide to justify an attack on Babylon 5 by the *Trigati*.

Remembering that the Minbari never fire first, Sheridan gambles by waiting for the *Trigati* to open fire and sends details of the ship's whereabouts to a nearby Minbari warcruiser. The cruiser hits the *Trigati*'s jump engines, and the ship explodes when it tries to enter hyperspace.

Lennier tells Sheridan and Ivanova that Sinclair and other humans were found to have Minbari souls during the Battle of the Line. As soon as they made the discovery, the Grey Council gave the order to end the war. He later refers to a prophecy which claims that the two sides of the Minbari spirit must come together to defeat the coming darkness.

Story arc: Captain John Sheridan assumes command of Babylon 5 while Sinclair pursues his destiny as the human ambassador on Minbar. Minbari souls are being reborn, either in part or in full, into human beings. Humans and Minbari must unite to win the battle against the darkness.

Revelations
(REVELATIONS)
Written by J. Michael Straczynski

Captain Sheridan's younger sister, Elizabeth, visits Babylon 5 to help her brother come to terms with the death of his wife, Anna. Anna was assigned to an explorer ship, the *Icarus*, when it exploded above an ancient world out on the Rim called Z'ha'dum.

Shortly after Elizabeth's arrival, Ambassador G'Kar returns to the station and claims that an ancient race is living on planets out on the Rim, including Z'ha'dum. When Sheridan expresses his doubts, G'Kar reveals that he will be sending a Narn ship to investigate and bring proof. However, Ambassador Mollari warns Morden about G'Kar's plans, and the Shadows destroy the Narn vessel just as it leaves hyperspace.

When all other means have failed, Dr. Franklin uses the Alien Healing Device to revive Garibaldi. With the help of a telepathic scan, the security chief remembers that he was shot by his aide, Jack. Jack is arrested and reveals that he is part of a new order on Earth. Shortly after his arrest, President Clark orders Sheridan to send Jack and all the evidence relating to the case to Earth. During his voyage home, Jack is transferred to a phoney security ship and disappears without a trace.

Ambassador Delenn emerges from her cocoon as a half-human, half-alien hybrid and explains that she has undergone the transformation in the hopes that she will act as a bridge of understanding between humans and Minbari.

Story arc: The Shadows dwell in the Rim. Anna Sheridan's ship "exploded" above one of their strongholds, Z'ha'dum. Delenn's first step in fulfilling an ancient prophecy is to transform herself into a half-human, half-Minbari hybrid. President Clark is linked to the conspiracy to assassinate his predecessor.

Points of interest: Garibaldi is revived using the Alien Healing Device last seen in "The Quality of Mercy."

The Geometry of Shadows
(GEOMETRY)
Written by J. Michael Straczynski

Ambassador Mollari forms an alliance with Lord Refa, whose associates plan to seize power when Emperor Turhan dies. When he learns that a group of Techno-mages have boarded Babylon 5, he becomes obsessed with gaining an audience with them. Instead, his efforts merely incur their wrath. Finally, as their leader Elric leaves the station, he predicts that Londo will rise to power—and that he will be responsible for the suffering and death of millions.

Ivanova is promoted to the rank of commander and is ordered to bring peace between the green and purple Drazi on the station. When she is kidnapped by the purple group, Garibaldi comes to her rescue. As she tries to talk sense to the Drazi, she removes the purple leader's sash and unintentionally becomes the group's new leader. Ivanova then orders them to dye their sashes green, thus ending their private little war.

Having saved Ivanova and helped her end the Drazi crisis,

Garibaldi realizes that he is needed aboard the station and resumes his post as security chief.

Story arc: Londo Mollari joins forces with a group of power-hungry Centauri who intend to seize the throne when Emperor Turhan dies and recapture the lost glory of the Centauri Republic. He is later told that he is touched by darkness and will be responsible for the death of millions.

A Distant Star
(STAR)
Written by D.C. Fontana

Captain Jack Maynard, Sheridan's first commanding officer, visits Babylon 5 to restock his explorer ship, the *Cortez*, before resuming his mission in the Rim. During the visit, Sheridan begins to question his assignment aboard Babylon 5 and starts yearning to be in command of a starship once again.

However, shortly after leaving Babylon 5, a severe explosion occurs on the *Cortez* and the ship becomes trapped in hyperspace. Sheridan sends the station's Starfuries to the rescue and they manage to show the *Cortez* a route out of hyperspace. During the rescue, the squad encounters a Shadow ship which kills Commander Galus and temporarily disables Keffer's Starfury. When his systems become operational a few hours later, Keffer follows the Shadow vessel out of hyperspace and returns to Babylon 5.

Meanwhile, Delenn learns that her authority is no longer accepted by the Minbari on the station, one of whom, Teronn, asks to speak to the Grey Council about the matter. Although she is distressed by their attitude, she manages to convince Sheridan that he is supposed to be aboard Babylon 5.

Dr. Franklin prepares diet plans for Sheridan, Ivanova and Garibaldi. However, the security chief is determined to cook *bagna cauda* for his birthday and has the ingredients smuggled aboard. When Franklin hears that Garibaldi is cooking the fondue as a tribute to his father, he relents and joins him for the meal.

Story arc: Sheridan is comforted by Delenn and is touched by her attitude to the universe. The Shadows dwell in hyperspace. Keffer sees a Shadow ship in hyperspace and vows to prove that they exist.

The Long Dark
(LONG)
Written by Scott Frost

A battered, 100-year-old ship from Earth, the *Copernicus*, is brought aboard Babylon 5. When the senior command crew enter the ship, they find two humans in cryogenic suspension: Will and Mariah Cirrus. Will died sometime during the flight, making Mariah the obvious suspect.

Once revived, Mariah is haunted by nightmarish visions and later tells Dr. Franklin that she believes that some kind of monster was inside her cryogenic chamber with her. Franklin becomes convinced that it killed Will and used her to stay alive.

Garibaldi befriends Amis, a shell-shocked GROPOS, who tells him that a Soldier of Darkness came aboard Babylon 5 from the *Copernicus*. When a series of strange deaths occur, Garibaldi begins to believe him and together they try to track the monster down. The Soldier is destroyed, but only after an enormous number of plasma hits.

Later, Sheridan learns that the Soldier of Darkness had reprogrammed the *Copernicus*'s course and was heading for Z'ha'dum.

Story arc: The Shadows are building their forces at Z'ha'dum.

Spider in the Web
(SPIDER)
Written by Lawrence G. DiTillio

FutureCorp executive Taro Isogi meets with Amanda Carter of the Mars Conglomerate to propose a peaceful solution to the Mars Crisis. However, shortly after their first meeting, Isogi is killed by a Free Mars fanatic. When the assassin tries to attack the only witness to the murder, Talia Winters, she scans his mind and experiences a flashback to the killer's own death. He then leaves, dazed and disoriented.

Shortly after, the murderer is identified as Abel Horn, a Free Mars fanatic supposedly killed during the Mars Rebellion in 2258. Sheridan speculates that Horn was used as a subject of Project : Lazarus and is now controlled by a computer in his mind.

Horn makes a second attempt on Talia's life and is again immobilized when she scans him. He then asks for the help of his former lover, Amanda Carter. Carter summons Talia to her quarters, where Horn demands to know who or what he really is. When Sheridan and a security team rush to Talia's aid, Horn tries to kill Garibaldi and is shot by Sheridan. Immediately after his death, Horn's body self-destructs.

Sheridan later tells Garibaldi that he believes that Horn was sent to Babylon 5 by Bureau 13.

Story arc: "Spider in the Web" introduces Bureau 13, a covert dirty tricks squad which exists within EarthGov. It is commanded by a mysterious woman known as Thirteen, who was once a Psi Cop.

A Race Through Dark Places
(RACE)
Written by J. Michael Straczynski

Bester arrives on Babylon 5 to investigate an underground railroad of unregistered telepaths. When the telepaths try to kill the Psi Cop, he manages to survive the attack but Talia Winters is kidnapped. The leader of the group explains that he was a friend of Jason Ironheart and that both of them were experimented on by the Psi Corps. The group then convinces her of the Corps' real nature and intent.

Dr. Franklin tells Sheridan that he has helped smuggle the unregistered telepaths onto Babylon 5 and gains his sympathy. When Bester discovers the group, its members combine with Talia to project a vision into his mind. The Psi Cop leaves the station convinced that he killed all the telepaths with Talia's help.

Sheridan and Ivanova are charged extra rent for their quarters by the Earth Alliance and face relocation, until Sheridan decides to remove the extra credits they require from the station's war readiness budget. Delenn also asks Sheridan to dinner, and the pair's relationship continues to grow.

Story arc: Talia's telepathic powers continue to grow as a result of Jason Ironheart's gift. When she learns the truth about Psi Corps she no longer wants to be a part of the organization. Talia then confides in Ivanova, and the pair's friendship starts to become close and intimate. Sheridan's relationship with Delenn also continues to develop.

Points of interest: Dr. Franklin's illegal clinic, first seen in "The Quality of Mercy" is actually a cover for the underground railroad of unregistered telepaths. The lurker who helped Garibaldi in "Chrysalis" is the group's leader.

Soul Mates
(MATES)
Written by Peter David

Ambassador Mollari is overjoyed when he is given permission by Emperor Turhan to divorce two of his three wives, Mariel, Daggair and Timov. While Mariel and Daggair try desperately to keep their positions and pretend that they love their husband, Timov makes no pretense of her feelings for her husband.

During a banquet given to celebrate the 30th anniversary of his ascension, Londo collapses and is rushed to medlab. When Franklin says that he needs a blood transfusion to survive, Timov agrees to give blood on the condition that the doctor doesn't tell the ambassador. When Londo awakens, he decides to keep Timov as his wife because she, unlike Mariel and Daggair, is genuine.

Talia Winters' ex-husband Matthew Stoner arrives on Babylon 5. Stoner claims that he left the Psi Corps when he lost his telepathic powers and offers Talia the chance to abandon the Corps. However, Garibaldi learns that Stoner is an empath and has been sent by the Corps in the hope they will have empathic and/or telepathic children.

Ambassador Delenn seeks Ivanova's advice on life as a human female.

Story arc: Londo begins to sever all ties as he heads for war and glory.

The Coming of Shadows
(SHADOWS)
Written by J. Michael Straczynski

When the elderly Centauri Emperor Turhan visits Babylon 5 to make a historic speech, Ambassador G'Kar immediately plans to assassinate him. However, the emperor collapses shortly before he was supposed to begin his speech. In medlab, he asks Dr. Franklin to tell G'Kar that he was sorry for what his people and his family had done to the Narns and had hoped to make amends. Hearing this news, G'Kar begins to consider the possibility of a lasting peace between the Narn and the Centauri.

While the emperor hopes to forge peace between the two races, other Centauri have rather different plans. When Lord Refa tells Ambassador Mollari that they need to do something that will distinguish their faction from their rivals, Mollari uses the Shadows to conquer Quadrant 14.

The emperor hears of the attack just before he dies and, in his last breath, tells the Ambassador they are both damned. Mollari, however, tells those around him that he ordered him to continue the fight for glory. Meanwhile, on Centauri Prime, the Centauri Prime Minister Malachi is assassinated and the emperor's nephew, Cartagia, assumes the role of emperor thanks to Lord Refa and his associates.

Following the attack, the Narns have no choice but to declare war on the Centauri.

Garibaldi receives a cryptic message from Ambassador Sinclair about the coming darkness. Sinclair reveals that he is building an army of light known as the Rangers and advises him to stay close to Kosh and away from the Shadows. Delenn receives a similar message.

Story arc: Londo uses the Shadows to send the Centauri into war against the Narn and helps his associates seize power on

Centauri Prime. He also has a dream in which he sees himself as the Centauri emperor and then sees himself on Centauri Prime watching thousands of Shadow ships fly by. Sinclair informs Garibaldi and Delenn about the Rangers.

GROPOS
(GROPOS)
Written by Lawrence G. DiTillio

Babylon 5 is overrun by 25,000 infantry soldiers, known as GroundPounders or GROPOS, under the command of General Richard Franklin. While the troops believe they are on their way to Io, in reality they are destined to lead an assault in Operation : Sudden Death, a top-secret Earthforce mission to quell the civil war on Akdor.

Commander Ivanova urges Dr. Franklin to make amends with his estranged father while he has the chance, and the pair eventually rebuild their relationship. Meanwhile, Lieutenant Keffer befriends his new roommates, Privates Large and Yang, and Garibaldi encounters a fun-loving GROPOS, Dodger.

The assault on Matok proves successful, but only at a heavy loss of life. Privates Large, Yang and Dodger are among the casualties.

Points of interest: Babylon 5's defense is revamped and becomes capable of fighting a warship. The station puts it to the test in "The Fall of Night."

All Alone in the Night
(ALONE)
Written by J. Michael Straczynski

While investigating unusual astronomical activity, Captain Sheridan is attacked and kidnapped by a group of unidentified aliens. Once aboard their ship, he is tortured and subjected to a series of experiments, which include fighting members of other species to the death. Sheridan befriends another of the "specimens," a Narn captain named Ta'Lon. Together the pair make plans to escape.

While aboard the ship, Sheridan has a strange dream about Ambassador Kosh and some of his crewmates. He later learns that his mind has made contact with the Vorlon.

Delenn is summoned before the Grey Council and stripped of her position as Satai. She is replaced by Neroon, of the warrior caste, but allowed to continue as ambassador to Babylon 5.

When Delenn hears of Sheridan's plight, she tells Ivanova that he has been kidnapped by the Streibs and helps her track them to their homeworld. When Ivanova leads the attack against the alien craft, they eject their captives into space. Fortunately, however, Sheridan and Ta'Lon manage to avoid being spaced by escaping from the Streib ship in a lifepod.

Back on the station, Sheridan discusses his current assignment with General Hague. Sheridan tells him that all of Babylon 5's senior command staff are loyal to Earth, while Hague reveals that President Santiago's assassination was just part of a wider conspiracy to seize power on Earth. Sheridan then invites Ivanova, Garibaldi and Franklin to join him in the battle against the corruption of Earth.

Story arc: Delenn loses her place on the Grey Council to Neroon, thus giving the warrior caste unprecedented power. Sheridan makes contact with Kosh's mind and is revealed to be part of an informal organization led by General Hague which is designed to fight the new order on Earth. He learns that President Clark is involved in the new order and played a role in the assassination of Luis Santiago. Sheridan then enlists Garibaldi, Ivanova and Franklin's support and tells them that they will fight within the rules—for now.

Acts of Sacrifice
(SACRIFICE)
Written by J. Michael Straczynski

As tension between Babylon 5's Narn and Centauri populations grows, Ambassador G'Kar seeks military intervention from the Earth Alliance and Minbari Federation. While the Minbari decline straight away, Sheridan tells him that he will consider the matter provided that G'Kar keeps the peace aboard the station.

However, G'Kar finds his authority being undermined by a younger Narn who is determined to start a war against all the Centauri on the station. When his group kills a loudmouthed Centauri, G'Kar has to prove his authority through combat. Later, G'Kar is heartbroken to learn that the Earth Alliance will not intervene in the Narn–Centauri War. Although Sheridan and Delenn arrange to provide unofficial civilian aid to the Narns, it offers little comfort to G'Kar.

Meanwhile, Ivanova tries to convince the Lumati to join the Babylon Project. Above all, the Lumati believe in evolution of species and decide to join the program when they see Babylon 5's Down Below, thinking that it is the Earth Alliance's way of separating "superior" humans from the "inferior." Ivanova is then shocked to learn that the Lumati seal all their alliances with sexual intercourse. After a great deal of deliberation, she decides to do a strange dance around the Ambassador which, she claims, is human-style sex.

Hunter, Prey
(HUNTER)
Written by J. Michael Straczynski

Earthforce Special Agent Derek Cranston arrives on Babylon 5 to coordinate the search for Dr. Everett Jacobs, a fugitive physician who supposedly misused his security clearance to obtain secret military information which threatens Earthforce security. Captain Sheridan learns from Sarah, an associate of General Hague, that Jacobs is really being pursued because he has a data crystal containing evidence that former Vice-President Morgan Clark was perfectly healthy when he disembarked from *Earthforce 1* 24 hours before it exploded, thus corroborating the claim that Clark was involved in the assassination.

Garibaldi and Dr. Franklin go undercover to search Down Below for the fugitive physician, and eventually rescue him from an amoral bounty hunter, Max. As Cranston orders a scan of the station which will locate Jacobs, the doctor is hidden in Ambassador Kosh's organic ship, which is impenetrable to scans. Once the scan is complete, Cranston becomes convinced Jacobs has left the station, and gives up the search.

Sheridan confronts Kosh about the dream he had on the Streib ship and the Vorlon agrees to give him lessons which will teach the captain about himself, the Vorlons and how to fight legends.

Story arc: Sheridan scores his first victory in the fight against the conspiracy on Earth and is also taken under Kosh's wing. The recovered data shows up again in Season 3.

There All the Honor Lies
(HONOR)
Written by Peter David

An unidentified thief steals Sheridan's communicator. The captain chases him and runs into a Minbari warrior, Lovell, who attacks him until Sheridan conveniently finds a PPG lying on the floor nearby and kills the Minbari in self-defense. When the only witness, Ashan, claims that Sheridan murdered Lovell without provocation, the captain finds his career in jeopardy.

Lennier investigates and learns that the murder was part of a plot hatched by the Third Fain of Chudmo to discredit Sheridan and have him reassigned. Lennier tells Ashan that he will inform Sheridan of the truth, thus discrediting his entire clan. Sheridan, however, decides that the entire, dishonorable truth does not have to be revealed, provided that Ashan issues a statement explaining exactly what happened.

Meanwhile, Centauri Prime sends a replacement attaché for Londo, but Londo threatens to quit as ambassador unless Vir stays. In a bid to boost the station's revenue, the Babylon Emporium is opened, but is subsequently closed when Sheridan sees that he has been immortalized as a teddy bear.

And Now for a Word
(WORD)
Written by J. Michael Straczynski

Babylon 5 becomes the subject of an Interstellar News Network (ISN) documentary, "36 Hours Aboard Babylon 5," hosted by Cynthia Torqueman. The one-hour program focuses on the growing tension aboard the station as the Narn–Centauri War threatens to spread into the sector, and features interviews with most of the station's leading command staff, plus Ambassadors G'Kar, Delenn and Mollari.

Knives
(KNIVES)
Written by Lawrence G. DiTillio

Londo Mollari is reunited with his old friend and ally, Urza Jaddo. Urza tells the ambassador that he has been charged with treason and asks for Londo's help to protect his family's honor. When Londo learns that Lord Refa is behind the action against Urza, he is unable to support his old friend. Urza challenges Londo to a duel to the death and allows the ambassador to kill him, so that his family will become part of the House of Mollari, as outlined in the rules of the morrargo.

Meanwhile, Captain Sheridan decides to investigate the Gray Sector, also known as the "Babylon 5 Triangle," and is attacked by the corpse of a dead Markab. Later, Sheridan begins to experience a series of visions until he realizes that he has been possessed by a noncorporeal life-form which had unintentionally been brought to Babylon 5 from Sector 14 by the Markab. Sheridan boards a Starfury and returns the alien to the region.

Story arc: Londo learns more about the coup d'état on Centauri Prime and, for the first time, begins to question his course of action during the past year.

In the Shadow of Z'ha'dum
(Z'HA'DUM)
Written by J. Michael Straczynski

Sheridan is sorting through his late wife's belongings when Garibaldi recognizes one of her crewmates on the *Icarus* as Morden, Ambassador Mollari's mysterious associate. The captain defies all regulations to question Morden about the event and ignores Garibaldi's resignation as well as the Centauri Republic's complaints. When Talia Winters refuses to perform an illegal scan on Morden, Sheridan tricks her into walking past him and she senses the Shadows accompanying him.

Finally, Ambassador Kosh and Ambassador Delenn tell Sheridan that the *Icarus*'s crew awakened the Shadows on Z'ha'dum and were captured by them. Those who would not serve the Shadows were killed. Kosh also explains that the Vorlons are planning to fight the Shadows, but are not yet ready. For the sake of the forces of light, Sheridan agrees to release Morden, on the condition that Kosh teaches him how to fight the Shadows. Sheridan tells him that he will one day travel to Z'ha'dum.

Meanwhile, Pierce Macabee of the Ministry of Peace visits Babylon 5 to launch several of the Ministry's programs, including the Nightwatch. Security Officer Zack Allen decides to join.

Story arc: Sheridan learns that the *Icarus* crew, including his wife and Morden, were captured by the Shadows and were given a choice between serving the forces of darkness and death. What did Anna Sheridan choose? Sheridan also learns that telepaths can sense the presence of the Shadows.

The Vorlons are revealed to be the last remaining First Ones, dedicated to fighting the Shadows when they return. Kosh says that "everyone" would recognize him if he left his encounter suit.

The sinister Nightwatch organization is established on the station.

Points of interest: If telepaths can sense the Shadows, why hasn't the Psi Corps detected any? Or are they in league with them already?

Confessions and Lamentations
(CONFESSIONS)
Written by J. Michael Straczynski

When Markabs suddenly begin to die without explanation both on their homeworld and on Babylon 5, Dr. Franklin learns that they were victims of Drafa, a fatal and extremely contagious disease. With the help of his Markab friend, Dr. Lazarenn, he races to find a cure.

According to Markab legend, Drafa was the gods' punishment for immorality. Consequently, all the Markabs on the station decide to be placed in quarantine where they will escape from the immorality of other aliens and repent for their misdeeds. As they continue to die, Ambassador Delenn and Lennier risk their lives to join them and offer comfort. Sheridan allows them to enter the zone, but is extremely worried for Delenn's safety. He tells her to call him John the next time they meet.

When a Pak'ma'ra dies of Drafa, Franklin is able to find the cause of the disease and then a cure. However, when he enters the isolation zone, he finds that all the station's Markabs are dead. Sheridan comforts Delenn.

Story arc: Dr. Franklin becomes increasingly dependent on stims as he races to find a cure for the disease. Sheridan and Delenn demonstrate their growing feelings for each other.

Divided Loyalties
(DIVIDED)
Written by J. Michael Straczynski

Lyta Alexander, the first commercial telepath assigned to Babylon 5, returns to the station with details of a new Psi Corps program which has placed sleeper spies in most of the leading EarthGov agencies, including Babylon 5. She explains that when a password is telepathically transmitted to his or her mind, a Psi Corps–induced personality will take over and the old one is destroyed.

Captain Sheridan is concerned about the invasion of privacy involved in letting her scan all of the station's command staff in search of the traitor, but agrees to let her do it when someone tries to kill Lyta. Ivanova once again expresses her unwillingness to be scanned and secretly tells Sheridan that she is a latent telepath.

When Lyta scans the majority of the senior command crew unsuccessfully, Ivanova becomes the prime suspect. She then relents and Lyta reveals that she is not the spy after all. Shortly

after, Talia enters the room and is exposed as the traitor by
Lyta. Talia is sent back to Earth, while Lyta leaves the station
after an unusual meeting with Ambassador Kosh.

Story arc: Talia Winters is exposed as a Psi Corps sleeper spy.
Once the password was sent into her mind, the Psi Corps
implanted personality took over and her own personality was
destroyed.

Points of interest: What was the significance of Jason
Ironheart's gift ("Mind War") and Ambassador Kosh's recording of her mind ("Deathwalker")? Could they be the key to
saving Talia's real personality?

The Long, Twilight Struggle
(TWILIGHT)
Written by J. Michael Straczynski

The Narn are on the verge of defeat when they decide to
mount a desperate attack on a heavily guarded Centauri supply world. Although the offensive will leave the Narn
homeworld defenseless, it is the Narns' only hope to turn the
war against the Centauri around.

Unfortunately for them, the Centauri intercept a
Narn transmission describing the attack and plan an offensive of their own. The Republic enlists the help of Londo
Mollari's allies, the Shadows, to protect the Centauri supply
world while the Centauri launch an attack on the Narn
homeworld.

The Centauri decimate the Narn homeworld using mass
drivers until the Narn unconditionally surrender. Ambassador
Mollari demands that G'Kar is removed from the Babylon 5
Advisory Council and sent back to Narn to stand trial for war
crimes against the Centauri, as a member of the Kha'Ri.
However, Sheridan grants G'Kar sanctuary aboard Babylon 5
and the Narn stays on the station.

Draal contacts Sheridan and offers him an alliance in the
coming fight against the forces of darkness. Draal also tells
Delenn to introduce him to the Rangers and she gives him
equal authority over all the Rangers in the area.

Story arc: The Narn are defeated and Delenn predicts that the Centauri will soon begin to expand into other worlds. Draal puts the incredible powers of Epsilon 3 at Sheridan's disposal and Sheridan assumes command of the Rangers in the area.

Points of interest: Draal reveals that there are others with him on Epsilon 3, including Zathras. Will Draal facilitate the events in which Sinclair steals Babylon 4 to use as a base of operation in the Shadow War? ("Babylon Squared")

Comes the Inquisitor
(INQUISITOR)
Written by J. Michael Straczynski

G'Kar launches a resistance movement against the Centauri. He buys weapons and, with Garibaldi's help, arranges to have them shipped to the homeworld. To prove he can still transport items to the homeworld, G'Kar is given 24 hours to supply a message from the relatives of a family of Narns on Babylon 5. He asks for Sheridan's help, who provides the message courtesy of the Rangers.

Ambassador Kosh summons an inquisitor to determine whether Delenn is right to ally herself with him during the coming war against the Shadows. The inquisitor, Sebastian, arrives and tells Sheridan he once lived in London, England, in 1888, before joining the Vorlons' service.

Sebastian then tortures, taunts and degrades Delenn until Sheridan rushes to her rescue. When Sheridan and Delenn demonstrate that they are willing to sacrifice their lives for the other and die unnoticed and alone, Sebastian tells them that they are the chosen ones: the right people at the right place at the right time. They are also the first to pass his test.

Shortly after the inquisition, Sheridan learns that Sebastian did indeed live on Earth in 1888 but disappeared after a series of murders. When the captain confronts him about his crimes, Sebastian admits that he was abducted by the Vorlons who taught him the error of his ways and now use him as an inquisitor. As he leaves the station, he says that he will always be remembered as Jack the Ripper.

Story arc: Delenn and Sheridan prove that they are the chosen ones and are fit to play their roles in the Shadow War. The Rangers manage to deliver a message from the Centauri-occupied Narn homeworld to Babylon 5.

Points of interest: Why is Sheridan the only one who can defy Kosh?

The Fall of Night
(FALL)
Written by J. Michael Straczynski

Following their victory against the Narn, the Centauri continue to expand their empire by invading Pak'ma'ra and Drazi territories. When Sheridan accuses them of destabilizing the whole region, Ambassador Mollari warns him not to become involved with matters beyond his jurisdiction.

Earth sends a representative of the Ministry of Peace, Frederick Lantz, to Babylon 5 to investigate the situation. Lantz is accompanied by a representative of the Nightwatch, Mr. Welles. While Sheridan believes that Lantz will negotiate some kind of pact against the Centauri, he is shocked to learn that Earth actually wants a non-aggression pact with the Centauri.

When a Narn warcruiser arrives at Babylon 5 seeking sanctuary, Sheridan agrees to shelter the vessel. Sometime later, Mr. Welles learns of the situation and informs the Centauri, who dispatch a vessel to the station. Sheridan warns that he will take any means necessary to defend the Narn cruiser while it is in Babylon 5's space, and is eventually forced to attack and destroy the Centauri vessel.

While Zeta Squad accompanies the Narn ship to safety, Lieutenant Keffer tracks a Shadow ship and pursues it. He manages to capture a picture of the vessel before his Starfury is destroyed.

Sheridan is ordered to apologize to the Centauri and travels to the Zen Garden for a meeting of the Advisory Council. While inside the core shuttle, Sheridan spots a Centauri bomb and jumps out of the shuttle just as it explodes. Just when it looks certain that the captain will die, Ambassador Kosh leaves his encounter suit and flies to his rescue. He reveals himself as a creature of light who appears in different forms to different races.

As the year 2259 draws to a close, Babylon 5's peacekeeping mission looks doomed. But, as Commander Ivanova points out, sometimes peace is another word for surrender.

Story arc: The Centauri begin to invade territories and Earth, rather than oppose the Republic's actions, chooses to sign a non-aggression treaty with it. Sheridan admits to being disillusioned with Earth. Kosh reveals himself as a creature of light.

•

SEASON THREE

Point of No Return

As the war against the Shadows escalates, Captain Sheridan finds it increasingly difficult to tell friend from foe and decides that the time has come to take a stand against the new order controlling Earth.

Matters of Honor
(MATTERS)
Written by J. Michael Straczynski

Earthforce investigator David Endawi travels to Babylon 5 to investigate the footage of the Shadow ship taken by Keffer's Starfury. He discusses the situation with Ambassadors Mollari and G'Kar, but is unable to find any concrete information.

When the Drazi colony Zagros 7 is blockaded by the Centauri, a Ranger, Marcus Cole, travels to Babylon 5 seeking assistance. Cole tells Sheridan and Delenn that Zagros 7 is the site of a Ranger training camp and that the blockade must be broken long enough for them to escape. Sheridan agrees to help and takes command of a new ship, the *White Star*, a hybrid of Minbari and Vorlon technology.

Meanwhile, Ambassador Mollari tells Morden that it is time to conclude their alliance. Morden seems indifferent and divides a map of the galaxy between the Centauri and the Shadows. He adds that the Shadows will be seizing control of one area within Centauri influence—Zagros 7.

The *White Star* arrives at Zagros 7 and breaks the blockade. While the Rangers escape, the *White Star* is pursued by a Shadow ship. Unable to attack the ship directly, Sheridan performs the Bonehard Maneuver and opens a jumppoint within a jumpgate. The Shadow ship is destroyed in the explosion, but the *White Star* just manages to escape.

Back on Earth, Endawi tells a senator that nobody aboard the station knew anything about the Shadow ship. After their meeting, the senator is joined by Morden as well as a member of the Psi Corps.

Sheridan starts the war council to share information and plan the war against the Shadows.

Story arc: Sheridan takes command of the *White Star* and experiences his first victory against the Shadows. Londo Mollari breaks his alliance with the Shadows. Morden is manipulating not only the Centauri but also the Psi Corps and the Earth Senate.

Convictions
(CONVICTIONS)
Written by J. Michael Straczynski

Babylon 5's command staff investigates a series of random bombings across the station. In one explosion, Lennier is almost killed while trying to save the lives of Ambassadors Delenn and Mollari. Sometime after, the Centauri diplomat narrowly escapes death again during another bombing and finds himself trapped in a transport tube with G'Kar. When the Narn refuses to help him find a way out of the tube, Mollari can do nothing but wait for a rescue team.

With the help of a group of monks led by Brother Theo, Captain Sheridan and Commander Ivanova learn that the bombings are the work of a crazed maintenance worker, Robert J. Carlsen. When they try to arrest Carlsen, he threatens to destroy the station unless he is allowed to leave. Security Chief Garibaldi realizes that Carlsen must have placed a bomb near Babylon 5's fusion reactor, and uses a security 'bot to move the bomb to a safe distance. As a result, when Carlsen tries to detonate his device, the station emerges unscathed. Carlsen is then arrested.

Story arc: G'Kar would rather die than help Londo Mollari.

A Day in the Strife
(STRIFE)
Written by J. Michael Straczynski

An alien probe reaches Babylon 5 and informs the station's inhabitants that they will have to pass a test to prove that they are worthy of contact. The probe then gives the station's crew 24 hours to answer 600 questions and promises to provide cures for every known form of disease as well as some highly advanced technology if all the questions are answered correctly. However, if the station fails to provide the correct answer to every question, the probe is set to explode with the force of 500,000 megatonnes.

Meanwhile, the Centauri-appointed Narn leader Na'Far arrives on Babylon 5 to take G'Kar's place on the station. He urges G'Kar to return to the Narn homeworld to stand trial, and then tells him that the families of all Narns aboard the station will be persecuted until he gives himself up for trial. G'Kar relents and decides to return home, but is stopped by the Narns on the station when they all demand that he stays with them.

Just as the probe reaches its 24-hour deadline, Sheridan realizes that its true intention is to destroy any intelligent race which could pose a threat to its creators and chooses not to transmit the answers. He then orders the command crew not to give the probe the answers. When the probe reaches its deadline, it recommences its voyage and self-destructs shortly after when a Babylon 5 security 'bot sends it the answers.

Ambassador Mollari arranges for Vir to be sent to the Minbari homeworld and finds himself truly alone aboard the station.

Points of interest: Ta'Lon, the Narn captain saved by Sheridan in "All Alone in the Night," travels to Babylon 5 as Na'Far's bodyguard and decides to stay on the station. He expresses his gratitude and debt to Sheridan for saving his life.

COMICS

In Darkness Find Me (1 of 4)
(DARKNESS)
Written by J. Michael Straczynski

Sinclair is recalled to EarthDome where he is summoned before President Clark and Rathenn, a member of the Grey Council. Rathenn uses a triluminary to restore Sinclair's memory of his encounter with the Grey Council during the Battle of the Line and explains that the Council gave the order to surrender once they had discovered that Minbari souls were being reborn, either in part or in full, into human beings. Rathenn then invites Sinclair to live on Minbar as the human ambassador. After a great deal of deliberation, Sinclair accepts the offer and leaves for the Minbari homeworld . . .

Treason (2 of 4)
(TREASON)
Written by Mark Moretti

Babylon 5 receives a distress signal from the Starliner *Chiyoda-Ku* and dispatches Zeta Squad to investigate. The Starfuries arrive, and find 24 of the ship's 25 crewmembers dead.

The lone survivor is slowly recovering in medlab when a dock worker, Jason Colby, attempts to kill him. The patient defends himself with a mind scan and flees from the medlab. Ivanova leads the search until Talia informs her that the man is with her.

The command crew learns that the survivor, Dexter Hall, was a Psi Cop who had infiltrated the pro-Earth group aboard the *Chiyoda-Ku* and had learned that it was supplying weapons for the assassination of the new Minbari leader. As a result of his fight with Colby, Hall enters a coma.

Ambassador Sinclair arrives on Minbar and meets with Delenn. Their reunion is interrupted by Kozorr, who opens Sinclair's case to reveal a rifle and plans to assassinate the Minbari leader. Kozorr places him under arrest and promises him that if he is found guilty the Minbari will declare war against Earth . . .

In Harm's Way (3 of 4)
(HARM)
Written by Mark Moretti

Senator Hidoshi tells Sheridan that Hall is a rogue telepath known as Cypher, and orders the captain to isolate him until Earthforce Internal Affairs officer Colonel Rabock arrives to lead the investigation.

Colby receives orders from his commanding officer in the Homeguard, Webster, to kill Hall. When Colby says that he wants to leave the station as soon as possible, his contact reminds him that he must continue the fight against the aliens who killed his wife. However, Colby is afraid that Hall described him to Talia Winters, and disobeys orders by trying to kill her. Fortunately, she is saved by Garibaldi.

When Dr. Franklin tells Sheridan that Hall's coma was irreversible, Talia completes a deep scan on the Psi Cop just before he dies and learns that he was indeed an undercover operative assigned to infiltrate the Homeguard. Then Colonel Rabock enters to assume control of the case—and is none other than Colby's commander, Webster.

On Minbar, Sinclair's trial begins. Neroon serves as head of the prosecution . . .

The Price of Peace (4 of 4)
(PEACE)
Written by Mark Moretti

After meeting with the station's senior command staff, Rabock/Webster contacts his superior and suggests that he should kill Colby. However, Rabock/Webster is told that if he did kill Colby he would expose the story about Cypher. During the course of their discussion, the commanding officer also mentions that Rabock/Webster killed Colby's wife. Unfortunately for them, Colby is listening to the conversation and realizes that Rabock/Webster is in fact Cypher. Colby takes him hostage and escapes from the station on a shuttle.

When Rabock/Webster attacks him using a telepathic scan, Colby opens fire and damages the shuttle's systems. Consequently, the shuttle explodes.

Sinclair is found guilty of trying to murder the Minbari leader. However, before the tribunal can pronounce sentence, he cites an ancient Minbari law and offers his life in exchange for war. The Minbari leader then enters the court chamber and pardons him. Later, Sinclair tells Delenn that he knew that the Minbari leader wouldn't allow him to be executed because of his Minbari soul.

Sheridan, Ivanova and Garibaldi's discussion of recent events is interrupted by the arrival of Colonel Rabock. Meanwhile, on Earth, a mysterious figure in a Psi Corps office deletes all records of Webster and Colby and begins the search for a new Cypher.

Shadows Past and Present (1 of 4)
(PRESENT)
Written by Tim DeHaas

Garibaldi becomes increasingly suspicious of Ambassador Mollari's numerous transmissions to Quadrant 37. When the ambassador arranges to meet with Lord Refa to discuss his ally (the Shadow emissary, Morden), Garibaldi decides to leave for their rendezvous to learn more about Londo's plans. As he boards a shuttle, he is joined by Lieutenant Keffer.

However, Morden stops the ambassador just before he leaves and tells him to go to Quadrant 37. He then arranges a reception party for Garibaldi's shuttle. Garibaldi starts to tell Keffer how he first met Lieutenant-Commander Jeffrey Sinclair on Mars, but his story is cut short when they are attacked by a Shadow ship. The shuttle crash-lands on a Centauri planet . . .

Against the Odds (2 of 4)
(ODDS)
Written by Tim DeHaas

Garibaldi sets the ship for self-destruct and leaves with Keffer before the Shadow ship arrives. After studying the wreckage, the Shadows erase all evidence of its existence before pursuing the two humans . . .

Survival The Hard Way (3 of 4)
(SURVIVAL)
Written by Tim DeHaas

Garibaldi continues his story as he and Keffer head for a Centauri city, unaware that their pursuers have actually overtaken them and are waiting for them in the forest. Once in the woodland, Keffer and then Garibaldi become paranoid and Keffer tries to kill the security chief. Garibaldi manages to dodge his fire, which instead hits the Shadows. Free of their paranoia, the pair manage to overcome the rest of their foes. Garibaldi wonders if the creatures have any connection to the spidery ship which he and Sinclair saw being excavated on Mars . . .

Silent Enemies (4 of 4)
(SILENT)
Written by Tim DeHaas

Garibaldi tells Keffer how he and Sinclair discovered and destroyed a covert alien–Psi Corps operation on Mars. Just as he finishes his story, they are captured by Centauri guards, who take them to the city. When they can find no trace of their crashed ship, the Centauri contact Ambassador Mollari, who vouches for their identities. Back on Babylon 5, Garibaldi tells Sheridan that the ship he saw on Mars was the same as Keffer saw in hyperspace.

Duet for Human and Narn in C Sharp (1 of 2)
(DUET)
Written by David Gerrold

G'Kar suddenly becomes desperate to leave Babylon 5 and kidnaps Garibaldi during his escape bid. Sheridan teams up with a strange Narn, Greegil, to pursue G'Kar's ship, but when they reach it they find it is empty and set for self-destruct. Meanwhile, G'Kar and Garibaldi are actually hiding in Babylon 5's core, where they are pursued by a cleaning 'bot . . .

Coda for Human and Narn in B Flat (2 of 2)
(CODA)
Written by David Gerrold

Sheridan and Greegil barely escape from G'Kar's ship, but their shuttle is damaged in the explosion. Sheridan dons a space suit to fix the damage, only to find that Greegil has locked him out. When the captain then reminds him that he has the code key to operate the ship, Greegil allows him back on board.

As G'Kar and Garibaldi continue to run from the cleaning 'bot, the ambassador reveals that he tried to leave the station to escape from Greegil, who vowed revenge when he refused to seal their clans' alliance by sleeping with his mate. Upon boarding the station, Greegil is arrested while Garibaldi and G'Kar are rescued when the security chief manages to display a message on the outside of the core.

The Psi Corps and You!
(CORPS)
Written by Tim DeHaas

A pamphlet in which the Psi Corps describes its function and value in the modern world. Naturally, most of the Corps' claims and information are false.

BOOKS

Voices
(VOICES)
Written by John Vornholt

Bester and Harriman Gray prepare for a telepaths' conference on Mars. When the conference is bombed, Gray suggests that they move the setting to Babylon 5.

Arthur Malten, the head of the association of commercial

telepaths, meets Talia Winters aboard the station and convinces her to attend the conference as a representative of the association. During the conference, Talia develops a headache and leaves the building, just before it explodes. Shortly after, she is arrested and taken to the brig, but later escapes with the help of Ambassador Kosh. Kosh provides her with passage to Earth. During the flight, she meets Deuce and the pair come to an uneasy truce.

Meanwhile, Talia is declared a rogue telepath by Bester as Garibaldi and Gray head to Earth on her tail.

Once on Earth, Deuce and Talia steal a Psi Corps shuttle before they decide to go their separate ways. Talia decides to travel to Mars just as Garibaldi and Gray's investigation leads them to the planet in search of Arthur Malten, who they have discovered was the leader of a revolutionary movement which had been planting the bombs in an effort to discredit Free Mars. By coincidence, they all happen to travel on the same transport and Garibaldi recognizes the telepath. Once on Mars, she meets her uncle, Ted, with Garibaldi and Gray in close pursuit. When the pair confront Talia, they convince her that Malten is the only one who can clear her name.

Bester meets with Gray and Garibaldi and the trio trace Malten to a bunker where he is being held by the Free Mars movement. Inside, they find Malten strapped to explosives set to detonate in 30 seconds and have no choice but to abandon him.

In spite of everything they have learned, Bester refuses to clear Talia's name until Garibaldi blackmails him with one of Ambassador Mollari's files containing details of Psi Cops gambling. Bester initially tries to use his mental powers against Garibaldi but is stopped by Gray. The Psi Cop then agrees to restore Talia's position in the Corps.

Accusations
(ACCUSATIONS)
Written by Lois Tilton

Ivanova receives a confidential message from J. D. Ortega, her former flight instructor at Earthforce, containing details of his arrival and asking her to meet him. When he fails to meet her, a computer search reveals that he was listed as a Free Mars terrorist suspect. Ivanova meets Garibaldi to discuss the situation and tells him that she couldn't imagine him as a terrorist. She is then called away to lead Alpha Wing against another Raiders attack.

Back on Babylon 5, J. D. Ortega's body is found in a flight locker. The security team also find a message for Ivanova: just one word, "hardwire." When Commander Wallace, Lieutenant Miyoshi and Lieutenant Khatib arrive on the station to assume control of the investigation, Ivanova finds herself under suspicion of terrorism and conspiracy. She is then placed on restricted duties.

Garibaldi continues his search and learns that Ortega had been killed by Yang, an enforcer for AreTech. He also discovers that the Mars-based mining company had been supplying information about its shipments to the Raiders. However, before Garibaldi can get to the murderer, Yang is killed by Khatib, who is then murdered by Wallace as part of an extremely elaborate cover-up.

With the help of a telepathic scan performed by Talia Winters, Ivanova recalls that Ortega always believed that a pilot should be "hardwired" to his or her Starfury, allowing Ivanova to realize that he stored information for her in her Starfury. While retrieving it, she is viciously attacked by Miyoshi, who is desperate to gain evidence to save her career. Garibaldi rushes to her aid and Miyoshi is killed by a security guard in self-defense.

The data crystal contains details of a new atom discovered by AreTech, supermorbidium, which could contribute to a potent weapon system. The command crew is left wondering about Ortega's intentions. Had he intended to give the information to Earthforce? Did he want to supply Free Mars with it to use in terrorist activities? Or was he going to sell it to the highest bidder?

Ivanova's name is cleared and she resumes her normal life aboard Babylon 5.

Blood Oath
(BLOOD)
Written by John Vornholt

Ambassador G'Kar receives a message from Mi'Ra, the daughter of Du'Rog, in which she reveals that her family has sworn a Shon-Kar against him. G'Kar insists on leaving the station immediately, but his ship explodes just as it enters the jumpgate. The Narn is pronounced dead.

Garibaldi and Ivanova travel to the Narn homeworld to represent the Earth Alliance at G'Kar's memorial service. Just before they leave, Garibaldi befriends Al Vernon, a human married to a Narn who trades a great deal with the Centauri, and Sheridan begins to suspect that Garibaldi is still alive.

During their trip to the homeworld, Ivanova, Garibaldi and Na'Toth discover that G'Kar is hiding aboard their ship. Once on Narn, G'Kar is reunited with his mate, Da'Kal, who decides to send money to the Du'Rog family in the hope that they will end their blood oath. While her family ponders how to spend their newfound wealth, Mi'Ra decides that money is not enough to stop her Shon-Kar and hires some assassins to kill G'Kar, Ivanova and Garibaldi.

After narrowly escaping a close encounter with Mi'Ra's reception party, the group confronts her. She prepares to kill the three of them when Al Vernon joins them and offers to give her a data crystal containing evidence which exonerates the Du'Rog family, if she disavows her Shon-Kar. She accepts his proposal. Al then reveals that he had been sent by Ambassador Mollari.

Back on the station, G'Kar thanks Londo for his help, even though he cannot fathom the Centauri's reasons. Londo tells him that he would prefer to see the Narn humbled and have to thank him than to see him killed in a family squabble.

Clark's Law
(LAW)
Written by Jim Mortimore

When a Tuchanq delegation visits Babylon 5, Captain Sheridan hopes that they will form an alliance with Earth. Shortly after arriving on the station, one of their delegates, Ambassador D'arc is involved in a near-fatal accident and left effectively brainwiped.

When D'arc is revealed to be a mass murderer, she is sentenced to death by President Clark. Thus Captain Sheridan finds that he must choose between his career and doing what his conscience dictates. To make matters worse, he knows that his actions will not only determine whether the Tuchanq become allies with Earth but might even convince them to join with the Centauri.

After a great deal of soul-searching, Sheridan decides that the only thing he can do is fake the execution. However, when the Tuchanq learn that he has not only deceived them but his own people, they decide that humans are dishonest and cannot be trusted. Consequently, they decide to forge an alliance with the Centauri. Sheridan is powerless as the Centauri and the Shadows conquer the Tuchanq homeworld.

APPENDIX III
Indexes by Group

Characters/People

Delenn
Delvientos, Alberto
Delvientos, Eduardo
Deuce
Devereaux
Dodger (Elizabeth Durman)
Draal
Drake, Nelson
Droshalla
Drozac
Dukhat
Du'Rog
Durza
Ellison
Ellison, Harlan
Elric
Endawi, David
Estevez
Fashar
Ferdinand, Ellasai, VI
Flinn, Mr.
Fosaro
Foster
Franklin, Richard
Franklin, Stephen
Franks, Aaron
Garibaldi, Alfredo
Garibaldi, Michael Alfredo
Gajic, Aldous
Galus, Ray
G'Drog
Geegil
G'Kar
G'Lan
G'Quan
Gray, Harriman
G'Sten
Guerra
Gyor
Hague
Hampton, Lise

Hanson
Ha'Rok
Hazeltine, Eric
Hedronn
Hernandez, Maya
Hidoshi
Horn, Abel
Ilarus
Ironheart, Jason
Isogi, Taro
Itagi
Ivanov, Andrei
Ivanova, Sofie
Ivanov, Gayna
Ivanova, Susan
Jack
Jackson
Jacobs, Everett
Jaddo, Urza
Ja'Doc
Ja'Dog
Ja'Toth
Jensen
Jha'dur
Jordan, Thomas
J'Quoth'Tiel
Ka'Het
Kalain
Kalika
Kat
Keffer, Warren
Kelsey
Kemmer, Frank
Kemmer, Lianna
Kha'Mak
Khatib
Kiro
Kleist
Knight One
Knight Two
Kobya

Santiago, Luis
Sarah
Sebastian
Sentauro
Shar, Mila
Sheridan, Anna
Sheridan, Elizabeth
Sheridan, John J.
Shinar
Shioshnic
Shon
Sinclair, Jeffrey
Sineval
Singer
Soul Hunter #1
Soul Hunter #2
Stoner, Matthew
Sykes, Carolyn
Takarn
Tennyson
Taq
Tasaki, Dr.
Tensus, Aria
Teronn
Tharg
Theo
Thirteen
Ti Korvo
Timov

Torqueman, Cynthia
Trakis
Tu'Lar
Tu'Pari
Turhan
Tyree, Adira
Una
Valen
Valo
Varn
Varner, Del
Venzann
Vernon, Al
Vin'Tok
Voudreau, Elise
Wallace, Commander
Wallace, Tonia
Welch, Lou
Welles
Wellington, Ombuds
Winters, Talia
Xon
Yang
Yang, Private
Zathras
Zento, Orin
Zimmerman, Ombuds
Zoog

Places, Worlds

Abbai 4
AirDome
Akdor
Amazonis Planitia
Ambassadorial Wing
Antares Sector
Arain Station
Babylon 1
Babylon 2

Babylon 3
Babylon 4
Babylon 5
Babylon Park
Balus
Bay 11
Bay 13
Beta 7
Beta System

Black Omega Squad

Blue Sector

Book Universe

Casinos

Centauri Prime

Central Corridor, The

Comac 4

Cobra Bay

Damocles Sector, The

Dark Star, The

Davo

Deneb Sector

Down Below

Downtown

Dug Out, The

Earharts

EarthDome

Eclipse Cafe

Epsilon 3 (Euphrates)

Europa

Finagle's Place

Fresh Air

Galactic Boutique, The

Garesh 7

Geneva

G'Kamazad

Glory Shop

G'Quan Mountains

Gray 19

Gray Sector

Green Sector

Green Tiger, The

Happy Daze

Hebka

Hyperspace

Hyach 7

Ikaara 7

Io

Isolab

Ja'komason

Ka'Pul

LaGrange 2

Lardec 4

Malax

Mars Colony, The

Matok

Maze, The

Medlabs

Mess Hall

Minbar

Narn

Observation Dome

Omelos

Orion

Passenger Lounge

Phobos Station

Proxima System

Proxima 3

Quadrant 14

Quadrant 37

Ragesh 3

Red Sector

Rim, The

Ritchie Station

San Diego

Sector 7

Sector 14

Sector 15

Sector 29

Sector 45

Sector 90

Sector 92

Sector 119

Sector 127

Sector 900

Sigma 957

Solis Planum

Station Phobos

Syria Planum

Tigris Sector

Tirolus

Vega Colony

Vega Sector
Yedor
Yellow Sector
Zagros 7

Zen Gardens, The
Zestus
Z'ha'dum
Zocalo, The

Vessels and Vehicles

Achilles, The
Agamemnon, The
Al Callisto, The
Alien Science Probe
Amundsen, The
Asimov, The
Black Omega Starfury
Black Star, The
Cartee
Chiyoda-Ku
Copernicus, The
Core Shuttle
Cortez, The
Crawler
Delta Gamma Nine
Earthforce 1
Earthforce 2
Flyer
Flying Dutchman, The
Frazi
Heyerdahl, The
Hyperion, The

Icarus, The
Ingata, The
Kawasaki Ninja ZX-11
K'sha Na'vas
Malios
Melori
N'Ton
Omega, The
Pournelle, The
Raiders' Battle Wagon
Skydancer, The
Starfuries
Sunhawk
Talquith
Transport Tubes
Trigati, The
Ulysses, The
Valerius, The
White Star, The
White Star, The
Zhalan
Zoful

Institutions/Organizations/Projects/Corporations

Alpha Squad (Alpha Wing)
AreTech
Babylon 5 Advisory
  Council, The
Babylon 5 Emporium, The
Babylon 5 Senate Oversight
  Committee
Babylon Project, The
Bureau 13

Centauri Republic
Chudmo, Third Fain of
Conspiracy of Light
Couro Prido
Delta Squad (Delta
  Wing)
Dockers' Guild, The
Earth Alliance, The
Earthforce

Earthforce Bureau of Internal Investigations
Earthforce Defense Bio-Weapons Division
Earthforce Special Intelligence
EarthGov
Fireflies Incorporated
Foundation, The
Free Mars
FutureCorp
Grey Council
Homeguard
Indonesian Consortium
Interplanetary Expeditions
Interstellar News Network
Kha'Ri
League of Non-Aligned Worlds, The
Mars Conglomerate, The
Ministry of Peace, The
Narn Regime
Nightwatch, The
Office of Planetary Security, The

Operation : Sudden Death
Project : Lazarus
Psi Cops
Psi Corps, The
Quartermaster Corporation
Raiders, The
Rangers, The
Russian Consortium
Senate
Shakespeare Corporation
Sh'lassan Triumvirate
SportCorp
Star Riders Clan
Techno-mages
Thenta Makur
"36 Hours Aboard Babylon 5"
Transport Association
United Spaceways Transport
Universal Terraform
Vorlon Empire, The
War Council
Wind Swords, The
Zeta Wing (Zeta Squad)

Battles, Wars, Historical Events, Treaties

Battle of Na'Shok, The
Battle of Salos, The
Battle of The Line, The
Dilgar Invasion, The
Earth–Centauri Non-Aggression Treaty

Earth–Minbari War, The
Euphrates Treaty, The
Mars Rebellion
Narn–Centauri Agreement, The
Narn–Centauri War

Devices/Technology

Acme Handy-Dandy Micro-Helper
Alien Healing Device
BabCom

Black Light Cammo Suit
Blast Doors
Breathers
Cardial Stimulator

Changeling Net
Credit Chit
Data Crystals
Encounter Suit
Energy Cap
Energy Pod
Exchange Machines
Gold Channel, The
Great Machine, The
HazMat
ICE
ICE-breaker
Identicard
InterWeb
Jumpgate
Link

Maintenance 'Bot
Medbracelet
Nano-Technology
Poison Tab
Recorders
Security 'Bot
Skin Tab
Slappers
StellarCom
Time Stabilizer
Triluminary
Vibe Shower
Vibration Detonator
Vickers
Virtual Reality Cybernet
XB7 Tracking Unit

Foods, Drinks, Medicines, Chemicals

Antarean Flarn
Anti-Agapic
Bagna Cauda
Brivari
C-15
Devalera
Duridium
Duridium Nitrate
Dust
Flarn
Florazyne
Japote
Jhala

Jovian Sunspot
Metazine
Morbidium
Morph Gas
Orca
Oxy Pills
Phroomis
Preslecomp
Quantium 40
Spoo
Supermorbidium
Treel
Yogtree

Alien Races/Creatures

Abbai
Antareans
Brakiri
Centauri
Children of Time
Dilgar

Drazi
Dubai
First Ones, The
Goks
Golians
Hyach

Ipsha
Liati
Llort
Lumati
Markabs
Minbari
Narns
Pak'ma'ra
Shadows, The
Shedraks

Sh'lassans
Slitch
Soul Hunters
Streibs
Ti Kar, The
Tukati, The
Tuchanq
Vree
Vorlons

Weapons

Defense Grid
Ka'Toc
Kutai
Mass Drivers
Needler

Paingivers
Phased Plaser Gun (PPG)
Shock Stick
Slaver's Glove
Starweb

Titles/Terms

Alyt
Conspiracy of Light
Custodian
Fortress of Light
Great Maker
GroundPounders
   (GROPOS)
Jarheads
Ka'Ti

Knives
Lurkers
Mutari
Muta-Do, The
Ombuds
Sho'Rin, The
Satai
Shai Alyt
Spacing

APPENDIX IV
Index of Sources

___

Pilot
The Gathering (GATHERING)

Season One—Signs and Portents
Midnight on the Firing Line (MIDNIGHT)
Soul Hunter (SOUL)
Born to the Purple (PURPLE)
Infection (INFECTION)
The Parliament of Dreams (PARLIAMENT)
Mind War (MIND)
The War Prayer (PRAYER)
And the Sky Full of Stars (SKY)
Deathwalker (DEATHWALKER)
Believers (BELIEVERS)
Survivors (SURVIVORS)
By Any Means Necessary (MEANS)
Signs and Portents (SIGNS)
TKO (TKO)
Grail (GRAIL)
Eyes (EYES)
Legacies (LEGACIES)
A Voice in the Wilderness, Part I (VOICE I)
A Voice in the Wilderness, Part II (VOICE II)
Babylon Squared (SQUARED)
The Quality of Mercy (MERCY)
Chrysalis (CHRYSALIS)

Season Two—The Coming of Shadows
Points of Departure (DEPARTURE)
Revelations (REVELATIONS)
The Geometry of Shadows (GEOMETRY)
A Distant Star (STAR)
The Long Dark (LONG)
Spider in the Web (SPIDER)
A Race Through Dark Places (RACE)
Soul Mates (MATES)
The Coming of Shadows (SHADOWS)
GROPOS (GROPOS)
All Alone in the Night (ALONE)
Acts of Sacrifice (SACRIFICE)
Hunter, Prey (HUNTER)
There All the Honor Lies (HONOR)
And Now for a Word (WORD)
Knives (KNIVES)
In the Shadow of Z'ha'dum (Z'HA'DUM)
Confessions and Lamentations (CONFESSIONS)
Divided Loyalties (DIVIDED)
The Long, Twilight Struggle (TWILIGHT)
Comes the Inquisitor (INQUISITOR)
The Fall of Night (FALL)

Season Three—Point of No Return
Matters of Honor (MATTERS)
Convictions (CONVICTIONS)
A Day in the Strife (STRIFE)

Comics
In Darkness Find Me (DARKNESS)
Treason (TREASON)
In Harm's Way (HARM)
The Price of Peace (PEACE)
Shadows Past and Present (PRESENT)
Against the Odds (ODDS)
Survival the Hard Way (SURVIVAL)
Silent Enemies (SILENT)
Duet for human and Narn in C Sharp (DUET)
Coda for human and Narn in B Flat (CODA)
The Psi Corps and You! (CORPS)

Books
Voices (VOICES)
Accusations (ACCUSATIONS)
Blood Oath (BLOOD)
Clark's Law (LAW)

APPENDIX V
Alphabetical Index of Sources

Accusations (ACCUSATIONS)
Acts of Sacrifice (SACRIFICE)
Against the Odds (ODDS)
All Alone in the Night (ALONE)
And Now for a Word (WORD)
And the Sky Full of Stars (SKY)
Babylon Squared (SQUARED)
Believers (BELIEVERS)
Blood Oath (BLOOD)
Born to the Purple (PURPLE)
By Any Means Necessary (MEANS)
Chrysalis (CHRYSALIS)
Clark's Law (LAW)
Comes the Inquisitor (INQUISITOR)
The Coming of Shadows (SHADOWS)
Coda for human and Narn in B Flat (CODA)
Confessions and Lamentations (CONFESSIONS)
Convictions (CONVICTIONS)
A Day in the Strife (STRIFE)
Deathwalker (DEATHWALKER)
A Distant Star (STAR)
Divided Loyalties (DIVIDED)
Duet for human and Narn in C Sharp (DUET)
Eyes (EYES)

The Fall of Night (FALL)
The Gathering (GATHERING)
The Geometry of Shadows (GEOMETRY)
Grail (GRAIL)
GROPOS (GROPOS)
Hunter, Prey (HUNTER)
In Darkness Find Me (DARKNESS)
Infection (INFECTION)
In Harm's Way (HARM)
In the Shadow of Z'ha'dum (Z'HA'DUM)
Knives (KNIVES)
Legacies (LEGACIES)
The Long Dark (LONG)
The Long, Twilight Struggle (TWILIGHT)
Matters of Honor (MATTERS)
Midnight on the Firing Line (MIDNIGHT)
Mind War (MIND)
The Parliament of Dreams (PARLIAMENT)
Points of Departure (DEPARTURE)
The Price of Peace (PEACE)
The Psi Corps and You (CORPS)
The Quality of Mercy (MERCY)
A Race Through Dark Places (RACE)
Revelations (REVELATIONS)
Shadows Past and Present (PRESENT)
Signs and Portents (SIGNS)
Silent Enemies (SILENT)
Soul Hunter (SOUL)
Soul Mates (MATES)
Spider in the Web (SPIDER)
Survival the Hard Way (SURVIVAL)
Survivors (SURVIVORS)
There All the Honor Lies (HONOR)
TKO (TKO)
Treason (TREASON)
A Voice in the Wilderness, Part I (VOICE I)
A Voice in the Wilderness, Part II (VOICE II)
Voices (VOICES)
The War Prayer (PRAYER)

APPENDIX VI
The Babylon 5 Jokebook

Q. How many Minbari does it take to screw in a lightbulb?
None. They always surrender before they finish the job and never tell you why.
(RACE)

Q. How many Centauri does it take to screw in a lightbulb?
A. One. But in the great old days, hundreds of servants would change a thousand lightbulbs at our slightest whim.
(CONVICTIONS)

Knock, Knock.
Who's There?
Kosh.
Kosh who?
Gesundheit